"I think the danger is gone now," she said, her voice as soft as the silk of her skin and as warm as the sun.

"Then why is your heart thundering with fear?" he said, pressing his palm against her chest.

She gasped sharply. "Your touch makes my heart race with desire."

He didn't need to hear more. He rubbed his hand against her breast, feeling the silk of her dress and softness of the flesh. She arched her back until the fullness of her breast filled his palm and she moaned deeply.

The sound ignited a hungering fire in him that went right to his groin, making his flesh there harden and throb. His mouth watered and his breath hitched. As a spirit being, his life had been one of service, of duty. Never had he felt this intensity of ecstasy.

Was she feeling the same way he did? He sent his spirit in search of hers, looking for the energy that made her heart race and her body shudder gently beneath his hands. And just as his wolf's spirit had seen the forest and the moonlight through her eyes in her dreams, he could see them together in her mind. But they weren't as they were now. For in her mind they lay upon a soft cloud of white and they were flesh to flesh, touching and tasting.

Turn the page for rave reviews of the passionate
romances by Jennifer St. Giles

"*His Dark Desires* easily stands out from the crowd. . . . Jennifer St. Giles writes smart. She writes sexy. She writes differently."

—All About Romance

"With its dark, dangerous hero and sexy storyline, this historical romance will appeal to contemporary romantic suspense fans who enjoy danger and intrigue."

—True Romance

"Teeming with menacing atmosphere. . . . St. Giles captures that Gothic essence . . . while maintaining a strong sexual tension between the protagonists."   —Fresh Fiction

THE MISTRESS OF TREVELYAN
**2004 National Readers Choice Award for
Best Historical and Best First Book
2004 Maggie Award for Excellence in Historical Fiction
2004 Daphne du Maurier Finalist**

"Full of spooky suspense. . . . [St. Giles'] story ripples with tension. . . . An engrossing read."   —*Publishers Weekly*

"[An] intriguing, well-crafted romance."

—*Library Journal*

"[An] excellent debut novel. St. Giles does a masterful job of evoking a Gothic atmosphere, and updates it nicely with smoldering sexual tension. . . . The story is compellingly told."

—*Affaire de Coeur*

Also by Jennifer St. Giles

Kiss of Darkness
The Lure of the Wolf
Touch a Dark Wolf
The Mistress of Trevelyan
His Dark Desires

JENNIFER ST. GILES

Bride of the Wolf

POCKET BOOKS

New York   London   Toronto   Sydney

Pocket Books
A Division of Simon & Schuster, Inc.
1230 Avenue of the Americas
New York, NY 10020

This book is a work of fiction. Names, characters, places, and incidents either are products of the author's imagination or are used fictitiously. Any resemblance to actual events or locales or persons, living or dead, is entirely coincidental.

First Pocket Books paperback edition May 2009

POCKET and colophon are registered trademarks of Simon & Schuster, Inc.

For information about special discounts for bulk purchases, please contact Simon & Schuster Special Sales at 1-866-506-1949 or business@simonandschuster.com.

The Simon & Schuster Speakers Bureau can bring authors to your live event. For more information or to book an event contact the Simon & Schuster Speakers Bureau at 1-866-248-3049 or visit our website at www.simonspeakers.com.

Cover illustration by Franco Accornero

Manufactured in the United States of America

10 9 8 7 6 5 4 3 2 1

ISBN-13: 978-1-4165-6341-9
ISBN-10:   1-4165-6341-5

To those who struggle in life to find light in their darkness, meaning in their personal pain, and answers to senseless loss. Know there is hope and there is love as long as there is a tomorrow.

God bless you.

Acknowledgments

Without the encouraging support of many people my dream of writing and this book wouldn't be a reality. Thanks to my friends and family who put up with a lot to enable me to share my stories with readers. And many thanks to the readers who send me notes of appreciation for the Shadowmen series. Your enthusiasm for more is what makes it all possible. Happy Reading.

Love,
Jennifer St. Giles

Nothing is so strong as gentleness.
Nothing is so gentle as real strength.

—Frances de Sales

Bride
of the Wolf

Chapter One

MARISSA VASQUEZ had known her escape from prison was too good to be true, but the suddenness and violence with which she'd been recaptured hours ago left her stunned. One minute she and her friends had been safe beneath an angel's protective shield at a ranger camp in Twilight, Tennessee. The next minute, the earth violently shook as Vladarian Vampires descended upon them.

Dios. Was Navarre dying? Was he already dead?

The gag in her mouth kept her from screaming, but her soul cried out in anguish. The blind warrior, a Shadowman from the heavens with a magical wolf spirit, had tried so desperately to save her. He'd been too drugged and injured to fight, and ended up facedown in the mud, blood gushing from a knife wound in his back.

What had become of Stefanie, Dr. Annette, Erin, and Megan? Her friends had been kidnapped with her, but taken somewhere different. Were they alive? Had the vampires sacrificed them as they'd threatened?

How could she bear it? It was all her fault. She hadn't stopped Navarre from being drugged, hadn't cried out to Dr. Annette that he might not be delirious when he'd pulled Marissa from the treatment room, warning of danger. It was true that he'd been in and out of consciousness since magically appearing the day before. Yet just before the vampires destroyed the angel shield and attacked, Marissa had had a feeling about Navarre and the threat he perceived, but she hadn't acted on it.

Even before he appeared to her as a man, she was sure he had tried to warn her. Over the past few nights a ghostly wolf with Navarre's golden eyes had come to her, crying a warning that only she had heard. She hadn't understood, though, which made her a poor *espiritista*, despite her grandmother's claims that she was gifted in talking to the otherworld.

Navarre had tried to save her and she'd failed to hear. Now she was in the hands of a monster and had no one to blame but herself.

She'd been tossed like a rag doll from limo to jet to Hummer. Hours and hours had passed since Hernan Cortes Herrera had leered at her through the limo's door, yet her skin still crawled as if it had just happened.

He'd laughed, his cruel, dark eyes gleaming in triumph as he spoke. "I am much smarter than Samir, no? He thought he had you and now you are mine."

Sheik Rashad bin Samir Al Sabah had captured her first at the ranger camp, but Herrera had somehow escaped with her after the others had been taken from the limousine. The fanged, twisted smile on Herrera's satanic features gave just a whisper of warning about his malevolent viciousness. She'd seen what Herrera had done to animals in her uncle's prison camp. She'd heard what Herrera had done to women over the years. She believed that he alone, of all Tío Luis's men, was responsible for her family's disappearance. And she was sure he'd been the one who killed her brother Rafael when he'd tried to escape their jungle prison several months ago.

"Your home awaits you," Herrera said, his grin widening as his goatee bobbed. "You are eager to be my bride, are you not, my little *novia*?"

Bound and gagged, Marissa glared her hatred at him.

He frowned at her. "You will be."

Reaching down, he grabbed her breast and squeezed until her vision went black with agony. She knew from experience at the brutal hands of her uncle that watching her thrash with pain would give Herrera pleasure, so she fought hard to show him as little reaction as possible.

She kept her eyes closed, bit down on the gag until her teeth ached, and focused her mind on the spirit of the black wolf she'd seen in her dreams. His majestic power as he ran through the moonlit forest. She saw the world through the wolf's golden eyes, watched his sleek grace, and heard the cry of his heart to the shadowed moon. She imagined what the night wind would feel like upon her face as she raced and what the pine-scented air would taste like as she ran free for the first time in her life.

Then Herrera grabbed her chin in a punishing grip. "Look at me," he demanded.

She opened her eyes, shuddering.

"You think you can play games with me, *puta*?" he said. "Think again. If I don't get what I want when I want it, you'll pay. In his will, *el jefe* said you had to be alive and undamned. That leaves plenty of room for all kinds of hell, *sí, mi novia*?"

Marissa glared at Herrera. She'd die before she gave him anything he wanted and he must have read her message loud and clear.

He cursed and slammed the car door.

She hadn't seen him since. She'd fruitlessly struggled against the numbing ropes binding her hands and feet until her wrists and ankles were raw. She'd been moved about by nameless, faceless men who'd kept her face covered with an oily rag. But she'd had plenty of time to think about what was to come. Soon the Hummer would stop. The door would open and she would enter hell . . . again.

What perverse turn of fate had caused Herrera and Sheik Samir to be so eager to be her groom? Besides keeping her alive and undamned, what else did Tío Luis's will say?

Even from beyond the grave her vampire uncle had his hands around her throat, choking the life and the spirit from her soul just has he'd done for years while—

Madre de Dios. She shivered with fear and her heart pounded so hard that her chest hurt.

The car had stopped.

• • •

By Logos! Death could not be worse. Submersed in a sea of darkness and pain he'd never known before, Navarre searched for a way out, but his wolf spirit kept drowning in turbulent waves he was helpless to fight against. Weakness was a warrior's greatest foe. Even nonexistence was preferable to powerlessness.

Aragon's mortal woman had done something to him. In trying to help—for he'd sensed that intent in her spirit—she'd stolen everything from him. He had no control over his mortal form and he couldn't seem to conjure either his wolf spirit or his Blood Hunter's were form. Even after Draysius's Pyrathian fire had rendered him unconscious, he at least had his wolf spirit. Now he was unable to help anyone, especially the mortal woman who needed it the most. The woman Aragon had called "Marissa."

Her name sounded like a gentle breeze beneath a starry, moonlit sky and he called to her with all of his might, but she didn't answer. She alone had heard and reached out to his wolf spirit when he'd been ensnared in the gray edges between the mortal and spirit realms. A vision of the future had come to him when he'd been trapped there, a horrible picture of what would happen upon the mortal ground and to all of Logos's creation if Pathos's son Cinatas and the Vladarian Vampires were not stopped. Saving Marissa was vital to seeing the evil destroyed.

Yet he could do nothing.

This total separation from his strength and his abilities was more torturous than the solitary limbo his spirit had been caught in since he'd been hit by the fire.

How much time had passed since he'd been stricken? How much time had he spent with his spirit caught between the mortal and the spirit worlds? How long had he watched the evil advancing upon his earthbound Blood Hunter brethren, Jared and Aragon, and the humans with them?

Too long. His heart supplied the answer, which might be

why he was drowning in a world of darkness now. Since he hadn't healed from the Pyrathian's fire, his warrior's strength must have weakened greatly. Likely to the point that he would no longer be able to fight against Heldon's Fallen Army in the spirit realm. He'd no longer be able to fulfill his sworn duty to protect the Elan upon the earth—those Logos had given special blood to. He wouldn't even be able to help Marissa against the horror of the future he'd seen.

By Logos, no! He couldn't accept such a fate.

Yet, how could he deny the truth of what he'd become? He'd have to leave the Guardian Forces, leave Sven and York, and leave Marissa.

He fought with all of his might against that fate, but couldn't move, couldn't free his spirit, couldn't stop the darkness from crashing down upon him again, sucking him deeper and deeper into nothingness.

The car door opened, bringing hot humid air rushing into the icy interior of the Hummer and crawling over Marissa's skin, reminding her of times when she'd awaken in the night to find either a fat-bellied rat or a vampire bat in her bed. Shuddering, she braced herself for the worst that would follow and Herrera didn't disappoint her.

"Let me see my blushing bride," Herrera commanded from somewhere outside the car. Rough hands dragged her out, taking little care in how they handled her body. Muscles trapped in one position for too long shouted in throbbing protest, while other parts of her refused to function. She couldn't feel her hands or feet and her knees wouldn't hold her weight when the men stood her up. With her blood semicirculating again, her bladder sent burning emergency signals to her brain. She would have crumpled painfully to the shelled concrete if the men hadn't held her armpits. As it was she hung in their digging grip with her arms bent awkwardly.

Dawn peeked across the sky, slashing red amid the black, weakening the night to a dull gray. She could hear a fountain bubbling behind her, as if laughing cheerfully at her imprisonment. A high wall surrounded her on all sides; the shadowy razor wire topping it reminded her of Corazón de Rojo—the compound her Tío Luis had kept her in. There, the white cement wall had been stained in many places from the blood of those who'd tried and failed to escape.

She couldn't believe she was back in another prison where cruel abuse would control her every move, her every function. She'd rather die first. Humiliation and anger overcame her fear as she stared at Herrera. The gag in her mouth kept her from naming him for the unholy bastard pig that he was.

"She does not look very appreciative of her new home, does she, Carlos? Does she not realize how hard I had to work to steal *centavos* from her uncle? How many years I was nothing more than *mierda* under Vasquez's boot—a blood slave for his perversities?"

"No, *jefe*," said the man on Marissa's right. He jerked her arm, pulling her painfully upright. "Should I teach her lessons she will never forget?"

Herrera whipped out a knife and held it to Carlos's face. "Touch her without my direct order and you die. She is my *puta* and no one else's." He swung the knife to her face. "You are still pure, *mi novia?* You saved yourself for Herrera, *sí?*"

She didn't answer, but wished like hell that she wasn't still a virgin.

"The priest is already here. We marry at dusk."

"Never!" She tried to speak despite the gag.

"You will," he said. Laughing, he flicked the knife near her ear and the gag flopped loose, but dryness and her swollen tongue kept it anchored inside her mouth. She tried to spit it out and failed. Then Herrera brought the knife down the center of her neck, grinning with malice as its tip cut a slit in her shirt and scratched her skin as he trailed it down her chest, exposing the tops of her breasts. "You've *grandes pechos* for Herrera, no?"

She spat at the gag again, this time dislodging it. Before she could tell him what she thought of him, he sliced through the rope binding her hands. Excruciating pain shot up her arms and she cried out, feeling as if he'd cut her hands off. She tried to lift them and more anguish throbbed through her as blood returned to her hands and fingers.

Tears stung her eyes.

He cut the ropes on her feet next. It was even worse. She sobbed as her vision dimmed and her stomach roiled.

The men snatched her back up as she sagged even more. "She'll faint at the sight of *el jefe's pene grande.*"

Herrera cursed. "Tell Ysalane *she* will be punished if my new bride doesn't please me in all ways." Then he grabbed her chin, snapping her head up. "Until tonight, *mi novia.*"

"I'll die first, *cerdo.*" Marissa forced the words out of her dry, swollen-tongued mouth.

"No," Herrera said, smiling. "You'll only wish you were dead."

Chapter Two

THE MEN dragged her across the courtyard and into a two-story manor with a tiled roof as opposed to the thatched roofs she'd always seen in jungle buildings. Icy cold air hit her as the double doors opened onto a lavish interior. The exact details of it all were lost in a blur as the men quickly hauled her up the stairs, not even giving her a chance to make her muscles work. Stabbing pain shot up her legs every time her feet thudded against a wooden step.

She gritted her teeth, determined not to cry out again. A short distance down a corridor, they brought her through double doors into a large, dimly lit bedroom.

"Up, *puta*," said one of the men as he kicked at a woman lying on a pallet on the floor.

The woman rolled to her feet, brandishing a knife in her hand. She lashed out at the man who kicked her, but sadly did not come close enough to his crotch to harm him. Her quick agility revealed a youthfulness that couldn't be seen in her harsh features and scarred visage. At some time point her face had been cut numerous times.

He laughed.

"Someday, Ysalane will cut your heart out." Her dark eyes and deep voice were filled with hatred.

"You aim too low, *bruja*."

"No, I aim just right."

"*El jefe* wants his bride ready to please him by tonight or you die," the man said. He then released his hold on Marissa, as did the other man. She stumbled and nearly fell before she gained enough balance to stay upright.

The men left, laughing.

"Bathroom, please," Marissa said to the woman, her words and voice barely discernible.

The woman pointed with the knife to a door across the room.

Marissa felt as if it were miles away. Nevertheless, she put one foot in front of the other, managing to latch on to the wall and a dresser to help her navigate the opulent room until her body began to function better. Herrera had to have stolen a great many *centavos* from her uncle to have built all of this. She wondered exactly where in the Belizean rain forest they were. Were they close to the remains of Corazón de Rojo? Or had Herrera built this compound close to the Guatemalan border, making escape even harder?

Reaching the door, she opened it to find a spalike bathroom meant for many—and considering the manacles installed in the tiled shower and huge tub, not all were willing. She shivered in dread. Somehow she had to get out of the compound, but first she needed to regain her strength and to find out where she was while managing not to get her throat cut by the knife-wielding Ysalane.

Marissa washed her hands, took several tentative sips of water from the faucet, then looked at her raw and bleeding wrists. She was sure her ankles were in as bad a shape. Suddenly the door she thought she'd locked swung open.

Ysalane entered with a pile of towels and brightly colored material in her hands. "You will do all that I command you to do or I will call Carlos and Emilio back to force you and they will have the added pleasure of watching you be groomed for *el jefe, bien?*"

No, it was not fine, but Marissa kept her mouth shut, closely watching the woman set down the bundle she carried. Lighting a candle, she went to dozens of dishes throughout the room, around the tub, upon the tables, along the counters, and set a thin trail of rising smoke from each. Soon a sweet aroma heavily scented the air. She then turned the water on to fill the huge, circular tub and added bubbling salts. Steam puffed up quickly, taking the chill from the room.

Marissa braced herself as Ysalane walked toward her. "Let me see your wrists." Surprised, Marissa tentatively held out her arm.

Ysalane shook her head. "It will sting badly in the water, but they need to be cleaned or the infection will come. Many in the jungle die from such stupid things. I have a salve that will help the healing. It is from my Mayan ancestors. You will like it."

Marissa pulled her arm back. "Why do you care?"

Ysalane narrowed her eyes; her upper lip had been cut on the right side in the past, causing her to have a twisted smile. Behind the scarred mask, Marissa could see that the woman had been pretty once. "I care for nothing but myself. The less you hurt now the more you'll be able to hurt later and the more you'll be able to please *el jefe*. Then I will not suffer more from his displeasure." She gestured to her face. "Whatever you prize most, he will destroy first."

Marissa grabbed her chest as her stomach flipped and her heart thudded to a standstill before racing with horror. In the dead of night at Corazón de Rojo, it was whispered that Herrera used knives on women, but she still found herself gasping. "He . . . he did that to you?"

"He is a vampire. He likes to drink blood, but he will never bite you to get it, for then you could become a vampire and be just as powerful as he is. You get him to bite you, you will be a very lucky woman."

Marissa shuddered. "You think being damned forever lucky?"

She shrugged. "I live in hell now. What would be the difference, except I would no longer be a slave *puta*? I could cut off all the *penes* I want and nobody could touch Ysalane, no?"

Swallowing hard, Marissa had no doubt the woman would do just that.

"Enough for now," Ysalane said. "We've much to do and you must have time to rest, as well. I will go fix fruit and cheese for you to eat and you *will* get in the tub to clean yourself. Otherwise Carlos and Emilio will put you there. They stand guard in the corridor, so do not think to escape. Also, there are many of *el jefe*'s armed *hombres* everywhere." She left, not waiting for an answer.

Marissa stood quietly in the steamy, smoke-filled room until she heard the outer door shut. There were no windows in the bathroom, so she raced to the bedroom. All of the windows were thick plate glass, tinted black, with no way to open them except shattering them. Moving quietly, she went to the double doors and set her ear to the crack between.

She didn't hear anything. Grabbing the handle, she slowly turned it, surprised to find it wasn't locked. Just before she clicked the door open, she heard a male voice. "Do you think *el jefe* is really going to marry that woman? She has breasts to suck, but no ass to squeeze."

"*Silencio.* Before he hears and kills us both." A loud pop followed.

"Ow. *Mierda!* What was that for?"

"Do you not know who she is?" Carlos's voice lowered to a hiss.

"She is Vasquez's *puta* niece. What makes her so special?"

"She inherited his billions. Oil stock and gold and money. *El jefe* marries her, he becomes one of the richest men in the world."

The blood drained from Marissa's head and she nearly fell forward into the door. *Heiress? Billions? Me?*

"Carlos, what gives *el jefe*, who is already rich, the right to become richer? Why can't you, say, or I marry the *puta*?"

"Maybe we will. Maybe she will try to escape and we can pretend she got away," Carlos answered with a laugh.

Instead of opening the door, Marissa slowly released the handle and locked it. She headed to the bathroom, not doubting that Ysalane would employ Carlos and Emilio if Marissa didn't bathe herself.

This time she made sure the bathroom door was locked. Steam and incense billowed around her as she quickly undressed and climbed into the bubbly froth in the tub. At first her wrists and ankles stung as if her uncle's flesh-eating ants were gnawing at her skin, but she gritted her teeth and sank beneath the water. Soon the pain lessened and the warmth of the water soothingly eased into her sore muscles.

Guilt descended on her the moment she began to relax, her mind immediately going back to Navarre and her friends in Twilight. Inhaling the sweet air, she tried to ease the heavy tightness in her heart with prayer. She hoped that miracles had found their way to her friends—then pleaded for a miracle for herself.

Fighting tears, she breathed deeper, and the more she did the more a floating sensation crept over her. She felt as if all that had happened weren't real, that it was an odd dream. When the water reached the level of her neck, she barely realized that she needed to turn it off, for her mind wandered between her bath and flashing images of the black wolf of her dreams.

She ran through a moonlit forest, the black wolf at her side. His sleek coat gleaming. His powerful form emanating majesty and grace. His golden eyes fierce . . . Navarre's eyes. Then suddenly, she could feel the heat of Navarre's skin beneath her fingers and the rough edge of his jaw as she'd bathed him when ill. His warlike features—strong brow, hooked nose, and square jaw—were too sharply angled for beauty, but so compelling that she couldn't stop herself from gazing at him. The wonder of his male body made her hands itch to touch more, to know more, to feel everything about him—the silky thickness of his long dark hair, the solid strength of his broad shoulders, and the supple heat of his taut muscles sculpting his chest and arms. He wore a large amulet of iridescent golden bronze that was warm as sunshine and as mysterious as the heavens. She couldn't stop herself from running her fingers across the soft hair of his chest and following its thin trail down his rippling stomach, but didn't dare dip below where the sheet covered him—she wanted to, though. She wanted to know everything about him. Her body grew hot, practically burning in secret places as she looked at him and touched him. He was a hewn and honed warrior from a place she did not understand, one who had fought hard to save her, a woman he didn't even know.

She didn't understand all of the magic surrounding Navarre and his wolf spirit, but she'd known such dark evil from her vampire uncle and men like Herrera that she had very little trouble in believing there were magical men like Navarre who fought against such depravity. There had to be, or all would be lost.

Even now she felt as if she were drowning in the darkness surrounding her, sinking into a deep, bottomless pit. When she thought of Herrera, what he would do to her tonight, she couldn't breathe. She couldn't face such violation of her body and heart. She'd rather die—

Pain burned her scalp as her long hair was jerked hard enough to pull her upward. She blinked the water out of her eyes and suddenly found that she could breathe again. Ysalane was there, shaking her, speaking loudly words that Marissa couldn't seem to understand, but it was all right. It didn't matter. Nothing mattered. All Marissa wanted to do was float, so she closed her eyes and dreamed . . .

The wolf. Navarre. The wolf. Navarre. She was with one, then the other, upon a misty cloud beneath the stars and the moon. With the wolf she ran free. With Navarre she tentatively touched what she'd never before desired—a man.

Suddenly a sharply pungent odor burned her nose. She tried to turn away from it, but someone held her down.

"*Mierda!* Wake up! Wake up!" Ysalane's voice was sharp and caused Marissa's head to ache.

"You used too much of the drug. Someday that Magic smoke concoction will kill someone," said a male voice.

Marissa blinked her eyes open to find Ysalane and a balding, leathery-faced man hovering over her. She was no longer in a tub with steam and smoke swirling around her, but on a bed in a dimly lit room. The man held a vial to her nose and Ysalane had a strong grip on Marissa's chin and forehead. Her body tingled from head to toe and she immediately realized that she was naked beneath the covers.

"Stop! Let go of me," Marissa demanded, reaching up and pushing the vial from her nose. She struggled to pull her thoughts together. Her mind didn't want to cooperate. Drug? Magic smoke? Ysalane had drugged her in the bathroom?

"You are lucky, Ysalane," the old man said, backing away, taking his vial with him. "Very lucky that she wakes. *El jefe* would have killed you if she died."

Ysalane let go of Marissa and Marissa crossed her arms over her chest, anchoring the blanket tightly to her breasts. *Dios.* What had happened to her?

Ysalane pushed at the old man. "You go now. She has much to learn and little time left."

"I go. But you may want to say good-bye to Pedro now. My heart cannot take too much more of going up the stairs here and down the stairs to the wine cellar. That is all I have done today. Up and down. Pedro, do this. Pedro, come here. Pedro, go there."

"Bah. Call that hellhole what it is. A *mazmorra,* where he tortures at whim. Who does he have down there now? Another man who decided he did not want to work for *el jefe* anymore?"

Dungeon? Herrera had a dungeon? Marissa shivered.

"No one Pedro knows. But *el hombre es muy grande. El jefe* brought him at the same time that he brought her and he needed Pedro's medicine, too. I go rest before someone calls Pedro again." The old man put a stopper on the vial he held and stuffed it into a black bag that had been sitting on the end of the bed.

Marissa's mind raced. *A very large man. Brought at the same time I was. Navarre? Was it possible?* She'd last seen him lying in the mud after being stabbed in the back. A monstrous-looking vampire called Cinatas had stepped on Navarre's back in triumph. No. It wasn't possible. There'd been too much blood gushing from the knife wound. For a man to bleed like that for so long and live was impossible. But her heart wasn't hearing any of the logic her mind recited. It thumped with hope. Somehow she had to get to the dungeon, which meant finding some clothes and leaving this bed.

She sat up and the room whirled around her before coming to a wavering stop. That all-over tingling feeling had yet to go away. She glared at Ysalane. "What did you do to me?"

"Gave you Magic smoke. It makes things much easier for Ysalane to ready you for *el jefe* and to assure him of your virginity."

"You drugged me and . . . and touched me?" Marissa shuddered, sure she would be sick at any moment. She swallowed hard. "You are an evil monster."

"No. Tonight you will have an evil monster and tomorrow you will beg Ysalane for Magic smoke to make the pain go away. Tomorrow you will beg me to touch you to help you heal. You think *el jefe* only likes to cut and suck blood from my face? Think again."

Marissa covered her mouth, fighting the nausea churning in her stomach. "Where are my clothes? I need my clothes."

"You cannot have clothes yet. Not until *el jefe* is sure you will not try and escape. It is the first rule for all women he brings for his enjoyment. Now you must prepare yourself for tonight so you will not be too frightened. He will be very angry if you faint and cannot show him how pleasured you are with his touch and the pain he will gift you with. You read first, then Ysalane will answer any questions or show you how to position yourself for *el jefe's* enjoyment."

The woman shoved a book in Marissa's lap. Marissa looked down at a sickening photograph of a naked woman, spread-eagled with her arms and legs tied upon a stone altar in a dungeon. There were chains on the walls and awful-looking apparatuses nearby that screamed torturous pain. The dark shadow of a man stood at the woman's feet and he held a whip aloft, ready to lash into her. The title swam in the tears filling Marissa's eyes. *The Ecstasy and Agony of Pain and Sex.* She threw the book aside as if it were a poisonous snake, her heart beating wildly. She didn't know much about the physical relationship between a man and a woman, but she knew that pain should have no part in it.

Ysalane picked up the book. Opening to an inside page, she shoved the picture in Marissa's face. It showed a woman on her knees. The man in front held her by the hair, his member stuffed into her mouth. "Carlos and Emilio would enjoy holding you still while I show you all these things. Maybe even give you a little taste of what is to come, *sí*?"

Marissa shook her head, choking on the rage inside her. She would not do this. She would not be a part of this, even if she had to die to keep it from happening.

Ysalane clearly took Marissa's cry as one of surrender because she turned to another page and lovingly caressed the awful image. "I have learned to love pain and you will, too."

Chapter Three

Deep within the inner circles of the spirit realm sat the Guardian Council's glittering Judgment Hall, where aged and true warriors, chosen for their wisdom and zeal, presided over all of Logos's forces. Twelve in number and robed in white, the Leader's spirit forms were blinding in their intensity and intimidating in their countenances.

York had peeked into the hallowed hall once, but he'd never sought entry.

Whether it was because he felt unworthy or because he harbored anger over certain judgments was up for wager. The bottom line was, he didn't trust himself in their presence, and Sven wisely didn't, either. Sven's extraordinary leadership and diplomacy always led him to face the Guardian Council over dire issues, of which there had been many of late—a situation that left York always waiting, an intolerable state of being.

"It is a wonder you have not paced a rut down to Heldon's icy realms by now," Sirius said, frowning at him as he passed.

York wanted to do something rash to ruffle the Pyrathian's calm, but his mind was too full of worry to think of anything. "How can you just stand there, leaning upon a saintly pillar with your arms crossed, as if Sven isn't in the Council right now, facing complete ruin?"

"Logic demands patience at this point," Sirius said. "No wonder Logos gave Pyrathians the gift of fire and not Blood Hunters. Your tempers run so hot you would have incinerated the universe millennia ago."

York swung on his heel and glared at Sirius. "By Logos. What does 'logic demands patience' mean? You, Sven, and I seem to be the only ones who realize the situation upon the mortal ground is dire."

"True, but are we right in taking the actions we have?" Sirius sighed, adding to the heaviness of his doubt. "Given the results, I find myself questioning it all with a much needed dose of logic and a great deal less emotion, which is how warriors are *supposed* to assess battle situations. I did not do that. I acted out of impatience, knowing my choices might not be what the Council would have wanted. I placed Navarre within the mortal realm, correct?"

York adamantly shook his head. "You're not shouldering that alone. We were in agreement. Given what happened to split Navarre's spirit after he was injured, Aragon taking him to the mortal realm and me bringing him back, there was no other way to save him. And we both thought he'd be able to help Jared and Aragon in battling Cinatas and the demons."

"But was it the wisest thing to do? Are we so involved in the situation that we have lost perspective? We both know the Council would have chosen to let Navarre die rather than for things to be as they are now. A warrior trapped in the mortal realm. And what of Navarre's feelings? You tell me. Would he have preferred death to weakness and blindness? As a warrior, what choice would you make?"

York cursed and turned away, yet could not deny the truth. "Death," he whispered.

"As would I," said Sirius. "So my impatience to act without the Council has led Navarre to a fate we both consider to be worse than death. It was my impatience that caused everything to happen in the first place. I led my unit in the hunt for Aragon when the Council called for his capture and execution."

"It was Draysius's blow that injured Navarre."

"Draysius was acting under my orders."

"Which you have more than made up for since."

"There are some things that can never be atoned for or made right," Sirius said.

York paused and gave Sirius a second look. More than

Navarre's situation burdened the warrior, but before he could ask, Sven returned.

York's breath caught and held at his leader's grave expression.

"York, you and Flynn are to join another Blood Hunter unit. The Council is allowing you to choose which and you may continue to mentor Flynn for now as they assess the situation. Sirius, you may return and remain leader of your Pyrathian unit."

After a long pause, York narrowed his eyes at Sven. "And?" he demanded. "Besides the fact that our band of five Blood Hunters have been reduced to only you and me, why are just Flynn and I joining another unit? What about you?"

Sven exhaled sharply. "I am relieved of duty until the Council can review my decisions since taking over leadership of our unit."

"By Logos!" Sirius's cry of outrage resounded louder than York's cry of disbelief. Sven was the greatest leader he'd had the privilege to serve under. Sven never failed to make a difference in the ongoing battle against Heldon.

"It's because I left Navarre upon the mortal ground, isn't it?" Sirius demanded.

"Navarre was my warrior and ultimately my responsibility. But the answer to your question is no. It is all of the choices I have made since taking over leadership of the unit. We've lost three of our five members. I've continually made controversial decisions that require Logos's intervention. And they are very displeased that I went above them to Logos's right hand, Elohim, the Guardian of Hosts, seeking special dispensation for our attack against the evil overtaking Twilight."

"A very successful attack," added York angrily. "Did they not consider that? What right do they have to punish you for exercising a privilege that all Shadowmen hold?" He punched the air with his fist. "Any one of us is allowed to seek Logos, Elohim, or his left hand, El Shaddai, provided we have a worthy cause and the courage to do so."

Sven sighed and set his hand upon York's shoulder. "Anger and resentment will not gain us wisdom and power, my brother. The Council rightly fears that I have been too focused on Jared and Aragon's battle upon the mortal ground. That I must distance myself and regain Logos's broader, eternal perspective in the fight against Heldon and the Fallen Army."

"I have thought the same," Sirius whispered, his voice taut with anguish.

York could tell there was a great deal Sirius was not revealing, but he was too angry to speak of it now. York shook his head and backed away from Sven and Sirius before he said something he'd regret, yet he couldn't hold his tongue completely. "You're giving up the fight. You're letting old rules and ways creep in and cloud the real issue here. We've all seen the balance between good and evil shift upon the mortal ground. We know that evil is gaining at an alarming rate. Jared and Aragon realized this, as well. They felt the call and they've found a way to fight against it. You can't abandon them now just because twelve warriors who haven't seen the situation and haven't been in battle for millennia are afraid to do something different or are resentful that you had the courage to act."

"York!" Sven cried, clearly shocked by what York said. "Listen—"

"No. Both of you have suddenly become too burdened with some private guilt to even realize what is happening." Biting his tongue before he could say more, York turned and left. He didn't even know where he was going. He just knew he had to escape the disappointment that Sven and Sirius would even begin to doubt what they had done to help in the fight. He also realized he had to face the crushing fact that he might be the only one left in the spirit realm who would help Jared and

Aragon stand against the overwhelming darkness moving across the mortal ground.

Twilight, Tennessee

Deputy Nick Sinclair felt as if the tornado that had hit the town last night had picked him up and had yet to spew him out. It had been a whirlwind twenty-four hours and the ride was just beginning, he thought as he studied the fax that had just come through.

"We have a lead on Marissa and Navarre," he said, sticking his head into the command center for the tornado relief efforts. The town had been lucky, no deaths from the twister despite major structural damage, but he and the rest of the team fighting against the murderous Dr. Cinatas, his Vladarian Vampires, and their corrupt medical corporation, Sno-Med, had taken a hard blow.

"Thank God," Dr. Annette Batista said as she moved his way, carrying a large box. Her response was amplified by cries of relief from the other two people in the room, Erin Morgan and eleven-year-old Megan Linton.

The people he needed most—Sheriff Sam Sheridan and the ex–Blood Hunters Jared and Aragon, along with Marissa's close friend Stefanie Batista, weren't there.

"Sam and Emerald aren't back yet?" he asked.

"Five minutes away. They just called. Jared and Aragon will be here by then, too."

"Good. We'll have a meeting then. I want our asses at the airport in an hour. Where's Stef?"

"She went to the chapel. She said she needed to be alone for a little bit." Annette's dark eyes were rightly filled with worry. When she was rescued last week with Marissa from Vasquez's hellhole, Stefanie had been close to the point of starvation, having lost her will to live. She'd made her first steps to recovery over the past few days and now everyone feared she'd relapse.

She hadn't eaten much at all today, despite working many hours to help with the tornado cleanup. She'd only drunk a milk shake at the Burger Queen Delight when everyone else had had the works, from cheeseburgers to banana splits.

Nick touched Annette's arm. "This news should help Stef. A private jet left Nashville about two this morning for a municipal airport outside of Belize City. We have a starting place and an approximate time with which to trace Herrera. I'll go tell her." He started to turn for the chapel then noticed again the box Annette held. "Do you need me to carry that somewhere for you?"

Annette shot him a wry look. "Actually, no, but you can bear witness to Jared and Aragon that the delivery did arrive. It's the ten pounds of truffles Jared ordered. I intercepted the UPS man. Erin and I are going to take charge of the chocolate."

Nick's brows lifted as he recalled Jared's plan to extract undisclosed favors from Erin in exchange for the mail-order truffles. A half smile tugged at Nick's mouth, the bit of humor amid the turmoil making things a little more bearable. "This is going to be interesting."

"Very," said Annette. "I'm on my way to hide them."

"Don't forget about me," added Megan Linton. "I'm sticking with Erin and Dr. Nette. Us girls will rule with the truffles and the men will just have to drool."

"What about me, squirt?" Nick asked. "Surely you're not putting me in with the other men. I'm special." A breath of relief whispered over his heart at the spark of humor in Megan's green eyes. Last night's kidnapping by vampires and Cinatas's heinous plan to make Megan his child bride hadn't set the spunky girl back for long. She'd gotten up first thing today wanting to help those affected by the tornado. Nick was still getting used to the idea that she and her mother were part angel.

Megan winced. "Sorry, but you'll have to drool, too, or it wouldn't be fair."

"Ah, Meggie, you're breaking me heart," Nick said. "You have to at least save one peanut butter truffle for me."

"Maybe," she said. Then her gaze turned serious. "Bring Risa back safe and I'll give them all to you." Tears filled her eyes. "And, and watch out for . . . I don't know. Just be very careful, okay?"

Erin set her hand on Megan's shoulder. "Hon, have you had another vision, about Marissa? About any of us going to find her?"

Megan shook her head and drew a shuddering breath. "Nothing that I can really see. Just a lot of darkness and pain."

Nick walked over and squatted down in front of Megan. "It's going to be all right. We're going to find Marissa and Navarre and bring them back here." He chucked her on the chin with his knuckle. "And we'll split the peanut butter truffles when I get back, okay?"

Megan nodded. Then before he could stand up, she wrapped her arms around his neck and hugged him. He hugged her back, knowing all the way to the core of his soul that whatever it took to send Cinatas and his minions back to hell for good, he'd do it or die trying.

They were all tired and stressed beyond what any human should have to bear. They'd been in this battle against evil for weeks now, and had made some progress, but last night had been the most harrowing altercation yet. Cinatas had taken over the town of Twilight, killing Nick's fellow deputy, John Michaels, and then kidnapping the women who'd been at the ranger camp. When Nick and the others had intervened, Erin had been minutes away from being beheaded and Megan was about to become Cinatas's child bride. Vampires wanted not only to sink their fangs into angel blood, but to get their hands on angel powers and twist them for the damned.

Unfortunately, Herrera had absconded with Marissa and Navarre while the team was saving Erin and Megan. The team had been searching everywhere for clues to where Herrera had gone. They'd logically assumed it would be back to Belize, but had waited a few hours for proof and an exact starting point for their search. They didn't have time for wild-goose chases.

Nick left the room and headed for the chapel. He braced himself for the sight of Stephanie's haunted eyes and pale, gaunt face, so different from the woman he'd known six months ago.

He knew better than anyone else how hard last night's events had hit Stefanie. A few days ago, she'd confided in him just a fraction of what she'd been through as a prisoner of Luis Vasquez with Herrera as her "personal" guard. The sexual abuse she'd suffered from both men had grabbed Nick by the guts and had him all twisted up inside.

He'd spent the last few hours before dawn this morning, sitting in the dark with Stefanie, listening and waiting for her to voice the few things she could. He could tell that she had lost all hope of ever being safe from the monsters who'd hurt her. And he really worried that her fear for what Marissa could be suffering already would send her over the edge of sanity— especially if they couldn't find Marissa.

Last night had made a complicated situation between them even more complex. Nick hurt for Stefanie so badly he couldn't see straight. He had to help her. He had to find Marissa. He also needed to figure out exactly what in the hell he felt for Stefanie apart from his empathy. She was special; he'd known it when he'd seduced her six months ago. But a one-night stand didn't a relationship make. Then again he was no longer the footloose and fancy-free player he'd been then, either. Her kidnapping and this battle against evil had ripped apart how he saw the world, and the pieces hadn't yet settled back into place.

The light spilling through the open door of the sanctuary

had a blue cast to it. Part of the left wall and its stained-glass windows had been destroyed by the tornado; relief workers had covered the gap with blue plastic tarps. The path of the twister had taken a hit-or-miss route all the way through the town, then up the valley to completely decimate the top of Hades Mountain. The Falls Resort, Cinatas's stronghold of demons and vampires, had been leveled. And the mushrooming black cloud of demonic power that had hovered over Twilight for the past two weeks was gone. The citizens who'd been under the spell of black magic were back to normal and didn't remember anything odd at all.

Though they'd seen the tornado suck up some of the Red Demons, Nick was way too jaded to think for a minute that Cinatas and his flock had been completely wiped out, not with the way they could disappear in the blink of an eye.

Nick crossed the threshold into the sanctuary and came to an abrupt halt, feeling as if somebody had slapped a pair of thumbscrews on him and cranked 'em down. Stefanie was up at the front of the church, but she wasn't alone. Staff Sergeant Jaymes Bond was with her and they were talking in hushed tones.

Not cool. Not good. Staff Sergeant Bond was the woman whose pretty neck and ass he'd saved twice now—first from a lynching, then from being iced by Red Demons. She was also the woman he'd kissed in the midst of that hell. If she and Stefanie got to talking about him, he'd be screwed. Before he could duck, turn around, or do anything smart, Bond looked up at him. Then Stefanie with her haunted eyes did, too.

Biting the bullet, he headed down the aisle, his palms sweating. He held the fax up for Stefanie to see, telling her about the middle-of-the-night flight to Belize.

"I knew he'd take her back to the jungle." Stefanie shuddered. "Back to Corazón de Rojo."

Nick shook his head. "Not unless they're camping out in

ashes. Sam checked that out first thing. The prisoners we freed from there burned it to the ground. And what didn't burn they destroyed beyond recognition. So far we get zero feedback on where Herrera disappeared to after we got you out of that hell-hole."

"Stefanie was just telling me about Dr. Cinatas and her kidnapping. I can't believe what the bastards are getting away with. Concentration camps? Deadly experimental treatments? My God."

Nick blinked with surprise that Stefanie had told even that much to someone else—especially someone she barely knew.

Stefanie shut her eyes. "Marissa could be lost in that jungle forever."

"Nope," Nick said. "Ain't going to happen. We're going to find her. The helo is sitting on go. As soon as I talk to Jared and Aragon, our asses can be at the airport and on my pal's jet inside of an hour."

Stefanie opened her eyes and the determination in them slammed full force into Nick. He'd been expecting last night's hopeless devastation. "I'm coming with you," she said.

Stunned, Nick grappled for words, his insides more twisted up than ever before. "Stef . . . you can't. That's insane. Not even taking into account what happened to you there, you're not well enough to go hiking through the jungle."

"I'm going," she said firmly, with more strength and resolve than he'd ever heard from her before.

"You can't deny me justice," she continued. "It wasn't your body and soul they raped. I worked all day helping here with the tornado cleanup. I'm regaining some strength. I can and I will do this or I will die trying. It's the only way I can get my life back. It's the only way I'll ever be able to live with what happened."

Bond reached out and touched Stefanie's shoulder. "I'm coming with you. You asked about my Special Forces experience and how you could get comparable training. I'm going to give it to you."

Nick wasn't exactly sure how, but his rescue mission had just gone to hell in a handbasket in less than sixty seconds. Not only was he screwed, but the men and the women of the team were so going to kill him—because he supported Stefanie's request completely.

Chapter Four

"THERE, YOU make a beautiful bride. *El jefe* should be pleased and will show Ysalane good favor."

"You will pay for your part in Herrera's evil," Marissa said through clenched teeth. "There is a God and you will pay." She kept her gaze directed at Ysalane rather than at the mirror she stood before. She wanted to shred the white satin and lace gown from her body on principle alone. But since she didn't know when or where she'd find any clothing, she bore the humiliating finery, hating every second that she was once again forced to do, say, and be what she despised in order to survive.

The pictures of the twisted sex, blood, and death she'd seen made her feel violated, ugly, and so sick that she would rather die than be subjected to such a hell. Yet hope still beat inside her, urging her to hold on, to believe that freedom would once again be hers and that Navarre might be the large prisoner of which the old man spoke.

She had to find a way to the dungeon before tonight. She had to find a way to escape, because she knew her courage had gone as far as it could go. She didn't have the strength to survive the rape of her body and her spirit that Herrera had planned. She shut her eyes against the travesty of the wedding gown, her heart crying out in protest.

Suddenly a sense of warmth washed over her, a gentle balm to her aching spirit. Ysalane screamed and Marissa opened her eyes. The woman had her knife out, thrusting it into the air as if she were trying to frighten or ward off an invisible attack. A quick glance revealed they were still alone in the bedroom suite. Ysalane cried out again and ran from the room like a woman running from death.

• • •

Hernan Cortes Herrera hung up the phone, satisfaction and anticipation pumping up his already thrumming libido. Dusk would fall shortly and everything would be his. The necessary witnesses had now arrived. The music played and the guests chatted, excited no doubt by their method of travel to his compound—blindfolded and driven an hour in the wrong direction before being brought here. The priest had arrived. His marriage to Marissa Vasquez would be an indisputable fact and he'd have the controlling shares of SINCO. Nothing would be able to stop him then. Guatemala was a ripe plum just waiting to be plucked in a smooth coup d'état.

He'd taken every measure to assure his compound remained secret from Cinatas and the other Vladarians, as well as from any humans besides the men he had stationed here. There'd be no interruptions of his wedding plans.

Nor of his wedding night. A virgin's blood would be spilled—and drunk—willingly, because he had the one thing that would insure her full cooperation. He picked up the phone. "Is Rafael Vasquez ready yet? I think his sister should have a chance to see her family before she marries."

"*Sí, jefe,* he is ready for visitors."

"*Excelente.*" Herrera disconnected and made his way to where Ysalane was preparing his bride. A night of pleasure for him, pain for her. He could already hear her cries, taste her blood, and feel the euphoria of having absolute sovereignty over the life and death of lesser beings.

He was destined for greatness, and nothing or no one would deny him. The power and wealth he had now were a step above the abuse, insignificance, and poverty he'd suffered as an orphan on the streets, but were nowhere close to the supremacy and riches that a descendant of Hernan Cortes de Monroy y Pizarro, the marques del Valle de Oaxaca, deserved. His ancestor had conquered, then left, but Hernan Cortes Herrera would conquer and rule.

Reaching the top of the stairs, he headed to the play suite, his lips tugging into a tight smile over his pulsing fangs. Besides his Heaven Room in the dungeon, it was his favorite arena for entertainment. He'd enjoyed many orgies with climactic blood-baths in the spacious bath adjoining the suite. Perhaps later, he'd let his soon-to-be wife watch such a moving event. Everyone orgasming and dying at the same time. Once he'd taken her virginity on the altar in the Heaven Room, the playing field for his enjoyment of her would be wide open. He wouldn't want another man to touch her, or impregnate her, of course, but seeing multiple women devour her treasures would be nice. By now, she should be dressed in the wedding finery he'd sent up a short time ago. He'd deliberated over what she should wear, but in the end the traditional white was the best choice— blood stood out against it in such a marvelous contrast.

Three steps from the double doors to the suite a scream sounded and Ysalane came barreling out. She held a knife in her hand, poised to attack anything in her path. Her eyes were wild with fear, more so than whenever he'd sliced her to drink her Elan blood. He stiffened his spine, outraged that she could possibly find something more frightening than him. He was the one with the life-or-death power over her.

"A terrible wolf god will come and we are doomed!" she cried as she rushed at him like a child seeking protection.

He stepped aside when she reached him and planted his fist against her back, shoving her to the floor. "What is this madness, *puta?*"

She scrambled to her knees and kept crawling away, desperate to escape.

Moving toward her, he grabbed her hair and jerked her head around to look him in the eye. "Answer me!"

"Ysalane has seen the future. You must send that woman away immediately or we will all die. Ysalane saw the god. Ysalane knows."

For a moment he just stared at her in disbelief. What could Marissa have said to have frightened this Mayan *bruja*? Ysalane had seen or been a party to practically every delicious depravity he'd committed at the compound since gaining power under Luis Vasquez. Drinking large quantities of her precious Elan blood was what had given him the strength to fight Samir and Cinatas for Marissa and control of SINCO.

She could ruin it all with her prediction of an avenging god. He had to be the only all-powerful one, or he'd lose his choke hold on everyone.

"*Silencio!* There is no god. You tell anyone of this madness in your mind and I will kill you, Elan blood or not. Nothing is to interfere with my wedding, do you understand?"

"You will see. The god will come."

He grabbed the knife from her hand and put it to her throat, nicking the skin just enough to draw blood. Then he leaned down and licked the sweetness, feeling it tingle warmly upon his tongue. "Go to my suite and wait for me. I will energize my body with your blood before the wedding. Nothing will defeat me, Ysalane, including your madness." He would decide later whether to drain her of her blood completely or not. If he had another source of Elan blood, he wouldn't hesitate, but until he did, he'd better keep her alive . . . barely.

First a little family reunion so that his blushing bride would know exactly what was at stake tonight and every night—literally—for her brother. It was one of his most gratifying tortures yet—the bed of sharp points piercing the flesh a millimeter at a time as heavy stones were added one by one. With a satisfied smile, he walked into the suite where Marissa waited. It was going to be one hell of a night.

For a stunned moment, Marissa just stood there, staring at the door Ysalane had slammed. Then it hit her. Her moment to escape had come. She rushed to the door and yanked it open, crying out at the sight of Herrera standing in the doorway, fanged grin and knife flashing.

Madre de Dios. Surely it wasn't time yet? She wanted to throw herself on the knife he held or rip off an electrical plate and thrust her hand inside. Do anything, even if it was cowardly and damning, just to escape his plans.

"What's this? An eager bride? So you liked the pictures of Herrera playing in his dungeon."

Marissa couldn't hold back the shudder that gripped her as the chill of his undead being and the pure evil of him tightened like a hangman's noose around her neck.

Herrara brought the knife to her throat. "Or perhaps you thought to escape?"

She pushed a little until she felt the knife prick her skin and warm blood ran down her neck. "Go ahead and kill me."

He leaned down and licked the blood on her throat, making her feel as if a thousand rats were crawling over her soul.

Jerking back, she glared at him. "Death would be preferable to being with you. Touch me and I will kill myself."

His nostrils flared with anger as he narrowed his gaze. "You think to have power over me, *puta*? You think you can escape me? I will show you who has the power. There is someone in my dungeon whom you need to see. Then you will understand what exactly the consequences will be if you don't willingly cooperate with *everything* I wish." He grabbed her arm and pulled her from the room and down the hallway.

His icy touch burned into her skin, but no matter the price, Marissa wasn't about to turn down a chance to see Navarre. It had to be him in the dungeon.

She carefully memorized the way, taking note of everything in the rooms she passed. One interesting display in a long corridor was of ancient Spanish armor such as the conquistadors wore. Several hefty swords and long deadly spears were in a cabinet with two full suits of armor at each end. Opposite the cabinet was an enormous tapestry depicting the Spanish defeating the native Aztecs in a battle that had rivers of blood running through the stone streets. It wasn't until she was even with the weaving that she realized the Spaniards all had vampire fangs.

In the dark of the night, her grandmother had whispered of bloodthirsty vampires descending and whole villages disappearing before dawn. Though Marissa had suffered greatly at her vampire uncle's hand and had lost five members of her family to the bastard, she hadn't believed her grandmother's stories about mass annihilation. Now she had to ask herself if whole civilizations had suffered such a fate.

Two armed guards with pitted faces and potbellies stood before a black iron door. It took both of them to pull open the heavy doors, which screeched horrendously as they moved. Beyond was nothing but darkness. Black stone made up the walls, the ceiling, the floor. It was like walking into a grave. Marissa's heart thumped more wildly with every step. Goose bumps covered her skin as the chill air penetrated the white silk of her dress like an ice pick to the bone. Surely, a man would die of hypothermia before he could be tortured to death down here.

A long corridor stretched out before her at the bottom of the stairs where garish red doors slashed through the blackness of the dungeon, enhancing its hellish effect. Sickening moans echoed from a large open area at the far end of the hall. Marissa's stomach churned. *Dios!* She'd been praying that Navarre was here, but not if it meant those tortured sounds were coming from him. She had to force herself to keep a steady pace because everything inside her wanted to run to help. Yet she instinctively knew that doing such a thing would only put another weapon into Herrera's hands.

"I've a little surprise for you, *pero* first let me give you a tour of my Heaven." He opened a door to a room painted in red, a room she recognized from the pictures Ysalane had forced upon her.

"This is the Virgin's altar of Goodness and Light." Herrera walked over to a white-draped stone altar shaped like an *X* with an elongated center. Heavy chains lay in wait for slender wrists and ankles. The image of the woman she'd seen on the thing with the man holding a whip over her turned into a motion picture in her mind. A wave of fear and dizziness slammed into her and she had to grab the nearest thing to stay upright. She nearly fell when the metal and leather strap she held swayed. It was suspended from the ceiling.

"That is the Flying Nun," he said, moving over to caress the contraption. "You lie on the straps facedown so that you are suspended horizontally, legs and arms wide like you're flying. You're naked, of course. There are no clothes permitted in Heaven. When you fly in this, Herrera then has access to every part of your body, your lovely breasts, your ass, your *cuchara*, everything. There is nothing I cannot do to you then. You will love the Flying Nun like I do, *sí*?"

Marissa locked her knees and released the leather, sure that any second she'd faint. He went on to other apparatuses in the room, but she tuned him out to focus entirely on taking one breath at a time. She would not cave in to the horror. She would find a way out of this nightmare. She had to.

"You are speechless? Perhaps you will find your voice when I show you *why* you will be Herrera's little *La Chingada*, eager to enjoy all of my heavenly treasures as often as I please," he said, motioning her from the room. She fled the horror of the room as fast as she could. Back in the corridor, she saw the wrinkled old man whom Ysalane had called to help her exit the last red door on the left.

"*Jefe,*" he said, as if speaking to God, then made a bow so deep that Marissa was sure she heard his bones crack. "There has been no change yet. Do you want for Pedro to bring *el doctor*?"

"*Mañana,*" Herrera replied. "What is it that you carry behind your back?"

The old man held up a fistful of long strands of black hair and grinned. "Hair for Pedro."

Herrera laughed good-naturedly, the almost human sound and response only making the vampire seem that much more wicked. "You need a *verga*, old man, not hair. A *pene muy grande*, like Herrera."

Marissa stared at the long black hair. Navarre had long black hair. No change? Doctor? Navarre had to be here.

Herrera grabbed a lock of her hair and gave it a tug. "Perhaps I will let him have yours, too. But then what would I hold on to when . . ."

Marissa shut out his voice and cried out to Navarre with her mind. He'd come to her that way before, in her dreams when she was in Twilight and then at dusk when his wolf spirit had appeared. This time all she could feel was the deathly chill of the air. All she could hear was the pitiful moaning from down the hall. All she could see was the horrendous fanged monster standing before her.

He released her hair and shoved her in front of him. "Time for a little reunion," he said.

She moved down the corridor, sure that whatever lay at the end was worse than anything Herrera planned to do to her.

She first saw the bottom half of a man lying upon a bed of what looked like sharp iron stakes. There were heavy weights on his feet, forcing the stakes to pierce his flesh. Blood dripped from his heels and ankles.

Madre de Dios. She couldn't look. She couldn't look away. As she entered the room, she saw more weights across the man's hips and holding down his arms. A black cloth covered his face. He moaned in agony. His every movement, his every breath, dug the dagger points deeper into his skin. She was devastated for him, even as relief that it wasn't Navarre flooded through her.

"What?" asked Herrera. "Do you not recognize your own brother, my bride?"

A black-robed *thing*—nothing that could do what it did could be human—pulled off the cloth covering the man's head and Marissa saw the weary and defeated face of her younger brother Rafael. The brother whom she'd been told had died when trying to escape her uncle's compound months ago.

"Rafael!" she screamed and clutched her chest.

"Kill me," her brother whispered. "Kill me."

"Now you see why you will do all that Herrera wants, *novia*. Every time you do not, your beloved brother will suffer this and worse."

"Stop this. I will," Marissa cried, falling to her knees. "*Dios mio*, I will. Please just stop!"

Herrera motioned and the black-robed thing pushed a button. The stakes retracted in a flash and her brother, screaming horribly, fell to the bed of checkered steel, then passed out.

"Rafe! Rafe. I'm so sorry," Marissa sobbed; the horror and the hatred and the anger raging in her consumed her.

Through her tears, Marissa saw the robed thing go over to the wall and push a button. She choked on a scream, thinking he meant to send the spikes back up, but instead doors opened. Inside was a rolling cart with metal buckets on it. The robed thing took one of the buckets and threw it on Rafe's face. He turned his face, but didn't completely revive.

"The wedding ceremony will begin shortly. Perhaps if all goes well, he will be in a better position to speak to you for a few moments next time." Herrera grabbed her arm, pulling her to her feet. Once standing, she jerked away from him and moved closer to her brother.

"Rafe!"

"Defiant so soon?" Herrera purred, from just behind her. "Do you need to see again what price your brother pays for it?"

Marissa stiffened her shoulders and tried to suck air into lungs that couldn't seem to breathe. "No," she whispered. "I will come." She had no choice.

• • •

Marissa! Navarre snapped his eyes open and this time the medicine Aragon's mortal woman had given him didn't steal him
away. The burning pain from the fire strike seared through his
mind, trying to rip away his consciousness. But by Logos, he
could hear Marissa's call to him, feel her over the pain, and he
latched on to her need, determined to stay with her.

So strong was her presence that he expected her body to be
resting firmly upon his as it had before when he'd first arrived
upon the mortal ground. She'd fainted at the sight of him and
had lain with the silk of her hair brushing his chest and the
thunder of her heart pounding against his. He could still feel
the soothing touch of her palm over his heated skin.

As it was then, he could only see darkness.

Another plea from Marissa's spirit slammed into him. This
time he heard the dire horror of her cry. His body jerked in response, his head and back rising from the hard, cold surface
beneath him. But that was as far as he could go. His hips,
wrists, and ankles were chained down. The metal links scraped
and clanked as he strained against them. He felt the pull and
ache of the knife wound in his back, an insignificant injury
that would have healed by now, were his warrior's strength
what it should be. That it hadn't let him know just how weakened he'd become from the Pyrathian's fire. He was also blind,
but other parts of his senses seemed stronger than ever. He
could feel the presence of Marissa and the wicked malevolence
surrounding them both so vividly it was almost like a picture
in his mind.

Marissa! He cried out with his spirit, but couldn't seem to
reach her through the horror pulsing from her. He tried to conjure his wolf spirit, but nothing happened.

Sucking in air, he pulled against the binding chains with all
of his might. He strained until the metal cut into his flesh, until
it seemed as if the very blood in his veins dripped from the

pores of his skin. Spent, he lay back gasping as frustration ate a deeper hole of uselessness in his warrior's spirit.

A warrior who could not fight, a being who could not serve, was less than the depraved, was less than nothing. His spirit screamed to the heavens, praying that Logos would strike him into nonexistence.

With Herrera's firm grip on her arm, Marissa walked into the crowded great room screaming so loudly on the inside that it was impossible no one could hear her. Since leaving her unconscious brother in the dungeon, she'd run dozens of escape scenarios through her mind—even contemplating appealing to the people gathered to witness her marriage to Herrera, for surely there had to be one among them who might help her.

Herrera had nixed that the moment they'd left the dungeon by telling her that if she tried to escape, not only would Rafe go immediately back into torture, but Herrera would have his men gun down the guests, bury them in the jungle, and there'd be a different set of guests the next night. All of that would be taking place while she spent the night as his flying nun.

She couldn't manage to smile as Herrera led her past the guests, but she did keep her mouth shut. Still, she desperately searched the gazes of the unnaturally euphoric men and women, hoping and praying that she'd find someone smart enough to question Herrera's farce, hoping that she could somehow find help. Not one of them gave her more than a moment's glance from glazed eyes, and she realized they had to be drugged, most likely through the punch or the hors d'oeuvres.

She wondered how she was even able to stand upright while every fiber of her being raged so violently against the overwhelming, undefeatable evil surrounding her. Were Stefanie, Dr. Nette, Erin, and little Megan facing the same thing? Were they dead or wishing they were? As she would be by tomorrow—Marissa turned to look at Herrera, suddenly recalling what he'd said to Stefanie last night when the vampires had descended into the ranger camp. *I have missed my* putica.

Stefanie had wanted to die. Had practically starved herself to death. And now Marissa knew why. She also deeply understood why Stefanie never spoke of it. Marissa had only heard about what Herrera wanted and had seen pictures of what he would do and she felt shamed. How much greater would that shame be afterward?

Knowing what Stefanie had suffered, yet bore silently, reached deeply into Marissa, giving her strength amid the seeming hopelessness of her situation. Evil had to fear something and God was all she had at the moment. She leaned closer to Herrera and whispered, "My *abuela* knew things, saw things. You heard the rumors in Tío Luis's compound. So you know she was always right. She said Stefanie was a saint, for one day she would be a god who devours her enemies with fire. You abused her. Hurt her. You raped Stefanie, didn't you?"

An odd look that almost had an edge of fear to it flickered in Herrera's black eyes, then he blinked and shrugged. "Jealous, *mi novia?* No need. She whored as often for your *tío* as she did for me."

Marissa finally found a reason to smile. "And now he's dead."

Herrera paled, his eyes widened in fear. She'd found a crack, a tiny crevice in the vampire's invincibility.

Clearly agitated, Herrera grabbed her arm and moved her more quickly to the opposite end of the large room. A priest, robed in rich purple and gold and wearing a jeweled biretta on his head, stood with his back to the room. Head bowed and hands clasped, he actually appeared to be praying. Then sudden hope flared in her heart when the priest turned around. She knew him.

It had been at least twenty years ago, before evil had killed her family and reshaped her life. She'd been a child then with only a handful of birthdays, but not too young to remember this priest. Father Dom had visited her grandmother many times.

She met his gaze directly, unable to stop the silent plea that surely had to be written all over her face. Was it her imagination that the priest recognized who she was? That he understood what was really happening? He'd blinked at her in a deliberate fashion twice, then nodded his head. Did she finally have an ally here after all?

Herrera tensed at her side and she lowered her gaze from the priest's.

"Let's see this done now," Herrera said. "Heaven awaits."

Father Dom nodded and gathered everyone's attention for the ceremony. He stated her full name, Marissa Isabella Tajeda Vasquez, Herrera's, and their intention to marry. Then the priest began speaking in Latin.

Herrera interrupted, telling the priest to speak Spanish.

Father Dom shook his head. "Canon law demands that marriage ceremonies outside the church must be performed in Holy Latin or they will not be legal."

"I've never heard of such *mierda*," Herrera said.

Father Dom lifted a brow. "When was the last time you saw a Catholic wedding ceremony outside of a sanctuary?"

Herrera waved his hand as if swatting a fly. "Just do what you have to do and hurry."

Father Dom then proceeded to marry her to Herrera. Marissa wasn't sure at what point her mind snapped, overloaded by all that had happened, and a surrealistic detachment took over. This just wasn't happening.

But it was. And how much more would come before someone, or something, could stop it?

Chapter Five

DESPITE THE cool, pressurized interior of the private jet, perspiration beaded Stefanie's clammy skin, trickling between her breasts and making her back itch. Her heart raced and every muscle of her body twitched with fear so badly that her insides shook from the strain of trying to stay absolutely still. She didn't want to talk to anyone, didn't want to argue anymore about the stupidity of walking back into the lion's den.

Her sister Annette had pleaded until she was blue in the face and now she fumed as she flipped through the pages of the same magazine for about the hundredth time. Though the noise was as irritating as the meant-to-be-soothing music piping into the cabin, the action was endearing. Stefanie knew with each turn of the page that her sister desperately wanted to heal her. Being a heart surgeon had trained Annette to solve dire problems with her hands, and she had to keep them in motion even though she couldn't do anything to help Stefanie's pain.

Stefanie kept her eyes practically shut, feigning a sleep that she could rarely find—not with the nightmare of her captivity still eating away at her. The images and the shame of Vasquez's and Herrera's rape of her body and her spirit were always with her. She'd been a prisoner for six months and the nightly abuse didn't stop until she starved herself to emaciation and Marissa's grandmother declared her a saint. Only then did Herrera and Vasquez leave her alone. As hideous and horrific as it was, it didn't compare to having to live with what had happened to Abe. What Vasquez had done to her friend.

She shuddered as the memory of Abe's screams reached out to her, as if by returning to Belize she could once again hear his cries as he was being eaten alive. Her soul would never recover from it. In returning to the Belizean jungle and hunting down

Herrera, she hoped to save Marissa and maybe vent the rage inside of her. By doing so, she hoped she might survive long enough to see an end to the Vladarian Vampires and their murder of innocents through Sno-Med.

The only thing left for her was the peace of death. She knew her spirit would find ease from the pain then because she'd already died twice and felt it. The fire man, the Pyrathian from the spirit world, had saved her both times, breathed life from the heavens into her, and forced her to live.

She didn't know why. She wished he would let her die. And when she was close to escaping the pain of this world for a third time days ago, he'd appeared to her and begged her to fight. So fight she would . . . for a time.

She thought she'd stuffed all of the horrors she'd lived through into a place deep inside her and locked the door tight, but with every mile that passed, more and more crept out. How could she do this? In her mind she knew Annette's arguments that she didn't have the physical or the emotional health and strength for this battle were true. Yet in her heart, she knew she had to do this. The idea of justice, of destroying the evil, was the only thing keeping her from being devoured by it.

A large, warm hand covered hers and she didn't have to look to know that Nick had joined her. She almost pulled her hand away, but settled on tightening her grip on the arm of the seat. There were moments when another's touch was too hard to bear even though she knew the person wouldn't harm her. Sometimes any interaction was too much and she felt as if she would shatter inside.

He leaned closer and whispered softly enough that his voice wouldn't be heard above the music and the sound of the jet's engines. "Your sister means well. She fought for so long to find you and get you out of the Vladarians' clutches that it's practically killing her for you to walk back into them."

"I know," Stefanie said. "And I understand why. But . . ." She searched for the right way to say what she felt.

This evening, the turmoil of arguing to join the fight against evil and rescue Marissa had left her raw. She'd been upset earlier and Nick thought her current tension a carryover from that. She was more than willing to let him believe it.

Annette had been completely against Stefanie going. Aragon had sided with Annette. Jared had reiterated several times that the main objective of the mission was to save Marissa—not spend what little manpower they had caring for the sick. If she slowed them down, she'd be sent back. He wasn't being unkind, but honest from a warrior's perspective. Nick had ridden the fence, not encouraging her one way or the other. Jaymes, a woman trained in special ops, had been her only supporter— something that surprised Stefanie.

"It doesn't matter where I am," she said, continuing. "Back in Belize. Sequestered at a ranger camp in Twilight. What difference does it make? Not even a church is sacred."

"You're right," Nick said, then sighed. "Cinatas's desecration and near crucifixion of a priest in broad daylight has taken this battle to a new level. We're fighting more than a corrupt medical organization murdering innocents for Elan blood."

"Whatever they are trying to do—get blood, control oil markets, desecrate churches—doesn't matter. As long as these monsters walk the earth no one anywhere is safe."

"I get that, but the big picture says that Cinatas and the Vladarians are after the whole global enchilada from the north to the south pole and from east to west. Jared, Aragon, and Sam all agree."

Imagining the entire world being like the hell she had lived in for six months was too much. She shuddered hard. "Taking the bastards down one at a time doesn't seem to be good enough fast enough."

"It's not. For every one we take out another one rises to fill the gap. Like Herrera trying to take over Vasquez's place with SINCO. Taking them down one at a time has been effective for Twilight, but we're going to have to do something big and fast to stop them completely. First, though, we get Marissa back."

"I pray that it won't be too—" Stefanie couldn't finish her sentence. Emotion closed her throat.

"It won't be too late," Nick said, clasping her hand tighter. "It won't be."

But Stefanie knew better than anyone else that it might. Not that she feared death for Marissa. It was the things Herrera could do to make a woman want death that she worried about.

"I hope to find the bastard who's using my father's name while we're here," Nick said.

She'd forgotten about Reed Sinclair. Nick's father had died when freeing Sam from Vasquez's clutches eight years ago. She figured that Nick had deliberately changed the subject to keep her from thinking about Herrera and Marissa. Not that the maneuver was any heroic deed, but it still touched her. She'd never forget the care he'd shown when he'd plucked her from her bed and forced her to obliterate images of Vasquez and Herrera with his kickass Glock. It was the first time she'd been able to channel the rage inside her at those responsible instead of swallowing it. Nick had given her permission to hate what had happened to her and to want justice for it.

He'd changed a great deal from the smooth-talking seducer who'd snowed her before, and some long-gone part of her wished that the Stefanie she used to be before had met up with the present-day Nick. That was about as far as she could think about a relationship with regard to herself—past wishfulness. Still, she loosened her grip on the arm of her seat and twisted her hand until his palm fell against hers. "You lost your parents when you were a lot younger than me. That had to have been hard."

Nick shrugged. "Shit happens and you deal. Though I

wouldn't have dealt with it well if it hadn't been for Sam. Instead of wearing a badge, I'd have ended up on the wrong side of the prison bars." He gave a short laugh.

"I think you're shortchanging yourself in that assessment. If you were just an ordinary guy who went to work then hung out drinking with your buddies, I might agree with you. But it takes initiative to learn to fly a helicopter as well as you do, and it takes a giving nature to spend so much of your time with LifeFlight. Annette's told me stories of just how handy you were in helping her save lives."

"Hey. She's the miracle worker. I just handle the helo." He squeezed her hand then lifted up both of his hands. "These babies go through withdrawal symptoms if I'm grounded for more than a week. Flying is like . . . like having heaven at your fingertips. I'm anxious to get off this plane and get into the helo waiting for us."

"Where are we going to go first?"

"Erin is already running through all the car rental agencies to see if any of them rented cars from around the Belize City municipal airport in the predawn hours. If she doesn't have a lead on Herrera by the time we land, we'll go to Corazón de Rojo and start asking questions of anyone in the area. Herrera has to be somewhere in the vicinity."

Corazón. Vasquez's compound. The hellhole she'd lived in. Hearing that it had burned to the ground hadn't been enough for her. She wasn't even sure if a nuclear bomb would do it for her. She blinked, suddenly realizing that Nick had been talking and she hadn't heard him.

". . . I know. I'm sorry, but Sam needed me to ask while we are at Corazón. Do you know where Abe Bennett's grave is? Sam wants to bring him home. His mother has been working with the embassy with little progress, but if there's any way we can help expedite that for her, it would help Abe's mother bring closure to her son's death."

"His bones might be left, but I don't know if you'll be able to get to them," she said softly.

"Shit. I don't know that I want to hear this. Why?"

"Vasquez locked him into a glass chamber of flesh-eating ants. Then they all sat there and watched him be eaten alive."

"Jesus help me," Nick said. "Just when I think I can't hear any worse, it gets ten times as bad."

"In comparison to what Abe was subjected to at the camp every night, he welcomed the death. Any death. The last I saw of him, his bones were in with the ants. That's why I never said anything about Abe. I couldn't talk about it before and it wouldn't have done his mother or anyone else any good to hear how he died. Sometimes having no closure is the greatest gift."

Turning her way, his eyes grave, he brushed a strand of hair back from her damp forehead and reverently touched her cheek. "You're a miracle. That you still breathe, think, or function at all takes more courage than anything I've ever heard of and more guts than I have. But someday you're going to have to sit down and let it all out. You're going to have to tell someone about everything that happened, because if you keep all that shit inside of you it will eat at you just like the ants ate your friend."

On some level Stefanie knew Nick was right. But that someday wasn't today. And she wasn't all that sure she wanted to live for a long time anyway. She had drawn Abe into the corruption at Sno-Med mess, so it was only fitting that she die, too.

Burgenland, Austria

Dr. Anthony Cinatas threw the bottle of merlot against the wall and watched Château Petrus's finest spatter red all over the snowy décor—silk wall, calfskin sofa, and centuries-old Turkish carpet. He'd had it all within his grasp and one minor miscalculation had jerked everything just beyond his reach. Temporarily so, but still aggravating.

Life had been a bitch before he died and he was finding out just how much bigger a bitch she could be now that he'd joined the ranks of the undead. Make that super undead, he thought, shifting his hand and sending out tiny bolts of electricity to zap a collection of ivory carvings. Snap, crackle, pop. Gone. Snap, crackle, pop. Gone.

Exactly what should have happened to Erin Morgan et al and didn't. *Snap*. Erin's head should have rolled and her blood flowed to the congregated damned. *Crackle*. The Batista sisters should have been reduced to dust by his crispy touch. *Pop*. The little angel should have become his bride. *Gone*. The spirit warriors and the town of Twilight should have been wiped out completely. He still hadn't figured out what went wrong. He'd had all of the citizens gathered in the high school cafeteria. All the armed demons guarding them had to do was open fire on everyone when the Shadowmen cavalry came to the rescue. But none of that had happened, thanks in part to the angel in their midst and her impenetrable wall of White Fire. He wasn't telling the rest of the damned world that, though. His story was that he alone had battled Logos after an entire faction of Shadowmen Warriors had wiped out all of the Red Demons. That Cinatas lived and escaped Logos to tell his story was a feat accomplished by only one other among the realms of the damned. That was Heldon.

It was the only way Cinatas could control the damage that Erin and the rest had done to his reputation among the damned. He was back at Zion and had yet to be officially crowned as emperor of his Unholy Empire. Still, the trip hadn't been a total loss. He'd discovered the secret to acquiring ultimate demonic power, something that Heldon had kept hidden for thousands of years.

A discreet tap at the door alerted him to Bastion's arrival. Cinatas waited enough time to keep Bastion properly humble, then bade him enter.

"Thank you, master," Bastion said as he bowed, his face touching the floor in his subservience.

"You may speak," Cinatas said after a time.

Bastion rose. "I have good news for you, master."

"Château Petrus is now mine?"

"Almost. Master Lacoste has agreed. Master Moueix has not, but given the incentives he now faces, I expect it won't be long. The news is that Conrad Pitt has accepted the modeling job and will board a plane for Dubai shortly."

"An eager boy. I didn't expect he would decide so quickly. This is excellent. Call Dr. Shahtar and tell him we'll be ready for the face transplant in two days. You have of course reserved rooms for Mr. Pitt and me at Burj Al Arab?" He slid his fingertips over his scarred cheek and chin. With plenty of Elan blood, it shouldn't take more than two days for him to be a new man.

"Yes, the Royal Suite for you and a spectacular room for Mr. Pitt. He will be thoroughly impressed and completely off his guard."

"Perfect. Any progress in locating Herrera?"

"Nothing past the flight to Belize City, master. You will find it interesting to know that another made inquires of the airport as well. The calls came from Twilight, Tennessee."

"They're after the woman Herrera took. An excellent turn of events. I'll be able to eliminate Erin, her warriors, and capture two angels as well. Monitor the situation for me, and as soon as you find Herrera, I'll want a full report. Samir is still looking for Herrera, too?"

"Yes, master."

"Good. Call Valois and have him meet me in Dubai. Herrera and Samir must die for their disobedience. No one walks from my coronation and lives. By getting Valois into the picture, I can blame the deaths of the Vladarians on Valois and avoid a rebellion among the vampires until I'm ready to annihilate them all. Unlike that cowardly Nyros hiding in hell, you serve me well, Bastion."

"Thank you, master."

"You are excused from my presence," Cinatas said absently, his mind already churning out a brilliant plan on how to kill a number of birds with one stone. Life might be a bitch, but he had what it took to screw her good.

Chapter Six

" . . . In final blessing, we ask humbly that their lives bear witness to the reality of love," Father Dom said, ending the ceremony in Spanish rather than the Latin he'd been speaking. He then pronounced them husband and wife.

Marissa couldn't believe it. The ceremony was over.

She gasped for air as a wave of dizziness swept over her. Father Dom reached out and steadied her. "Wisdom and light will come with patience, child," he said, then turned away from her.

That was it? All the patience, wisdom, and light in the universe weren't going to save her.

"Congratulations, Señora Herrera. Your home is as beautiful as you and as magnificent as your new husband," said a woman, dressed in black and crusted with diamonds. She had bloodred lips and pale, plastic-looking skin. Her dark eyes oozed with resentment as if she envied Marissa's position as Herrera's bride. Marissa backed away from the woman, returning only a nod of acknowledgment. If the woman wasn't a vampire, then she obviously aspired to be.

As with Ysalane, Marissa found herself shocked that anyone would seek to be damned or to be with a monster like Herrera. True, Herrera had dark hair, intense eyes, and features drawn from a strong Spanish heritage. Some who didn't know him might call him handsome. To her he was the personification of hideous evil.

The rest of the greetings and congratulations passed in a surreal blur. Everyone spoke to her as if nothing were wrong. They called her "Señora Herrera," told her how lucky she was, and gave her advice. Couldn't they see she was screaming inside?

"I commend you, Herrera," said an impeccably dressed man with stylishly cut silver hair.

"And how is that, Otto?"

"You have chosen the perfect woman to complement the arm of the future *presidente* of Guatemala."

"I told you she was perfect. You did an excellent job in getting the guests and the priest here," Herrera said.

"It will cost you, of course."

"She's extremely rich, General. So money for anything, anything at all, is no problem. It's time to put the power back into the hands of those who are born to rule, no?"

The General smiled and clapped Herrera on the back. From their conversation, it was clear the General and Herrera planned to take over the country in the next election, either by coercing the vote or by military force. Guatemala's turbulent political history made it vulnerable to vultures. Herrera as a dictator would make Hussein and Hitler angels in comparison.

She'd yet to figure out if she was in Guatemala, where escape over the border would be more difficult, or Belize, where everything would be easier.

"I've some news you'll find interesting," said the General.

Herrera leaned closer. "I'm listening."

The General flicked his hard black eyes at her. "Perhaps a moment alone would be advisable."

Herrera nodded and led the man to a far corner of the room. Marissa drew a deep breath. She had expected that the second the priest finished the ceremony, Herrera would have whisked her away to his torture chamber. So she wasn't going to complain about standing stiff-faced and socializing, though the triviality of it in comparison to her dire needs made her silent screaming even louder.

When Herrera and the General pulled out cigars, Marissa decided that it was her chance to do something, anything, to help herself. Bubbling with frustration that she couldn't just run off like a madwoman, she eased a fraction at a time toward the refreshment table at the other end of the room, where the exit was located. She occasionally spoke to one person or another, but tried to stay as removed yet as aware as she could.

After about ten steps, she realized that a guard at the wall closest to her was staying parallel with her movements, his gaze centered on her. Glancing to her left, she saw another one on the other side doing the same, hemming her in.

Edging to the middle of the room, she stopped delaying and headed directly for the punch and cake. Under the guise of accepting the food and drink from the serving maid, Marissa studied what lay beyond the exit doors. She was able to make out a clear path to the kitchen.

A svelte woman wearing a red, formfitting suit and an elegant hat that dipped an intriguing layer of black netting over her upper face turned at the table and clasped Marissa's arm as if to quietly get her attention. At that exact moment, the serving maid handed Marissa a cup of the deep red punch. The movement caused the liquid to spill over the sleeve of her wedding gown.

"*Dios.* Forgive me," the woman said in American-accented Spanish. Marissa jerked to attention, her heart thumping with hope that she might have found a person she could confide in. "I only wanted to congratulate you on your marriage."

Marissa grabbed a napkin and blotted her sleeve. "Don't worry," she said. If it wasn't for the fact that the punch looked disturbingly like blood she wouldn't have even bothered to clean the stain, for the dress, though beautiful, was part of the nightmare.

"You must dilute it with water quickly," the woman said. "Is there a bathroom close by?" she asked the maid.

The maid was staring at the stain as if she would be executed over it then snapped to attention. "*Sí,* this way please." She motioned them to follow her from the room in the direction of the kitchen. Marissa didn't wait for a second invitation to leave her two watchdog goons behind. She went with the maid and the other woman accompanied them, as well.

She heard the guards scrambling, but didn't look back. The maid took them through the kitchen, where Marissa saw at least twenty-five people preparing large dinner plates, letting her know that a banquet was about to ensue. She'd choke on anything she tried to swallow.

They passed the small elevator, which stood open with a rolling cart inside that had four metal bowls of food scraps on it. All too quickly, they entered a corridor that Marissa immediately recognized from the conquistador display cabinet and tapestry. The steps leading to the dungeon lay to the left. Thankfully, the maid turned to the right and soon opened a door to the bathroom, just as the guards rounded the corner of the hall.

The woman who had followed them waved off the maid. "I can help her. Why don't you get those hardworking men a piece of cake while I clean her sleeve?"

The maid hesitated.

"It's all right," Marissa assured the maid, realizing the woman had gone to great lengths to get her alone. "It was my fault. We'll be fine." Still looking doubtful, the maid nodded and left. Marissa then turned to the stylish woman and held out her hand. "I'm Marissa Vasquez."

The woman lifted a brow. "Don't you mean Herrera? I'm Chanel Langston, General Menendez's fiancée. Let me see what I can do about that stain."

Marissa blinked and had to bite the inside of her cheek to keep from crying out in disappointment. No help would be forthcoming from this quarter. The woman took charge, turning on the tap, adjusting the temperature, and dabbing at the stain with a cloth off the counter.

"You know, I was surprised by Hernan's sudden wedding plans. Have you known him long?"

"He worked for my *tío* Luis," Marissa replied, taking the cloth from Chanel. "I think I can take care of this myself."

She sighed. "I've offended you. I didn't mean to."

"But you did mean for the punch to spill and you did mean to get me alone to ask questions, *sí*?" Marissa challenged.

"Yes," said Chanel. "The General asked me to find out more about you."

Marissa deliberated for only a moment. This woman might be her only chance ever to get a message out. Surely someone who'd known decency and freedom all of their life would help her? And if it backfired? Maybe she would have escaped with Rafe by then. "You want the truth?" she whispered. "Herrera kidnapped me for my money and for the controlling shares in the SINCO Oil Corporation. If I don't cooperate with everything he wants then my brother, who is being tortured in the dungeon under our feet, will die. Also, if you say anything about this to anyone now and Herrera finds out then everyone here will die. If you can secretly contact Sheriff Sam Sheridan in Twilight, Tennessee, and tell him, maybe you can help. Do you know where I am?"

Chanel paled and grasped the edge of the vanity. "No. We came by helicopter, but were blindfolded after changing to Herrera's personal aircraft at a heliport someplace in the jungle. That port was a forty-five-minute trip from Belize City. I'm sorry. I will . . . uh . . . see what can be done to help you."

A loud commotion sounded from the kitchen, startling both of them.

"Put some soap on the stain," Chanel said. "I'll go tell them you'll be but a moment more. Be very careful." She squeezed Marissa's shoulder then left.

Marissa peered into the hallway, surprised to see Chanel going in the opposite direction from the way they had come— and the guards who'd followed were nowhere in sight. The noise in the kitchen continued. Marissa turned the water in the bathroom on full blast then, as she left, locked and shut the door. It wouldn't delay searching for her very long, but every second counted. She inched her way to the kitchen. There she saw most everyone, including her guards, fighting a fire that encompassed the top of the huge stove. The water they threw on it only made it flare higher.

A fire extinguisher was on the wall right next to her and she reached for it. But once she had it in hand, she glanced at the service elevator and didn't think twice. She pulled the cart out, ducked down, and climbed in, taking the extinguisher with her as she hit the down button.

When the doors opened below, she blasted the robed thing who'd tortured her brother full in the face with white foam. He stumbled against the steel bed her brother had been on, trying to deflect the foam. His hood fell back, revealing a bald man with a face ten times more scarred than Ysalane's. Marissa moved closer, forcing him back until he landed on the bed. Showing no mercy, she located the button controlling the spikes. The steel daggerlike points rose too slowly for her taste and she took the heavy extinguisher, hitting the robed thing on the head twice, refusing to consider there was anything human about it.

Then, seeing no other guards inside the chamber, she grabbed two long bars with branding arms at one end. One she wedged in the elevator and the other she slid through the looped handles of the double doors. All of the red doors were locked, except for the one that opened to Herrera's "play" room. She wasted precious moments searching for keys, even went back to the creature she'd knocked out on the steel spiked bed, but couldn't find any. Frustration ate at her as she picked up another iron bar and a thick wooden-handled mallet.

She returned to the corridor and heard a moan that sounded like her brother from the first door on the right. She went directly to that door. The old man who'd held the long hair in his hand had exited from the door on her left. She prayed that once she got to Rafael, she'd find Navarre behind the other door.

Hammering the iron bar, she wedged it into the door lock and popped it open. Inside, she found Rafael wrapped in blood-soaked bandages and bound by chains to a steel-framed bed.

"Rafael," she said, rushing to his bedside. He didn't turn her way or answer and she saw from his flaming cheeks and slurred mumbling that he was delirious with fever.

Madre de Dios. Would he even live long enough for her to get him to help? She wedged the iron chains binding him loose from the bed frame. Then taking the hammer and the rod, she headed for the other door.

"Going somewhere?" Herrera asked, appearing before her.

Marissa screamed in frustration and fear. She had stupidly lost sight of the fact that Herrera wasn't bound by the physical laws of mortals.

"I had no idea how resourceful my new wife could be. It will require keeping a closer eye on you in the future. I saw the priest signal you. If you think he'll help you escape, think again. Luckily for our wedding, I've stopped you from escaping. Afterward, my men will handle our guests and the priest will be taken to his church. Once the documents for our marriage are filed, he'll be crucified there."

She went to hit him with the hammer and the rod, but he deflected them both with blows so strong that it left her arms numb. He grabbed her wrists and wrenched her arms behind her. Her struggles were like the fluttering of butterfly wings against the strength of a vulture.

"Since we don't want your brother to die yet, you're the one I'll teach a little lesson to tonight," he purred. "Very convenient of you to come to my dungeon so soon. I was tiring of the wedding niceties and yearning for Heaven. So we'll go ahead and start our fun while they enjoy their own meals upstairs." He dragged her from Rafael's room, down the corridor, and into his sick room to the stone altar. She fought hard to no avail. Within minutes he had her manacled, spread-eagled in the X, her arms and legs stretched out painfully tight with no room to maneuver. She was completely pinned down.

He pulled out a sharp, gold dagger. "Remember my rule. No clothes allowed. You are overdressed, no?" He smiled.

"You're going to burn for this," Marissa choked out, finally able to force words past the solid lump of fear and desolation in her throat. "You're a coward whose power comes only through force rather than any true strength."

He slapped her face. Her teeth cut painfully into her cheek as the taste of blood filled her mouth. "Look above you, my dear, and watch what Herrera does to you. I'm going to tear your soul apart a piece at a time, starting with your virgin body."

Dios mio, she already felt as if he'd ripped a part of her away when she saw what he'd done to her brother. She'd never be the same. Above her on the ceiling was an enormous mirror. He ran an icy hand up her leg, pushing her dress up, until he exposed her panties and cupped her silk-covered sex. The evil in his cowardly touch pierced to the very heart of her, ripping more of her away as he caressed her. She struggled hard to escape him, but couldn't.

"Time to spill your virgin's blood and drink it as you watch. I'm going to use you every way possible until you're near death from the abuse. After that, perhaps you'll learn you cannot escape me." He smiled then. "Hopefully not, though, because I'll enjoy giving you the lesson again and again." He grabbed the crotch of her underwear and jerked hard. The cloth cut sharply into her thighs before the silk ripped.

Navarre! Navarre! Marissa's heart cried out against it all, her spirit reaching for the one man whose wolf spirit had given her so sweet a taste of freedom. She couldn't bear this. She couldn't survive this.

"No!" Navarre's yell roared into the darkness as Marissa's call for him pierced his mind. It was more painful than the Pyrathian's fire strike and went directly to his heart. He jerked hard against the chains binding him, fighting with all of his might to free himself. The burning in his head intensified to an excruciating throb as he fought its almost overwhelming pain.

"No! No!" He refused to succumb to the pain and the darkness! He would not give up! Suddenly his body convulsed and his wolf spirit broke free from the gray edges of the spirit realm and plunged to the mortal ground.

The moon and stars glittered in the night sky and the cool wind stung the wolf's face, rippling over his thick fur as he dropped from the heavens. The moment his paws hit the earth, he ran through the jungle, his entire being focused on Marissa's beckoning need. He knew she was close.

The wolf could feel her. He saw the house, the lights, then the people. Men with guns shouted at him, but he kept running right at them, toward Marissa's call. They screamed and fired their weapons. Some ran away when the bullets passed through his spirit form, others kept firing. With bullets flying in his wake, he passed through the wall of the house, hearing glass shatter behind him. Inside, he paused in the dim room to gain direction. Moonlight from the shattered window reached into the shadows and the wolf froze, startled. His mortal form lay before him, chained to a bed, straining horrifically to free himself. The phenomenon of being in two forms at the same time had never happened to him, to any of the Shadowmen as far as he knew. The wolf howled in confusion.

"Go! Go to Marissa! Save her," Navarre's mortal form shouted at his wolf spirit.

The wolf ran through the wall, down the corridor, and into

the room where Marissa's spirit cried out desperately for him. Bound cruelly tight, she cringed from the knife that Evil held at her throat. She screamed for him to stop, but Evil laughed and cut slowly down her dress, leaving a thin line of welling blood to mark her exposed neck and upper chest. The beads of blood bled into the white of her dress.

The wolf howled with pure rage and attacked the Evil. Leaping over the table, he went for Evil's throat, but passed right through it. Evil screamed and backed from Marissa, holding the knife before it.

The wolf raged louder, howling with his frustration. He wanted to sink his teeth into Evil and tear it apart piece by piece. He leaped at the Evil again, ripping at it, but passed through it again.

"What beast is this that burns?" Evil cried.

"The beast that will deliver your death," Marissa shouted.

"You bitch," Evil yelled. "Call him back now or I'll kill you." Evil disappeared only to reappear next to Marissa. It held the knife over her heart, ready to plunge.

The wolf paced, gnashing his teeth.

"Kill me, and you'll only die faster," Marissa yelled.

Navarre, though blind in the room he lay bound in, saw everything happening through the eyes of his wolf spirit. A Vladarian Vampire had her chained to an altar, her legs spread, her dress pulled up and body exposed. Some blood already stained the top of her dress. Her voice was hoarse from the fear and the desperation of her cries. Her heart and spirit were defiled by the vileness of the vampire's intent. Rage, anger, frustration, hate—there weren't words strong enough to describe the emotions overwhelming him.

Navarre's being cried out against the vampire's violation of Marissa so strongly that the stone walls shook with the force of his howl.

Suddenly as the hot night air from the broken window

blasted over him, Navarre felt his body tingle. The tingle became a burning that quickly turned into a volcanic rush of savage energy unlike anything he'd ever felt before. In one herculean wrench, he ripped the binding chains from their anchors. Rising from the bed, he felt his way along the wall until he found the door. Jerking hard, he pulled the knob free, broke the lock, and kicked the door open.

He followed the call of Marissa's spirit, turning right and feeling his way down the corridor as he ran. He saw through the wolf's eyes that the Vladarian had a knife poised over Marissa's heart and his own heart thundered with fear.

By Logos! he raged, flinging himself around the doorjamb where his wolf spirit joined him, enabling him to see his way clear to Marissa. He ran forward, jerking hard at some contraption hanging from the ceiling. Cement rained down as he shoved the leather and metal mass at the vampire's head, forcing the vampire to deflect the blow rather than stab Marissa.

Before the vampire could reposition for a killing strike, Navarre was on him. He wrapped his hands around the Vladarian's throat as he slammed into the fanged monster. Hell and all of the tortures of the damned were too good for this bastard. In the millennia he'd fought Heldon's depraved creatures, Navarre had never hated as deeply and as strongly as he did at this moment. "Seeing" what the vampire planned to do to Marissa sent Navarre over the line to a savagery he couldn't understand or control, but before he could vent the justice and rage consuming him, the vampire disappeared into thin air.

Navarre yelled and attempted to follow the vile creature into the very depths of hell itself to satisfy his hatred, but his body didn't shift to the spirit world. He leaped into the air, tried again and failed.

"My brother is here," Marissa yelled. "Please save my brother. Herrera might be trying to kill him now."

Navarre spun around and reached Marissa's side. Through

the wolf's gaze, he assessed her bruised cheek, bloodied lip, and the welling cut down the center of her neck and chest. By Logos! All of hell would pay for this. "Where is your brother?"

Marissa stared at what she thought was Navarre, then blinked the tears from her eyes and stared again. "Down the hall. Last door on the right," she said, shaking her head.

"Go," Navarre said to the ghostly black wolf she knew and had loved so well from her dreams. The wolf ran from the room.

Surely she had to be seeing wrong. Navarre wasn't Navarre, but a creature. If she could have moved, she would have recoiled, repelled by the changes in him. What had Herrera done to him? He wore the black sweatpants she'd last seen him in, and the golden-bronze amulet that marked him as being from the spirit world, but the noble warrior had been replaced by a creature that was half man and half wolf . . . with . . . with hated fangs and claws. She knew the creature was Navarre. It had Navarre's voice and—she nearly sobbed—his golden eyes, but he was no longer a man. She shuddered as the creature touched her wrist when he grasped the manacle and pried it open, a feat that had to require superhuman strength.

Even though he was freeing her, the sight of his claws and the brush of thick hair covering his skin brought more tears to her eyes, tears of sadness and of revulsion. She pulled her arm up the moment she could, groaning at the pain in her muscles.

Dios mio, what had happened to him? Her heart wrenched at the changes. She wondered what had happened with the knife wound in his back. He didn't seem to be hurt from that at all. Too much hair covered his body for her to see where the wound was, so she'd have to ask later.

He felt his way to her legs as a blind person would and she bit into her cut lip to keep from crying out at the injustice and the horror. She had thought what Herrera had done to her brother heinous, but what he'd done to Navarre was worse. As soon as she could cover herself, she pushed down her dress, and brought her stinging legs up as Navarre freed her.

"The Vladarian is with your brother," Navarre said. "We must hurry."

Fear clenched her gut. She didn't question how Navarre knew. He broke the last manacle and she scrambled off the altar, ignoring the pain. She ran to the door. When she didn't sense Navarre behind her, she turned back and saw him feeling his way. Her heart twisted again. Whatever Herrera had done to Navarre, she had to remember he was still the injured warrior who'd done everything he could to save her.

She returned to him and, wincing against the sharp-clawed hairiness, she grabbed his hand, reminding herself that the creature was still Navarre. "Follow me," she said softly.

Navarre stiffened in response then after a second sighed as if broken and she realized his blindness hurt him. His claw clasped her hand and she tightened her grip. "Lead me," he whispered. "My wolf spirit is protecting your brother, but the Vladarian must die."

Guiding Navarre, Marissa ran, wishing she could burn this dungeon and the whole house to the ground and kill Herrera in the worst way possible. They reached her brother's room to find the wolf attacking Herrera. She cried at the sight of a knife sticking from her brother's chest and rushed to Rafael's side, sure Herrera had killed him, her heart wrenching with hurt and rage.

She breathed a dizzying sigh of relief when she saw the knife was embedded in the left side of her brother's chest, close to his shoulder and collarbone. Herrera had missed her brother's heart, which Marissa was sure he meant to stab, and likely the ghost wolf had stopped him.

Glancing up, she saw Navarre attacking Herrera and turned her attention back to Rafael and the knife. He still burned with fever. His eyes were shut and he thrashed his head back and forth in his delirium, but his breathing wasn't that of a man in mortal distress. The knife hadn't hit anything vital. Bleeding would be a problem, though.

"Rafe?" He didn't answer, only moaned. Clenching her teeth as her stomach roiled, she grabbed a roll of leftover gauze off a table by his bed then pulled the knife from his chest and stuffed the gauze into the wound, packing it tight. She found tape as well and plastered the bandage down. Tears streamed down her cheeks at his suffering even as she raged at the lies she'd been told. If her brother was still alive months after she'd been told he died, was there yet hope her mother and sister were alive, as well?

A claw landed on her shoulder and she bit her lip, fighting to stop the instinctive reaction to pull away. She looked up at the creature Navarre had been turned into. "Herrera?" she asked, seeing quickly that the vampire was gone.

"I failed. The coward disappeared again. We must go." Easing her back with a gentle touch, he picked her brother up. "Follow me," he said.

"How can you see now?" Marissa asked as she searched the room for a weapon. She found the iron rod and the heavy hammer that Herrera had knocked from her hands earlier. Every fiber of her being was tied into knots, wondering if Herrera would appear again. She knew from experience with her vampire uncle that Herrera could only appear at will to a place known to him, either by having been there before or by seeing a photograph of a specific destination. Once they made it out of the compound, Herrera would be forced to rely on his sense of smell or his guards to find them.

"I can only see through the eyes of my wolf spirit like in a dream," Navarre said as he led the way to the corridor with the ghost wolf at his side.

Marissa understood. When the wolf spirit had invaded her dreams, she'd been able to see through its spirit as it ran free through the moonlit forest. Marissa stepped from the room and heard shouting and banging. At the end of the corridor the dungeon's double doors groaned and creaked, bulging from the force of men trying to open it. The iron bar she'd pushed through the handles earlier was holding them off, but at any moment it or the steel handles would break loose.

"This way." Navarre directed her down the hall, turning into the last room on the left. The door hung from its hinges.

Entering, she immediately saw the broken window, felt the damp warmth of outside air, and caught the perfume of frangipani blossoms scenting the air. Jagged glass still hung from the frame.

"Stay back a moment," she told Navarre, and lifted a blanket from the bed to wrap around her hand. Then using the hammer, she knocked out the remaining glass. After she finished, she laid the frayed wool over the glass shards and set a nearby chair under the window. Though not full-sized, the window seemed large enough for Navarre to squeeze through. She climbed up then wedged herself on the sill until she could scramble out into the night. The bottom of the window was level with the grass outside. From the placement of the huge wall and its razor-wire top, she figured they were on the left side of the house, toward the back. The compound was lit with floodlights and confusion reigned. Both guests and armed guards were running around.

So far, no one had noticed her, yet she knew their moment of opportunity wouldn't last long. She heard Herrera's men shouting at the guests to go to the courtyard where arrangements for their trip home would be made.

Marissa's heart stopped then thundered. Were the men rounding up the guests to murder them because of her attempted escape? She had little doubt that Herrera would commit such an atrocity. Guilt flashed the images of Chanel Langston's concern, and Father Dom's kind face at her. She had

to do something. First she had to hide Rafael somewhere safe—
if such a place existed. "Hurry and lift Rafael to me. I think
Herrera is going to murder everyone here. *Dios*, we have to stop
him. He told me that if I didn't cooperate with his plans he
would do it."

Navarre handed up Rafael headfirst and Marissa caught her
brother beneath his shoulders and pulled him onto the grass.
He moaned and groaned but mercifully didn't regain consciousness. She couldn't imagine the kind of pain he must be
in, with puncture wounds covering his backside from shoulders
to heels. Her stomach roiled and she had to take several deep
breaths to calm the rising horror and anger. She would focus on
their escape now and think about it all later.

When she looked up, she found the ghost wolf at her side
and Navarre struggling to fit through the window. He was even
bigger than she thought, but part of the problem was that his
raging frustration and use of brute force was working against
him.

"Wait, Navarre." Leaving Rafael, she went to the warrior-
turned-creature. "Slow down, exhale, and pull all your stomach
and chest muscles in tight."

Navarre eased his movements, his golden gaze focusing on
her. He exhaled hard and adjusted his bulk enough to force his
way through the opening. Blood and fur marked the top and
sides of the window, telling her he'd been seriously scraped. She
winced, wanting to reach out to him, but he moved away and
picked up Rafael.

"Hey, Carlos. Look what Emilio has found. A pretty heiress
playing right into our hands, no? I think we give her and her
amigos a ride in the truck, no?"

Crying out, Marissa swung around to face the hard black
muzzles of two machine guns and the greedy gazes of Carlos
and Emilio.

Chapter Seven

CARLOS LAUGHED. "Why bring her *amigos*? Kill the *hombres*, especially the hairy one, and tie her up in the supply truck with the priest. Once we off him, there'll be no record of the marriage and—"

"*Sí,*" Emilio interrupted eagerly. "I will marry the *puta* and share her and the money with you."

"No, I will marry the *puta* and share her and the money with you," Carlos insisted.

Emilio glared at Carlos. "It was my idea to—"

Navarre moved so quickly, Marissa wasn't exactly sure what happened. He turned and made a sweeping back kick, hitting the guards' gun arms with such force that Marissa heard bones crack before anyone could react. They screamed in pain while their weapons flew high into the air and clanked onto the tiled roof thirty feet above. Navarre landed smoothly on his feet, poised to strike again, still holding Rafael. The feat wasn't human.

The guards looked dumbfounded as they scrambled to draw hidden weapons from their pants, but the ghostly wolf sprang at them, growling with menace. Eyes wide with fear, Carlos and Emilio backed away, gesticulating and muttering for the saints to save them. After five steps they turned, yelling for people to run for their lives. "*El Lobo Diablo está aquí!*" The Devil Wolf is here.

Heart pounding with urgency, Marissa urged Navarre to the back of the compound. "We have to help Father Dom."

With his wolf spirit in the lead, Navarre ran, carrying Rafael so effortlessly that it was as comforting as the power he'd shown in his lightning attack on Carlos and Emilio was frightening. All she had to carry was the hammer and the iron rod, but they taxed her aching muscles. She hadn't even thought to use them when faced with the machine guns, but then Navarre's action had come so quickly that she still reeled from it.

"They fear my wolf spirit more than me," Navarre said, sounding amused as he moved into the shadows cast by a line of mahogany trees and a towering kapok. The spirit wolf stayed in front, its gaze searching in every direction. The dense overhead foliage and strangling vines diminished the reach of the floodlights surrounding the house and left them less exposed.

Marissa blinked, surprised by the humor that made him human for a moment. "You're right. Your spirit could probably chase Herrera and all of his soldiers back to *infierno*."

"No," Navarre said grimly after a moment of silence. "That I cannot do. I failed. I was unable to follow the Vladarian who threatened you into the spirit realm and deliver justice. I am no longer a warrior worthy of being among the Shadowmen. I can no longer fulfill my Blood Hunter duties."

Marissa opened her mouth, ready to argue that he was every bit a warrior, but then clenched her teeth. In all honesty, did she know anything about the world he came from? No. Nor could she deny that Herrera had done something terrible to him. So instead of offering false platitudes, she touched Navarre's arm, forcing herself to accept the feel of the thick fur. "You've . . . you've fought well. If it wasn't for you and your wolf spirit . . ." She shuddered. "What Herrera would have done to me and what more he would have done to my brother would have killed us both. You saved us at a cost to yourself. No warrior could do better than you."

Navarre only grunted. Then she heard the voices and the sounds of men tramping noisily through the vegetation, coming right toward them. Navarre slipped behind a thick tree trunk, set Rafael down, and motioned for her to stay with her brother.

She moved to Rafael's side and offered Navarre her weapons. He grunted, taking the iron bar and testing the feel of it in his hands. "This will do."

Moving so silently and swiftly that he became a whisper and a blur, he slipped off to the left, his wolf spirit guiding the way. She felt Rafael's brow, wincing at the heat of his fever, and quickly checked the bandage she'd placed over his chest wound even as she wondered what Navarre planned to do.

Loud cries of surprise and a peek around the trunk showed her that he'd crept up behind the group of six men. Navarre's superhuman strength, lightning movements, and the iron bar proved to be more lethal than the guards' submachine guns. He dispatched half of them within seconds with three well-placed hits and a few kicks that sent them flying. Two more moved in to attack, managing to bring the muzzles of their guns up to fire, but a rushing attack from the ghost wolf had the men shooting far to the left of Navarre. Still, her heart raced with worry and she almost stepped out from behind the tree and called to the men to distract them, but by the time the men shifted their aim to shoot Navarre, he was on them.

One guard, looking repeatedly back over his shoulder, ran her way. Marissa gripped the hammer tightly and, when he passed, she brought it down hard on his head. He groaned, fell to his knees, and started to raise his gun, but then keeled over.

Uncertain what to do with a machine gun, but sure she'd rather be armed with one than not, she took the man's weapon, then decided to search his pockets. She dumped everything into the middle of the bandana she pulled from his neck and made a sack, tying the ends to the belt laden with bullets that she stole from him, all of which she'd sort out later. Then spying the man's heavy boots, she took his shoes and socks and tied them to the belt, too. Rafael was barefoot and her silk slippers wouldn't last long. Once belted to her waist, the ensemble felt clunky, but made little noise against the silk of her dress.

Only a whisper of air against her skin alerted her to Navarre's return. She stood as he picked up Rafael, his massive muscles bunching beneath the thick black fur covering him. He wore no shirt or shoes, only the black sweatpants, a creature that looked monstrously sinister with his claws and fangs, but was so gentle and good within his heart, whereas Herrera, who would be considered handsome according to the world, was hideously vile inside.

This time luck was on her side. They didn't encounter any more guards and quickly found several large buildings. Staying in the shadows, they crept closer. One building was a massive garage with all ten double-door bays open. Another had to be the barracks for the guards. Camouflage clothes hung on a line stretched out in front and boots lined a windowsill inside the screened porch. She almost asked Navarre to stop so she could get some of the clothes and a few pairs of boots, but the telltale smell of cigarette smoke let her know they might not be as alone as she thought. They moved deeper into the darker areas edging the trees and kept going.

The garage contained over a dozen vehicles, from limousines to jeeps and different-sized trucks. Moths and bugs zinged around a lantern sitting on a desk next to where a man talked loudly on a phone. He swatted absently at the bugs, squashing them with his bare hands and wiping the remains on his pants. Four other guards had gathered around a table along the left wall of the garage. From their conversation, she realized they were rolling dice to see who would stay in the garage on guard duty and who would go to the house to help with the *fuego* before all burned.

Gracias a Dios. The fire from the kitchen must have spread, which explained the chaos of the guests and guards milling around the house and possibly why Herrera had yet to come after her again. That and the fact he could be looking for Father Dom. She prayed that everything burned all the way through to the dungeon's floor, so no one would ever suffer Herrera's tortures again—at least not here.

The gravel driveway led to a medieval-looking wrought-iron gate complete with spikes and a two-story watchtower about a hundred yards away. She had no doubt armed guards manned the tower. That escape route appeared almost as daunting as the twelve-foot-high fence topped with razor wire, though breaking through the gate in a truck should offer more protection and take less time than trying to scale the wall.

She'd never had the opportunity to drive before, but didn't think it would be too difficult from what she'd seen. Turn the key, push the gas, and steer.

Raucous laughter brought her attention back to the garage to see two men being slapped on the back as they left the table. They'd obviously lost. One of the men climbed into the passenger's door of a large truck and the other went to a pegboard on the back wall then jangled a set of keys as he climbed into the driver's side. He revved the engine and sent gravel spattering as he made a sharp right turn toward the house. Marissa cursed under her breath, praying that Father Dom wasn't tied up in the back of *that* truck.

Two down and three to go.

"Wait here." Navarre set Rafael gently down, took the iron bar, and stealthily edged his way toward the garage with the wolf spirit at his side. He lost his element of surprise when Rafael let out a loud moan. All three men jumped to attention, guns ready, and started advancing from the garage. Another sound from her brother and they'd likely start shooting in her direction. The men hadn't seen Navarre yet. He stood just to the right of the doorway, but they'd be on him in a second.

Even if she knew how to use the gun she'd stolen, it would

only draw fire in her direction. She acted before she thought twice about it. Unbuckling and dropping the belt and the gun, she jumped up from the bushes and waved her arms at the guards as she pleaded. *"Ayudeme! Por favor!"* Help me! Please!

"I'm hurt," she said, limping slowly toward them. They lowered their weapons and began talking.

"Come here," one of the guards ordered. "Tell us your name?"

"Señora Herrera," Marissa told them. "There was a fire and when I was escaping two men called Carlos and Emilio tried to kidnap me. They wanted ransom from my new husband. They hurt me." She pointed to the blood on her dress.

This declaration caused a stir among the men. They were so involved in her and the situation that they didn't see Navarre and his wolf spirit until it was too late. He disarmed them and dropped them like flies, but she was surprised to realize that he only knocked them unconscious. He didn't kill them when he so easily could have.

After he finished, Navarre scowled in her direction. "I may be a failed warrior, but I do not need you to endanger yourself to protect me."

"But . . . but—"

"We must hurry. I'll get your brother," he said, turning away.

That her action caused him to feel shame shocked her and left her confused. Why shouldn't she help when it made sense to do so? He was right that they had to hurry. So though she wanted to explain and even apologize—for what, she wasn't sure—she shoved it all aside and focused on what they had to do to get out of there.

"Get the gun and the belt that I left with Rafe and I'll look for the priest." She didn't wait for an answer but snatched up a flashlight and rushed toward the trucks. The search for Father

Dom almost had her screeching, heartsick that he might have been inside the truck that left. It wasn't until she reached the last truck—a small moving van—that she found him. And if it hadn't been for the light reflecting off the jeweled biretta on his head she would have missed him among the mess of mismatched junk. Bound, gagged, and blindfolded with his robes and cap askew, the priest was so still he didn't seem to be breathing at all.

"Please be all right," she whispered, slipping the blindfold off.

He stirred then, blinking against the light of the flashlight until his eyes widened with recognition and surprise. She loosened the knot for the gag and he shook it from his mouth.

"My child, what are you doing? You must leave. You must save yourself."

"We go together, Father, for Herrera plans to kill you. Hold still while I get a knife to free you." She climbed back over chairs, boxes, and blankets to the back of the truck. Navarre had arrived with Rafael, the gun, hammer, and laden belt.

Marissa spread out a blanket and Navarre placed Rafael on it. She then unclipped the knife from the belt and returned to Father Dom, cutting him loose.

The priest sat up, rubbing his wrists and shaking his feet. "Who do you have with you, child?"

"My brother Rafael. Months ago Vasquez told everyone Rafe had died trying to escape Tío Luis's prison. Herrera has hurt Rafe badly to force me to marry. There's also a warrior called Navarre helping us, but Herrera has done something awful to him. We must hurry now and talk later."

The priest scrambled up.

"Marissa." The deep, gentle timbre of Navarre's voice startled her. Her heart thumped hard and the air rushed from her lungs.

"Yes." She hurried to him, focusing on his golden eyes and not the covering of black fur.

"I have sent my wolf spirit to chase after the guards at the gate."

"Which leaves you blind now." She reached out. "Take my hand and I will help you find a place to settle back here with Rafe, while I drive."

"No. We all stay together. I cannot protect you both as well."

Father Dom climbed over the boxes and joined her. He gasped, jerking back from her. "*Santa María y Madre de Dios*, protect us from the deformed creatures of hell," he whispered.

Shocked, Marissa turned to the priest, strengthening her hold on Navarre's claw. "No, you don't understand. He isn't evil. He has more good in him than you or I or anyone and he is injured, blind, but there isn't time to explain. We'll all get into the front of the truck."

Navarre's muscles tensed beneath her fingers and she could almost feel the fur on his skin rise up in agitation. "He is not to be trusted," Navarre said succinctly.

"No, Navarre, you don't understand. Your appearance, what Herrera did to you, has frightened him. Father Dom was a good friend of my grandmother's. We must hurry and leave now and talk about this later." She guided Navarre's hand to Rafe. "Carry my brother."

"Herrera didn't—"

Rafe cried out in pain and Navarre didn't say more. He scooped up Rafe, who now thrashed in his delirium, and spoke gently to him. Rafe's struggling immediately eased. Marissa guided Navarre to the cab of the truck, thinking the warrior definitely had magic in his voice.

There was a small bench seat behind the front one and Navarre laid her brother there after she pushed the boxes of Twinkies and candy bars onto the floor.

"You sit here." She settled Navarre in the passenger seat, placing the machine gun and her other booty on the floor at his feet.

When she turned around, she found Father Dom looking as if he were waffling between running away on foot or coming with them. "If Herrera finds you, he will hurt you. He told me he would. Navarre has the strength to protect us all. You must believe me when I tell you he is not evil."

"How can he protect you if he's blind?"

"He can." She left him to ponder that as she ran to the back wall for keys. The pegs were numbered, as were the parking places. She took the keys for space ten then saw a metal first-aid kit on the wall above stacked cases of bottled water. Surely she was pushing her luck, but she couldn't bring herself to leave behind what might help. She opened the kit and pulled all of the first-aid contents out of the cabinet onto the top case of water then picked up the water and ran for the truck.

"Hold this," she said, dumping all of it into Navarre's lap and slamming the door shut.

Father Dom still hadn't climbed into the truck.

"I'm leaving. Get in now or stay."

"Child, you don't—"

"Have time for talk," she said, opening the driver's door. "In or out?"

Gesticulating as if the devil had him in his grip, the priest got in, scooting to the middle. Marissa climbed in then tried to make heads or tails of all the gadgets in front of her and which one did what.

"Here," Father Dom said, taking the keys. He put one key into a slot on the dash and turned it. A loud noise filled the garage. Seeing the pedals on the floor, she pushed the first one and grabbed onto the steering wheel. The engine roared louder, but nothing happened.

"You have to put the truck into gear." Father Dom reached for a lever and pulled it down. The truck jerked forward.

"I've got it now!" Marissa yelled and pushed on the gas, ecstatic that the truck moved in response. When she looked up she saw she was off center of the openings, the middle concrete post was in her way. She steered right then left quickly, unsure of which way to go.

Father Dom grabbed the wheel and jerked it to the right just as they hit the opening. The post scraped the left side of the truck.

"*Santa María y Madre de Dios,* have you ever driven before?"

Marissa blinked at him. "No."

At the sound of gunfire, she took back control of the wheel and pointed the truck toward the gate. "But I think I have it now." She pressed the gas as far as it would go.

Father Dom pulled a knob and lights came on. Then he began shouting the name of every saint known to man.

"The guards are confused," Navarre said. "Only two of them have not run from the wolf and they are shooting at it now. The gates are partway open and another car is on the left outside the compound. The guards are turning toward the truck coming. One is running up to the road, aiming his gun at the truck."

"How can he see if he is blind?" Father Dom asked.

"I see him," Marissa said, and directed the truck at him. The guard stumbled back, falling as he tried to get out of the way. She saw Navarre's spirit wolf revealed in the headlights as it ran across the road and leaped at the other guard.

"What was that?" Father Dom shouted.

Marissa didn't have time to answer. She edged the truck to the right and hit the partially opened gate. The truck jolted hard from the blow, throwing them about before settling on the road. The iron gate flew high into the air and landed on top of the black limo on her left.

Just then Navarre's wolf spirit leaped onto the hood of the truck and came through the windshield into the cab. Marissa hadn't expected it, but then the wolf didn't frighten her, and she realized Navarre wanted to see where they were going.

Father Dom screamed and passed out. Navarre caught him and held the priest in the seat. Marissa winced, supposing she should have found a way to warn the priest, but there hadn't been time. She just hoped he woke before she had to stop the truck, because she wasn't exactly sure how to do it.

Chapter Eight

"YOU ARE very lucky, señores," the attendant said as Nick signed for the eight-passenger Bell helo he'd reserved. They'd landed in Belize a short while ago to the bad news that Erin hadn't located any car rental place that had picked up passengers from the municipal airport in the predawn hours. Which meant Herrera had used his own transportation and thus was untraceable from that angle.

"How is that?" Nick pocketed the keys and papers he needed to lay his hands on the helo. He couldn't wait to have the joystick in his hand and start eating up the sky.

"This morning, all the *helicópteros* in the city were rented for the whole day and night just to fly guests for a big wedding tonight. If you had needed a *piloto* as well, you would have not been so lucky."

"A wedding?" Nick asked. He heard Stefanie's hopeful gasp and saw Annette, Aragon, and Jared turn their attention toward the clerk. "Must be a big one. Who's getting hitched?"

The man rolled his eyes. "I don't know. Nobody tells Juan anything."

Nick slipped out his wallet. "I'd be extremely interested in finding out," he said, patting the soft black leather.

Eyes wide, the clerk smiled. "Perhaps I may be able to find out for you, señor. *Un momento.*" Going to the phone, he made a call. Then looking puzzled, he made two other calls. After that, he held his finger up and disappeared into a back room. At that point, Nick tensed, his police-trained radar bleeping. He motioned a warning to Jared and Aragon and turned to Stefanie and Jaymes. "Go wait with the door open. I don't like the delay, or the guy's look after he called."

Jaymes caught Stefanie's arm, moving quickly. Annette followed. Aragon and Jared took up positions in front of the women. Nick moved a few feet from the desk, his hand on the gun in his jacket's pocket.

Nick heard the murmur of voices from the other room then footsteps, and he braced himself to react. The clerk returned with a file, shaking his head. "It is the strangest thing," the man said. "Our *pilotos* as well as the others carried passengers to a *helipuerto,* but they were then taken by another *helicóptero.* They are all waiting for the return of the passengers, who are hours late."

The whole scenario sounded just strange enough to fit the bill for Herrera. "Who rented them?"

The clerk hesitated, glanced about, then whispered, "I dare not say."

Nick drew a fifty from his wallet and the clerk leaned over the counter, open file in hand. He pointed to a name, making Nick completely understand the clerk's reluctance. General Otto Menendez—a dangerous man and a major power player in Guatemala's violent political arena.

"Where?" Nick said, drawing out another fifty.

The clerk turned the page. All that was listed there were coordinates. Nick memorized them and handed over the money with a card that had his cell number on it. He pocketed his wallet. "You've been a great help, Juan. Call me if you hear more and there'll be a bonus for you when I get back."

"Muy bien, señor . . ." He looked at the card. "Sinclair," he said, then frowned. "You know, I'd be careful telling people your name during your archaeological *expedición.* There is a very bad man in the jungle called Sinclair. The drug wars between the *policía* and the drug lords make it a very unsafe place to be. Five *policía* were executed yesterday." The clerk tucked the card into his pocket as he shook his head. "The world is a very bad place."

"Thanks." Nick managed to force the word past the large

lump in his throat. His hand automatically clutched the Glock in his pocket. The bastard sullying his father's name was going to pay. Reed Sinclair died a hero saving Sam from a jungle hellhole and Nick was going to make sure it stayed that way.

"Surely you're not going to tackle anything that might involve Menendez," Jaymes said, falling into step beside him.

Nick blinked. He'd left the building and was already halfway across the parking lot without even knowing it. He had to force his mind off his father and back to the primary reason they were here—to rescue Marissa and Navarre.

He'd been avoiding Jaymes since she and Stefanie declared their intention to make the trip to Belize. He hadn't figured out yet how to handle the situation of his interest in her and his past involvement with Stefanie. No, scratch that "past involvement." He'd turned a new leaf and wasn't going to sugarcoat anything, even to himself.

He and Stef *had* had a one-night stand that *might* or might not have gone somewhere if she hadn't been kidnapped. But what had once been a selfish interest in a night's entertainment with a beautiful woman had now changed. He was more emotionally tangled up with Stefanie than he'd ever been with a woman. What she'd suffered wouldn't leave him alone. Day and night it was with him, whether she was around or not. He thought about it and about her constantly now. She obviously had wanted to be alone on the flight here, but he'd watched the expressions on her pale face and had felt the stress and fear pouring off her on the plane and couldn't stop himself from going to her.

Whereas Jaymes was another piece of work altogether. The special ops officer was a mixture of sexy soft and hardass that had him clenching his teeth and fisting his hands to stay anywhere close to respectable and decent when he was around her. He couldn't remember wanting to get down and dirty with a woman at first sight more than he did with her. It was more than ironic that for the first time in his footloose life, he wasn't doing any horizontal dancing. Not while his head was wrapped up in Stefanie. His dick wasn't listening to him, though. All it could hear was Jaymes's sexy voice. She was warning him against pursuing anything that involved General Menendez.

"Don't tell me Jaymes Bond is afraid of a little intrigue," he said jokingly. She needed to lighten up a bit. He had no idea if Menendez and this wedding had anything to do with Herrera and Marissa. From what was said when the Vladarians kidnapped everyone, Herrera and another vampire named Samir had both claimed to be Marissa's fiancé and that had something to do with SINCO.

She grabbed his arm. "Listen, you can diss me and my ability all you want, but when it threatens the lives of others, I'll kick your ass to the curb for it. This is no time to joke and if you call me Jaymes Bond that way again I'll make you eat it."

"Whoa, lady. Take a chill pill." Nick stopped and nearly recoiled from the force of her anger. Damn. How had he pissed her off? He held his hands up. "No dissing going on here. Don't know what I did to give you that idea."

"How about ignoring me since the moment I signed up for this trip? One would think that you'd welcome another combat-trained person on this mission. Obviously a female doesn't qualify. But screw that. What's important here is that if you start playing in Menendez's league, you're likely to be found dead before you even get to the batter's box."

"And you're jumping the gun. Crying wolf when we don't even know who's at the door." Nick raked an unsteady hand through his hair. Maybe he was dissing her because right at that moment he wanted to take all of the energy she exuded and kiss it right into one hell of a sex fest, starting with a grand slam to home plate. "We don't know if he is even acquainted with

Herrera or not. And we don't know if this wedding has anything to do with Marissa."

"Do you know who General Menendez is?" she asked, letting go of his arm.

Nick bit his lip to keep from asking her to hold him harder. She'd probably kill him for saying it, but she was cute when riled, her eyes practically sparked purple fire. "I didn't just drop off a turnip truck, but I'd bet hands down that you know more since you're inside the military shark tank. So if we decide he's involved, I'll expect you to give us a report on the dirty general who likely had a hand in several massacres and a number of assassinations during the civil war. Right now, we need to get this helo in the air and make some progress."

She narrowed her gaze at him as she slowly nodded. "Okay, flyboy. I'll give you a chance and apologize for thinking you hang your hat with the good ole boys' club. We'll talk about Menedez's ass later, but realize the bastard has a long arm and you might run into it without even knowing he's there. Just so you know, if you don't fly the helo like a breeze, I'm taking control of the stick."

"You fly?" *Man oh man, could this woman get any better?*

"Like a dream, so watch your ass." She turned from him then and walked a dozen feet back to where Stefanie and Annette were following.

Jared and Aragon reached him and he fell into step with them.

"Six weeks," Aragon said.

"No, four. Two if we're lucky," Jared replied.

"What are you two arguing over? More truffles? Don't tell me you placed another order?"

"Hey," Jared said, smacking Nick on the back and knocking him a bit forward. The warriors didn't know their own strength sometimes. He lowered his voice to a conspirator's whisper. "That's a great idea."

"Yeah," said Aragon, glancing over his shoulder at Annette. "I've got a number of ideas for some strawberry and coffee truffles." He slapped Nick on the other side of his back. "You're a lifesaver. We were thinking they'd got the upper hand."

"If you weren't talking about a truffle order, then what?" Nick asked.

"You," said Jared.

"Yeah," added Aragon. "We've noticed that mortal men are notoriously stupid when it comes to accepting their fate in regard to Logos's greatest gift to man."

"Huh?" Nick shifted his gaze between the two beasts. They stood four to five inches taller than his six two.

"Your life's mate," Jared said.

Nick practically tripped over his own two feet. "Hey, guys. Don't know what planet you're from, but I play the field. I might be on a little sabbatical at the moment, but choosing just one forever isn't my style."

"Eden," Jared said. "We were created in Eden along with all other spirit beings. So no other planet was involved. And I hate to tell you but every Adam eventually meets his Eve—and she's yours."

"I think you two are swimming in too many hormones to even think logically. Why pick just one fish when there's an entire sea of them?"

"Like I told you," Aragon said. "Six."

"Nope. Didn't you see the way she looked at him?"

"What way?" Nick asked, nearly forgetting to keep walking.

Jared shook his head. "Sorry I mentioned it. I forgot you weren't interested."

"Hey. Who said I wasn't interested? What look?"

Aragon and Jared leaned forward and looked at each other. "A week," they said simultaneously.

Nick missed his step and would have fallen if they hadn't caught his elbows.

"Hey," Annette called out. "Is Nick all right?"

"Yeah, yeah. I'm fine." Nick regained his balance and shook off Jared's and Aragon's hands as they laughed.

"I hope he flies better than he walks," Jaymes said, laughing.

"You have no idea," Nick yelled back. He definitely was going to take her soaring and she'd never forget it. Problem was, he wondered if he ever would, either.

Dubai, UAE

"Quite frankly, I need a second in command, Valois, and I need to know if you're up for the position," Cinatas said, keeping a sharp eye on Victor Amadeus Valois's reflection in the mirror. The leader of the Royals, the blue-blooded faction of European vampires, could barely contain his disdainful frown. Clearly, second in anything was far beneath a direct descendant of William of Normandy.

"Let me explain," Cinatas added. "As you know, Wellbourne was a major disappointment. So it's just as well that he perished at the Falls. At least I am assuming that is the case. He has yet to return to his estates or appear in the damned realms, correct?"

"Yes, that is what all reports indicate. I have sent trusted lawyers to settle his affairs." Valois's accompanying smug smile said it all. The men would no doubt see that Wellbourne's assets ended up in Valois's coffers. Just as Cuthbert's assets had Cuthbert's widow was reportedly in Valois's bed.

"Excellent." Cinatas smiled. The more Valois did, the more assured Cinatas was that his ultimate plan would work. "Then here's the deal. I'm sure you're not aware that before my beloved father, Pathos, was taken from us, he set a new world order in motion. A strategy to rule not only the world, but Heldon's and Logos's realms as well."

Valois's usual expression of droll boredom fractured to an openmouthed gasp, which he quickly covered up with a yawn.

Hook baited.

Cinatas paced across the glassy-smooth, white Carrara marble—the only decorative feature in Burj Al Arab's Royal Suite worth taking note of, in Cinatas's opinion—and gazed at the panoramic view of Jumeirah Beach's coastline. Crystalline blue waves as gentle as a mother's caress rippled through the Persian Gulf and lapped at the shore.

It was a city of opulence and opportunity and only fitting that he'd be reborn—so to speak—here.

"As my trusted second in command, you would of course be called upon to rule the world, while I oversee the heavenly and the damned realms. I don't think one man can do it all, do you?"

Valois cleared his throat and stood, chest thrust forward and nose in the air. "Depends on the man, but why work so hard? I may have the time available to help you, especially if I delegate my current duties to my nephews. Can you detail exactly what you have in mind? Gaining rule of the world is simple enough, but eliminating Heldon? That would be next to impossible and Logos's demise completely impossible."

Bait taken.

Cinatas cupped his hands and created a marble-sized ball of zapping static electricity. "Catch," he said, tossing the tiny ball at Valois.

Valois reacted and caught the ball then immediately cried out in pain as smoke smoldered from the resulting burn. "You bastard, I kill for slights less than that," he yelled, shaking his hand.

Cinatas smiled in satisfaction. "Forgive me, I thought you'd appreciate a demonstration of how to eliminate both Heldon and Logos."

"You'll need more than trickery and fire," Valois snarled.

"You misunderstand. I'm not planning on attacking either Heldon or Logos, but as I work on becoming more and more powerful, I will subtly create more and more situations where they are forced to destroy their forces and eventually themselves, a little at a time. Already Logos is losing warriors in the spirit realm. In just a few weeks three Blood Hunters have come to the earth; more are sure to follow. As for Heldon, I've proven desecrations are the key to power. He'll now be fighting every damned power-hungry Tom, Dick, and Harry that rises up to challenge him. Anything can be done if you time it just right." *Even the death of all the Vladarians,* Cinatas silently added. Once he had the power he wanted, he'd waste no time in ridding himself of the thorn in his side.

Before then, Cinatas expected Valois to try and overthrow his rule. He and Wellbourne had been as thick as thieves about something, and Cinatas was sure that was the only thing the two could have agreed on. *Keep your friends close and your enemies even closer.* Cinatas didn't have any friends so he was going to keep his enemy right up his ass.

"If you think you're capable"—Cinatas smiled sweetly—"then the first order of business will be Herrera's and Samir's elimination. Despite my warning, they disrupted my coronation and therefore forfeited their lives. I will be tied up for the next two days, after which I expect that you'll have located them and prepared everything required to take them out. We'll act as soon as I join you."

"But the coronation didn't even happen because—"

"They left before the attack. What happened after they left is irrelevant. I get control of Marissa Vasquez and we'll split their current assets," Cinatas added. "I'm of the opinion that the oil-rich Vladarians in SINCO have become too self-important and need some guidance in humility—if you think the Royals are up to the challenge."

"Now that is an offense of which they are undoubtedly guilty. The Royals made repeated complaints to Pathos about the dangers of so many plebian vampires attaining power and influence, but he refused to listen to our advice."

"I'm all ears," Cinatas said, grinning from ear to ear. The

trap was now set. Valois and his Royals would soon garner more hate than they could imagine. Maybe even enough to resurrect the guillotine. As Valois droned on, Cinatas turned his mind to tonight's expected events. Cover model Conrad Pitt would be arriving shortly. He'd be wined, wooed, drugged, and dead by morning, and Cinatas would be the proud bearer of a new face. All of the monstrous burn scars would be gone and who knew what doors would open for him then.

By all predictions, the Antichrist was supposed to be a handsome devil.

If the shoe fit . . . why not?

"Keep them in sight, but do not let them know they are being followed, and call me if they stop or meet with anyone," Herrera ordered. A mass conspiracy had to be underfoot and he would get to the bottom of it or his name wasn't Hernan Cortes Herrera. The fire. The appearance of the werewolf and Marissa's escape with her brother. The missing priest. The unauthorized evacuation of his wedding guests—the servants said that General Menendez gave the order, but the General denied doing so before he left. Too many things had gone wrong in too well-ordered a manner to be coincidence.

He'd get Marissa back, but first he'd find the snake in his camp. Most of the back of the house had burned, part of the rest was too damaged to use. Only the front, Ysalane's usual domain, remained habitable.

She came up behind him and his nostrils flared at the sweet scent of her Elan blood. "Herrera must drink and regain his strength," she said in his ear as she held out her hand. She'd cut her palm and cupped it, creating a pool of the nectar for him to drink.

Leaning forward, he gripped her wrist and drank the treat, sucking deep from her cut until the skin blanched and very little blood trickled out. She was naked, according to his standard order, but tonight she'd added a little enticement for him. She wore a barbed strap around her neck, so that little droplets of her blood slid tantalizingly down her body. Pulling her around, he licked a red bead off her nipple then followed a trail of red up her chest to the barbed necklace and sucked a little at each wound.

Aroused, hungry, and needing to vent, he propped her ass upon the desk, spread her legs, and used the letter opener to puncture the blood-swollen flesh. She cried out in pain and he licked and lapped until she shuddered with pleasure. After, he flipped her over and took his frustration out amid her cries of pain and pleasure.

She caressed his cheek when he'd spent his last. "See, Herrera doesn't need that *puta*. Ysalane can take care of you."

Herrera froze. Then, pulling back, he shoved her to the floor. "Was it you? Did you conspire against me? What did you do?"

Ysalane held her arms out to block his angry kick. "No, no. Ysalane didn't do anything. Only cast a spell to protect Herrera from the wolf god that will kill you."

Herrera paused. Had Ysalane's black magic saved him in the dungeon?

"Get up," he told her. "We'll do more of this spell to protect me from the wolf and I will get Marissa back from him just as soon as they reach their destination."

Ysalane climbed to her feet. "Ysalane must dress to do spells."

"Then go dress," he said, waving her away.

"Ysalane will do the spell, but it will do no good if Herrera takes the woman back. The wolf god will kill you."

"Just hurry. I expect the guards tailing them to call at any minute and we must be ready to move then." Herrera was sure he could handle the werewolf now that he was expecting the beast. Meanwhile, if the snake wasn't Ysalane, there were only a few more people who knew about Marissa—trusted people. Obviously, he needed to clean house.

Chapter Nine

Navarre's right claw punctured the padded handle he gripped as Marissa careened around a bend in the road. His left arm held the priest upright because the man had gone limp upon seeing the wolf spirit, and every muscle from Navarre's chest down was clenched to keep him wedged in the seat. On top of that, he'd placed his wolf spirit in the back to avoid frightening the old man again when he woke and now found his limited vision from that position frustrating enough to howl over.

Then again, the wolf kept looking at Marissa in the moonlight and not the road ahead or the jungle passing by in a blur—at least he blamed the unwarriorlike behavior on the wolf and not the growing desire inside him to do nothing else.

It didn't help that with every jolt and jerk, his fangs gouged his lip and the burning in his head from the fire strike throbbed to the point of madness. He couldn't think clearly—a condition that worsened beneath the full light of the moon.

From the spirit world, he'd seen the effects of the moon on Jared and Aragon when they'd first come to the mortal ground, but he'd never imagined how strong the lunar influence could be. Just as the moon held sway over the great seas, its gravitational force hit him and drew from his warrior's spirit a gnawing, unfamiliar hunger.

He didn't know what he hungered for, only that his mouth watered at the primal scents filling the jungle air and his pulse throbbed with an excited awareness that had nothing to do with Marissa and the danger they were in. The sensations were frightening, for the intensity of them rivaled his savage hatred of the vampire Herrera. He instinctually knew to fight hard against them—anything so dark could not be good.

Added to this were the hundreds of sensations bombarding him, all new and different and drowning him in a whirl of irritations. The first of which was this contraption the mortals called a "truck."

Marissa plowed through bumps and dips, making the burning in his head so painfully sharp that his teeth hurt from the constant throb. If it wasn't for the fact that he wanted to stay as close to her as possible, he would have jumped from the vehicle and run. At least then he wouldn't feel so completely useless sitting here while she propelled their escape.

He should be doing something—fighting, making things right for her. He should be carrying *her* away from the danger rather than her carrying him away. "Why do mortals use these death traps, anyway?"

"I'm sorry," Marissa said, startling him. "*Dios,* I must not be driving this truck right."

He hadn't realized he'd spoken his irritation about the truck aloud and now struggled to explain what he meant, for he didn't want her to blame herself for his discomfort. "I understand the necessity of this vehicle for the moment, but is there anything right about an object that traps one inside, taking away the freedom to move?"

"You feel trapped?" she asked, surprised. "I have been *en prisión* so much of my life that vehicles are freedom to me. Though I've never had so rough a ride as this. Maybe I'm going too fast, no? Giving it too much gas? I was worried about Herrera's men coming after us, but I don't see any headlights or darker shadows to indicate a car or truck on the road behind us."

He wanted to ask her about being imprisoned, but she hit a huge bump that threw them all sideways. The priest groaned, and Navarre moved his arm away as the old man came awake with a shout. Though Navarre had never met a mortal claiming to be Logos's servant, his senses told him the man wasn't who he claimed to be. There was much more darkness clouding the priest's spirit than there should be. Navarre expected Marissa would have sensed this as well, for she connected with spirits well. She was the only one who had heard and communicated with his wolf spirit long before he came to the mortal ground when he'd been trapped in the gray edges of the spirit realms.

From the backseat, Marissa's brother moaned loudly with pain.

"I'm sorry, Rafe," she called out, glancing back. The spirit wolf's gaze met the concern in her dark eyes.

"Look out, child!" the priest yelled as the truck swerved toward a dense clumping of bushes and trees. They barely avoided the foliage as she pulled sharply back to the road. "Stop and I will drive," he said.

"How do I stop?"

"Ave María y Madre de Dios y Parce Domine!" the old man cried in a mix of Latin and Spanish pleas. "Push upon the other pedal at your feet."

"*Por Dios!* I thought it was for more gas. Why do they have pedals in the same area that do opposite things?" she asked.

Suddenly the truck slammed to a halt. Unprepared, Navarre fell forward and hit the windshield. In the back with his wolf spirit, Rafe slid to the floor, cushioned by the thick blanket. The priest landed on the floor in the front and Marissa cried out as her cheek hit the steering wheel. The truck's engine quit.

Navarre gave a silent prayer of thanks and hoped the engine was somehow broken. Perhaps they had gained enough distance from Herrera and his men to leave this death trap behind. To him it made more sense to escape by leaving no trail through the jungle than to rush down an already paved road that the enemy can use as well.

Pushing back in the seat, he felt his head but found no injury. The constant burning throb inside had not worsened and, in fact, it seemed less, or he'd become accustomed to the discomfort.

"What did I do wrong?" Marissa asked, sounding so worried that Navarre felt guilty for his thankfulness.

The priest crawled up from the floor. "You pushed too hard."

"I pushed too hard? *Pero,* I pushed just the same as I did for the gas."

"Tomorrow," the priest said. "We'll talk *mañana.* My heart cannot take more tonight. You were fearless in driving to escape from Herrera, child, but now it would be foolish to continue when I can drive."

Marissa sighed, and Navarre suddenly realized that apart from the escape, driving itself was important to her.

The priest noticed, too. "Tomorrow," he said. "You will learn more. Dawn will be coming soon and Herrera will have many men looking for you and this truck then. We must get as far away as we can and try to hide or disguise it."

She nodded and opened her door. Navarre did, too. Exiting the truck, he pulled the back of the seat forward as he'd felt Marissa do earlier. Guided by the wolf spirit's sight, he resettled Rafe by gathering the side edges of the blanket and lifting him in the cocoon to lie on the seat.

He touched the young man's forehead, then felt for his pulse, discerning his heartbeat was strong, though his pain and fever were great. Navarre focused what healing energy he could summon from his weakened state and sent it to ease the young man's spirit and his pain. Later, when Navarre had more time, he would try to do more, but given that his body had lost the ability to heal itself, he didn't have much hope he could help in that way.

A gentle hand on his arm let him know Marissa had crossed to his side of the truck. "Is Rafe all right?"

Navarre turned her way, blindly at first. "He is in pain and fevered, but his heart beats strong." His wolf spirit leaped to the front seat in order to see her completely in the moonlight, for it was their first moment free of immediately dire circumstances.

Though disheveled and bloodstained with a bruised cheek and a cut lip, beauty never had had a more exquisite face—heart shaped with wide dark eyes, pale, creamy skin, and dark, wavy hair that fell to her waist. She was as intriguing as the starlit heavens he'd often wanted to explore, but never had.

A warrior's time was never his own. Once he became one of the elite Shadowmen and served as a Blood Hunter, his life belonged to the Guardian Forces. Even now that he was too weak to fight, time still wasn't his. Not with Herrera threatening to destroy her.

He couldn't resist taking a moment more, though. He went to brush his finger along her cheek just to feel the realness of her, but saw her stiffen and an expression of pain settle upon her features. She'd been through so much. Instead of touching her face, he brushed the bloodstained front of her dress that Herrera had cut. A thin red line marked the center of her chest, dipping down into the swell of her breasts.

What kind of evil marred such perfection? What kind of evil caused such pain? Anger surged through him and he had to pull back from her as he fisted his hands so tightly his claws cut into his skin.

"Are you hurting where he cut you?" he asked harshly.

She drew a deep, shuddering breath. "No, it stings but it is nothing in comparison to what Herrera did to Rafe . . . and to you. I'm so sorry, Navarre. This is all my fault. And I wasn't afraid of you just now. It just hurts me badly to see what Herrera has done to you."

"What do you think he—"

"From the snares of the devil deliver me!" the priest screamed. He held a jeweled cross in front of him like a shield as he stared in horror at the wolf spirit. "SATAN BEGONE!"

The distant hum of an engine—one much quieter than the truck's—reached Navarre's sensitive ears. "Someone comes this way," he said. "We must go." He urged Marissa into the truck as he sent his wolf spirit racing into the night to see who followed them.

"Father Dom," Marissa called out above the old man's continued rant. "*Por favor,* someone is coming. Either get in and drive, or I will."

Navarre felt Marissa climb into the truck. Gritting his teeth and resigning himself to more torturous riding, he followed, hating the blindness that rendered him useless in his mortal form.

The priest, despite his fears of the wolf spirit and Navarre, must have wasted no time in getting in. The engine roared to life, and the truck started moving ahead even before Navarre could locate the handle and close the door.

"You must understand, Father Dom, the ghost wolf is not from the devil, but from the spirit of one who *fights* evil. It and Navarre saved me from Herrera's attack."

Marissa's defense of him touched Navarre's spirit.

"You are too quick to trust, child," Father Dom said. "We'll speak of this later."

"I agree with the assessment," Navarre said, pointedly inferring who couldn't be trusted. Marissa tensed in the seat. He was sorry for that but she had to understand the danger. The priest's guarded reticence bordered on a warning and edged up Navarre's distrust of the man.

As Navarre turned his attention to what his wolf spirit saw, he begrudgingly had to admit that with the priest driving, the ride went much smoother and seemingly faster than before.

The wolf sprinted down the road with its every sense alerted to the danger following Marissa's trail. As it ran, it caught the scents of the night and felt the primal pull of the moon and the jungle. It howled in response and rushed faster toward the engine's hum until the gleam of a sleek black car glinted just ahead.

Taking a huge leap, the wolf landed on the hood of the car

and looked at the men inside. They wore odd devices over their heads and eyes that gave a greenish cast to their faces. One of the men pointed at the wolf and shouted, *"El Lobo Diablo!"*

The wolf bared its teeth, growling, and leaped through the windshield, snarling wildly at the men. They scrambled and screamed and the car crashed into a tree before coming to a stop.

Navarre welcomed the return of his wolf spirit and kept it in the front near his feet despite the priest's cries to be saved from the devil. "Those who follow are delayed in their journey," he said once the priest quieted.

"How?" Marissa asked.

"Frightened by a wolf. They stopped their car with a tree," Navarre said, and settled back in the seat until his shoulder brushed hers. Despite the hungers teeming inside him, for now he was just grateful to be with Marissa without death knocking at the door.

After Father Dom started down the road, Marissa turned in the seat and checked on Rafael, surprised to find that he was doing better than she expected. Rather than thrashing and delirious, he actually appeared to be resting. He still had a fever, but it didn't feel as hot as before. "Navarre, *por favor,* can you hand me a bottle of water? They are at your feet."

He gave it to her. "What is this for?"

She looked at him oddly before she realized that the wolf was still looking at the case of water on the floor and Navarre couldn't see her expression. Did he not know what water was? "Water is an element necessary to sustain life. You drink it."

"Sustenance," Navarre said. "Spirit beings do not need it."

"*Pero,* are you a spirit being now?"

He frowned, angling his head to the side. "No. In truth I am completely subject to the laws of the mortal realm, yet I do not think I am mortal, either. I don't know."

"Then we will see, no?"

"Spirit being? Mortal? Is he insane? How can the wolfman not even know what water is?" Father Dom asked, incredulous.

"Navarre is from the spirit world. Herrera took him from a place where there were two others from the spirit world on earth to fight men like Tío Luis and Herrera. In fact, they are the ones who rescued me and my friend Stefanie from my uncle."

Father Dom grunted in response and focused his attention on driving. Marissa turned back to Rafael. She dampened his dry lips and bathed his face in the cool liquid. He was pale and gaunt as if he'd been locked away with very little to eat for a long time, cheeks sunken in, bones protruding, very little muscle mass to his tall lanky frame. His dark hair was matted with sweat and oil and had turned gray at the temples; his face was unshaven, beard tangled. A year younger than her twenty-four, he had the appearance of an old man. What hell had he lived through since she last saw him? She ached inside for him.

The bandage on his chest from the knife wound showed some leakage of blood, but not a lot. As soon as they found shelter, she'd tend to his wounds with some of the supplies she'd taken from the medicine kit. She prayed that with time and care, her brother would regain his strength.

Satisfied that he was as comfortable as he could be for now, she sat back in the seat and drank the rest of the water, realizing that she was terribly thirsty. She then retrieved three more bottles, giving one to Father Dom, opening one for herself and one for Navarre.

"Here." She placed the bottle in his hand. "I've already opened it."

Navarre drank, spilling some, but not much. He finished it all before she'd drunk half of hers. She gave him another bottle.

"Thank you," he said. "It helped with the strangeness I feel inside me."

"Strangeness?"

He shrugged. "Cravings that are so strong they hurt."

"Ah. You are hungry. You need food." And so did she. Turning around again, she scrounged around the floorboards until she located three Snickers bars and three Twinkies from the boxes she had pushed to the floor earlier. Seeing again that her brother rested more peacefully than ever, she handed the snacks out to Father Dom and Navarre, keeping one of each for herself.

"These are very good. One is chocolate with nuts and the other is vanilla cake with cream." She unwrapped part of the Snickers and handed it to him.

Navarre took one bite and the pleasured intensity in his gold eyes as he looked in her direction took her breath away, bringing to mind the rough-hewn, handsome warrior as she'd first seen him. He gave a soft moan and she felt her mouth go dry.

"This is . . . indescribable," he said, moaning again.

Water, she needed more water. Several gulps later, she felt as if she'd regained her senses, though it seemed much hotter in the truck than before. When she looked back at Navarre, he'd finished the Snickers bar and had opened the Twinkie. He licked the cream spilling from the golden cake. "This is good, too. How much of this food can I have?"

"As much as you can eat when we reach a place that has them for sale. But there are many other things to eat that taste just as good," she told him. Hungry herself, she quickly set to her own. It was safer than looking into his eyes. She was exhausted, hungry, and grateful to Navarre for saving her and her brother. That had to be why she'd been overcome with emotion from the look in his gold eyes.

Surely that was what had happened . . .

She'd think about it later.

The longer Father Dom drove, the sleepier she became. Now that the need for adrenaline had eased, her body began to shut down after almost thirty-four hours of fear and fighting to survive. At first she tried to watch how Father Dom was able to drive so much more smoothly than she had, but the warmth of Navarre's body next to hers seeped through her aching muscles, relaxing her. That ease, combined with the comfort of his presence and the knowledge that the wolf spirit could stop Herrera's men even from a distance, wrapped around her frightened soul and released her, for now, from the horror she hadn't thought she would survive.

Navarre touched her arm. "Stop fighting your needs. You must rest."

She shook her head even as she appreciated him caring for her, so attentive to her despite his own horrors. "There is too much to do."

"What can you do now?"

"Shelter must be found. My brother attended. Help sought." The list went on and on in her mind. Navarre needed special help, too. Whatever Herrera had done to turn him into the half-wolf half-man creature had to be undone and she'd have to make it happen for him. And what about her friends in Twilight? Were they already safe or in need of saving just like her? One thing she knew stronger and deeper than anything she'd ever felt before—the evil that had brought them all to this point had to be destroyed.

"None of that can be done at this moment. You must rest now so that you'll have strength later. We have not seen the last of Herrera and his men. But soon we will, for I will obliterate him."

Navarre's voice rang with conviction, as if he had no doubt that he would "obliterate" Herrera. She'd never used that word before, but liked the sound and the meaning of it. "Yes," she said slowly, adding her conviction to his. "We will obliterate him."

The words were empowering and so different from how

she'd been raised. Her family had been manipulated and abused most of her life, but could they have chosen differently? The answer she found was uncomfortable to her heart. Yes, somehow, some way, they could have banded together and done then what she and Navarre had accomplished tonight.

"Thank you," she whispered to Navarre.

"For permission to rest?"

"No, for helping me to thwart the power Herrera tried to hold over me tonight. I've realized evil only begets worse evil. My uncle shaped Herrera into the monster he is now. There is no placating wickedness, as my mother and grandmother had urged. There is no coexistence with it, for its sole purpose is to destroy good." She thought of Ysalane and how the woman had become evil to survive it. "If you try and do those things it only gets worse."

"You speak true. Rest, and we'll talk of this later."

Sighing, she let her eyes close and her head drooped toward Navarre. Too tired to dream of running with the wolf in the moonlight, too tired to think of the mighty and handsome warrior Navarre had been, she fell into a very deep sleep.

Wrapped in a cocoon of warmth, Marissa snuggled closer and felt hair tickle her nose. She wiggled and shifted, wanting to sink back into the place of comfort and peace she'd been in, but unfamiliar sensations teased at her, the feel of strong arms holding her tightly, the solid beat of another's heart close to hers, the gentle caress of warm fingers upon her face and her lips. They were dreamed-for sensations and she sighed at the heavenly feel of them as heat tingled in every place her blood pulsed.

She moved closer, wanting more.

"You are awake?" The timbre of Navarre's whisper, so close to her ear, sent tiny shivers of pleasure everywhere.

Dios, you're not dreaming!

"Navarre?" Marissa popped her eyes open and stared,

stunned. Surely she had to be dreaming or dreaming that she wasn't dreaming. She was in the truck. Shaded light streamed in through the window. She lay sprawled across Navarre's lap, facing him with her head resting in the crook of his shoulder, cushioning her from the hard door. Her legs stretched along the seat and onto the floor. Her chest was pressed so tightly to his that she could feel the heat of him, the imprint of his amulet, and the beating of his heart as if there were nothing between them. Her palm rested upon the smooth, hot skin of his muscled arm that lay against the side of her breast as he caressed her face. Father Dom was nowhere in sight and Navarre was no longer a creature, but a man—a very large warrior with rough-hewn features, intense golden eyes, full parted lips, and a hard arousal pressing against her bottom.

"I hunger," he said, and her lips parted as he slid the pad of his finger along her bottom lip.

The dream was magical and perfect—a bit heart-wrenching because Navarre was no longer this golden warrior, but a misshapen creature. Perhaps it was wrong of her even to imagine herself kissing him as he once had been, but she didn't have the strength to deny herself. This one little moment in a dream wouldn't hurt.

"Me, too," she said, then closed her eyes and brought her mouth to his, marveling at her imagination. His hand fell from exploring her face to rest against the swell of her breasts. Sensations exploded inside her that were so different from the ugliness and fear Herrera had thrust upon her, and she pressed herself eagerly to Navarre, needing something that she wasn't sure how to express.

Chapter Ten

MARISSA FELT Navarre stiffen for a moment as if surprised; then he pressed his lips harder against hers and the stubble of his beard roughly brushed her skin. She fleetingly wondered why she would dream that but the thought was swept away by a hot wave of need. Her heart swelled and pounded, racing as wildly as the desire rushing through her.

Then . . . nothing. Wasn't there more to a kiss?

She drew closer, moving her lips against his, wanting that more. He groaned, a deep rich sound expressing satisfaction greater than when he'd eaten the Snickers bar. She automatically slid her free hand up his sculpted chest through the smattering of soft dark hair there then along his neck, relishing the sensual nuances of supple skin, burning heat, and hard man. She threaded her fingers through his silky short hair, sighing with utter pleasure at every sensation. Short?

Her eyes snapped open, bringing her fully awake from dreamland. Navarre the warrior she dreamed had long black hair to his shoulders. This Navarre had unevenly chopped hair, as if someone had taken a knife and sheared it off at an odd angle—like an old man wanting a toupee? Her gaze sought Navarre's golden one. The fire in his eyes stopped her breath, making her feel as if she could drown in the molten pools, but his gaze was directed at some point a little down and to her right where her face had been when she'd first awakened. His hand at her breast was tentatively tapping up her neck like a blind person seeking an unfamiliar way.

This wasn't a dream. This was real. Navarre was no longer a hairy, clawed creature with fangs, but he was still blind. How was it possible? Where was her brother? Was his fever worse? Where was Father Dom?

She backed away, flooded with questions and mortified over her forwardness in kissing him.

"*Dios*, I'm sorry!" she cried.

Navarre frowned. "Why? Was that not pleasurable for you?"

"Yes, but—"

"Good. This hunger grows like a fire that must be allowed to rage. You taste better than Snickers or Twinkies." He slid his hand up her neck to her chin and brought his lips back to hers, hitting the corner of her mouth. Then he quickly dragged his mouth to perfectly fit hers. His hips shifted, pressing his arousal tighter to her bottom and she gasped, losing her thoughts to his sensual need. His tongue brushed over her lips, tasting her as he had the cream from the Twinkie, and he moaned with pleasure.

Her heart flipped. She opened her mouth wider. His tongue swept over her lips again. This time she brought the tip of her tongue to his, wanting to taste him. He responded by delving his tongue deeper into her mouth in a wild seeking of hers. Her stomach clenched and the fire of desire exploded inside her. This was the more! She needed to feel him everywhere against her. She wanted nothing between them.

"*Madre de Dios!* What is this . . . this . . . abomination?"

Marissa jerked away from Navarre to find Father Dom staring at her in horror. He had a wet cloth in his hands and a damp face, clearly having just refreshed himself. She blinked at him, desperately trying to find her wits and her voice.

"What is wrong? Is there danger?" Navarre tensed. Shifting and sliding his hand, blindly searching, he landed on her breast. An electric jolt went right to Marissa's sex and a hot rush of embarrassment heated her face.

"Have you forgotten that you're a married woman, Señora Herrera?" Father Dom asked.

"Herrera!" Her brother sat up in the backseat. "I will *kill* Herrera and follow him to hell." Her brother's voice was weak and hoarse, yet he seemed stronger than ever. Marissa wanted to cry out in joy, except the mad glow of murderous hatred in her brother's eyes had her practically fainting in fear. *Dios* help them all.

Dawn broke across the sky in a revelation of pink, purple, and blue that failed to touch Stefanie's soul. Once sunrise and sunset were her most treasured times of day. She would stop whatever she was doing and take a few moments to revel in the beauty of the unfolding majestic tapestries. Only there were no more bright possibilities in her life and today wasn't the dawning of a new day for her, but a return to the past. A return to horror and death. The death of her friend and the death of her spirit.

Corazón de Rojo lay in the jungle below the hovering helicopter and she braced herself for the landing.

Last night Nick had flown to the coordinates the clerk had given him. It was in Guatemala, not far from the border—a fact that had Jaymes bristling with warnings. Many drug lords and gangs would execute before asking questions if their territory was breached. Apparently, General Menendez, while demanding and promising a hard-line policy against drug lords and gangs in his political campaigns, was in fact up to his neck in the trade. Fortunately or unfortunately, they had found nothing but a helipad in the center of a dark, empty field with one metal building at the far end. Caution made them just fly over, using infrared and night-vision technology to scout out the area. Nick, Jared, and Aragon planned to go back later today and do a ground check of the area just to be sure, but the likelihood that it had anything to do with Herrera and Marissa had lessened in Stefanie's mind. Why would Herrera go to Guatemala when he was so powerful in Belize?

Nick set down about half an hour closer to Corazón than Xunantunich's Archaeological Park, the place he had landed last time. Stefanie was stunned to see how relatively close to civilization she'd been kept a prisoner. It proved just how powerful Vasquez had been to get away with what he had.

Then again, Belize's rain forest was so dense that a few bends in the road took you to the middle of nowhere. It wouldn't have mattered if she had known where she and Abe were—escape over the high wall of the compound had been impossible.

Stefanie waited with Annette just beyond the gust of the helicopter's rotor draft as the men and Jaymes armed themselves. Rather than guard the helicopter as he'd done the last time, Nick planned to lock up the cab and, for extra measure, do a little something to disable the engine. Something that he said was easily fixable if you knew what it was.

With every step she took upon Belize's soil, flashes of memory assaulted her, but she refused to retreat. She had to move forward and face the past she could never forget.

"I'm sorry about yesterday," Annette said. "Sorry that I made it harder for you to come here. It's just that it kills me to see you hurt and it kills me more that I can't help you."

"I know," Stefanie said, reaching out to clasp her sister's hand. "You know, I said the same thing to Abe when . . . when we were here."

Don't go there. Don't remember that much. You can't or you'll be completely lost. Marissa needs you.

Stefanie breathed deeply and focused on letting the memory of Abe's torture just wash over her rather than allowing herself to drown in the atrocities. She kept functioning . . . just barely.

"I wish there was something . . . anything I could do to help," Annette said, her voice thick with emotion.

"You are. You did. You got me out of here. And just knowing how much you care helps—even if it doesn't seem that way sometimes." Stefanie brought Annette's hand to her cheek. "Were I you and you me, I would have argued just as strongly to talk you out of returning to hell. I don't even understand completely why this is something I have to do. I just know that

I must, and that I had to be here for Marissa. I know what Herrera does . . . and I had to come."

"Stef. I know bad things happened to you. Things you haven't been able to talk about. I just wish you could—"

"You want to stop the pain and feel you can't because you don't know the root of the problem. That's the doctor in you, Nette. But you have to understand that what happened to me will never go away. I haven't told you because it would hurt me more than I already do to cause you that pain. I love you too much. Please try and accept that. I promise to go and talk to someone objective when the time is right." Annette didn't need to know that the time might not ever be right.

Stefanie could see the men and Jaymes rushing across the field. She was surprised at how heavily armed they were, carrying machine guns and machetes. She and Annette were the only ones unarmed and she made a mental promise to herself that it would be the last time. She wanted to have a weapon in her hands. She wanted to have that power, the option to fight.

There was no more time for talk as they moved through the jungle to the compound, Jared and Aragon in the front, Nick and Jaymes bringing up the rear. Still, despite her resolve that she had to take this step, returning to this dark cave of torture brought wave after wave of paralyzing fear. Everything about the place seemed to welcome her back, lush fat leaves and towering trees waving in the breeze, tangled vines spiraling down like gnarled fingers pointing the way, squawking macaws preening scarlet plumes. Even the bright morning sun warmed the rain forest to a steamy bath. But every fiber of her being rejected it. She shivered with cold; her palms were damp, her muscles were tightly drawn, and her heart thumped at a sickening pace. Breathing became harder and a nauseating vertigo swirled at the edges of her vision.

She had to do this. She had to. But God, every minute was harder than the last, every step more grueling.

"Stef, hold on," Nick said.

She stopped, thankful for a brief respite, and turned to face him.

"I meant to give you this," he said, taking her hand and sliding a light pistol into her palm. "This is the safety. It is on, but still be careful. Do you remember what I told you the other day?"

Her mouth was so dry she could barely speak, but she clasped the gun tightly. "I'm going to obliterate the bastard. I'm going to put this gun in my hand and I'm going to shoot and shoot and shoot. And I'll do it every day until when I shut my eyes and that son of a bitch pops into my mind, I see myself offing him. I'm not going to be a victim ever again. Not in my nightmares and not in my life."

"That's my girl." He squeezed her arm. "Just do me a favor. Let us know when you're going to start shooting so we can get out of the way."

Unbelievably, a slight grin tugged at her lips. "Thanks," she whispered as she slid the weapon into the pocket of her windbreaker. Logically she knew she wasn't any safer now than she had been minutes ago, but the feel of the gun in her hand helped anyway. The dizziness receded and her heart eased to a slower pace.

Jaymes, who'd been standing quietly beside them, spoke up. "A man with guts enough to arm a woman can't be all bad. You'll need this for the tight spots." She, too, held out something.

"What is it?" Stefanie picked up the slender object made out of some strange material. About the length and width of her finger with a clip on the end, it fit into the palm of her hand.

"A knife you can hide practically anywhere. I thread it through my hair like an oriental stick. Squeeze the buttons on both sides at the bottom and the blade will eject from the top. But as Prescott said at Bunker Hill, 'Don't fire until you see the whites of their eyes.' Literally."

"Thank you." Stefanie gripped the knife, then took Jaymes

up on her suggestion and twisted her hair into a knot, securing the knife into the mass with the clip. She drew a deep breath. "I'm ready." And she was.

The group moved more quickly after that and she realized that they'd been adjusting their pace to hers. Minutes later, they reached a wide opening and her breath caught in surprise. There was nothing before her but a large area of burned rubble. Corazón de Rojo had been leveled. Completely.

She wanted to laugh, but couldn't. No matter what physically lay before her eyes, in her mind the horrid place was just as big and whole and real as ever.

A breeze riffled the tiny weeds that had found root among the rocks.

"Aragon, did you smell that?" Jared asked, sniffing the air, turning in a circle, gun at the ready.

Aragon shifted to a defensive stance. "No. What?"

Jared sniffed again then shook his head. "A foul but odd smell. It's gone now. It would be better if we hurried, instead of standing in the open."

Stefanie moved to the left, seeing things as they were before. Then when she reached a place, she turned to Nick. "You can mark this spot. Have them look here for his bones. This is where Vasquez's ant house was."

"Ants?" Annette asked, puzzled.

"You don't want to know," Nick said. "Let's just say Abe was the bread that fed thousands." He pulled some sort of orange plastic from a pocket of his camo pants and began placing it in the area, weighing it down with rocks. Suddenly the screech of howling monkeys cut a raucous wave through the jungle, setting everyone's nerves on edge. Though distant, the sound was still disturbing.

Just as Nick finished, his cell phone twanged some "love 'em and leave 'em" song.

"Yo," Nick mumbled, shifting his gun. "Come again? . . .

Shit, we were sort of already on that but thought we'd landed a lame duck . . . Yeah . . . We'll call you back. It changes the game big-time.

"Guess what?" Nick muttered. "Sam received an anonymous call from a CIA buddy undercover in Central America's drug shit. Seems as if General Menendez attended a wedding of one Hernan Cortes Herrera last night where he married a very reluctant billionairess by the name of Marissa Vasquez. We're heading back to Guatemala, *amigos*."

"I don't think so," shouted a heavily accented voice. Four armed men slipped into view, weapons aimed directly at them. Stefanie clutched the pistol in her pocket.

York found himself pacing in the twilight edges that separated the mortal ground from the spirit world. The mushrooming surge of evil that had threatened Jared and Aragon and the mortals with them had been beaten back by the ex–Blood Hunters' efforts and by the fighting whirlwind of power York had built with Sirius and Sven. They'd sucked the demons into the spirit world and spewed them back into hell where they belonged. The Guardian Forces fighting that gathering of Heldon's Fallen Army in the heavens had won their battle, too. A peaceful blue sky and bright warm sunlight ruled the new day. If the Shadowmen hadn't intervened, York was certain all would have been lost on the mortal ground. Evil would have taken over the Sacred Stones and all of the area surrounding the ancient worship site. He knew that as deeply as he knew his own soul. So why were Sirius and Sven suddenly doubting the wisdom of their decision to fight?

He didn't understand it, nor could he accept it. He wasn't going to abandon Jared and Aragon, and if he saw an opportunity to act on their behalf, then damn the rules, he was going to help. The unraveling of his Blood Hunter unit left him raw and alone. None of them could have predicted that day when Jared had been bitten by a Tsara, a spiritual assassin for the damned, that they would have come to this end—a tattered remnant of the powerful band of warriors they'd been.

He didn't want to do as the Guardian Council ordered. He didn't want to join another band of brethren and lose himself within their ranks. He wanted to gather several new warriors and mentor them with Sven, share with them the story of Jared's and Aragon's greatness, bring about a new awareness of how the battle between the Fallen Army and the Guardian Forces was changing. The path for warriors to join the fight upon the mortal ground had been tentatively forged, and Logos needed to open the gateway by providing special dispensation to Shadowmen who were willing to make the necessary sacrifices and join that fight against the growing numbers of the damned.

York had thought both Sven and Sirius believed in this course of action. Now he didn't know.

A hand landed on his shoulder and he whipped around, expecting to see that one of them had come to their senses. Instead he found the young warrior he'd been mentoring, Flynn.

"You are late for my lessons," Flynn said.

York glanced at the sun. "It appears more time has passed than I realized. My apologies. Do you think you are ready for the mortal realm?"

"Do I even need to answer?" Flynn asked with a wide determined grin that told York the young warrior was ready to get his hands dirty.

"Then we shall go now." York led Flynn through the gray edges between the spirit and mortal worlds.

"I spoke to Sven," Flynn said after they passed the spirit barrier and glided down into the atmosphere. "He said we are to be reassigned. Have you considered which band of Blood Hunters you wish to join?"

York exhaled harshly. "No. In truth I have little desire to

subject myself to another leader's stringent adherence to the Guardian Law. Both Aragon and Sven are leaders who realize that circumstances in battle sometimes mitigate the rules."

Flynn nodded. "I know. My brother Exeter sent me to your band for mentorship for that reason. He and two of his brethren are suffering greatly from just such a situation."

"That is interesting to know." But York said no more. Instead he turned to the matter of instructing Flynn on the differences between the spirit and mortal worlds and the Blood Hunter's role in protecting the Elan.

As they patrolled throughout the continents, York ran through a number of rising possibilities. What if he could band together a group of Shadowmen who skirted the edge of the Guardian Law? Might they be convinced to help with the fight on the mortal ground? Might he even bring that band to Logos, seeking permission for them all to go? The longer he considered the ideas, the more possible they seemed. He would have to make it happen a step at a time, which meant he had to follow the Guardian Council's directive and join a Blood Hunter band.

"Flynn," he said as they approached the end of their patrol. "It may be that your brother might need a couple of warriors around that see things the way he does. What say you, after our lesson today, we join his Blood Hunter band?"

"I say there couldn't be a better choice."

"Good." They soon reached Stonehenge, their last stop before returning to the spirit realm, and shifted from their spirit forms into their mortal ones. Dawn had yet to break across the horizon, and gray twilight wavered between the promise of the rising sun and the dark force of the night.

"Excellent performance for your first venture into the mortal realm and adeptly shifting forms," York said. "You have spent time practicing."

"I have, but shifting here is different somehow." Flynn

frowned and walked to the center of the monoliths. "Being in this realm weighs upon one's spirit."

York joined him in the misty circle. "You will become accustomed to the gravity over time."

"It is more than that," Flynn said. "There is a feeling of age here, of many lingering spirits that press upon me."

York lifted a brow, surprised by Flynn's perceptiveness. "You sense what the spirit realm with its timeless infinity doesn't know—a finite existence. Though the spirits of mortals are eternal, their bodies are not. Here they live for a short time, then die. The mark of their life upon this earth remains, creating the ancient, almost sacred feeling you sense. It is especially strong in the places we've visited tonight. Those marks of mortal lives gather most where the spirit barrier separating this world from our realm is thinnest."

"Which is where Blood Hunters are supposed to find the damned trying to cross into the mortal realm; but we found nothing tonight."

"Usually that is true, especially with a nearly full moon, but all has been eerily quiet tonight." Which was a shame in York's mind. A good fight with some Underlings, a few demons, or any sort of Blood Hunter action would lift York's spirits. "The damned are still licking their wounds from the beating we gave them."

Flynn grinned and rubbed his knuckles against his broad chest. "More likely they knew I was coming and fled to their frozen caves in fear."

York rolled his eyes, wondering if he'd ever been as impatient and arrogant as Flynn. Well, the arrogant part at least. Larger than most Blood Hunters, Flynn had quickly moved his way up to the top echelon of training warriors. York cuffed Flynn playfully on the back of the head, then ran ahead and yelled back, "They probably decided to save their energy for a foe worth climbing out of hell to fight."

Flynn gave chase. "Come back and say that to my face like a real warrior, old man."

York darted to the right and ducked around a monolith, but instead of moving ahead, he turned on a dime and went in the opposite direction.

Flynn came barreling outside the circle, finding himself farther behind.

"Old man?" York laughed, sprinting faster.

Just then a swift breeze cut across the lingering mists and with it York caught the vile scent of a Tsara—one of Heldon's spiritual assassins whose bite delivered a fate worse than death by irrevocably turning their victims evil.

Even its smell clawed at York's spirit. He stopped dead in his tracks and brought forth his sword. "Tsara!" he called out, warning Flynn almost too late. Three Tsaras broke through the spirit barrier almost right on top of them. There was a moment of surprise and then they attacked.

Two of them went straight for Flynn, who was closer. One came at York. The air crackled with the Tsaras' rabid excitement. Shaped like mortal men, the thick black creatures had red eyes, red claws, and a mouthful of dagger-sharp teeth.

He and Flynn were in a fight for their immortal souls and they couldn't even fight back to back. There was too much distance between them.

By Logos! It was unprecedented for three of the practically undefeatable beasts to appear together and so boldly, practically at daylight. Something seriously foul was afoot. York had only fought one Tsara at a time in the dark of the night. There was something very wrong in the mortal realm and they had to find out what. That is, if they survived.

Chapter Eleven

Señora Herrera? Rafael in hell? Denial and outrage bubbled up from the very depths of Marissa's heart.

"No!" She pushed herself from Navarre's warm arms and sucked in a bolstering breath before voicing her outrage as she glared at Father Dom, wondering how he even dared to declare her married. "*Por Dios,* no matter what words were said last night I am not and never will be the wife of that vile demonic creature. Do not *ever* refer to me as Señora Herrera. And you." She pointed at Rafael. "Are not going to kill yourself or go to hell. We will, however"— she touched Navarre's arm—"obliterate Herrera *together* once we have the proper weapons and a plan."

The priest shifted his gaze between her and Navarre, pointedly looking at her hand on Navarre's arm.

Marissa automatically pulled her hand back, as if it were sinful of her to touch the warrior, but doing that really did feel wrong. She had a difficult time believing any part of the wonder and pleasure she'd shared with Navarre was wrong. It seemed the most right thing that had ever happened in her life. And that was followed by the miracle of Navarre's restoration to the handsome warrior he'd been.

No one appeared happy with her decree. All three men scowled as if they were being forced to engage in the most unpleasant of tasks, and for once, she decided it didn't matter. She was sailing full speed ahead, regardless. "First we wash, and eat, then take stock of our situation and decide where we are. Since you've refreshed yourself, Father Dom, why don't you see what we can use from the back of the truck. Navarre can help me with Rafe. Then we'll gather what snacks might be left in the cab."

"Beware, child," Father Dom said, glaring at her then at Navarre. "Shapeshifters are of the devil. Satan, the first shapeshifter, became the snake and deceived Eve."

Shapeshifters? Marissa wondered what the priest was getting at. But she felt Navarre stiffen at her side and she clasped his hand.

"Those who speak from ignorance," Navarre said, his voice low, but hard, "still bear the responsibility of their lies. Shadowmen serve Logos with a pure heart and never deceive. What say you, priest? Do you serve so well?"

Giving a final rheumy glare at Marissa's hand clasped in Navarre's, Father Dom tossed his damp rag into the truck, adjusted his jeweled biretta on his gray straggle-haired head, and left them. Soon impatient, angry knocks and bangs echoed from the back of the truck.

"Shapeshifters? Shadowmen? Logos?" Rafe finally asked, dark eyes narrowed with distrust as he looked at her and Navarre. "*Mierda!* Do I dream? Have I died?"

"No." Navarre spoke quicker than Marissa could. "I will explain to you both before the priest poisons your minds, but first I must be free of this death trap." He released her hand and used both of his on the door, pulling and tugging on different things until he found the handle and popped open the lock.

"Where is the ghost wolf?" she asked when she realized he didn't have his wolf spirit seeing for him.

"Gone," Navarre replied. "Disappeared with the rising of the sun." He pushed the door open and felt his way out of the truck, inhaling deep breaths of air as if he'd escaped a coffin. She couldn't blame him. Though the truck was large, his size turned it into a sardine can.

"*Mierda!*" Rafe said. "He is blind? You are *loco* if you think a woman, an old priest, and a blind man can kill Herrera. Honor demands he must die by my hand for what he has done to me and now to you, no matter what the cost."

She had no doubt that if her brother could have moved, he'd have gone after Herrera like a madman . . . and gotten himself killed. *Dios,* Rafael's eyes were haunted, and she did not have the courage to ask what more Herrera had done to him. The bed of stakes was too horrific to remember and the thought of losing Rafael now that she had found him hurt too much to consider.

"And you will do this when you cannot even walk unaided?" she asked, then felt guilty as his cheeks stained with shame. "Rafe, *por favor,*" she said softly. "You must give yourself time to heal, *hermano menor,* little brother. Plus, do not be so quick to judge. This woman and that blind man are what got you out of Herrera's dungeon and saved Father Dom from execution."

Marissa followed Navarre from the truck's cab, feeling as if she were made of stone. Every bone creaked and every muscle groaned in protest. She flipped the seat forward to help Rafael out, but then saw Navarre step away from the truck, and she twisted to catch his arm, more aware than ever of the supple, heated strength of his body. Naked from the waist up, he seized her attention with his every move. She needed to find him clothes so that she could think properly.

"Where are you going?" Marissa pulled on his arm until he stopped. Granted, he had his arms out feeling his way, but another step would have had him sliding into a ditch.

"I don't know. I just know that I must do something or go insane," he said harshly, turning her way. The expression of anger and loss on his face tore at her. What would it be like to be blind and in a strange place, knowing nothing save what you remembered from a different world?

"Then help me with Rafe first. After I get him comfortable, I will take you down to the water so we can clean up," she said, urging him back.

Navarre grunted. "I do not need pity."

"And I don't need help," Rafael muttered. Though he'd

moved to the opening, he was shaking so badly that she doubted he could stand, but the look in his eyes told her his fragile ego would never admit it.

Marissa wanted to walk away and leave both of them to their own miserable devices, but her heart wouldn't let her.

"All men who've survived hell and have been ravaged by fever need help," Marissa declared to her brother. "And understanding another's pain and trouble, and needing to be with them during that time, is not pity," she informed Navarre. "Bruised egos and foolhardy bravado aren't going to give me food and shelter, or keep me from Herrera's slimy hands. Are you two going to help me or not?"

Neither of them said anything, but they did cooperate with her commands. While Navarre helped Rafael from the truck, she ran to grab blankets from the back to make her brother a pallet in the shade.

She took note of how well hidden the truck was beneath a canopy of kapoks, gumbo-limbos, and thick, tangled vines. Father Dom had chosen well. The waterfall and surrounding area didn't seem large enough to be on anyone's map.

"He is dangerous," Father Dom whispered as she picked up the blankets.

He looked worried, haggard, and old. He had to be close to seventy, the same age her grandmother had been. Marissa's heart squeezed. She'd lost her grandmother last week when the Blood Hunters had invaded Corazón and rescued Stefanie. It was as if her grandmother had only breathed to see Marissa free, and once that happened, she went on to the spirit world she loved. She had to remember that like her grandmother, Father Dom saw the world through different eyes—wise ones, but ones that also assumed the unknown and inexplicable was bad.

"Only to evil, Father Dom," Marissa said. "Last night Navarre could have chosen to kill men rather than disable them and he didn't. He saved us all. So I do not understand your dislike of him."

"Nothing good can come from one who is a hideous creature by night and a seducer by day. You've lived a sheltered life, child, and do not know the ways of the world."

"I've lived an imprisoned life and know the ways of evil, and its ways are not Navarre's. You will see. I don't know what Herrera did to make him a creature, *pero gracias a Dios* it is no more. Now I must help Rafael and we will talk again later."

Father Dom looked as if he wanted to say more, but she left. Hurrying back, she placed the blankets in a comfortable spot then led Navarre, who carried Rafael, to them. Her brother had wrapped the blanket around his waist to cover himself. He was naked beneath the mummylike bandages he wore.

"It's unbelievable how well you are doing," she told Rafael. "Last night, I thought it would take weeks for you to heal enough from all of the cuts to even move."

Rafael froze and stared at her dumbfounded. "Last night? You mean it was only last night?" He shook his head. "I feel as if it's been days, if not a week."

"You had a very bad fever. You were delirious when we found you and didn't wake until this morning. I've bandages and medicine in the truck that will help. I'll be right back." She left and gathered the supplies, adding water, candy bars, and the knife tucked into the sleeve of her dress. She left the gun and the other things she'd stolen in the truck.

Returning, she found Navarre kneeling beside Rafael, speaking in hushed tones with his hand on her brother's forehead. For a moment Marissa feared her brother had had a serious setback. A collapse or a heart attack after the severe treatment he'd suffered wouldn't be unusual. She'd heard of it happening with her uncle's prisoners and the men had always welcomed death. Sequestered as she'd been, she'd never witnessed her uncle's tortures, but she'd heard—their screams, the rumors. Had Herrera subjected Rafael to such horror? Had the bed of stakes and starvation, which were terrible enough, been the extent of what he'd suffered? She prayed so.

Before she could speak, Navarre moved away from her brother and Rafael sat up. He stretched his back, his legs, and then paled, looking at Navarre oddly. "What did you do? I hurt a little now, but I am no longer in unbearable pain. It's just not possible. *Dios mio.*"

Marissa walked up, completely stunned.

Navarre must have sensed her presence, for he turned her way. "Your brother has healed well. I must not be as weak a warrior as I thought."

"How have you done this?"

Navarre shrugged. "I gave him healing energy several times. Last night when we stopped for the priest to drive, and then again after we reached here. I thought I would only be able to lessen his pain and fever, because if I still had the strength to heal then I would no longer be blind."

"It is a miracle," Marissa whispered. She went to her brother. "Herrera tried to stab you in the heart but missed," she told Rafael. She eased the bandage from her brother's chest and found the gauze she'd packed into the wound loose on top and the wound itself scabbed over. Then she remembered Navarre being stabbed when Herrera had kidnapped her.

"Your back, Navarre? I wondered about it last night. How you moved so well, as if uninjured. Maybe you can heal." She went to Navarre and ran her hand down the smooth skin of his back in awe. He jerked a little, then relaxed. He was completely healed. She touched him again to be sure. This time she registered all the things she'd missed. His heat. The rippling muscles. The power beneath his supple skin. It was hard to see straight from all the wonder and the sensual feelings zinging her fingertips and darting to every secret place inside her.

Navarre must have felt it, too, for his breath caught and he leaned into her touch. It was almost like kissing. She took longer than necessary to determine that only a slight pink line marked where the knife had lodged and a few healed scratches where he'd forced his way through the dungeon's window.

"You're healed," she said. "You can cure others and yourself of grave wounds. *Madre de Dios,* that is a miraculous gift."

Navarre shook his head. "Then why am I still blind?"

She leaned into him, pressing her cheek to his back. "I don't know, but we will find the answer."

"Prophesies of the Antichrist say he will heal," Father Dom said.

Marissa looked up to find the priest watching them from the corner of the truck. She didn't pull away from Navarre as she had before, but instead leaned closer.

Father Dom glowered and said, "There are some canned goods in a box back here. Cherries, different vegetables, and soups."

He disappeared before Marissa could reply. Navarre wasn't evil. The priest would soon learn that.

"Cherries?" Rafael whispered hoarsely, seemingly more stunned at that prospect than the healing. He rose to his feet and took several steady steps then looked back at Navarre. "I don't know who you are, but I am grateful for this and for your rescue of Marissa."

"You are welcome. But no warrior needs thanks for doing what his heart and soul deems to be right."

"Try and explain that to Father Dom over cherries, Rafe. I'm taking Navarre down to the water." She desperately needed a few moments to gather her mind and absorb what Navarre had just done. It was a miracle and her heart was overwhelmed by it all. "Come down to the water when you finish eating, and remember not to eat too much too soon or you'll feel ill."

"I remember," Rafael said solemnly. "There are things I will never forget." The haunted shadows in his dark eyes let her know that as it was with Stefanie, deep hurts weighed upon her brother's soul. Something Navarre's physical healing couldn't help.

Navarre waited impatiently while she located a long, solid tree branch to serve as a cane and wrapped a cloth over the end. Then she showed him how to tap the ground around him to "feel" where to step.

It was slow, but Navarre, with minimal guidance, was able to follow the leaf-strewn path down to the pool of emerald water. Yet by the time they found a flat rock near the water's edge and sat down, she could feel the tension pouring off him.

Cutting them off from the truck was a large copse of trees, and bushes that dripped with plants and wild orchids. Marissa welcomed the perfumed air and the moment of privacy with a sigh of relief. She'd have to talk to Father Dom. Had to make him understand that he was all wrong about Navarre.

"Wait here. I'll be but a moment and then I'm going to wash my face." She went into the trees to relieve herself, smelling the damp freshness of the earth and air. She still wore the ripped, silken underwear Herrera had touched. Shuddering, she shed them, burying them in the dirt beneath her feet. Though being uncovered below felt strange, she *felt* cleaner without them.

Reappearing, she found Navarre sitting perfectly still and she went to the water's edge.

"What is that noise?" he asked.

Marissa bit her lip to keep from crying out at the injustice of him not being able to see the beauty around them. "You hear the waterfall. About thirty feet above us on the right, water has carved a path from the side of a lush green flowered cliff and spills into a deep emerald pool at our feet. The bright morning sun is so warm that steam is rising from the damp ground and the air is sparkling like a diamond from the droplets of water. It is very beautiful."

"I can see that," he said.

"How is that?"

"In your voice. I can see the beauty of the land in your voice, Marissa."

The way he said her name was like a caress that whispered tantalizingly over her heart. Her knees were so shaky that she had to kneel before she melted into a puddle. Cupping the cool water, she splashed her heated face and arms, wondering what it was about Navarre that went right to the center of her being. From the very first, even as his golden-eyed wolf spirit in her dreams, he'd touched her soul deeply.

Shaking her head, she reminded herself that there was no time for daydreaming now. She assessed her dress, now a ruined travesty of a wedding gown. Its destruction made her feel good and she couldn't wait to cut it into pieces. She'd start in a few minutes by shortening it with the knife she'd brought. Hopefully soon she'd be able to burn it.

As she brushed water over the back of her neck and her chest, she gasped in shock. The thin cut that Herrera had made down her throat all the way to her cleavage was now only a smooth pink line that would likely fade in a day or two.

"What is it?" Navarre tried to rise quickly, but then stumbled over a rock on his left and fell to one knee.

She jumped up. "Nothing. I'm fine. I just saw that you healed me, too. Herrera's cut is practically all gone."

"By Logos! I cannot bear this," Navarre said. "Not knowing where I am. Not knowing what things are. Not knowing if danger is nearby or not."

"I'm sorry." Going to him, she placed her hand over his clenched fist, wishing she could help him. "I didn't mean to frighten you."

Taking her hand in his, he felt his way up her arm and cupped her cheek in the palm of his other hand. "No. It is I who apologize. I should not vent my frustrations when there is naught to be done. A wise warrior does not waste his strength on fruitless journeys of emotion. I'd always considered myself wise until now. Now I am humbled to learn how foolish I am."

She turned and brushed her lips against his palm. "But I want to know your thoughts and troubles. I want to know about you. Where you came from and why you are here. Who is Logos?"

He touched the medallion he wore. "The Creator that all the Shadowmen and the Guardian Forces serve. This amulet I wear is a symbol of my oath to serve. Just like Jared and Aragon, for over a millennium I've been a Blood Hunter, a chosen warrior who protects those of Elan blood within the mortal realm. I come from the spirit world. Why am I here?" He released her cheek and turned from her. "I don't know. For the moment I am trapped within the mortal realm. A mistake, perhaps? Warriors who cannot heal go to a place where their spirit becomes one with the universe for eternity. We sometimes call it death, but it isn't the finite end a mortal's body faces. Yet even that fate is preferable to this darkness."

She grabbed his shoulder and turned him toward her, wanting to see his face. "Surely you can't mean that."

Physically he looked so strong and capable. Tall, so tall, and shoulders so broad that he had completely filled the overlarge doorways in the dungeon. His chest rippled with powerful muscles as did his arms and thick legs. Sparse, dark hair spread across his chest down to a thin trail below the waistband of his black sweatpants. She remembered with a quick, strange clenching of her stomach the hard press of his arousal against her this morning. He'd found kissing her very satisfying and she wondered what more pleasures lay within the secret world of desire and intimacy. But there were so many other things involved in her attraction to him, his noble stance, the wisdom and tone of his words, the gentle brush of his spirit against hers, and the molten heat in his eyes when he kissed her.

"I do not know what to think anymore," he finally said.

"I do," she replied without question. Even if she were blind, to know the pleasure of his touch and kiss would mean the world—but she couldn't tell him something so . . . so forward. "Why . . . I'd . . . I'd think about all of the good things I could experience and not dwell upon those I couldn't. How long have you been blind? What caused it?"

"Only since I awakened in the mortal realm have I been unable to see. I was hit by a Pyrathian fire strike."

"Pyrathian? Is that some evil beast in the spirit world?"

Navarre laughed. "No, though there have been times I would like to call them such. Pyrathians are Shadowmen like Blood Hunters. They serve Logos as well."

"Then how could one have been stupid enough to harm you?"

"A long story, but they were following the Guardian Council's orders and I was defending Aragon from them. I do not know how that was resolved. Aragon obviously was not executed because he now lives on in the mortal world with Jared."

Marissa's mind raced through the pieces of conversation she'd heard among Annette, Stefanie, Aragon, and the others. It was just last week that Aragon had returned to Twilight and the ranger camp. "It hasn't been long since this injury happened to you, then." She caught Navarre's arm and pressed her hand over his heart. "You can't become discouraged. And there are so many good things to experience."

"Like you," he said softly, laying his hand over hers. "Touching you. Tasting you."

He unerringly leaned down and brushed his mouth over hers. Her heart thudded hard. It took her several seconds to realize the pulsing wasn't her rushing blood, but the approaching sound of a helicopter.

Dios mío. It could be Herrera's men. "Hurry!" she gasped,

pulling Navarre into the copse of trees. A quick glance back at the truck revealed that everything was hidden.

"What is it?" Navarre demanded harshly.

She explained.

He pulled her close into the circle of his arms, against the solid beat of his heart, and she rested gently with him until he spoke. "Good things become a two-edged sword that cuts a warrior to his soul when he can't protect them."

The pain in his voice was so deep and full of disgust that, though she stood with her arms wrapped around him, she wondered if she could reach him at all.

Chapter Twelve

"I'M SURE they had help, Otto. Who besides you knew of my plans?" Herrera watched the General's expression closely as he sipped the creamy smooth scotch. The fifty-year-old Chivas Regal Royal salute had been released to honor a queen's coronation. It was the best he'd ever tasted and he decided then he'd have the finest liquors to commemorate a Cortes's return to power.

"I've given it a great deal of thought since last night. Even asked a number of questions, discreetly, of course," said the General. Then he shrugged. "And have come up with nothing."

Herrera dug his fangs into his gums. The General had always been a difficult man to read, but something about his confident, suave demeanor wasn't hitting the right note of innocence. The inept guards following Marissa had lost track of her after an attack from the ghost wolf and his men had yet to pick up the trail.

The search by ground and air continued, but he'd been unable to sit by the phone any longer. Herrera had taken out all the frustration he could on Ysalane. Any more and she'd likely die. For now he was forced to vent his anger by unraveling the conspiracy against him.

"I'm afraid you'll have to look to your own men," the General said. "The guests knew they were coming to a wedding, but not where it was being held. Even I didn't know that, if you recall. I am surprised her escape happened at all. Not with how closely you guard your location and the number of armed men guarding your compound. But I am really shocked to hear that your men haven't found her yet."

Herrera smiled slightly, wanting badly to expose his fangs and show the General his true place on the food chain, but the timing wasn't right. "Actually, they are trailing her with orders to wait and see who she meets with. I want to know who helped her."

The General's brows lifted high. "You're so sure she couldn't have effected the escape on her own? In my long years I have learned never to underestimate what a woman can do. I'd much rather face my own interrogators than a woman with an agenda. And all women have agendas."

"Even the lovely Ms. Langston?"

"Especially the devious Ms. Langston, but currently her agenda and mine are the same, so I'm enjoying the fringe benefits." His lips curled into a leer. "But enough of this. Since you have Mrs. Herrera in hand, let's talk of the campaign. I'll be meeting with our principal backer this afternoon and want to assure him you are in complete agreement with the direction the new presidency's military will take."

"Who is this backer?" Herrera asked as he stood, feeling a trap closing in around him.

Menendez walked to the window and looked outside. As Herrera passed Menendez's desk, his gaze caught a letter sitting on top. *Otto, have no doubt. You will be Guatamala's president. My men are in place.*

"The backer is someone important who must remain anonymous," Menendez said, turning from the window. "All you need to do is what we direct you to. Guatemala is ready for a dynamic new face, and yours is it."

They were using him, Herrera realized. Using his face and charisma to get into power and then they likely planned to assassinate him.

"Of course, Otto. You are, after all, the one with the experience," Herrera said with a smile. The man was going to die as soon as the election was over. He drank down the rest of the scotch. "But now I must go." He stood and clapped Menendez on the back. "A man who can serve a great scotch is a man Herrera can't do without."

"You're worth it," Otto said, grinning. "At ten thousand a bottle, I don't share it lightly."

"Remind me to send you a case of it when I win," Herrera said, and quickly took his leave. Hopefully he had time to set up a team of men to follow the General. Waiting until after the election to find out who he was dealing with politically didn't fit into Herrera's agenda. Once the vote was final, he'd be the only man standing.

The helicopter ride back to the resort he'd commandeered went entirely too fast. Darkly tinted windows and sun-reflecting fabric gave him all the daytime freedom he needed. That's what made living beneath the canopy of the rain forest so appealing. By the time the sun's rays reached the ground they were practically harmless, even to his sensitive skin.

He expected to find Ysalane bedridden. Instead she was moving well as she worshiped in front of her Mayan altar. A sweet odor permeated the room: her Magic smoke. He was beginning to think there was something to her ramblings. After all, she had known of the wolf before it appeared last night.

Could she be strong enough in her magic to have conjured the wolf herself?

Before he could accuse her of it, she turned to him. "Ysalane can help you find the wolf spirit tonight at midnight. But you must promise Ysalane to kill the wolf and the woman. For if you do not, you will die."

He considered hitting her for her continued impertinence. No one made demands of him, but then he decided to play along with her game for a while. He'd kill the wolf, but as for Marissa, he had plans for her that nobody would stop him from fulfilling.

"Tonight then, Ysalane. You will tell me and I will take care of them both."

She nodded and turned back to the altar. "It will take me time to ready myself for the journey into the spirit world and summon forth the god who sees all for you to find this wolf. So do not bother Ysalane until then."

Do not bother *her*? Herrera saw red and had to leave before he destroyed what might be his only chance to locate Marissa. Exiting the room, he went in search of the resort's owners. If his men hadn't killed the women yet, Herrera would have a little fun first.

As he crossed the room, the sound of several approaching helicopters became almost deafening. At first he thought his own men were flying over the resort in their search for Marissa, but as the sound increased along with a punishing wind slamming the windows, he realized the helicopters had landed. Shouts and gunfire erupted.

Cursing, Herrera marched to the door and yanked it open. Who in all of hell had the balls to come after him?

"Where is she?" Sheik Rashad bin Samir Al Sabah appeared, fangs and rich robes flashing, dark eyes murderous. It was the first time the coward showed he had a dick. Vasquez, who'd led SINCO for years, had always questioned it, because Samir never stood up to anything or anyone. If SINCO had been in Samir's hands then OPEC would have slurped them up for lunch.

Herrera laughed at the oil-rich Valdarian who'd been so sure he was going to come out on top and have all of SINCO for himself. "What does it matter where Señora Herrera is? You lost. I won."

"And your immortality ends today," Samir snarled.

Herrera bared his fangs. "Touch me and the entire Valdarian Order will move against you, Samir, and then you'll die, too."

"Haven't you heard? Cinatas has ordered our extermination because we left his little ego party. I now have nothing to lose."

"You're pathetic," Herrera said. "You're going to let that usurping little bastard have power over us? It's time the Vladarians united and signed Cinatas's death warrant. None of us wanted Pathos's bastard son to rule in the first place. Have you even contacted the rest of the order to see if they support Cinatas's pompous ass?"

Samir paused, doubt replacing the fire in his eyes. "We both will take action against Cinatas. But first, I will have what Vasquez contracted to me." He snapped his fingers and a studious, blue-tinged demon with glasses appeared. His scrawny limbs literally shook with fear. In Heldon's realm, Blue Demons were the lowest of the lot, even beneath the odorous Frankensteinian Black Demons, who attached the heads and appendages of their vanquished foes to their own slimy bodies.

It was very telling to Herrera to learn Samir carted a Blue Demon around as an assistant.

"The contracts." Samir held out his hand and the Blue Demon gave Samir a folder. Samir opened the folder and held the papers out for Herrera. "You will see here, signed by both myself and Luis Vasquez six months ago, a legal transaction. I purchased Marissa Vasquez as my wife for the sum of one billion dollars. She is my first wife among my concubines and was to be delivered to my harem one week ago when the last of my payments to her uncle was complete. So any marriage between you is null and void. She is mine."

Herrera shrugged and smiled. "It would appear that Vasquez lied to us both, then, Samir, for he promised her to me as well. *Pero,* I do not have legal documents to prove it so." It would seem that Marissa was even richer than Herrera dreamed possible.

"Then you must give her to me, for I do," Samir said smugly.

"You'll have to find her first, Samir. She escaped after the wedding ceremony saying she'd rather die than marry either of us."

"Escaped? To where?"

"The jungle, *mi amigo*. It is a very dangerous place," Herrera said, thinking that for once good fortune was truly going to smile upon him.

Stefanie's heart thundered and a cold sweat broke over her quivering body. She stared at the four armed men holding machine guns and all she could think was she was going to be a prisoner again. All she could see was Vasquez and Herrera as they raped. . . .

Oh God . . . don't go there now! Fight! These men were just like the men who'd held her down, watching and laughing at her degradation. She slammed shut the door to the past and zeroed in on her rage and the scene around her as she gripped the pistol in her pocket. "Never again," she whispered to herself.

"And who are you?" Nick asked, holding his hands up with his gun pointing toward the sky.

Stefanie glanced about. There had to be a way to turn the tables, and if she knew Nick, Jared, and Aragon, that way would come fast.

Nick moved forward two steps, taking the lead in front of Jared and Aragon. Jaymes edged in closer, too.

"Your worst nightmare, *sí*?" the man said, chuckling, waving his gun. The other men laughed, moving in closer to their leader.

"Sorry," Nick said. "You don't have fangs. You're not red like a demon. And you're not as handsome as Lucifer himself. So you aren't my worst nightmare. But we might be yours. Jared, care to give them a little taste of what we are?"

"Thought you'd never ask," Jared said.

Jared changed to his were form, muscles bulging, seams ripping. The attackers stared, slack-jawed, and Stefanie tensed, ready to act.

Nick moved fast. Slashing down on the leader's arms, he jerked the man's weapon away and jammed the muzzle under the man's chin. Aragon and Jared went for the two men on Nick's right, and Jaymes took down the man on the left with a twisting double kick that had the bastard's gun flying and him grabbing his groin even as he reached for a pistol at his waist.

Stefanie ran forward and shoved her pistol against the man's head. "Don't move," she said, her hand shaking. He glared at her and even though he released his pistol, he seemed to smile.

"You'll pay, *puta*," he said under his breath.

For Stefanie, his look, his tone, was part of the nightmare of her past. She didn't remember him as being one of her captors, but it didn't matter. "No," she whispered. "You will." She pulled the trigger . . . twice . . . but nothing happened. Her hands shook and her lungs burned for air that she couldn't seem to get. A dizzy roar made her vision begin to fade.

"I've got him," Jaymes said, stepping in and twisting the man's arm behind him as she shoved him onto his stomach.

Stefanie stepped back, her face numb. Some part of her realized that were it not for the safety, she would have put two bullets right between the man's eyes.

The men had the others disarmed and on their knees with their hands behind their heads.

"Now," Nick said to the leader. "Since you aren't my worst nightmare and I might be yours, who are you and what did you want with us?"

"Jose," the man said. "Anybody who comes in a helicopter with guns must answer to El Diablo Sinclair. He pays us well to bring him guests."

"El Diablo Sinclair," Nick said. His face paled and his expression turned murderous.

"*Sí. Por favor*, you mentioned General Menendez? He is a very good *amigo* of El Diablo, and I've heard the General visits him today."

"And you just happen to know this?" Nick scoffed.

"No. I am a smart *hombre*. El Diablo always says to bring him guests, but then some days he says to me, do not bring guests until after dark. I ask myself why and one day I have men stay and spy on El Diablo. That day the butcher General came. I do this *uno, dos, tres,* more times and each time the General comes. So today when El Diablo tells me not to bring guests until after dark, I know Menendez is coming."

"Maybe we need to pay this Sinclair a little visit today," Nick said. "Menendez could lead us to Herrera and Marissa. Provided Jose here isn't lying."

"No, Nick," Jaymes said. "No. It would be suicide to go after Menendez."

"Who said anything about going after the guy? It wouldn't hurt to get a bird's-eye view of what is going on with Sinclair. Hell, Marissa could even be with them," Nick said softly.

"We're likely to get our ass shot right out of the sky," Jaymes snapped.

"Wasn't thinking of taking the helo to pay dear old dad a visit. I hope you're up for guard duty, Agent Bond."

"That's Staff Sergeant Bond to you, flyboy."

"Jared, Aragon, what do you say?"

"Makes sense to check the story out rather than trying to chase down where the General was yesterday," Aragon said.

Still in his half-were state, all bulging muscles and fangs, Jared came up behind the leader Nick held at gunpoint. "If he isn't telling the truth, I will just make a meal out of him."

Jose's eyes bulged. "It is the truth. I swear it upon *mi madre*'s grave."

"How far is Sinclair?" Nick demanded.

The man shook his head. "Sinclair will kill Jose."

Jared growled deep.

"An hour on foot," the man said, gulping furiously. He nodded his head toward the heart of the jungle.

Nick smiled. "You'll get the distinct honor of leading us to El Diablo Sinclair. If you're smart, you'll live long enough to get your family and move to Brazil before Sinclair finds out how we found his camp."

"Brazil is not far enough," Jose cried. "I will just tell you where his camp is."

"No can do," Nick said. "Better get your family on a boat, because you're coming with us."

The man started praying and Stefanie turned away from the group, realizing she still had a death grip on the pistol, with her finger holding down the trigger. The safety had stood between her and what could only be described as murder. Rage had her more than willing to kill and she wondered if she hadn't just take her first step to becoming just like Vasquez and Herrera.

His back to Stonehenge's monoliths, York slashed up with his sword as the first Tsara made a screeching dive, red nails of poison clawing too close for comfort. The sword glanced off the Tsara's stone-thick hide. The beast lunged, deadly teeth clashing. York barely had time to drop and roll to the side to escape the imminent bite.

His roll brought him closer to where Flynn, whipping around like a whirlwind, held two of them at bay. The beasts dove in at him in a constant barrage and it was only a matter of seconds before one broke through Flynn's defense.

York made another roll toward Flynn as the Tsara tried to impale him again. One more roll and he'd be in a position to join his whirling force with Flynn's.

Suddenly Flynn stumbled, off balance because he didn't have a counteracting Blood Hunter's force with him. A Tsara gave a victory death screech as it closed in for the kill.

"No!" York turned, twisted, and thrust his sword like a spear, aiming for the Tsara's yawning mouth. It was a gamble that might save Flynn, but left York totally vulnerable. The sword hit dead center and the Tsara convulsed into death throes, its horrendous screeching deafening.

Flynn landed on one knee, the dying Tsara at his feet. Flynn looked up, and from the horror filling his eyes, York knew the air on his back wasn't the morning breeze but the only warning he was going to get of the Tsara's bite.

Flynn flung his sword before York could stop him. Even if Flynn killed the Tsara, the third would destroy them both before they could retrieve their weapons.

York heard the Tsara's victory screech cut off by Flynn's sword. The Tsara landed on York's back, convulsing in death.

York rolled, trying to escape the cold, burning evil of one of Heldon's most vile creatures. But the Tsara's claws swiped across his back. Pain cut through him as if the frozen depths of hell were trying to grab him and drag him under.

He shook his head with disbelief. This couldn't be happening. Not now. He might have escaped certain assassination from the Tsara's bite, but if enough of the poison was in the scratch, it would eat at him until he became too weak to fight.

There was no time to think about it now. One more Tsara was left. Grabbing Flynn's sword from the Tsara's mouth, he rolled toward Flynn. Flynn had retrieved York's sword and already had it lifted in defense, but the creature was gone. Scrambling to his feet, York looked across the horizon to see the Tsara flying quickly away.

"We have to follow it," he told Flynn. "We have to stop it."

"Are you all right?" Flynn asked.

"Of course. Do you think I'm an old man or something?" York said, rolling his eyes, but he had to keep from wincing as a cold finger slid down his spine. Already the dead Tsaras were turning back into their human forms. Heldon, unable to create himself, harvested Tsaras from the most wicked of men in the very seconds after their executions on earth. Heldon loved serial killers and the death penalty. They kept him rolling in assassins.

Chapter Thirteen

NAVARRE HEARD Marissa's ominous description of the danger approaching them, felt the frightened racing of her heart and heard her breath catch, just as he could feel everything about her soft body pressed so tightly to his. Rage filled him. His spirit and soul shouted at fate for rendering him so helpless upon the mortal ground.

The rhythmic sound from above had lessened, but did that mean the danger was stalking her now, coming in for the kill? He strained with every functioning sense for the slightest change in the air around him, but could discern nothing different. Yet, how would he know? This was the first time he was experiencing the mortal ground so strongly.

He cradled Marissa to his body as closely as he could. Her back was protected by a wide tree trunk and his arms were wrapped along her sides. Anything wanting to harm her would have to get through him, but it wasn't enough. It would never be enough.

"Tell me what is happening. Tell me what I can do to protect you. Where is the danger now?"

"I'm sorry," she said, her voice as soft as the silk of her skin and as warm as the sun. She raised her head from where it rested against his chest and he knew she was looking at him. He turned his face in that direction and he felt her palm slide to his cheek. "I think the danger is gone now. The helicopter passed over without hovering or even dipping lower. I don't think they're turning back for another sweep of the area, either. The sound is becoming more and more distant."

"Then why is your heart thundering with fear?" he said, easing back and feeling his way up to press his palm against her chest.

She gasped sharply and pressed closer to his hand. "Your touch makes my heart race."

He paused, suddenly struck by something he hadn't considered before. "Do you fear me?"

"Not fear," she whispered. "Not as I did last night with the creature Herrera had turned you into. Now it's excitement. Pleasure. Desire for more, especially when you touch my breast."

He didn't need to hear more. He rubbed his hand against her breast, feeling the silk of her dress and softness of the flesh swelling above the material. She arched her back until the fullness of her breast filled his palm, and she moaned deeply.

The sound ignited a hungering fire in him that went right to his groin, making his flesh there harden and throb as it had when he'd tasted her earlier. He caressed her breast, fascinated by how wonderfully perfect she felt, like something fashioned especially for him. A hard point rose up beneath the silk and teased the palm of his hand. When he brushed over that nub again and again, she shuddered in response. He caressed her more and pressed his hardening flesh tighter to her, rubbing against her until he, too, shuddered from the pleasure.

Impatient with the cool material and wanting to feel her warm skin, he pushed his fingers beneath the silk and moaned at the heat of her and the firm softness as he delved in search of her aroused flesh. His heart pounded as fast as hers when he closed that velvety crest between his fingers. His mouth watered and his breath hitched. As a spirit being, his life had been one of service, of duty, and what pleasure he'd experienced in the spirit realm had been found in the beauty of the universe, the cradling warmth of Logos, and the exquisite sounds of heavenly music. Never had he felt this intensity of ecstasy. Never would he have imagined or believed such personal pleasure possible.

"Marissa, I hunger greatly. I must taste you." He bent his

head until he found her welcoming lips, where he thrust deeply into the well of her mouth and drank of her with strong swirls of his tongue. He wanted to experience all of her just this way. Flesh to flesh. Mouth to mouth. He wanted to explore her, wanted to know if there were more places to caress, more points to harden with pleasure.

By Logos, this wasn't enough. Something in her was driving him, urging him forward. He felt as blind in this quest as he did without the sight of his wolf spirit, but this frustration was different. This he could do something about.

Was she feeling the same way he did? He sent his spirit in search of hers as he'd done when she'd slept in his arms. Except, this time, rather than imbuing her with healing energy, he went looking for the energy that made her heart race and her body shudder gently beneath his hands. And just as his wolf spirit had seen the forest and the moonlight through her eyes in her dreams, he could see himself together with her in her mind. But they weren't as they were now. For in her mind they lay upon a soft cloud of white and they were flesh to flesh, touching and tasting.

He didn't need to know any more; he had to take this burning quest to that white cloud right now.

"I am ready. Where do we go?" he asked, surprised at his own breathless desperation. "How does this material come off?" He tugged upon the silk at her breast, wanting to free her from it, and heard a slight tear.

She pulled back from him. He could no longer taste her but his hand still cradled her breast. He heard her gasp for air as if she hadn't taken a breath in forever. "What?"

"The white cloud. I see in your mind where we can lie down flesh to flesh and explore this pleasure."

Marissa stared at Navarre, desperately trying to absorb what he'd just said over the wildfire consuming her mind, body, and spirit. *Madre de Dios.* His touch, his kiss, went to the very center of her being and made her crazy. She wanted to forget there was anything or anyone else in the world but the two of them and she wished they had nothing to do but to pleasure one another. Unfortunately, they were standing in a copse of trees with Herrera likely looking everywhere for them. Father Dom was calling for her, his voice getting closer by the second, and Navarre's fingers were inside her dress, playing with her nipple and making her bones melt into a puddle.

"Shh," she said, taking his wrist in both her hands and pulling his hand from her bodice just as she saw Father Dom pass them and look along the emerald pool, first to his right and then to his left. Navarre's arousal pressing against her was so hot and insistent that it was a wonder he hadn't burned a hole through their clothing. She pushed him back, nearly groaning at the loss.

"We're here," she called out to the priest as she prayed to a thousand saints that she and Navarre didn't look as if they'd been doing what they had been doing. None of the saints must have been listening to her because Father Dom's expression said it all. He made the sign of the cross over his chest.

She reacted instinctually by trying to camouflage her disheveled state with pretended fear. She waved her hands wildly at Father Dom and took several steps over roots and around vines toward him. Navarre followed as if glued to her backside. In fact his hand rested suggestively low on her hip, making her more aware than ever that she'd buried her underwear a short time ago. She felt very exposed at the moment.

Swallowing nervously, she spoke up. "*Por Dios,* are you sure it is safe to be in the open, Father? Can they not return and see us? It could be Herrera up there!" She brushed her forehead with the back of her hand. "I was so frightened."

Father Dom frowned and she bit her lip as guilt washed over her. She was confused. Why should the pleasure she felt with Navarre be something to feel shame over?

"The sound grows more and more distant," Father Dom said curtly. "Should he come back, we will hear in time to take cover. What kind of helicopter was it?"

Marissa's cheeks heated. She'd never even tried to look. "I was too far back in the trees and too afraid to look. Besides, I wouldn't know what I was looking at except to tell you what color it was. Were you and Rafe well hidden?"

"Inside the back of the truck," Father Dom said. "They couldn't have seen us." He glared at Navarre, who stood there with a fierce scowl on his face as if he could make the priest evaporate. "I think it would be safer for you if we all stayed together from now on."

"I think Marissa and I need to find the white cloud first," Navarre said.

"White cloud?" Father Dom asked.

"Nothing!" Marissa cut in. "Uh, just something I described to Navarre about the steam over the water. It is like a white cloud. He's saying he wants to clean up first and so do I. Once I . . . we finish washing we'll be up to eat. There is soup?"

"Yes." Father Dom looked between her and Navarre. "The jungle is a dangerous place, with many unknown beasts to devour the innocent and unsuspecting. Be careful." On that ominous note, he walked back to the truck and Marissa led Navarre to the water, her legs shaky and her heart fluttering. She quickly set about cleaning herself as well as possible then took a knife to her dress, cutting it off just below her knees, enough to protect most of her legs but allowing her to move more easily.

Then she looked to Navarre. He sat quietly, seemingly gazing in her direction, looking as if he were upset about what happened. She went to him.

"Let's see about cleaning you up. That old man who sheared off your hair in the dungeon left it uneven. I wish I had scissors but the knife will have to do. It seems sharp enough."

He reached up and touched his hair, grunting. "I had not realized."

Working carefully, Marissa cupped water in her hands and fingered it through Navarre's dark hair. She grabbed a piece of scrap silk from her dress, dipped it into the water, and began bathing his face, then his back, shoulders, and chest. His strange amulet glowed with a subtle inner light whose radiating warmth seeped into her when she touched it. Every contour of his body was sculpted perfection. In some ways he seemed too beautiful to be real, yet in other ways so roughly hewn, he couldn't be anything but the embodiment of raw, elemental man.

She could close her eyes and picture every nuance of him, see him so clearly that—

"Navarre!"

"What is it?" He turned so sharply she had to step quickly back to avoid cutting him with the knife.

"You saw. You saw a picture in my mind. How?"

"Part of my gift as a warrior and Blood Hunter is to reach within another's mind and body to heal. I wanted to know when I was touching you and tasting you if you felt the great pleasure that I did, so I sent my spirit in search of yours, and when I did, I saw the image in your mind. The image of us together, flesh to flesh, touching and tasting."

"You saw detail? My naked body and your naked body?"

"Yes."

"You saw color? The white cloud? Your black hair? The color of my skin?"

"Yes."

She grabbed his shoulders and did a little dance. "Don't you understand? If you can see pictures in my mind, then if I put a picture of this place into my mind, you could see it!"

He caught her arm, becoming very still, his expression wavering among disbelief, wonder, and hope. "Possibly."

"We must try." She gazed out over the waterfall and the emerald pool, committing every detail she could to her memory then shut her eyes and recaptured it all in her mind. "Okay, I am ready."

She felt Navarre's hands on her head, his palms to her temples, his thumbs gently brushing over her eyes. Then she felt the force of his spirit enter her. The full heat of him and the potent maleness of him brushing her to the very center of her feminine core. It was hard to keep the serene beauty of the landscape in her mind when she wanted to delve back into the passionate embrace she imagined they'd share as lovers.

"I see it," he whispered. "I see it. Everything is as you described. It's beautiful." He bent down, resting his forehead against hers. "Show me more."

Giving him his cane, she sent him picture after picture of the surrounding area. He was soon able to navigate with accuracy and speed, as if he were only slightly visually impaired instead of totally blind. Then they sat down and she finished cutting his hair.

Still wrapped in a blanket, Rafael joined them, carrying a large box. He appeared stronger than before, which made his haunted dark eyes more pronounced. He studied Navarre intently then brought his gaze to hers, his mouth grim. Father Dom had likely given Rafael an earful.

"Father Dom wants you to come eat," Rafael said. "He has heated chicken soup. For the first time in months I've eaten real food. The slop Herrera gave us wasn't fit for pigs."

Her conscience smiting her, Marissa set down the knife and went to her brother. She squeezed his shoulder. "I'm sorry we haven't talked. Months ago Herrera told everyone that you were killed trying to escape. Even Tío Luis believed you were dead. He . . . he . . . let's just say he made my grief worse. You must tell me what happened to you."

"I escaped Corazón and had made it almost all the way to

San Ignacio when Herrera caught me. He took me to his dungeon, killed the two guards that were with him when he found me, and said, 'Now no one knows you are here or can save you. You will help make Herrera a very rich man.' I knew then he planned to get you. I told you I'd heard rumors that Tío Luis would use you to increase his power in SINCO."

Marissa shivered as tears filled her eyes. "So you've been in Herrera's dungeon for months. *Dios mío,* I am so sorry."

Rafael pulled away from her touch. "It doesn't matter anymore. Nothing matters anymore but seeing Herrera pay. When that is done then I will be done. I need to bathe and would like some privacy."

"Do you need help? You need clothes. I can try and make something from the blanket for you."

Rafael shook his head. "Father Dom gave me the pants that he had on under his robes. I need no help. I would be too shamed for anyone to see what Herrera has done."

"Rafe, *por favor.* You cannot think that way. You did not have a choice about what happened. You mustn't blame yourself. Everything will be all right now. We're free."

Rafael leaned forward and whispered. "You do not understand. Tell no one about this. I only tell you to save us both the pain of you trying to save me. There are some things of which one can never be free. If he had raped you, could you walk with no shame?"

With dawning horror, Marissa reached out to her brother, wanting to assure him she would, but couldn't force the words past the lump of outrage and pain in her throat. She had felt that way. She had felt that if Herrera had defiled her, she wouldn't be able to survive. There were no words to describe the pain she felt for her brother.

"Please go and try and understand. Herrera's death is my future and there is nothing more," Rafael said, turning his back to her. Many of his bandages had loosened, revealing the multitude of scabbed-over cuts from the bed of stakes, but in the middle of his back, between his shoulders, she saw a word had been branded into his skin. PUTO.

She turned and rushed up the hill, past the truck, uncaring of the vines and thorns that grabbed at her dress and skin. She ran until she could run no more before she gave way to her tears and cried her heart out. It had to stop. Somehow this evil had to be stopped before others could suffer so horribly. *Madre de Dios,* how could she help her brother? How could anyone help him? She cried until she had no more tears left. Her stomach hurt, her face ached, her eyes were a blurry mess, and her heart felt just as horrified and just as burdened as before. Tears solved nothing.

"Marissa," Navarre called to her.

She looked up to see both Navarre and Father Dom coming toward her. "I'm here," she said.

"That *I* can see, child," Father Dom said. "What happened to upset you so?" The glare he sent Navarre's way blamed the warrior.

"No matter what your pain, Marissa," Navarre said softly, "you shouldn't have run away alone."

"In this, I agree with him," Father Dom added. "What happened?"

Marissa gulped for air. "I . . . I saw Rafael's wounds, his scars, and it was too much. I had to be alone." She stood, trying to collect herself as she wiped the tears from her cheeks. But suddenly she couldn't stem the tide of her anger rushing through her. "What God can allow such evil as Herrera to exist? How can he be God and let it happen?"

"None can know the mind of God, child. One can only pray and hope that their prayers will be heard," Father Dom said.

"Marissa, I understand your pain," Navarre said, "and the pain of your brother. The existence of evil within the mortal realm is not a simple matter. But neither is its presence something so shrouded in mystery that one cannot understand why. And its demise isn't contingent upon prayer, though the fueling energy of all prayers are welcomed and needed within the spirit realm. Logos created a universe with rules to govern it and even he must obey those rules or the world would cease to exist. Those rules of choice and will and order and balance stop him from destroying the wickedness, but it can be fought and one day will be once again contained. Within the spirit world, the Guardian Forces' battle with Heldon's Principalities of the Damned never ends. Heldon knows that ultimately he can never win. That is why he turned to the mortal realm. By destroying souls that Logos created and loves, Heldon hopes to demoralize and defeat Logos. The Shadowmen fight within the mortal realm to save each soul."

"And what happens when you fail to save one?" Marissa asked. Tears filled her eyes again for surely Rafael was lost. Where were the Shadowmen when her brother needed saving?

"Until one pledges his soul to Heldon, then he is not lost no matter what has happened. But when one does join Heldon then Logos and all of heaven grieves."

Dared she hope for her brother? If the light and the wisdom in Navarre's golden eyes were any indication of that, her heart could cry yes. There was hope.

Navarre reached out his hand to her. "Come. You must trust that I will defeat this evil. I will eliminate Herrera. You must believe that the Shadowmen will stop Heldon's sudden surge of power upon the mortal ground and bring balance back to Logos's creation."

Marissa set her hand in his, finding comfort in both his words and presence.

Father Dom turned away, muttering to himself. But Marissa found it interesting that he hadn't disputed anything Navarre had said. She was too exhausted to delve deeper into any of the problems swirling around her. They returned to the truck and the sight of Rafael down by the water burdened her heart even more. He'd bathed and changed into Father Dom's pants and had fashioned a shirt from cloth. He wore the boots she'd stolen and had the machine gun propped next to him. He'd sheared his hair close to his scalp and now was shaving himself with the knife using a mirror from inside the truck. Rafael was no longer the handsome young man she remembered or the haunted invalid from this morning. She almost wished that Navarre hadn't healed her brother, because Rafael was now a man on a suicide mission.

She didn't know what she would say to him. She didn't know what she *could* say to him. She could only give him her love and understanding, and respect his wish to keep secret what Herrera had done to him. And somehow she had to find a way to save him from what had happened to him and from this doom he'd embarked upon.

Father Dom followed her gaze and sighed. "I'll go down and talk to him," he said. "The way of the gun has its purpose and sometimes is the best revenge, but not always."

His words surprised her. She thought he'd condemn violence without exception. She waited until he reached Rafael before she collected the can of chicken soup and joined Navarre, making sure her shortened dress covered her properly. Though her brother and Father Dom were now just out of sight, her thoughts stayed with Rafael and his turmoil, so much so that it seemed surreal to be sitting on a blanket in a gently humming forest.

She had expected the soup—indeed all of life—would have lost its flavor. But it hadn't. The soup comforted the ache in her stomach. The dappling sunlight warmed her, and Navarre's relaxed but assured presence as he asked her questions about her life and the world as she knew it helped reel in her jumbled emotions.

After finishing, he stretched, then lay back upon the blanket. "The soup was fine, but nothing tastes as good as the Snickers or Twinkies—or you," he said softly.

Marissa nearly choked on a noodle. She'd yet to adjust to his shirtlessness, and to have all of his muscled self reclining next to her sent her senses whirling to places they shouldn't go.

She might have succeeded in turning her mind to something proper, had he not laid his hand on her leg. Darts of heat sizzled right up her dress and she imagined the fire of his hand following those darts to her practically bare sex. She grew damp everywhere, especially *there*, and her heart pounded.

He inhaled sharply, his hand gripping her leg tighter. "I feel your excitement, Marissa. I can see in your mind again." Shifting to his side to face her, he slid his hand several inches up her leg. "Show me, Marissa. Look at my hand upon your leg and show me what you see. I want to see me touching you."

Oh, she wanted that, too. This was supposed to be wrong, yet she had never felt more right. She was supposed to be proper. She was supposedly married to another man. Yet her heart rebelled against all those things she was supposed to be. She wanted to be the person she was in her heart—a woman whose body burned and whose soul soared at this man's touch. She should at least tell Navarre why intimacies outside of marriage were considered wrong. She should tell him she was married to Herrera in the eyes of the church, but she couldn't seem to find the words.

A quick glance toward the water showed no one coming. She looked at Navarre's hand on her thigh, just above her knee, saw how his fingers splayed, pressing into the softness of her skin, and closed her eyes, giving him the image.

He groaned. "Show me more, Marissa," he said, moving his hand higher, sliding her dress up as he rubbed her leg. "I can tell this pleasures you as much as it pleasures me."

"Yes," she whispered.

He moved higher as she watched and she sent him another image of him caressing her inner thigh, molding the muscle to the cup of his hand. Her breath hitched and her stomach flipped as he did exactly that and then pushed her dress all the way up, exposing her sex.

When his questing fingers brushed the edges of her sex, she shuddered and moaned. Almost unable to stay upright from the dizzying flood of heat, she leaned back on her shaking hands.

"That pleasures you the most? To touch you here?" he asked.

"Yes."

"You are so hot here and so soft beneath the silky hair. Show me again. Show me touching you here." She watched him caressing her, his fingers delving and exploring her dark sex, making her stomach tighten into a knot of almost painful pleasure. Her heart raced faster than her mind could think, but she managed to send him the image of what she could see. He caressed her more and more, sliding into the damp groove of her sex until he hit a place that made her hips jerk upward.

"Yes," he said. "I feel it, Marissa. You've a pleasure spot here, too." He flicked his finger over it, her hips arched closer to his touch, and she groaned deeply. Her body spiraled out of control as he relentlessly rubbed that special spot faster and faster until she shuddered and cried out from the burst of pleasure. Stars exploded in her mind and her spirit soared to what she could only describe as heaven.

With his spirit touching Marissa's as intimately as his hand brushed over the slick little point of pleasure he'd discovered, Navarre could feel the rising fire of her passion burn through him. Never in all his millennia had he experienced such beauty, such an exquisite peak of unforgettable pleasure. It made him ache for more, to be even more connected to her than he already was. He wanted everything of himself to be melded to her, to be inside of her.

"I see your pleasure," Navarre whispered, moving closer to her as he brought both his hands to her temples to penetrate deeper into her mind. "I see the stars. I feel your passion. This is more than heaven, Marissa," he said softly. "This is ecstasy."

He brushed her lips with his, then went back and tasted her sweet mouth before he pulled her so close that their hearts seemed to beat as one. Her body quivered again, as if his embrace pleasured her, as well. He pulled the edge of the blanket over her to keep her warm and listened to her breathe as her body relaxed in sleep, his warrior's soul touched to the core by the beauty, frailty, yet fearlessness of her spirit.

Chapter Fourteen

IN SPIRIT FORM, York, with Flynn at his side, trailed the surviving Tsara. They'd stayed far enough back to keep the assassin from sensing their presence, but they needn't have worried because the beast never once looked back. Flying low to the trees or slipping in the shadowed contours of the land, the Tsara moved across the English countryside with purpose.

The odd behavior had York wondering if he and Flynn were flying into a trap, but they had no choice. They had to follow the Tsara and stop it from carrying out whatever demonic mission it was on. Soon the scents of forest and sea permeated the morning air and the Tsara dipped down into a darkish mist.

The moment York delved into the dark cloud a stench enveloped him and the Tsara's scratch on his back began to pulse. Icy chills shot through his spirit with such paralyzing force that he tumbled from the sky. Tree branches snapped as he crashed downward, digging into his skin and whipping his body. He landed on his back in the decaying leaves on the forest floor in his mortal form.

Flynn dipped down, hovering over him. "What happened?"

York sat up, groaning. "I do not know. My spirit froze and I could no longer fly or maintain that form."

Flynn landed on the ground next to him and whirled into his mortal form. "Your spirit froze? I've never heard of such a thing."

"Nor I," said York as he gained his feet. His mortal form ached badly and the Tsara scratch continued to throb, making even the slightest movement an agony. "We must continue after the Tsara and work this out later." York leaped to change into his spirit form. He flew through the air and landed unsteadily on his mortal feet. His heart pumped with growing fear. He hadn't changed. He tried again, this time nearly plowing into Flynn.

The young warrior adeptly stepped to the side. "What are you doing?"

"Can you change to your spirit form?" York demanded.

Flynn leaped and easily shifted.

"By Logos," York cried. "It's just a scratch. How could it affect me so quickly? Why isn't it healing?"

"What scratch? I knew it! The Tsara at Stonehenge got you!" Flynn shifted back, his expression thunderous.

"Look," York said, showing Flynn his back. "It's just a scratch. A minor scratch. Warriors have been scratched before, have usually healed, and lasted through entire battles, sometimes even centuries of fighting, before their hearts slow."

"But there is no cure for it, correct? Eventually a warrior will no longer be able to fight." Flynn cried out in frustration. "You suffered this while trying to save me."

"No. I suffered this in battle with one of Heldon's assassins just as other warriors have done in the past. But we've no time to waste on talk. You must follow the Tsara by air and I will move as quickly as I can on the ground. We must stop its mission before it's too late."

Flynn looked as if he would argue, then leaped into his spirit form and soared up through the trees.

York took a moment to orient himself before running in the direction the Tsara had headed. The deformed trunks and gnarled limbs of the forest exuded an aged wickedness, as if twisted over time by a malevolent hand. An odorous stench seeped from the black bark and dark leaves. No creature stirred as he sprinted through. No birds, no squirrels, no butterflies or bees. It was a dead forest, and by night it was likely the hunting ground of undead creatures.

Shaking off the suffocating feel of the place, he focused on fighting the throbbing cold in his back and sensing the waves of goodness radiating from Flynn's wake—they stood out like a bright beacon in this world of darkness.

York's lungs labored. His blood pounded and he was sure he couldn't take another step when the black walls of a spiked castle appeared in the dark mists. From his vantage point, he could see not just one Tsara circling it, but a multitude of them, flying like vultures over a kill.

By Logos! He'd never seen such an unholy gathering.

Where had Flynn gone? York's soul wrenched with worry. He'd sent the young warrior off to thwart the Tsara. What if Flynn had blindly flown right into the middle of the murderous fray?

Flynn! York's spirit cried out.

"Behind you, old warrior," Flynn said softly.

York turned with relief.

"I think for the first time I understand the logic of 'retreat to fight another day,' " Flynn said.

"We're definitely ill equipped to even discover their purpose, which doesn't appear to be the immediate assassination of an Elan. Why is it that I don't even know of this place?"

"As I followed the Tsara by air, I came to a strange shield covering the area, one that reflected a quaint village toward the heavens. The Tsara made a ripple in this barrier that I was able to push through, but just barely. It became solid again within minutes. It was only when I passed beneath a covering of clouds that I saw the castle and the hovering Tsaras."

"Interesting, I didn't encounter a barrier through the forest," York said.

"Then we at least know how to escape and how we can return," Flynn muttered. He sounded more than a little concerned.

York couldn't blame him. Being trapped within an encompassing realm of the damned wasn't exactly a smart move. "Let's leave before they decide to do something besides chase each other around in circles." York led the way through the forest. Flynn ran at his side until he suddenly heard Flynn cry out.

Looking back, York saw Flynn on the ground, a shocked expression on his face. York went to Flynn's side. "What's wrong, old man?"

Flynn didn't even grin. He sat up blinking at York as if he couldn't believe what he saw. "You just walked through the barrier," Flynn said.

"What barrier?" York glanced around.

"This one." Flynn stood and flung out his fist. It bounced off with stunning force.

York frowned and followed Flynn's action. York's fist swung unhindered.

"I'm not sure I want to know why, York, but you can pass easily through the damned's barrier."

"I wonder if it has anything to do with the Tsara's scratch. Take my hand and follow in my footsteps."

Flynn grabbed hold and together they passed through the barrier. Once on the other side, York turned back. All he could see from this vantage point was the twisted black forest and the dark spires of the castle in the distance. "What do you see?" he asked Flynn.

"Blue sky, sunshine. Acres of green forest, tall trees, and flowering bushes."

York turned away, his heart grim. He was in terrible trouble.

They crossed through the rest of the forest without mishap and when they reached the edge they found themselves standing at the choppy shore of a slender inlet.

York saw a quick, bright flash and almost dove for cover before he realized the beam of light had come from a device held by a mortal woman. She stood on the deck of a white boat that bobbed up and down on the waves as wildly as her red hair whipped in the wind. As he watched, she put the device back up to her face and took a step forward as if to see closer.

At that moment, a wave hit the boat and she pitched into the water.

"Did you see that?" York said, moving closer to the water.

"See what?"

"The mortal woman that just fell into the water. She hasn't come back up."

"No."

"By Logos, I can't just leave her." York dove into the icy water and pushed his way through the waves, reaching the boat in moments. As soon as he surfaced, he could smell the sweet blood of an Elan and instantly located her from the air bubbles rising to the surface. Somehow her clothing had caught on the bottom of the boat and she was struggling to free herself by taking it off.

He pulled the material over her head and shoved her toward the surface, then followed her up after wrenching her clothing free.

She'd grabbed a ladder that hung from the side of the boat and turned to look at him with eyes the color of the sky as she wiped water from her face. He could tell from her shivering that she was cold. "Thank you."

"Can you get back on your boat?"

"Yes," she said. Her teeth chattered and her body quivered as she pulled on the ladder and made it partway up.

York frowned as he watched. He'd never thought about what a mortal woman looked like before. The way her full breasts moved and swayed with every movement fascinated him. She suddenly fell back into the water with a groan.

He caught hold of her from behind to lift her back to the ladder. Her breasts were an intriguing combination of softness and firmness, with hard points at their tips. A strange burning shot through his body. "What happened?" he asked close to her ear.

She gasped and then coughed as if she'd breathed in water,

but wasted no time in grabbing the ladder and pulling from his hold.

He followed her up, quickly surprised to find his body quivering from the cold, too.

He couldn't remember his mortal form ever reacting to the elements of the physical world before.

She turned to him, her arms crossed over her fascinating breasts. Then she gasped, her eyes wide with surprise. "My shirt! You got my shirt."

He held out the material to her and she took it, plastering it over her chest.

"Bloody hell! You're naked!" She held her hand up as if to block the view, but then spread her fingers and peeked through. "Does Valois have a nudist colony hidden on the Forbidden Grounds?"

"Valois?" York asked. "Forbidden Grounds?"

"The royal bastard whose estate you were just standing on." She glanced back at the shore then at him. "How did you swim that far that fast?"

York shrugged. "I just did."

"Where's your friend?"

"Flynn?"

"I guess. You had another man standing with you on the shore."

York looked around. "I don't know. Flynn," he called out. "Flynn?" Concerned, York moved to the side of the boat and looked across the water. Nothing. Flynn must have changed to his spirit form, but York had to make sure.

York leaped to change, but crashed through the boat's rail and landed back into the water; shocked that he hadn't changed, then stunned that he'd forgotten he couldn't. The Tsara's poison was working quickly.

The woman ran to the side of the boat, looking down at him. "Are you bloody insane?"

York had to wonder the same thing. By Logos, what had happened to him? And where was Flynn?

Cinatas submerged himself again in the tub of Elan blood, the proverbial Fountain of Youth for the undead. The special proteins in the blood sustained and energized a vampire's body for months rather than the measly hours or days of normal blood, but this was the first he'd experimented with the blood as a healing solution. The results were remarkable. He thought he'd require several days of recovery, but after twenty-four hours, he was almost good as new.

Fortune had favored him with a gift and he'd decided to make the best use of it. Not only did Conrad Pitt have the perfect face for Cinatas, but he had the perfect blood, too, and there was no sense in wasting that. Conrad's severed head went to the doctor with enough money to kill any questions. Then the model's body was hung upside down until the last drop of Elan blood plopped from his veins. The only drawback at this point was that the perfect face remained perfectly expressionless, something the surgeon said might or might not change over time.

As soon as Cinatas was sure his new face was functional, the doctor and his staff, so isolated on their island of paradise in the Persian Gulf, were going to suffer a little massacre. For now he had an empire to build and vampires to exterminate. Valois had better have the Royals up in arms against SINCO. It was time for Herrera and Samir to die and for Cinatas to bring the Vladarian Order to their knees. He had returned to his favorite motto: *If a man cannot control those who serve him, then he deserves to die.*

Stefanie swatted at a beetle on a kamikaze mission with her nose and glared at the slow-moving hands on her watch. She sat with Annette and Jaymes in the cockpit of the helicopter while time dawdled and her emotions flew in circles. Three of the four men who'd tried to capture them at Corazón were tied up and bound together by their feet about twenty yards in front of the helicopter in the middle of the small field. Far enough away to be easily shot if any of them tried to make a run for it or attack, if they even managed to get loose.

Nick, Jared, and Aragon had taken Jose and loaded up with climbing gear and weapons headed for El Diablo Sinclair. She knew it made sense for the men to move fast and for the women to hold Jose's friends hostage, especially since Jaymes could fly the helicopter if the men called for it. But the seeming fruitlessness of sitting here twiddling thumbs while Marissa was suffering untold horrors at Herrera's hands rankled. She wanted to be doing something.

The men would be gone for at least three hours and only thirty minutes had passed. Jaymes tapped her fingers on the control stick looking as if she'd power up the helicopter and take off at any second. Annette flipped through another magazine faster than a speeding bullet.

Stefanie tried to focus on the emotions spinning wildly inside her. If she could get a handle on those, she'd be a more effective part of the team. Though she hadn't done badly in the altercation at Corazón, she considered her reaction more frightening than the men taking them at gunpoint. If the safety hadn't been on, she would have killed the man.

Now she was left with her thoughts and emotions and the raw questions she didn't want to face. Could she become the very thing she hated? Would empowering herself turn her evil?

She exhaled, exasperated with herself and with everything.

"What's wrong? Are you ill?" Annette leaned forward from the seat behind and felt Stefanie's forehead. "You're very pale."

Ill? Pale? Who wouldn't be after facing the ghosts of horror? Stefanie was likely insane or close to it by now. She thought to yell no, but then tried to laugh instead. The sound came out as a strangled croak, which had her doctor sister feeling for a pulse.

"We're what's wrong," Stefanie finally managed to say before Annette could think about dragging out the emergency med kit and starting an IV. "Look at us. By the time the men get back, we'll be ready for an asylum. Sitting here watching the seconds tick by is worse than every step I made in returning to Corazón."

"She's right," Jaymes said. "Ladies, it's boot camp time. We're going to slip some silencers on some hardware and have target practice." Jaymes settled an intent look on Stefanie. "By the time we're done you two are going to know a gun backward and forward—*and* how to slip the safety off if you intend to kill someone." She ended with a question in her eyes that Stefanie couldn't answer.

She knew. Jaymes knew she'd actually meant to kill the man. Stefanie met the woman's gaze head-on. "That would be important."

"Whoa. I don't know about this," Annette said, holding up her slender surgeon's hands. "It's not that I'm squeamish about annihilating the damned. I'll be the first one torching one of those bastards, be they demon, vampire, or rogue werewolf. But guns don't stop the damned, they kill men, or leave me bullets to dig out of maimed bodies."

Irritation brushed Stefanie's raw heart. She blinked at her sister. Here she thought Annette was in the forefront of this battle against evil and instead she was waffling on the sidelines. "You can't be serious," she said, turning to face her sister. "Turning the damned into burnt offerings is just fine, but it wasn't the damned who held me and Abe at gunpoint on Spirit Wind Mountain. It wasn't the damned that transported us to Corazón. It wasn't the damned that carried out Vasquez's and Herrera's orders and helped keep us prisoners. And it wasn't the damned that would have riddled us with bullets just now. It was mortal men doing the damned's will. You can't sit on the fence, Nette, because you or someone you love could die. You either fight all elements enabling this evil to exist or you get out of the fight."

Annette's eyes grew wider with every word. When Stefanie finished, a tense silence filled the air.

"Stef?" Annette whispered. "I . . . you're . . . you're differ . . . you're right." She set the magazine aside. "Boot camp it is."

What followed were the most intense, most grueling hours she'd ever spent. Jaymes accepted nothing less than perfection and made both her and Annette repeat a task, faster and faster, until patterns and routines were ingrained in their minds. Actually hitting a target dead center wasn't as important as making the actions automatic. Next time Stefanie wouldn't forget to flip off the safety. Next time she aimed and pulled the trigger, she'd kill.

Chapter Fifteen

Nick hung sixty feet above the ground, hidden by the thick foliage of the rain forest's lower canopy. El Diablo Sinclair's compound stretched below him, surrounded by a fifteen-foot electric fence that made any covert approach nearly impossible. Nick bet that at night they had the grounds lit up like a Christmas tree as well. Four single-story buildings with three-story watchtowers on each end made a square around an elaborate two-story mansion complete with gardens and fountains on the outside and chandeliers visible within.

Armed guards patrolled the perimeter with military precision—alert with weapons at the ready. These men had been trained well, Nick thought, observing them through high-powered binoculars, an air of expectation energized the busy camp.

Jose, the man who'd led them to Sinclair, was bound, gagged, and lashed to a tree trunk below. He knew if he moved, made a noise, or was discovered, Nick had a bullet with his name on it. Like Nick, Jared and Aragon were suspended in trees, each on a different side of the compound. They were all armed with some kickass grenades and machine guns, just in case any of them was discovered. Hell would rain down long enough to give them all the opportunity to escape.

Nick hoped it wouldn't be necessary. They were counting on Jose being a man of his word. According to Jose, the red flag flying in the air about twenty feet above Nick was Sinclair's signal to Menendez that the coast was clear to land. Once Menendez showed, Nick would be able to put a GPS tracker on him.

They had all their bases covered. Nick hung near the helipad. Aragon was above the front entrance and Jared covered the back. No other way out was visible, but that didn't mean there wasn't one. Corazón had had an escape tunnel leading over two hundred yards into the jungle.

The howler monkeys were at it again, this time much closer and louder. Their nerve-racking screams sent shivers down Nick's spine. Mentally he knew they were harmless, but still, something that can make that kind of noise could easily be underestimated. He'd seen *Planet of the Apes,* both versions and the sequels, so he kept a wary eye out.

The primates were so loud that he felt the pulsing vibrations in the air and actually saw the helo before he heard it. As the helo drew closer to land, Nick realized the quiet approach was also due to the machine itself. The "Stealth" helo had first made an appearance in Nam. Menendez had connections.

Nick kept his binoculars trained on the cockpit, waiting to confirm whether or not General Otto Menendez had arrived. Once the occupants left the helo, Nick would fire "sticky" tracing darts at the helo's frame until he had a sure hit. Then he'd activate the GPS tracker. The General's signature gray hair and politician's smile came into view.

"Menendez is here," Nick whispered into the radio.

"About time," said Aragon.

"Wish we could move in now," Jared added.

Nick seconded that emotion. Tonight would mark twenty-four hours that they'd been in Belize and he had mixed feelings about what they'd accomplished. The helo touched down and two guards exited, giving the immediate area a sweeping search before signaling an all-clear. Thankfully, they didn't look up. Next, Otto Menendez stepped out and turned to help a svelte, very tall blond woman descend from the aircraft.

Nick kept the binoculars trained on the couple as they cleared the rotor's downdraft. A golf cart fashioned after a Hummer drove up. Its driver got out and shook the General's hand, then greeted the woman. Nick's body tensed beneath a rush of disgust. This had to be Sinclair. From the back all Nick could see was the man's tall, impressive build and a Indiana Jones hat cocked on his head.

After a moment, the man turned back to the golf cart and revealed his face.

Nick gasped, "Fuck." Luckily the sight of his father sucked all the air from his lungs, or his curse would have drowned out even the screeches of the howler monkeys. He rubbed the sweat from his eyes and blinked twice just to be sure, but there was no mistaking it. Reed Sinclair was alive and well and apparently living high on the hog as a drug lord in the middle of the jungle. "Double fuck."

"Your overuse of the graphic euphemism brings pleasant memories to mind," Aragon muttered, "but I doubt that's your intent. What's up?"

"El Diablo Sinclair is my dear old dead dad."

Marissa woke with a start to find herself alone and wrapped snugly in the blanket she and Navarre had been sitting on. More time had passed than she'd imagined. Evening shadows had crept into the day, filling the area with a murky gloom. The scents of sweet frangipani and night-blooming orchids were already lacing the cooler air. For the first time in too long, Marissa felt refreshed and energized, ready to face what had to be done.

She lazily stretched, then awareness and memory shocked her fully awake. Her dress. She slid her hand down to her hips. Her dress was indeed pushed to her waist. She hadn't imagined or dreamed the intimacy she'd shared with Navarre.

His touch had made her body burn, then sing with pleasure. A sweet yearning ache was centered between her legs and in her breasts. She wanted more from Navarre. She wanted to share everything possible. This desire went beyond the pleasure of his touch, for her heart ached to know him so much she thought she would burst from want.

She could hear Father Dom, Rafael, and Navarre close by. She quickly tugged her dress down, making sure she stayed completely covered by the blanket. Guilty heat stained her cheeks.

How could she have let such a thing happen? How could her heart's need and her desire for Navarre be so great that she'd allow such an intimacy while her brother—and a priest!—were so close? It didn't matter that they couldn't see her or she them. Or did it?

If she were married to Navarre and lived in a home as most married people did, she would have welcomed any intimacy in the privacy of their bedroom, even if her brother and Father Dom were staying in her home. So was being with Navarre here any different? Did it matter that there were trees and bushes and a truck between them instead of walls and doors?

Did it matter that the law and the church saw her as Herrera's wife? Did any of the circumstances that had trapped her into such an untenable position matter at all?

Her upbringing insisted yes, but her heart cried no. Everything with Navarre seemed so right. What did he think about the intimacy they'd shared? She searched for him in the shadows and found him, Rafael, and Father Dom all staring at her expectantly.

"What is your opinion in this matter?" Navarre asked.

She blinked. "I'm sorry. I didn't hear what you were discussing. What do you want to know?"

"Should we stay here tonight or try and reach Father Dom's church in San Ignacio by morning?"

Marissa shook her head, alarmed that they'd even consider such a move. "We can't go there. Even if we weren't with you, Father Dom, it's not safe for you to go back. Herrera vowed to kill you when he caught me freeing Rafael in the dungeon. He thinks you helped orchestrate my escape."

"I will declare sanctuary for you all before God and my entire congregation. He can't touch you then. It is much safer than being alone in the jungle with no one to help or bear witness to his crimes."

Marissa shook her head, wondering how Father Dom could even think such a thing. "You can't honestly believe Herrera would honor or respect anything, even God? He'd slaughter everyone in the town of San Ignacio if it suited his purposes. There are no rules or decency in his book."

"We can't just sit here forever," Rafael said. "I say we arm ourselves and go to where he'll find us so we can kill the bastard."

"How and with what?" Marissa demanded. "We need time to plan and we need help to act. I say we stay here tonight, then as soon as we can, find a phone. I will call my friends in Twilight. The lawman and two of Navarre's warrior friends from the spirit world are there. They can help us more than anyone else."

"How?" demanded Rafael. "If Herrera kidnapped you from there once, he can do so again. He will be expecting you to go to them."

Marissa opened her mouth to argue, but then couldn't deny what Rafael said. "Even considering that, they can help us the most."

Rafael stood, hands fisted. "No. I don't need a stranger's interference. We stay hidden until we can trap Herrera. I've never asked you for anything in my life, my sister, but I demand this. Herrera is mine to destroy."

He stalked off with the machine gun slung across his back before she could reply.

Father Dom threw his hands up. "The foolishness of youth. It appears that staying here for tonight is the best thing to do. And we'd better do what we can before it becomes too dark to see."

Her thoughts about Navarre and the intimacy they'd shared

were still a jumbled mess. All of her life she'd been taught that certain things were wrong, and now that she faced them, she couldn't see them as wrong. "I need to refresh myself. I'll be down at the water," she said, needing some time to think about everything. She found the waterfall and the evening to be a soothing balm. There were so many things in life she had missed because of her uncle's evil. Simple things like the forest . . . and passion.

She turned quickly at the sound of wood tapping on stone. Navarre joined her by the water, as she had secretly hoped he would.

"You're becoming very good at that, you know," she said, walking to him and taking his hand in hers.

He gripped her hand tightly and turned his face toward hers as if trying to see her. "Much of it is memory and part of it is trying to sense other things around me," he said. "After seeing the picture of the path in your mind and counting the steps to each change in the level of the ground, I can now find my way back and forth. When I smell the flowers I know I'm close to the trees. The water is fifteen steps from the large root at the bottom of the path. But you are different," he said softly.

"Than roots?"

"Than everything. I don't have to memorize details or try and sense things. With you I know. I know when you're near. I know what you feel. Now, instead of feeling warm pleasure from my touch and the ecstasy we shared, you feel angst. Why?" The moon crested over the trees and sent a slice of light down, casting the shadows from his face.

Her breath caught at the thrill of his rough-hewn features, towering strength, and yet gentleness. How could she explain her confusion? "I . . . I feel the pleasure. *Dios,* it is something I've never known and will never forget, but—"

"Aaah!" Navarre cried out, his back arching and his limbs shuddering. His cane flew from his hand and he nearly flung her off balance before he released his death grip on her hand. He cried out again and his body twisted forward. He landed on his knees and looked up to the sky.

"By Logos . . . save me!" he yelled.

"Navarre? *Dios mío*, what is wrong?" Marissa grabbed his shoulder, wishing she could see into his mind as he saw into hers.

A scream of pure torture ripped from his lungs and suddenly his muscles bulged, everywhere, nearly doubling his body mass. It seemed to her that bones cracked and stretched in painful succession, one after another. His neck, back, arms changed, then his hands, his fingers turning into sharp-nailed claws. Legs, thighs, calves, and feet. Black hair erupted from his smooth skin, covering his chest, back, arms, and face. Fangs projected from his upper jaw.

He was the creature again, only this time even bigger. But it was more than that. She sensed a primal savagery oozing from him. She stumbled back, lost her step, and would have fallen into the water if he hadn't reached out and grabbed her arm. His claws painfully scratched her skin.

"Navarre? *Madre de Dios*, what has happened? You're . . . you're the creature again. What has Herrera done to you?"

Breathing heavily, he released his hold on her arm and she saw she was bleeding.

"Blood," he said harshly. "I smell blood."

He grabbed her arm again, bringing her scratches to his nose and inhaling. Then he licked the blood on her arm.

She cried out and he jumped back, pulling away from her.

"Hurt you," he said, his voice grating like broken glass. "Sorry. Hurt you."

"Marissa! Marissa!" Father Dom yelled. He ran toward them with a large branch in his hand and shoved its sharp, jagged end at Navarre. "He's evil. The shapeshifter is evil. This creature will kill you."

"No!" Navarre roared. He snatched the branch from the priest's hand and snapped it in half with his claw as if it were no more than a toothpick.

"Marissa, to your right!" called Rafael.

She twisted around and saw that Rafael had the machine gun pointed their way. She cried out, moving closer to Navarre to protect him. "No, Rafe, no. Don't shoot. It is Navarre. It is something Herrera did to him."

Rafael didn't lower the gun, but he didn't advance closer, either. "What did Herrera do?"

"Nothing," said Father Dom. "Herrera didn't make this man a werewolf. Satan did. All shapeshifters are born of the devil."

"No," Marissa cried. "That's not true."

"Tell her," Father Dom shouted. "Tell her. Are you a shapeshifter?"

"Yes," Navarre said, his breathing ragged as if he could barely hold on to his control with his fisted hands.

Though she kept her body between Navarre and the machine gun in Rafael's hands, she backed away from Navarre.

Navarre cried out in pain and before she could say anything, he turned and ran up the incline and past the truck into the jungle. His spirit wolf appeared suddenly, running at his side.

"Navarre!" She started after him, but Father Dom grabbed her arm, pulling her back.

Rafael ran past her and before she could stop him, he sprayed bullets through the jungle where Navarre had just been moments ago.

"No!" she screamed, jerking free of Father Dom.

She ran to her brother and pulled hard on the machine gun strap slung over his shoulder. He wobbled off balance, and the next spray of bullets went high into the trees. "How could you try and kill him, no matter what he is? If it weren't for him you'd still be in Herrera's dungeon and so would I!"

"What do you mean? That's not a man. It's a creature I've never seen before," Rafael said, shaking his head.

"It's not a creature. It's Navarre and he looked almost like that last night when he carried you to freedom." She turned to Father Dom. "And you would be dead if it weren't for him." She ran from them toward the jungle. "Navarre! Navarre! Can you hear me?"

Vines and branches and bushes ripped at her dress and scratched at her skin, but she kept moving, calling for Navarre as she searched the area. The farther she went the darker it became. She ran until she could see no more then came to a gasping stop. She'd made a very foolish move that might just mean she'd spend the night alone in the jungle. She'd lost her sense of direction and didn't know which way led back to the truck.

She should have taken time to get a flashlight and she should have brought Rafael with her, but she'd been so angry and so upset and worried about Navarre that she hadn't thought clearly. She had to think now or she'd be in worse trouble. Dragging in deep breaths of air, she calmed herself, then took stock of her surroundings in the almost blinding dark.

She had to feel around, trying to discern what the black, hulking shapes surrounding her were. Her heart pounded with a growing fear that she beat back. She kept telling herself that this was what Navarre faced, only worse. He couldn't see anything at all. She tripped over something and landed hard on her hands and knees as she fought to stem another rush of panic.

Navarre did this. I can do this. As she felt her way back up she discovered a solid tree branch, light enough for her to pick up, but heavy enough to defend herself with. Then she ran into a strangling shower of vines from above and fought her way past them, her heart pounding.

Tears filled her eyes, but she refused to cry. Next she found the gigantic, smooth roots of a huge kapok tree and settled herself with her back to its trunk. She'd wait here until either Rafael or Father Dom found her or morning came.

Just when she had herself calmed enough to breathe without gasping, a loud cry rent the jungle silence and turned her blood to ice. It was the cry of a jaguar on the hunt. Judging from the volume and ferocity of the scream, it was hungry, agitated, and very close by.

Chapter Sixteen

CONFUSED AND in pain, Navarre ran as far and as fast as he could. His were form was out of his control. Never had shifting been as painful or as deforming as what happened to him tonight. He'd seen what he looked like through the eyes of his wolf spirit and the size and ferocity of the beast he'd become frightened even him.

Yet the creature didn't even come close to the hideous repulsiveness of the hungers boiling inside of him. He'd smelled Marissa's blood and had become ravenous for it. He hadn't been able to stop himself from tasting it, and that ignited a fire that grew stronger by the second. All he could think about was blood.

He ran as hard as he could, hoping to cleanse the burgeoning evil and regain a warrior's control over his body. But the world and its temptations kept dragging him back under. His senses were more developed than ever before. Everything had a discernible scent. The trees, the vines, the forest floor, the creatures hiding beneath the cover of leaves and even the smell of the blood pounding in their veins.

Though he could see through the eyes of his wolf spirit, he found that he didn't need his vision to locate other creatures in the night. He could sense them, smell them, smell their blood. He reached through a thick wall of vines and grabbed a small animal. Its high-pitched bark of terror rang through the air and he wanted to snap its neck just like he'd wanted to break the priest in half when the man had jabbed him with the sharp stick. He let the small animal drop from his hand before he could tear into its heart and lap up the blood. Some small part of him cried out in horror at the thought.

Still his mouth watered, his fangs ached, and his stomach

rumbled. He started to chase after the little creature with four white stripes along its back, but then heard the roar of a fiercer beast that had to be larger—and more of a meal to feast upon.

Time to hunt.

He drew closer to the beast, sensing it, too, was stalking prey within the teeming wildness of the jungle. Then a breeze broke through the brush and vines and he caught the scent of humans. Marissa's image flooded his mind. Remembered pleasure with her exploded through his body and brought him to a standstill. The driving hunger for blood lessened beneath his rising tide of lust for her.

He heard a woman's laugh, and though he knew it wasn't Marissa, he followed the sultry sound. The rain forest thinned, giving way to a clearing where six small bungalows clustered around a larger building. He circled the place, listening for more of the woman's voice. A sign read GREEN WATER JUNGLE RESORT. Each of the smaller houses were separated by tall grass walls and each had a raised pool of hot bubbling water behind it. The laugh sounded again. It came from his left and he followed until he saw a mortal man and woman in the bubbling water.

"My, what big eyes you have," the woman said.

"The better to see you with," the man said softly, moving closer to the woman.

"My, what big hands you have," the woman said.

"The better to touch you with," the man said as he reached her. He pulled her up to stand in front of him and cupped her breasts with his hands. She moaned and arched her back just as Marissa had done. The man growled and leaned down, covering one of the woman's breasts with his mouth, making loud sucking noises before he released one breast and moved to the other. The woman grabbed his shoulders.

"My, what a quick tongue you have," the woman said, panting with every breath.

"The better to eat you with," the man said, growling again.

He suddenly grabbed the woman by her bottom, sliding her up his chest. Then he moved to the side of the bubbling pool and set her down on its edge before he spread her legs open. Surprise and a yearning hot desire flamed through Navarre's blood as the man lowered himself to taste the woman's dark secrets, just where Navarre had found Marissa's hard point of pleasure.

The woman squirmed and jiggled, but the man opened her legs even wider and pinned them down against the sides of the pool. She then thrashed her head and rubbed her breasts and moaned louder and louder.

Navarre's groin grew hard and throbbed. He ached to be with Marissa.

"Little Red Riding Hood doesn't think she can take any more," the woman said as she gasped for air. The man stood up, his groin as swollen as Navarre's. "Especially as big as this bad wolf is," the woman said.

The man laughed and brought both his hands to his groin, stroking his swollen flesh. "She's going to take everything this big bad wolf has ready for her." The man scooped the woman up and they disappeared inside the building.

Navarre couldn't turn away. He moved closer, sending his wolf spirit after the man and woman. Inside the man laid the woman on a soft, white cloud. She arched her back, lifting her hips for him, and he put little white clouds beneath her. Then he slid his hardened flesh deeply between her legs.

Navarre thought the man would hurt the woman from the ferocity of his thrusts, but she cried out for more in a manner that left Navarre's body throbbing with as much need as her obviously mounting pleasure.

Marissa. He needed Marissa. His wolf spirit returned, allowing Navarre to see that he'd changed back to his mortal form. His hulking were form had disappeared as his lust for blood had been erased by a greater need for Marissa. His desire for her had given him control over the beast within. He had to bring Marissa here, to this place of warm bubbling pools and fluffy white clouds.

He sent his spirit in search of hers. That's when he felt her fear and knew she was in danger. The predatory cry of the other beast roared through the jungle as if he'd caught his victim.

Marissa!

"Ysalane is ready to show *el jefe* where the wolf god and the woman are." Ysalane entered the room unbidden.

Samir looked up from his financial reports on the computer screen. It was the first time the vampire had surfaced from his business even though Herrera had hardcore porn on the big screen. "The wolf god and Marissa?"

Herrera clenched his teeth and glared at Ysalane. With Samir's intrusion, Herrera had forgotten her witch-magic promise. Even at that she'd said she wouldn't be ready until midnight and it was several hours before that now. Didn't the woman have the sense not to reveal her magic to Samir? The bastard was sure to want Ysalane now.

Herrera shrugged. "She thinks she can use Mayan magic to find Marissa."

"You will see, Ysalane will show you." She held up a large crystal jaguar.

"Then by all means, show us," Samir said.

Herrera fisted his hands. She was his *puta* to command, not Samir's. "Do it quickly. We've already wasted too much time waiting on worthless mortals to find her."

Ysalane went to the center of the room and placed the jaguar on the floor. Then she brought forth a knife, cut her palm, and smeared her blood over the jaguar as she chanted in a strange language. What appeared in the air over her head was a ghostly image that faded in and out. But Herrera immediately saw the wolf ghost inside a room where a dark-headed man was screwing the brains out of a dark-haired woman.

Herrera roared and would have hit Ysalane but for the fact that Samir got up and stood in his way. "Let the Elan finish. Her blood is sweet and there must be more we can see through her eyes. Where are they, Elan? Where does my adulterous wife sin?"

Herrera watched Ysalane blink with surprise at Samir's protection and gentle question. Or was it that Samir was calling Marissa his wife when he knew Herrera had married the woman?

Samir moved to Ysalane and swiped a finger of blood off the jaguar then sucked his finger. "Sweet. Very sweet."

Ysalane's cheeks reddened and she bowed her head. Herrera pictured Samir and Ysalane dying in the worst possible ways he could imagine. Vasquez had taught Herrera well and he couldn't wait to let his evil wings spread—just as soon as he held Guatemala in his dictatorial fist. Ysalane began to chant louder and the wavering, ghostly picture panned out to reveal a sign: GREEN WATER JUNGLE RESORT.

"Beautiful," Samir said, brushing a gentle hand over Ysalane's head.

"You will do as you promised now," Ysalane said, looking at Herrera.

He'd had more than he could take. He snatched her up by her hair, which she twisted and pulled against until she had her hands on her bloody jaguar. "No, *puta*. Now get out of my sight." He shoved her out the door.

"Ysalane's jaguar will kill the wolf god and his woman. You will see!" she said, holding up her bloodied crystal jaguar as she backed away. He'd never before seen the dark rage in her eyes and felt a chill of apprehension run down his spine. He shut the door and dismissed the feeling. Wolf gods and magic had his imagination running wild.

"What did you promise the woman?" Samir asked.

"Nothing," Herrera snarled. "Touch my *puta* again, taste her blood again, and I will kill you, Samir."

"I have Marissa. I want nothing of your whore, but I've learned to get more by hiding the wolf of ruthlessness beneath the lambskin of gentleness." Samir shrugged and went back to his computer.

Herrera tried to calm his rushing blood and figure out how to locate the resort while sending Samir on a wild-goose chase.

Samir laughed. "This is ironic," he said. "We've men searching miles and miles of the jungle from here to the priest's church in San Ignacio and Marissa is only a few miles from where we sit." He stood and opened his cell phone. "I'm glad we were able to settle this in a civilized manner, Herrera. Once I have properly taken care of my unfaithful wife, we will form that coalition against Cinatas and take control of the Vladarian Order. While you were watching your movie, I e-mailed the other members of SINCO and have heard nothing but praise for the plan. I have an excellent relationship with them all and have scheduled everyone to meet at midnight in my new palace in Kassim the day after tomorrow."

Herrera saw his plans for leadership of the SINCO's coup evaporate. Samir had to die, but first Herrera had to get his hands on Marissa. "I'll go with you to the resort, just to make sure all goes well. You are aware of Vasquez's legal stipulations for maintaining control of Marissa's SINCO shares, *sí*?"

Samir frowned. "What are you talking about?"

"Vasquez's will. You can only maintain control of her SINCO assets as long as you continue to meet his requirements in regard to Marissa's treatment and well-being." Herrera turned away, smiling with satisfaction. "I'll send you a copy of the document."

Maybe he'd let Samir live a little while longer, just so he could see the righteous bastard squirm. Meanwhile, he'd have to think of a punishment great enough for Marissa. Her virgin's blood was spilled and he hadn't had the pleasure of doing it.

"Marissa!" Navarre ran faster, harder, feeling her fear as another predatory cry vibrated through the jungle. Some instinctual part of him felt a change in the jaguar. Its scream was diffcrent than before, for its ferocity went beyond primal hunger or territorial warning into the realm of possessed rage.

Navarre let out a challenging roar, desperate to distract the beast that he was sure was after Marissa. He could feel it. He wasn't even sure why, but he'd lived and fought for a millennium by following his intuition and he wasn't going to question it now. Marissa was in mortal danger and he could curse himself for an eternity for leaving her side. It just proved how greatly his were form had controlled him, stealing away rational thought and driving him to the very edge of evil.

When he hit a road that cut back toward the truck, he moved even faster toward Marissa, his senses at full alert. The moonlight hit him full in the face and he felt his body changing again. This time less painfully, more like his usual Blood Hunter's were form. His senses heightened and he ran even faster.

He howled at the jaguar this time, the sound powered by his were strength. The jungle trembled at his chilling cry and the night exploded in chaos as animals everywhere scurried in terror. Navarre heard an answering challenge from the beast, one that was closer to Navarre than before, and he hoped the animal was now stalking him.

I'm coming. He sent the warm wave of assurance to Marissa's spirit, praying that she'd be able to hear him above her pounding fear. He smelled the priest and her brother before he found them running along the road. The priest let out a scream at the sight of him and Rafael aimed the gun toward him.

"Where's Marissa?" Navarre demanded. The creature cried

again, much closer, and he could hear Marissa's heart shouting for him. "She's in danger from that beast."

Rafael lowered the gun. "We're looking for her. She ran into the jungle after you. But that is only the cry of a jaguar. They never really attack people in the jungle unless they are trapped and under attack. There's another more dangerous beast, though. One whose scream I've never heard."

"That was me," Navarre said. "Go back to the truck and get inside. This jaguar is out to kill. I will find Marissa and bring her back when it is safe. Don't worry."

"In sixty-five years I've never been attacked by any of the rain forest creatures," the priest said, pointing his finger in disapproval. "Propriety demands that you bring her back immediately—"

Suddenly a red-eyed beast leaped from a tree overhead, flying at the priest and Rafael, its fangs snarling and its claws spread.

Screaming, Rafael lifted the muzzle and fired. The jaguar jerked from the force of the bullets, and screamed louder, clawing wildly. Both Rafael and the priest were knocked over backward and the beast went for the priest's throat.

Navarre saw it all through his wolf spirit. With a primal yell, he launched himself on the animal, grabbing its upper jaw and yanking it back before it could close its jaws on the priest's throat. The moment Navarre touched the jaguar he could feel the evil spirit inside it, like acid burning his soul. He could also smell the creature's blood—and a craving to taste that blood clenched Navarre's gut.

The beast twisted under Navarre's hold, lashing out with its claws. Navarre wrestled with the animal, giving it blow after blow as it snarled with what could only be described as a demonic intent to rip Navarre's throat out. Then it suddenly leaped free and ran into the jungle, roaring loudly as it fled, but its cry didn't echo defeat. It rang with victory.

"It's a demon, an abomination," gasped the priest.

"It was a jaguar, but then it was something else, too," Rafael said. "I shot it in the chest. It should be dead."

Navarre only had one thought. Marissa.

"Go to the truck and wait inside." He left Rafael and the priest and followed the beast in the direction of Marissa. Being smaller and on all fours let the beast move faster through the jungle than Navarre could run upright with only his wolf spirit to guide him.

Frustration ate at him. The beast could kill Marissa with one swipe of its claws or sink its teeth into her throat before Navarre could reach her.

By Logos! This would not happen. Navarre channeled all of his angst into his anger and his were form became even more ferocious, more primal, more animal than man. He dropped to all fours, enabled now to run faster with his wolf spirit at his side, showing the way.

He hit a small clearing, saw Marissa with a branch in her hand, heard her scream, and saw the beast fly through the air, jaws open for Marissa's throat.

Navarre leaped for the jaguar, digging his claws into its back as he desperately tried to snatch the animal away from Marissa. She lashed out with the branch, hitting the beast's mouth, before she curled into a ball.

Navarre ripped at the beast's flesh, but its demonic force kept it going after Marissa, and he had no choice but to sink his fangs into the beast's throat and rip it open to stop the animal. Blood spurted everywhere. In his mouth, over him, over Marissa.

He felt as if he were suddenly drowning in the very same thing he'd been dying to taste. It sickened him. With Marissa near, he needed her more than he needed blood. He released the beast and spat out the blood, then pulled her into his arms.

"Are you all right? Please be all right," he whispered. "I'm sorry I left you."

"I'm okay," she said, shaking her head. "But I'm the one who needs to apologize. Father Dom and Rafael were wrong. *I* was wrong to pull away from you in fear." She set her hand on his chest, then pulled it back. "*Dios mío,* you are covered in blood. So am I." She shuddered.

Navarre knew she'd been right to pull away from him. There had been much to fear, could still be, but he would have to explain it to her later. He'd also have to let her know the jaguar had been possessed by an evil spirit, one bent on killing her. That had to have come from the damned.

"Come with me," he said, taking her hand, so glad to have her safe that he wanted to share with her the beauty he'd found before anything else could happen. "There is a place I want to show you. One with white clouds and warm water to clean yourself in."

Marissa didn't hesitate to take his hand or follow him. "We should see if my brother and Father Dom are all right."

"They are fine," Navarre said. "I have just seen them and told them I would bring you back when it was safe."

"They'll worry about me."

"We will not be long. You must clean yourself first and see this Green Water place with the white cloud. It is just as you pictured in your mind."

Chapter Seventeen

York treaded water, staring up at the woman looking down at him.

"Are you all right? And what about your friend? My God, is he in the water? Has he drowned? Do I need to call for help?" the red-haired Elan shouted down at York before he could answer her question about his sanity. She appeared seriously panicked.

"No," York yelled back. "I am certain Flynn is fine." Now that York had time to think, he was sure Flynn must have returned to the spirit realm for help. With the Tsaras congregating behind some unknown magical shield and York presently trapped in the mortal realm, it was the logical course of action for a warrior.

York swam to the ladder and climbed into the boat, trying to decide what he should do next. Investigate what he could about this Tsara situation while he was in the mortal realm, search for a way to return to the spirit realm, or find out why an Elan was hovering around a Vladarian Vampire's lair?

"Then where is he?" the Elan demanded as soon as he reached the deck. "Where did he go? What kind of friend would abandon you while you're swimming through rough water trying to save me?"

York wiped the water from his eyes, grimacing at the cold and her questions. The Elan had moved to a different part of the boat and she'd put on her shirt, but that didn't stop him from remembering what she looked like beneath, or wondering why she would cover such beauty in the first place. "I am sure Flynn went for help."

"Unless he flew like Peter Pan to Never-Never Land that means he went to Valois, because there is no other help for miles." She pulled out a gun and pointed it at him. "I'm sorry to have to do this, considering you practically saved my life, but I can't let you go and I don't have time to be nice about it, either. I've got to get out of here before Valois shows up. I'm not ready to fight him yet. Turn around and put your hands behind your back."

York blinked, cocked a brow, then felt a smile tug his lips, thoroughly amused. "You want to make me your prisoner? What is your name?"

"Yes." She leveled the gun more firmly, attempting to hide her shaking hands. "You can call me Kassandra. What's yours?"

"York," he said as he considered his options. He decided that the Elan's desperation and what her possible connection was to the man who was hoarding Tsaras outweighed his searching for a return to the spirit realm at the moment. "Kassandra, I will be your prisoner for a time then." He turned around and put his hands behind his back.

She gasped. "Good Lord. You're bleeding. How did you cut your back?"

He started to turn back, surprised to hear the Tsara's scratch hadn't begun to heal.

"No! Don't move. Not yet." A second later she bound his arms together with metal bracelets, and his heart beat just a little bit faster at the feel of her hands on him. His groin grew heavy and the image and feel of her breasts filled his mind. "Okay, you can move now," she said.

He turned around.

"Oh my God." She still had the gun pointed his way but she closed her eyes. Almost closed them, he noted as he saw a sliver of sky blue between her red lashes. He looked around, wondering what had disturbed her this time. It seemed that this Elan wasn't a very logical mortal. Still, for some reason he found himself very interested in being her prisoner for a time.

• • •

Move, you bastard. Nick tore his frustrated gaze from the blinking dot on the computer screen that had yet to obey him and paced across the small sitting room. He was sure he'd spontaneously combust at any second and set the three-bedroom hut on fire. He wanted, *needed,* to do something besides wait for General Menendez to depart from El Diablo Sinclair's compound, and flying after Menendez's ass in hopes the General would lead them to Herrera and Marissa was something Nick could sink his teeth into.

He almost wished Jared would call for help just so Nick could go into action. Jared, with plenty of provisions, had stayed to keep the camp under surveillance in case Menendez left by car after all. Nick had expected Menendez's visit to last an hour or two and then they'd be in business tracking the SOB. Unfortunately, Jared and Aragon had seen Menendez's men unload two small suitcases from the helo and put them in the back of a Hummer golf cart.

Nick hadn't seen anything past the fact that his father, Reed Sinclair, was alive. He still couldn't. They'd waited three hours for Menendez to leave. When he didn't, Nick and Aragon had left Jared and returned. After a full meal, everyone had gone to bed early to be ready whenever Menendez took off. They'd let Jose and his men go under the dire threat that the werewolf would kill them and their families if they ever spoke to Sinclair again, or if they told anyone about what happened. Given the men were thoroughly humiliated, they wouldn't be likely to spread the news.

His father was alive. His father was a drug lord.

God, the questions were driving him crazy. Nick still couldn't quite believe it. Eight years. For eight years his father had never once tried to contact him.

A hand settled on his shoulder and he whipped around, surprised at being caught off guard. Stefanie stood behind him, her shadowed blue eyes full of concern.

"You're sure it was your father?" she asked softly enough not to wake the others.

"As sure as I can be without DNA."

She tightened her grip. "I'm sorry. There has to be an explanation, a reason—"

"Is there any excuse for abandoning your kid? Hell . . . you know what? It doesn't really matter." He pulled away and paced across the room. "I'm too old for this shit."

"No one is ever too old for pain," she said quietly.

Nick swung around. "That's not what I said. Besides, the shit you're dealing with is real crap. I don't know anyone who could have held up like you have. My baggage from being a messed-up kid with screwed-up parents isn't important."

"Yes it is."

"No it's not." He exhaled hard. "I've got to get out of here for a while, take a walk or something. You mind watching the computer for a bit? Jared is supposed to call if there is any movement, but it wouldn't hurt to keep an eye on it from this end, too."

"Yeah, I'll watch the screen for you, but a walk isn't going to help," Stefanie said, glaring at him. "You're about to explode because you're sitting on your pain and aren't opening up." She turned her back on him. "And thanks for letting me know my problems are so important that nobody else matters."

"That isn't what I said." Nick's eye twitched as he exhaled again, adding exasperation to his frustration and emotional tornado.

"Yes you did." She glanced back over her shoulder. "I don't need a friend who won't let me be one back."

The zinger hit him between the eyes. "Stef . . . I . . . shit. I don't need this right now, either. We'll talk later," he said, clamping down on his temper.

He left the hut, welcoming the cool night air. Moonlight bathed the area in a soft glow and the distant sound of a classical guitar from the main building joined the pulsing music of the jungle—buzzing beetles, droning cicadas, and croaking frogs. The "huts" or cottages of the Saturno Archaeological Inn were pods semicircled around a hotel that housed more guest rooms, a dining and entertainment facility as well as meeting rooms. Spreading out behind it were tropical gardens and a lagoon-shaped pool. Both were empty.

Deciding he'd let off more steam swimming laps than wandering the garden, he stripped to his Jockeys and began plowing through the water. Instead of easing the pressure inside him, every cutting stroke seemed to feed his anger. He wasn't sure how long he swam, but he didn't pull himself out of the water until his arms were Jell-O and his lungs ached from his ragged breaths.

"Leaving your clothes on the ground is one way to get bitten in very sensitive places," Jaymes said, raking him with a sharp glance that lingered on . . . his "sensitive places" before meeting his gaze. She lay on a chaise longue, wearing hug-me jeans and a tight, scoop-neck tee that left him begging for more skin and less shirt.

"You offering?" he said, lifting a brow as he moved into the danger zone—any distance that put her within reach. She had his clothes stacked on a patio table next to her. He slipped his shirt off the top and began patting himself dry.

"After the way you bit Stef's head off, I'd hesitate to offer anything."

He paused. "Eavesdropping part of your daily routine?"

Her mouth quirked up, flashing dimples at him. The woman was deadly enough without more ammo.

"Stef's right, you know. You're a powder keg ready to blow." She gave him another once-over. This time his dick got into the action, a fact his wet Jockeys made more than obvious. Jaymes lifted a cool brow at him and he wondered how in the hell any special ops anything functioned with her around. He sure as hell couldn't ignore what she did to him. Well, at least his body couldn't.

He tossed his shirt to the table and moved another step closer to the lounge chair. He was in no mood for talk or bullshit. He needed a big distraction. "Again. You offering to *blow* off . . . some steam?"

She rolled her eyes with disgust. Adeptly gaining her feet, she put the lounge between them before he could even blink.

"FYI I have a vagina, not a relief valve for assholes." She started to march off and Nick mentally slapped himself upside his head.

"Hey," he called out. "I'm sorry. You're in the wrong place at the wrong time. I'm just . . ." Hell, he couldn't even begin to describe what he was.

To his surprise, she turned around. "It's not me you need to apologize to. It's Stef. I heard her crying before I came out looking for you. How could you do that to her? Turn her down when she was doing her best to reach out?"

Nick uttered a string of expletives he'd never put together before and raked his fingers through his wet hair. "Why don't you tell me what in the hell I was supposed to say to her? Whine about my screwed-up parents? A drunk mother who accidently killed herself trying to hurt herself so my dad would have to stay home and be *her* hero rather than out saving the world? Or do I complain about a father so addicted to danger that he couldn't stay home more than a few days at a time? He left after her funeral and I saw him twice over the next three years. It wasn't until Sam showed up with the news that Reed Sinclair died a hero that I realized I'd been sitting in limbo waiting for my father to come back and get me. Now I find out he's been dealing drugs and living high on the hog for the past eight years while I grieved? The SOB can just stay dead for all I care. End of story. What is that bullshit compared to the abuse and torture Stef went through? It's like complaining to a starving kid that my steak is tough."

Shaking his head, Nick turned back to his clothes. How had he just spewed all of that crap? It was like once his mouth started running he couldn't stop it.

Damn, but he was too old for this shit. Screw his dear old dad. Snatching up his jeans, he put them on and drove the zipper home. He wouldn't get any rest tonight. His mind wouldn't shut down, his gut would bother him about what an ass he'd just made of himself, and more importantly, his conscience would eat at him until he talked to Stef. Had he really been an asshole to her? He hadn't meant to be.

"Sit down," Jaymes said from behind him.

He grabbed his shirt and turned around, to find her a foot away. Too close. He didn't want any more psychoanalysis. "Listen, I'm not up for chitchat, even if you're dishing out the miracle cure for excess baggage. I've said too much already."

"No cure for baggage, just for tension. It's called 'Jin Shin Jyutsu.' "

"Sounds kinky," he said.

"Sit here." She directed him to the bottom of the chaise. "Do you ever turn off the lines?" She placed her hands on his neck. Heat as well as an electrified zing went zigzagging through his body and bounced back to his groin. Nice distraction.

"No." He leaned into her touch, figuring replacement therapy was better than no therapy. He'd trade FUBAR emotions for sexual tension any day.

"Why?"

She had such magic in the light touches of her hands that it took him a few minutes to put his glib tongue into gear. "Cast no lines, catch no fish. A man could starve that way."

She laughed. "Well, take it from a woman who has heard them all and seen it all, you've got more going for you without them."

His mind snagged on that assessment. Had she just told

him he was better off with his mouth shut? Whatever she was doing to him turned his muscles into putty and somehow it didn't matter what she thought as long as she kept doing what she was doing.

Tension evaporated beneath the heat and magic of her hands. He'd expected hard, tough-as-nails pounding, not this barely there but powerful pressure. He would have groaned from the relief working its way through his body and mind, but all he could manage was a yawn. He hadn't slept well since learning what Stef had suffered at the hands of Vasquez and Herrera. He was so relaxed that he almost forgot about getting Staff Sergeant Jaymes Bond horizontal.

Almost, but not quite.

"You're amazing." He reached back and placed his hand over hers. She paused in caressing his neck. Then before he could say anything else, or pull her around to face him, her cell rang.

She backed away. "I had Grayson call in some markers. Sinclair has been operating for eight years. Somebody knows it, has been letting him get away with it, and we're going to stop it."

Nick bit back a curse, feeling as if she had somehow betrayed him. He didn't want his father investigated. Did he? Nothing was ever that simple. Now that Grayson knew Nick would have to call Sam, and let him know there was a dead man walking. Somehow that was worse than facing Reed.

Running ahead of Marissa and his physical body, Navarre's wolf spirit rushed from the cover of the jungle into the open moonlight. Marissa stopped in her tracks at the sight of a number of buildings.

"Do you know what this place is?" she whispered, pulling sharply on Navarre's arm to keep him safely within the shadows. "It is a resort. There are people here. If anyone sees you as a . . . wolf creature, they won't understand. They might try and hurt you. If we're seen, word could even get to Herrera."

"Do not worry." Navarre placed her hand over his heart, and though she could feel the jaguar's blood matting his fur, she didn't pull back from him as she'd done earlier by the waterfall. He'd shown her nothing but selfless acceptance and brave courage and she could do no less. "Watch this."

She stood in stunned silence as he changed back into a warrior without the agonizing pain from before. The metamorphosis occurred rapidly in a gentle, almost natural blending from creature to man.

"I don't understand. How does this happen? What happens to you?"

Her hand trembled as she touched his chest. He was back to normal, except for the jaguar's blood covering him. The thick fur, the overbulging muscles, and the fierce countenance were gone.

"Shadowmen are spirit warriors who can shift into different forms. Blood Hunters take on the spirit and gifts of the wolf to protect the Elan. Changing form is usually as simple as you just saw, but everything is so different for me now that I do not know if I can explain the changes. Part is the effect of the mortal world and the pull of the moon on my being. They are stronger than I expected, and tonight the savage tide was worse than last night, turning the Blood Hunter in me into a beast that hungered for blood as if I'd become unworthy of my service, as if I'd become evil." He clasped his amulet in his hand as if he might tear it off.

She set her hand over his fist. "No, not evil. Never that. And never question your worthiness. You have fought like no other to save and protect me." She knew every word was true without even thinking twice.

"You don't know what happened inside me."

"Herrera is evil. You're not. Not now and not as the wolf

beast, either. There's a difference between animal instinct and malicious intent. Surely you know that. Even though you felt different inside, both times you've become a wolf, last night and tonight, you used your power for good. You didn't selfishly feed your hunger no matter how badly your body urged you to do so. That shows the core of your heart is good."

"I'm not as sure as you." He shook his head, but released his amulet instead of breaking it. Then he clasped her hand. "Unbridled, the beast could become evil. It was only thoughts of you that saved me."

"What do you mean?" She looked into his eyes and wished things were different. That instead of the sightlessness in his golden depths, he could look into her eyes and see how much she believed in his goodness.

"Through the eyes of the wolf spirit, I saw a man and a woman sharing pleasure in this place and I wanted to share pleasure with you more than I hungered for blood. That is how I discovered that my desire for you enables me to control the beast. I can think of pleasure with you and the beast disappears. I can fear for your safety and it returns."

Having known the evil of vampires, Marissa had little trouble embracing Navarre's wolf magic in her heart even though part of it made him beastly. He'd shown her only goodness and kindness and had fought the wickedness that wanted to destroy her.

She slid her hand into his. "I am glad thinking of me helps you. When Herrera tried to hurt me, thoughts of you kept me from giving in to the pain and his madness."

"It is good then. We find strength in each other. Now, you must see the white cloud." He urged her into the moonlight where the wolf spirit stood looking their way.

"What about the people here? Won't they—"

"I can sense when strangers draw near. I will keep us safe. Trust me."

She followed him along the edge of the clearing with the wolf spirit leading the way. They passed a clothesline and she looked longingly at the fresh garments hanging behind a large cottage. "*Dios*, I would give much to have something besides this dress to wear."

Navarre paused. "What would you need to give? If I can find it, I will get it for you so that you can."

Marissa's heart squeezed. "We can't. Not now. I would need to ask them to buy their belongings, and if they agreed, I would need to give them money for it. There is money in the truck that I took from Herrera's guard, but I don't have any with me now." Stealing to escape from Herrera was a different matter than stealing from an innocent person.

Navarre grunted. "We can't ask them and remain hidden, too. They appear to have much and you are in need. Surely they would let you buy something."

If they were like Stefanie and her friends in Twilight, they would give her many things. "*Sí*, I think they would."

"Then can you take what clothing you need now and I will bring the money back here later to pay for it?"

Marissa glanced at her dress, looked at the fresh clothes, and could barely speak. "*Sí*. Somehow when this is all over, I will make it right." Heart pounding, she went to the line and chose a shirt and pants for herself and the same for Navarre, then raced back to him.

"No one is in this building," he said, leading her to a small hut in the back that was reassuringly closer to the jungle than the others.

The sticky blood covering her head and back was nauseating and the steamy hot tub did look very inviting. Five minutes wouldn't hurt. Would it? "You're sure no one is here?"

"Yes. Come see." With the wolf spirit leading, he went to the glass doors of the hut and opened them.

She couldn't resist looking. She'd seen pictures of such nice places and had always dreamed of staying in one. Once she had her head in the door, she had to explore what she'd never had the freedom to do before. Moonlight streaming through the windows in the ceiling showed a large room with chairs, tables, a television, a kitchen, and a huge bed that was as big and white and fluffy as a summertime cloud.

The "white cloud" she'd imagined being naked with Navarre on. He'd seen the image in her mind and hadn't forgotten it. Neither had she, and he would know it immediately if he tapped into her mind again. Cheeks burning, she left the intimacy of the bed and crossed the wooden floor, finding an instant answer to her prayers.

She turned to Navarre, who was still standing and gazing at the bed. "Do you think I could take a shower? *Dios,* that would be heaven."

"Shower?"

She pointed to the bathroom. "In there."

He and his wolf spirit moved to look through the doorway and then he asked, incredulous, "You want to take that with you? It is . . . extremely large and couldn't be carried all at once. Do you pay money for it, as well?"

"No, you don't understand." She shook her head, smiling, then grimaced at the blood drying on her skin. " 'Take a shower' means to bathe in the water that comes from the pipes. I'll show you." She set the clothes down in a chair and moved through the shadows to the tiled shower. It, too, had a large window in the ceiling that let in the bright moonlight and even gave a glimpse of the stars overhead. To be indoors and yet see the heavens made the place magical.

Opening the shower door, she was delighted to find two shower heads on opposite sides of the stall and an array of soaps, shampoo, and lotions on a shelf. Navarre and his wolf spirit filled the opening as she stepped inside the large area to turn on both faucets, adjusting the temperature and flow of the water. She then stepped beneath the double spray, clothes and all, groaned in relief as the water pounded away the sticky mess. She couldn't wait to be rid of the satin wedding dress.

"Can you wait in the other room?" She turned to Navarre. "I'll be only a min—"

He was right behind her! In the shower *with* her! And *Dios mío*, he was *naked*!

It was scandalous . . . sinful . . . she should cover her eyes instead of stare at what the moonlight revealed to her water-drenched gaze . . . but he was magnificent.

She should leave the shower and wait for him to finish . . . only she couldn't make her feet move.

She should tell him this was improper, yet she couldn't speak.

Instead, she couldn't stop herself from touching him. She laid her hand on his chest, splaying her fingers over his warm, muscled chest, feeling him and the heat radiating from his amulet.

He paused from enjoying the spray of the water and she pulled back, embarrassed.

Moving closer to her, he said, "Touch me again. I have never experienced anything within the spirit realm that can compare to the pleasure you give me."

Marissa hesitated only a moment before the inner fire of her desire burned away the strictures she'd been taught. She opened herself to Navarre—a man who continually gave everything of himself so completely and innocently to her.

She slid her hand to his cheek and brushed her thumb across his full mouth. "Nor I. I've never known anything in my life as wonderful as the pleasure you give me. Touch me, too."

Navarre slipped his hand to her shoulder and tugged on her dress. "I want to touch you flesh to flesh, to feel your body against mine as I saw in your mind."

"So do I," she whispered, unzipping the ruined silk. When

the dress loosened, he urged it down her shoulders and over her breasts and hips. It fell to the tiled floor where she kicked it into a corner, then drew a satisfying deep breath of steamy air. Free. She felt free.

"You're so beautiful," he said. She looked up at him then remembered he didn't see her directly, but through his wolf spirit watching from the doorway. She faced the wolf, letting him see her fully, and Navarre inhaled sharply. Her breath caught on the electric excitement charging the air between them. It was all so strange and magical to be standing naked with him. So many sensations tingled through her—freedom, exposure, decadence, need, desire—that she didn't know what to do. She nervously grabbed the shampoo because showers were for bathing, right?

"Let me help you bathe," she told him. "We'll start at the top and work down. Close your eyes so the soap won't sting them." She had to stand on her tiptoes and stretch to scrub his head. The shower steamed and a woodsy herbal scent permeated the air. That in combination with the warm water was heavenly. "You're so tall I can't reach the top of your head."

"Let me," he said.

She thought he meant to take over washing his hair, and she stepped back, but he planted his hands on each side of her bottom and lifted her up his body. Her breath flew from her lungs as her breasts rubbed up his soapy chest and she felt the full hard length of his arousal before he anchored her sex tight against his stomach. She could feel him, feel his amulet intimately against her. Fire raced along her nerves and exploded in her mind. Her nipples hardened and her hips arched to him, aching for more.

"Can you reach now?" he asked. The tickle of his breath over her nipples made her moan.

She nodded, unable to speak, and began scrubbing his hair, sure that at any moment she would expire from the sweet ache filling her. While his eyes were closed, she bathed his face and neck and shoulders. She'd just finished rinsing the soap from his silky hair when he shifted her a little higher, placed his mouth over her nipple and sucked.

She cried out in shocked pleasure as she grabbed his shoulders, her back bowing into an almost painful arch. She groaned, urging him to give her more as the heat of his mouth and the feel of his tongue branded her. He moved to her other breast, adding more flames to the fire consuming her. She wrapped her legs around his back and pulled him closer, arching her back even more to give him all of her breast. He suckled her until she thought she would scream from her building need—then he suddenly set her back down. She wavered on quivering legs as she blinked up at him—consumed, amazed, and dazed.

"Close your eyes," he said, picking up the shampoo. "I will wash you, too, from top to bottom."

She wanted to protest. Her whole body ached for more pleasure, but he poured shampoo on her head and she didn't have a choice. She shut her eyes and gave herself over to his ministrations. He soaped up her hair, his strong fingers massaging her scalp and cleaning away any of the lingering ugliness of the past few days, making her feel fresh and . . . free.

But he didn't stop there. Shampoo-slick hands and fingers moved over her face, neck, and shoulders. She rinsed her head and opened her eyes when he moved to her back, where his slow caresses sent her pulse speeding faster than she thought her heart could beat. Butterflies fluttered in her stomach when she thought about where he might touch her next. Everything inside her whirled into a dizzying vortex of desire that had her breasts aching and her sex throbbing.

As she glanced over her shoulder toward his wolf spirit, she knew he'd positioned her so that he could see his hands moving slowly down her spine, over her bottom, and—as he knelt on one knee—her legs. She shivered, unable to take any more without touching him back.

Spinning around to face him, she buried her fingers in his hair. He was still on his knee and she leaned down to kiss him, urging him to rise so she could touch him, too. He kissed her hard, a tantalizing meeting of their lips and tongues that left her breathless, but then he didn't follow her lead. Easing her back, he put more shampoo in his hands and, starting at her feet, massaged his way quickly up her legs until he reached the dark curls of her sex. Then he slowly slid his hand between her legs, slipping his soapy fingers back and forth over her aching flesh.

"Navarre!" Clutching his shoulders, she cried out as her muscles quivered weakly and her hips thrust for more.

"You have great pleasure here," he said as he used both his hands and opened the folds of her sex to rub a very sensitive spot. "I will show you how great."

She felt as if she would faint. "I want to touch you, too, but I can't because you keep touching me, and when you touch me . . . *Dios mío,* I cannot do anything else but feel the pleasure you give," she cried.

He laughed. Rising, he splayed his hands over her stomach, inching upward until he cupped her breasts, rubbing the hard points of her nipples with his thumbs. "When I am touching you I cannot think about anything but to keep touching you."

"*Pero* that's not fair," she said, grabbing his wrists, intending to make him stop. Only it felt too good and she pressed her breasts harder into his hands.

Driven to desperation by her own weakness for the pleasure of his touch, she gave up thoughts of exploring his body as well as he'd explored hers and reached for his hard arousal, pressing hotly against her abdomen. She wrapped her hand around his throbbing shaft and slid down until she felt the brush of the thick, dark hair of his groin—then she caressed him again and again.

He suddenly stilled, and groaned deeply, his expression one of surprise. His hips moved, thrusting his arousal in the tight glove of her hand, and she caressed him more, exploring the long, thick length of his sex. His body trembled, and it awed her to know her touch could render this large warrior as weak as his caresses made her feel.

Before she could explore further or even revel in her newly discovered power, he scooped her up and kissed her as he left the shower. He carried her to the bed and laid her down upon the fluffy softness, which made her feel as if she were floating on a cloud.

She reached for him, wanting him to lie beside her, but he shook his head.

"Wait. There is a pleasure I wish to show you," he said, standing over her. His gold eyes glowed in secret anticipation. Then before she could ask him what pleasure, he spread her knees, bent down, and, *Madre de Dios,* put his mouth on her sex!

This had been in that depraved pain book Ysalane had given her and Marissa's heart thundered with fear. She would have pulled back, except Navarre had her legs pinned firmly against the soft mattress. A surrendering sigh of pleasure escaped her as his tongue intimately licked her aching flesh and set her on fire.

He kissed her there and sucked upon her until she was sure she was dying. She couldn't breathe right. Her heart couldn't beat right. Her body couldn't do anything but respond to the firestorm he ignited. Intense sensations consumed every part of her until the burning coil of desire became unbearable.

"Please, Navarre," she cried, reaching for him, needing to feel him everywhere against her, needing an answer to the sweet flames claiming her soul. He looked up and she felt everything inside her melt in the heated passion in his golden gaze. Moving up her body, he brought his lips to hers and kissed her gently.

"Together," he whispered, his deep voice, full of emotion, rumbled through her. "We shall feel the fullness of this ecstasy together."

He kissed her again, his tongue delving into her mouth as his mind penetrated her mind. It didn't matter that he couldn't see her directly with his eyes, he could see into her soul and that was everything. As his spirit wrapped around hers, he slowly pushed his hard arousal against the slick folds of her sex and slipped himself just inside her. His groan of satisfaction took her breath away. Still, she tensed at the strange sensation of being filled inside.

"Is this not right?" He paused, raising up on arms that trembled. His warm amulet dangled between her breasts.

"This is right." She brought her hands up, touched the amulet then caressed his male nipples, finding the hardened peaks upon the dark discs. "I have never done this and it feels different, but also good."

He moved then, easing in a little, then out, and a fiery dart shot straight to her core.

"Yes," he whispered, "I felt that." He repeated the motion again and again until her hips thrust up to meet his and he went deeper inside her. She felt a slight twinge of pain, but that soon gave way to the pleasure again as he moved out then in. The next thrust went deep and sent and an even greater shock of pleasure burning through her.

She moaned, arching her sex up and wrapping her legs around his hips to bring him closer as her need for this new, more fulfilling pathway to shared pleasure opened to her in a firestorm that consumed every fiber of her being. A universe of stars burst before her eyes and her body spasmed wildly in Navarre's arms.

Navarre groaned in response to the vibrating pleasure inside of Marissa, his entire body quivering with the passion burning through him. He couldn't thrust deep enough or fast enough.

His heart slammed against his chest. His groin drove harder and harder against her softness, delving deeper and deeper into her sheathing heat as he felt the propelling rise of her pleasure. Through the eyes of his wolf spirit he saw every move her body made in response to his. He loved how her full breasts rose and fell faster and faster, their hardened points brushing his chest as he plunged into her until her pleasure shuddered through her and shattered his universe.

His body went wild in response as wave after wave of her rapture washed over him. His mind, body, and soul shuddered uncontrollably, propelling him to his own, unbelievable pinnacle of ecstasy.

Chapter Eighteen

"AMAZING," NAVARRE said, lying with Marissa wrapped in his arms. It was frustrating to watch her from the distance of his wolf spirit eyes instead of seeing her as closely as she saw him, but then he did have the added pleasure of watching himself as he touched her and tasted her, which excited him greatly.

Even though he'd just shared an unbelievable heaven with her, something inside him hungered for her again. He cupped his hand over her breast, marveling at how well her fullness filled his hand. Her breasts were fascinating—soft and firm and deliciously pliable—he couldn't stop himself from enjoying the feel of them or from watching them. He brushed his thumb over the hard point there and her hips jerked in response as she groaned.

"Your pleasure and your body are amazing." He shifted so that he could caress both her breasts at the same time and she moaned softly, her back arching in response. "Why do mortals not do just this all of the time?" he asked.

"*Dios,* because maybe they would go insane from too much pleasure? You have already stolen my mind once and now you are running away with it again." She arched, thrusting her breasts toward him.

"I do not think there can be too much pleasure," he murmured. Bending down, he brushed Marissa's mouth with his, dueled with her tongue, and then moved to suck on her breast. He couldn't get enough. His groin was already hardening, wanting to delve into her hot sheath again. Suckling her breasts, one after the other, he slid his hand down to find the hard point of pleasure hiding in the heated, wet folds of her feminine flesh. It only took two strokes to find the nub and center his caresses on it.

Marissa cried out and arched her back, lifting her hips, and he remembered how the man he'd seen pleasuring the woman had put small white clouds beneath her hips. He wondered if this would bring Marissa even more pleasure. Sitting up, he gathered several white clouds.

"Lift your hips again."

"What?" Marissa blinked at him, looking dazed.

On his knees, he moved between her legs as he'd seen the man do to the woman. Then sliding his arm beneath Marissa, he urged her back up until she had to bend her knees and arch herself to him. He placed three clouds beneath her and sat back on his heels, satisfied with the result. Her secrets were open to him and positioned just right for him to slide inside her, and he did.

"This feels strange." She gasped and fisted her hands in the fluffy material beneath her.

"This feels perfect," he said. With his weight upon his knees, he found he could caress her breasts and the secret hard point of pleasure as he thrust into her. She cried out in awe as he did so, and he caressed her relentlessly as her passions unleashed in a flash flood of mounting pleasure that had her crying his name out again and again as she thrashed her head from side to side. He delved into her body and into her mind again, going deeper than ever before. This time the soul-consuming pleasure overcame them both at the same instant, melding their entire beings into one soaring entity upon an incomparable peak of rapture that forever bonded him to her.

On the last wave of pleasure shuddering through him, Navarre heard the sound of approaching engines and felt an encroaching darkness descending upon the beautiful serenity of the area. Pulling Marissa to him, he rolled to his side, slipping from her pleasuring heat with regret. Then he stood and scooped her into his arms.

"We must go. I fear Herrera is coming. I don't know how he found us, but I feel his presence." He moved to the door.

"The clothes," she whispered. "Please. They are on the chair."

Now that her body was fully known to him, he thought clothes were unimportant, but he could tell by her voice that they were essential to her. He swung around and went to the chair, leaning down for her to grab them. Then he ran through the building and out into the moonlight. The full impact of Herrera's malice hit him, and he realized the Vladarian Vampire was closer than he thought. Men's shouts filled the air.

"Find everyone and bring them to me. Marissa will not escape."

It was Herrera.

"*Dios nos ayude,* God help us," Marissa said. "Will he hurt the people because of us?"

"I will not allow him to." Anger surged through him as he ran into the jungle with Marissa, his wolf spirit guiding the way. A hundred feet in, he set her down. "You must lead me and I will send my wolf spirit back to help the others."

"*Sí,*" she said.

His wolf spirit ran back to the Green Water Jungle Resort, leaving him blind with Marissa in the darkness of the jungle. In his mind's eye he saw the blur of trees and the distant lights of the resort.

Marissa pressed clothing into his hand. "Hold these as I dress and then I will help you. What is happening at the resort?" she asked.

Navarre focused on his wolf spirit, which ran immediately for the building that he'd seen the man and woman in before. Navarre told Marissa what he saw through the eyes of the wolf as she dressed and helped him put on clothes.

The people were being forced at gunpoint from the buildings. The woman he'd seen before was crying and holding her arm as if it hurt. The man with her was stumbling, bleeding from a cut to his head. In the area near the large center building there were more people being held at gunpoint by many guards. Herrera was there, accompanied by another vampire.

Herrera yelled at the man. "Tell me where the wolfman and the woman are and maybe I will let you live. That is importante *to you and your guests, no?"*

The other vampire stepped up, his demeanor quiet and genteel. "There is no need to threaten these people, Herrera. It is a very simple matter. We will search the place. If we find no evidence of Marissa and her lover, then we will allow them to live. If we do find signs of their presence, then we will extract information from them one at a time beginning with the women until we have Marissa."

"Sheik Rashad bin Samir Al Sabah, we believe we have found evidence. Bloody clothes and a shower left running, but the water is very cold as if it has been running for some time," said an armed guard after exiting the empty cottage where Navarre had been with Marissa.

"Impossible, that cottage is empty. I have no guests staying there," said the man Herrera had been threatening.

Herrera and the vampire hurried to the cottage.

The moment they disappeared inside, the wolf spirit attacked the remaining guards. Running at them, fangs gnashing, it jumped for their throats. The wolf spirit passed right through them, but that seemed to frighten them even more. They yelled and shouted and began shooting at the wolf spirit.

The man whom Navarre had seen before grabbed one of the guard's guns. "Everybody run," the man yelled, shooting at the guards before he wrapped his arm around the woman and ran for the jungle. That seemed to galvanize the others. They ran, too. More guards ran up and raised their guns at the fleeing people, but the wolf spirit attacked again and again, chasing each and every guard. Herrera came running out and the wolf spirit turned for him. Herrera screamed and ran.

"Navarre," Marissa said, touching his arm. "They will search

this area heavily for us. We need to hinder Herrera's and Samir's men from following. They must have arrived in cars, because I heard no helicopters. Maybe we can break the cars or steal the keys or something, but we have to do it fast."

Navarre sniffed the air. "The engine smell is in that direction."

Marissa bit back a groan. That direction took them practically back the way they had come, right into Herrera's reach. She pulled up the décolletage of the shirt she'd borrowed, slightly uncomfortable with how much of her breasts the scoop-necked shirt exposed. At least the pants were comfortable. Not too tight or loose. She would have to cut Navarre's pants into shorts, but the drawstring waist fit him well. She took his hand and swallowed the lump of fear rising in her throat.

Both Herrera and Samir were now after her and she was walking right toward them. She knew that making it harder for the vampires to follow her was the smart thing to do, but the urge to run and keep running made every step painful.

When they reached the road, she pulled back into the shadows. A man and a woman were already there.

"Seth, why do you think the men are after the woman and what is a wolfman?"

"Drug wars. In this part of the world it always boils down to that. 'Wolfman' must be a code name for a drug lord, like El Diablo."

"Where did you learn how to do all of this gun stuff and blowing up cars?" the woman asked.

"Sugar, if I told you, then someone would kill us both. So don't ask. Just get in the Hummer and be ready to roll. Once I set the rags on fire, the shit will blow in less than sixty seconds."

The woman got in the Hummer and the man, who carried a machine gun, went to another Hummer and a large open-bed truck. He lit white rags stuffed in the gas tanks of each, then ran for the Hummer.

He was just driving away when the truck and the remaining Hummer exploded into a ball of fire. A blistering wall of heat hit Marissa, knocking her off her feet. *Madre de Dios!* What happened?

"Navarre?" she cried, pushing herself up from the ground and searching the shadows. "Where are you? Are you hurt?"

She heard him groan from behind her and rolled to her feet. He was sitting up holding his head in his hands.

"*Dios,* I am so sorry. I knew the man was going to set the vehicles on fire, *pero* I didn't know the explosion would reach us. Where are you hurt?"

"My head." He looked up, blinking at her. She could see him in the bright light of the fire. He held his hand up in front of his eyes. "My eyes hurt and my head burns inside."

From the direction of the resort, she heard the sound of shouting. Her heart sank with dread. She and Navarre were going to be captured and it would be all her fault.

"Herrera and Samir and their men are coming. Can you rise? Can you walk?" She caught Navarre's arm, urging him to get up.

"I am a warrior. It will take more than that to render me incapable," he muttered, gaining his feet and turning his face away from the fire.

At that moment his wolf spirit appeared. She took Navarre's hand in hers and tugged him deeper into the jungle.

"We must hurry. We have to reach Rafe and Father Dom and get as far from this area as possible. Herrera and Samir will slash and burn everything for miles trying to find us. I worry about the man and the woman who just escaped. Herrera may mistake them for us." Navarre followed her lead, rushing into the darkness with the wolf spirit running ahead.

"I would not worry," Navarre said after a moment. "I think the man will do well. He was knowledgeable in fighting. What did he do to cause the explosion?"

"Put a rag in the fuel tank and set it on fire. Gas makes the engines work and it is extremely flammable."

The sounds of guards and machine guns shooting grew louder, making Marissa wonder if they were now so spooked from the wolf spirit and the explosion they were randomly shooting at anything.

"A good thing to know," Navarre said, then scooped her off her feet. She protested and he shook his head. "We will move faster this way and it pleasures me to hold you."

"But your head?"

"Holding you eases me, just as touching you and tasting you gives me great pleasure." He bent his head and kissed her thoroughly and she realized that since his wolf spirit was seeing for him, he could flee and kiss her at the same time. Her slippers were back in the cottage. Her feet were already stinging from the terrain. She settled into his embrace with a sigh as her heart swelled with emotion for him, a connection that began when he'd entered her dreams and blossomed to fulfillment when he'd joined his body with hers. This gentle warrior, this fierce shapeshifter, had claimed her heart. No matter what the church, the law, or Father Dom said, she and Navarre were one.

Navarre jerked his head up and swung around as if to shield her. "I feel your anger, brother of Marissa. Show yourself."

"Rafe? Rafe is here?" Marissa urged Navarre to set her down and he did.

Rafael stepped from the shadows with the machine gun pointed at Navarre. "I could not cower in safety with you in the jungle and that crazed jaguar about. I heard the shots and the explosion and ran this way. And what do I find? You making love to this man! Father Dom is right. The shapeshifter is a seducer and now he has ruined your honor, Marissa. He must pay for this sin with his life. As your brother it is my duty to take care of you. Go back to Father Dom, Marissa, and I will see this done."

• • •

"They were here! They were right here, and your incompetent men allowed them to escape," Samir said as he paced the room.

Herrera glared at Marissa's virgin blood staining the bed in front of him, raging that he'd been cheated of that treat. He could smell her here—and him! That wolf creature with whom she'd committed the abomination. His only thread of sanity was that Samir saw the evidence of Marissa's adultery. Herrera wanted to rub Samir's face in it while he killed the bastard. It would seem they'd reversed roles. Samir was agitated and Herrera felt calmer than ever.

"If you recall, Samir, I wanted to sneak up to the place, surround it, and take it by storm, but you were in too big a hurry for that."

Samir waved his hand like a god dismissing a fly. "No excuses. Incompetence is incompetence. We need more men and we need them immediately. Using demons won't work as it will soon be daylight. I want an army of men now! Then your whore can show us again where Marissa is hiding with her lover. They'll not escape the next time."

"An army on such short notice will cost you billions, but justice is worth any price, *sí*, Samir?" Herrera asked slowly, the gears in his mind spinning rapidly through a number of scenarios. Samir was a problem and needed to be eliminated, but still, he had money and what appeared to be legal documentation to Marissa's billions. For Herrera to get his hands on both Samir and Marissa's money, he had to bide his time and not kill the man just yet. Herrera also had to wait until after they met with the rest of the SINCO Vladarians to plot their takeover of the Order from Cinatas.

But . . . there was one man Herrera could kill with this fortunate opportunity. General Menendez. The man was bitter about losing the last election and the letter on the general's desk addressed to *el presidente* was a clear indication of Menendez's future goal. The bastard was plotting to assassinate him after the election and take over so he could finally rule. That was why he wouldn't reveal his other supporter.

Herrera was sure Menendez's army could be bought for the right price. And Samir had the money to make the price right. The possibilities of taking over Menendez's army were . . . intriguing.

Complex and cunning, a plot worthy of his extraordinary mind, Herrera thought and smiled with satisfaction. "It will cost you a lot but I think I know of a nearby army that can be bought. But we will have to act quickly. The general who runs this army is only away until morning and if we wish to steal it from him, we must to do so before then."

"Where?" asked Samir. "It is worth any price."

Cringing, Herrera held out his hand. "I've been to the camp. I will take you there through the spirit barrier."

Samir hesitated. "Betray me, Herrera, and you'll spend eternity wishing you weren't among the undead."

"Have faith, Samir. We both have much to gain, no? *Pero* let me tell you about my plans for Guatemala and beyond. Ruling SINCO isn't my ultimate goal, but just a means to my great end. If you buy me an army"—Herrera shrugged—"then I have no need of Marissa or SINCO, true? Did you know that the famous conquistador Hernan Cortes is my ancestor?"

Pasting a smile on his face, Herrera took Samir through the spirit barrier, landing them in General Menendez's camp—and into the midst of a drunken orgy. It would seem when the General was away his men liked to play dirty—a good sign. Herrera would keep their appetites in mind and feed them on a regular basis. He hadn't considered he could control an army of men by their dicks.

He located the man in charge, slaving away between inviting legs. "Colonel Estrada! General Menendez would be outraged by this lack of discipline in his absence, no? As future *presidente* of Guatemala, how can I have any confidence that this drunken army will be of any use to my regime!"

Colonel Estrada looked up from his whore.

"You call this an army?" Samir sneered. "This is what my money will buy me? You waste my time, Herrera!"

Colonel Estrada leaped to his feet, pulling up his pants and saluting.

Herrera smiled. He had Estrada between a rock and a hard place and would glean even more money from the deal than he first anticipated. "*Cinco minutos,* Samir. I promise you will not be disappointed."

Herrara pulled Estrada aside and the deal was made. All of his life, Herrera had known big money could move mountains. He just didn't know how quickly. It took a little longer than five minutes, but in short order five hundred trained and armed men were at his disposal, and more could be called upon if needed.

The hunt was on.

The wolfman, Marissa, and now Menendez himself were all on the agenda.

All that they lacked for the final coup was Ysalane's magic.

Chapter Nineteen

MARISSA MARCHED angrily over to Rafael, shoved the muzzle of the machine gun up, and planted her finger in the middle of her brother's chest. "*Dios,* I think Herrera must have sickened your mind more than he tortured your body." Rafael winced with deep pain, but she did not ease her anger. "How dare you *again* threaten to murder someone as noble and selfless as Navarre! He has given me nothing but goodness, which is more than anyone has ever given to me! Do not speak to me of false honor! Right now we must hurry and escape from here. Herrera and Samir, another evil vampire who wishes to have Tío Luis's putrid fortune, are not far away and they know we are nearby.

Rafael glared at her then at Navarre, but he lowered the machine gun. "This is not over," he said and turned around.

Navarre stepped forward and put his hand on Rafael's shoulder. "You will tell me of Marissa's honor and how I have harmed her."

More shooting echoed in the jungle not far away and Marissa took the machine gun from her brother. "If Herrera or Samir catch me, *then* I will truly have no honor. I am leaving immediately. You two may stay here or come with me and Father Dom, *pero* I do not want to hear another word about it now!" She marched off, thankful to hear both Navarre and Rafael follow.

When Marissa drew near the truck, she heard Father Dom talking and it wasn't to himself or in prayer. She stepped from the jungle, mouth agape in shock. "You! You have a phone!"

Father Dom let out a string of saints' names then cursed himself. "I will call you later, *amiga.*" He hung up the phone. "Marissa, child. You must listen. I am on your side. On the good side."

"You have a *teléfono* and you did not tell us? What possible reason can there be for that?"

"It is very complicated, *pero* I can explain."

Rafael stepped to Marissa's side and took the machine gun back. He pointed it at Father Dom. "Explain."

"I am trying to save her from Herrera, but his plans are much greater than recapturing your sister. He does not wish to be just *el presidente* of Guatemala. He wants to become *el dictador* and take over everything. He must be destroyed."

"Dios." Marissa had no doubt that Father Dom was telling the truth about that, at least. "We've no time to talk about this. We must leave here now. We are lucky Herrera's vehicles were destroyed or it would already be too late. Give me the phone. I will keep it until we can talk about this."

Father Don hesitated for a moment then handed the phone over. "The batteries are low, so it would be best to turn it off until it is needed."

Marissa looked at the phone and couldn't tell exactly which button was for what. "Turn it off, then."

Father Dom did so and sighed. "You have to believe me, I have only wanted to help."

"We will see. For now, we must leave." She put the phone in the pocket of her borrowed pants.

"I will drive," said Father Dom. "I can get us away from here quickly and quietly."

"I say we leave him here," said Rafael. "How can we trust him?"

"Taking over as dictator would be something Herrera would do," Marissa said. "He had a man at his house by the name of General Menendez and I think that is exactly what they spoke of doing after the election. Besides, I would not leave my worst enemy for Herrera. Also, do you know how to drive, Rafael?" Marissa knew her brother, like her, had not had the opportunity to learn such simple things.

Rafael shrugged. "It cannot be difficult. I am sure that I can."

"The priest goes and he drives," said Navarre in a tone of voice that wouldn't brook any argument. "And if he does anything to harm you or your brother, Marissa, he will meet the God he serves before his next heartbeat."

The back of the truck was already closed and the supplies put away. They all climbed into the cab. Father Dom drove with Rafael next to him. Marissa sat squashed between her brother and Navarre. She supposed that instead of all cramming together in the front, one of them could have sat in the backseat with Navarre's wolf spirit for company. But Navarre was too big for the cramped space and Marissa wanted to be next to Navarre in case she needed to protect him from Rafael or Father Dom. And Rafael was keeping an eye on every single move that Father Dom made. So it was a wary and weary group that drove off into the moonlight. Dawn would soon arrive and they needed to be as far away as possible.

For once, luck or fortune was on their side and they didn't encounter anyone. As soon as they were at a safer distance, Marissa pulled out the phone, hoping that she could call Sheriff Sam. Following Father Dom's instructions, she turned on the phone and found there was no signal in this area. She turned the phone off again and focused on their escape, quickly realizing that Father Dom wasn't making last-minute decisions and taking random turns as he had before.

"*You* know where we are, don't you?" she accused.

He sighed. "Yes, that was part of what my phone call was about, to find if we were where I thought. I had my suspicions about the river we were next to and wanted to be sure. We are in Guatemala, close to the Belizean border. I have some friends, a couple that has a mission and church not far from here. They will hide us today and help us get to Belize tomorrow night."

"How do we know we can trust them?"

"Menendez killed their son and daughter. Believe me, they will do anything to stop the General and Herrera from taking over their beloved country."

Marissa had no doubt that when it came to his country the old priest would help, but what about when it came to facing vampires? Wherever they ended up, she had to make sure nothing and no one would hurt Navarre.

She slipped her hand into his and he tightened his hold. "Do not worry. All will be well."

As much as she wanted to believe in his reassurance, there had never been an instance in her life that anything had truly been all right for any length of time. So while she believed in Navarre with her whole heart, she didn't hold any hope that fortune would shine their way. If they survived this, it would be because they fought every step of the way.

Cinatas walked the length of the throne room, sure Valois had deliberately had the butler escort him here to wait—fifteen minutes and counting.

Cinatas's fangs were on edge and his hands were clenched in envy. Not only because king after king lay in Valois's family history, but also because Cinatas now knew for certain that Valois was up to something very big. The numerous Tsaras hovering about the castle's spires spelled serious trouble and a close tie to Heldon. The strong scent of many with Elan blood wafting in the salty breeze told Cinatas Valois had been collecting his own supply of Elan blood for some time and was not dependent on Cinatas for transfusions.

During his twenty-four-hour recuperation, Cintatas reflected over his failure to eliminate Erin Morgan and her cohorts with growing rage. He'd had the perfect coronation ceremony planned. Erin's beheading and the drinking of her blood. His marriage to an innocent angel whom he could shape to his will. An orgy of demons destroying the others while the Blood Hunters fruitlessly tried to save a town that was already supposed to be dead. But the angel's mother had destroyed it all with her wall of white fire and the help of the Blood Hunters.

Cinatas could not afford to go up against her again and fail. Therefore he had to make sure he was powerful enough to squash them the next time. That meant not only did he have to gain as much power as he could from every source possible, including multiple desecrations of the world's most holy sites, but he had to get his own house in order. Every Vladarian not one hundred percent working for Cinatas had to go, and Cinatas had to collect all of their assets for himself. Samir and Herrera were first on his list, since they'd blatantly left the planned coronation ceremony, and SINCO would be the first golden pot Cinatas would acquire.

He'd chosen his third victim well, too. All signs pointed to the fact that Valois was working against Cinatas. Most likely all of the Royals were in on the plot, which meant they, too, would have to go the way of the oil-rich Vladarians.

Valois's castle, hidden on a tributary off the Solent in coastal England, was black from the ground to its deadly spires. Even the forest surrounding it was black. Cinatas hated black but he could visit the place on occasion. The castle didn't compare to Zion in size. Zion was much bigger, but Zion *didn't* have a throne room.

And Cinatas didn't have kings in his ancestry. Amid the black marble and gold accents dominating the décor, there were tapestries of elaborate coronations of different kings, and one of a family tree going from William of Normandy through his son Henry and line after line of monarchs leading directly to Valois.

It was nauseatingly pompous. It was infuriatingly daunting. It made Cinatas feel every inch the poor, discounted Puerto Rican boy of a voodoo priestess. His new face could do little to fix that but changing a few stitches on the tapestry could re-place Victor Amadeus Valois with Dr. Anthony Cinatas with very little trouble. Who would dare to deny him?

Yes, an occasional night in a black castle to see his name cast among histrory's great kings would be worth it.

"Well, this is an unexpected and honored surprise," Valois said, walking down the marble steps and passing beneath the five-tiered gold chandelier. The ceiling thirty feet above sported scenes of naked Greek gods in various states of revelry and bat-tle. Zeus was clearly recognizable as the largest, most powerful, and best endowed. His features were also very familiar—Val-ois's face adorned the body of the god. That would have to change as well.

Valois continued with a sneering smile. "I don't believe Pathos ever bothered to visit anyone of the Order. We always had to come to him."

Cinatas ground his fangs. The only reason he was here was to get a feel for what he stood to gain when he took Valois out of the game. Though couched as a compliment, the demeaning implications of the Valdarian's remark were clear.

Before turning to face Valois, Cinatas pasted on an admiring smile and pushed back the hood of his cloak. "Nice *little* castle you have."

"Who in the bloody hell are you?" Valois drew his dagger from its sheath, fangs snarling.

Cinatas laughed, lovingly caressing his own cheek. "Amaz-ing what a little bit of surgery can do these days. You should try it. I would think that you'd tire of looking at the same face these many centuries."

Valois narrowed his eyes then replaced his dagger and shrugged. "Why mess with perfection? It would be like burning these tapestries of my ancestral kings and putting up pictures of insignificant rock stars."

Electricity crackled over Cinatas's hands and he smiled

harder. "Life is full of the unexpected, which brings me to the reason for my visit. What progress have you made in locating Herrera and Samir?"

"Why don't we step into my formal study while I explain? I'll call for refreshments. Do you prefer tea, wine, or something stronger?"

"Nothing, unless of course you happened to have something from Chateau Petrus, in which case any vintage would do."

"Excellent choice." Valois walked over to a gold phone on a carved black desk and pushed a button. "Rothschild, remember that imperial of Petrus I bought last year? Bring me a bottle . . . Yes, I know it's not quite sixty years yet, but I'm making an exception for a special guest." Valois hung up the phone. "My general rule of thumb is a wine isn't drinkable until it has passed the sixty-year mark. This Petrus vintage lacks one year from that, but the vineyard produces such perfect wines, I can always break my rule in their case."

Cinatas's mouth watered even as his gut churned. He'd tried several times, but hadn't been able to get his hands on any Petrus older than 1961. That Valois had an imperial of it rankled sourly. How Cinatas would have loved to turn to Valois at this moment and say, "Thank you for the compliment. I own Petrus." But because of Nyros's incompetence, Cinatas couldn't call the vineyard his yet. It was just one more little torture Nyros's cowardly demon ass would suffer just as soon as Cinatas desecrated enough churches to go into hell and take on Heldon.

"Not to rush you, but you were about to tell me something about Herrera and Samir," Cinatas reminded Valois.

Valois smiled with satisfaction. "I've no need to search all over the jungle for them. I've the perfect place to catch them both in the act of treason, along with all of the oil-rich Vladarians. They're having a meeting at Samir's palace in Kassim, midnight the day after tomorrow. We can swoop in and eliminate them all. I've arranged factions not only from the Royal

Vladarians but from the Russians and the Europeans as well. They'll be adequate witnesses to the rest of the Vladarian Order as to why it was essential for us to take over SINCO."

Cinatas barely curbed the scream raging in his throat. That was exactly what he didn't want. He had instructed Valois to use only the Royals to eliminate the oil-rich Vladarians. The point, besides annihilating Samir and Herrera for skipping out of Cinatas's failed coronation ceremony, was to generate enough strife between the Royals and the other factions so that once the SINCO Valdarians were gone, he could then get the other factions to take out the Royals.

"And the Vasquez woman?" Cinatas asked. It wouldn't do for her controlling shares of SINCO to end up in anyone else's hands but his.

"Nothing yet," Valois said tightly. "I will let you know as soon as I have word."

"Oh, Vickie boy," a lilting voice called. "Come out, come out, wherever you are. Sabrina is a bored witch and wants to play. You left me quite unsatisfied with the lesson and I'll have to tell on you."

A redheaded woman popped her head into the study. She had sky-blue eyes that twinkled with mischief and a bewitching smile that had an evil little twist to its corners. An almost visble aura of power surrounded her.

"My, what handsome devil do you have with you?" she said, looking at Cinatas with interest, from head to foot.

"You've no idea," Cinatas said, at first a little shocked. He'd never garnered the interest of women before, but with his new face, he supposed he would have to get used to it. He smiled at her then turned to Valois. "Vickie boy, do you think Sabrina can join us for wine?"

Valois looked as if he were about to explode and Cinatas relaxed for the first time since walking into Valois's dark castle. The visit was turning out to be more than just slightly interesting. It would seem that Sabrina was also an Elan. The sweet scent of her blood made Cinatas's fangs throb.

"By Logos!" Navarre cried out as white pain shot through his eyes. He sat up, trying to shield himself from the brightness and the burning sensation pounding through his head. He covered his eyes with his hands, pressing his palms against his eyelids to ease the sharpness of the ache.

"What is wrong?" Marissa set her hand on his shoulder. "This is from last night and the explosion. I caused you to hurt yourself."

"No. I do not know what is causing this increase in the pain. It must now be morning. I cannot bring forth my wolf spirit."

"*Sí*, the sun has just arrived. I was at the window watching it rise like a huge bright ball and this beam shot through the window and crossed the room and . . . Navarre!" Marissa grabbed both of his shoulders this time. "It's the light. The light is causing your eyes to hurt! Last night it was the brightness of the fire and now this morning it is the sun. You may be getting some of your vision back."

He eased his hands from his eyes and the pain came back, but he also realized that a sense of whiteness came with it, instead of the total darkness that he remembered from before. "I think I can sense light but that is all and it is painful." He covered his eyes back up.

This would not work. How could he hope to protect Marissa like this? It was worse than being completely in the dark. "I must stop the light from hurting them."

"I think these things take time, but I am very much encouraged that you can sense the light. Wait here, I have something that will help."

Navarre reached for her arm. "No. Don't go until you give me a picture of where we are and where you are going. I need to know that I can reach you quickly." They had arrived in the dark hours of the morning and the priest had asked Navarre not to have the wolf spirit around yet. It would only frighten Señor and Señora Castillo, the old man and his wife at the mission. Though he hadn't been able to see the couple, Navarre had been able to quickly tell they were kind and generous. They'd fed them Guatemalan sweet cakes and dragonfruit, which weren't Snickers and Twinkies, but close.

"We are sleeping on pallets on the floor of a very simple church. Father Dom and Rafael haven't awakened yet. Can you see it in my mind?" She handed him his cane.

"Yes." Navarre focused his thoughts and saw the one-room building with its many windows, wooden chairs, and at the very front an altar with a single cross hung above it. The priest and Marissa's brother lay on the floor near the altar between Navarre on his pallet and Marissa's empty pallet. Rafael had declared this arrangement necessary for Marissa's honor. Navarre was going to have to find out exactly what Rafael meant by her honor and how Navarre could have possibly harmed it.

"I am going to get the dark red cloth from the altar. By putting that over your eyes, I think we can ease some of your pain."

Navarre nodded, feeling uncomfortable that he had to too often rely on Marissa's help in order to take care of simple matters. By Logos, this was not the way of a warrior. If he'd had a choice he would have rather died nobly in battle than to suffer this . . .

Speak the truth! his heart demanded. *Forget your pride and speak the truth. You would suffer anything to be with her and to share the pleasures of the flesh with her. You would also suffer anything to see her face with your own eyes while sharing that pleasure with her.*

"Here," Marissa said.

He felt a cool soft cloth slide over his hands and he moved them away, letting her cover his eyes. Then she tied it behind his head, anchoring the cloth in place. The darkness and the pressure it provided eased his discomfort.

He sighed. "Thank you." With that done, he could now turn his mind to more important matters. "Did you feel me in your dreams last—"

"Shh." She set her finger over his lips and he couldn't resist tasting it with his tongue. *"Dios,"* she whispered. "Come with me."

She led him across the room and down some steps. He could feel the warmth of the sun on his skin and the freshness of the air, but also sense a mystic feeling of ancient worship. They were now outside of the building. "Show me what it looks like."

"It is like being on top of the world," she said.

Looking into her mind, he saw a wide, flat mountaintop with several buildings on one end. A large area of brightly colored flowers and white stone figures. Across a stretch of bright green grass there were ruins half covered with vines. The stairs seemed as if they were climbing their way right into heaven. "It is very beautiful. Like you. I wish you could show me yourself as clearly as that."

She laughed. "I'm afraid you would be disappointed, but if we find a mirror I can do that."

"A mirror?"

"It is a glass that reflects one's image in it. I could look into it and show you exactly what I look like."

"Then we will have to find a mirror soon for I cannot wait to see you so closely. I want to see all of you that way. I see you through the eyes of the wolf spirit but it sometimes feels too distant. Did you not feel me in your mind last night?"

"I felt you everywhere," she whispered. "In my mind. In my heart. On my body. Inside me. It felt as if you were making love to me all over again. I could barely sleep because of what you made me feel. But *Dios,* you cannot do that in there."

"In where?"

"In the church. It is not proper."

He reached for her and pulled her into his arms. "We are not in the church now," he said softly, and then kissed her the way he had been wanting to kiss her since Herrera had so abruptly appeared at the resort last night. She moaned.

"Remember for me, Marissa. Picture in your mind me pleasuring you last night. Let me see your memory."

"*Dios,*" she whispered as if afraid to, but the images came to him. Of him touching her breasts. Of him tasting her secret flesh. Of him thrusting into her.

His groin burned and he bent to kiss her again.

She spoke as he brushed his mouth over her lips again and again. "We cannot . . . do this . . . now. Tell . . . me . . . about . . . your . . . world—"

"You cannot even honor her on sacred ground!" Marissa's brother cried, from just a short distance away. Navarre heard him coming at him and felt the man's anger. Navarre swung Marissa behind him just as a fist slammed into his chin.

Instincts took over and Navarre grabbed the fist, twisting Rafael's arm until the man turned from the pain. Then Navarre brought his other arm around Rafael's neck. "Before I face your anger, you must explain how I have hurt Marissa's honor. I would never do anything to harm her."

"You use her like a *puta.*"

"No, Rafael. No!" Marissa cried.

Navarre heard the pain in Marissa's voice and hated Rafael's tone. "Explain what you mean, for the only one hurting your sister right now is you and it is making me very angry!"

"You are making love to her and you are not her husband. You are not married to her. This shames her. It is a sin and takes away her honor."

"Then there is no need to be angry. I will be her husband. I will become married to her."

"No, Rafael. Don't," Marissa cried, pulling on Navarre's arm.

She was in even more pain than before. Navarre released Rafael and reached for Marissa.

"You can't marry her because she is already married!" Rafael shouted. "Herrera is her husband!"

Navarre felt everything within him freeze then wrench as if torn apart. "What is this marry, then? Explain this to me."

"Go away, Rafael," Marissa cried. "You are not my brother if you can be so cruel."

"I speak only the truth to protect you from further harm. You should have told the shapeshifter the truth."

"Marissa?" Navarre turned to her.

"To marry someone is to bind yourself to that person forever through your vows. To become one with that person and share your life with them."

Pain and anger centered itself in Navarre's stomach. "You bound yourself to Herrera in this way?" He couldn't believe it.

"I didn't have a choice," she cried. "Herrera was torturing Rafael in the dungeon and would have tortured him even more if I had not cooperated. It was the night we escaped. Father Dom married me to Herrera, but I did not give my vow. I could not speak, I was so sickened. Herrera spoke for me."

"Wait!" Navarre shouted, his heart thundering with rage. "Herrera forced this upon you and Father Dom helped him?"

"Yes, but he had no choice. You don't understand what Herrera does to people to make them do his will. I am sorry. *Madre de Dios,* I am sorry, but I will see this ended. As soon as I can. I will annul the marriage."

"Hush." Navarre pulled Marissa into his arms. "I am not angry with you. I am angry at the priest. I may not protect you from dangers I cannot see, but I can guard your heart from such wrongs. We will see this done now. Come with me." Navarre drew Marissa with him, back to the church. He knew the general direction, but stumbled a little with his cane until Marissa took the lead.

"There is nothing Father Dom can do," she said. "I must seek this annulment through the courts and then through those who have the authority within the church."

"Priest!" Navarre shouted as he reached the last of the steps and pushed open the door. "Priest! You're the evil here!"

"You're the shapeshifter!"

"Put the gun down, Father Dom!" Marissa yelled, thrusting herself in front of Navarre. "Would you shoot an unarmed blind man in the house of God?"

Gun or no gun, Navarre set Marissa aside. "It would be better to ask him how he can be a servant of Logos and marry you against your will to Herrera! That is the true abomination here. YOU will undo this wrong you have done to Marissa immediately or you will be facing Logos before you can draw another breath! And do not doubt that I know of what I speak." By the sheer force of his anger Navarre sent to the priest's mind an image of Logos and all of his burning, fiery glory that created life and warmed the universes.

"Stop!" the priest cried out in pain.

Marissa wanted to smack and kiss Navarre at the same time. The fool was so outraged on her behalf that he didn't care what danger he put himself in. At one time she would have never believed Father Dom would shoot Navarre, but then she wouldn't have believed he had a phone and kept it secret, either. They had yet to hear his explanation for that. Everything had been put on hold last night to escape. Then when they'd arrived and Señor and Señora Castillo had opened their home, it had not been the right time to discuss Father Dom's role in the situation with Herrera. Marissa did know for certain that the priest was against Herrera, and that had to count for something.

Marissa moved in front of Navarre again and glared at Father Dom, who looked dazed but still had the gun pointed at Navarre. "Navarre is only trying to protect me. *Por favor,* just tell him what happened and how this can be fixed later, *pero* not now."

Father Dom lowered the gun and sighed heavily. "I didn't do it, child."

"What?" Marissa felt her heart thump and her lips go numb with shock.

"I did not marry you to Herrera. I performed a burial ceremony in Latin. All that Herrera vowed to do was to give all of his wealth to the poor. And even if I had married you to him, the very fact that you didn't consent to it would have been grounds for annulment."

"If you did not marry me to him then why did you say you had? *Dios!*" She scrubbed her face with her hands, attempting to bring back feeling, since as all the blood had drained from her head. "Do you not know the anguish my heart has been in?"

"We cannot trust him," Rafael said from the back of the church. "First he lies about the *teléfono* and then about the marriage."

"I lied about the phone to protect Guatemala and I lied about the marriage to protect Marissa from the shapeshifter. And it would seem to my wizened eyes that her heart cannot have been too anguished for she has given it to him after all." Father Dom laid down the machine gun and went to Navarre. "Shapeshifter, was that truly God that I just saw?"

"Logos, as I know him," said Navarre.

Marissa watched in amazement as Father Dom fell to his knees. "I am forever in your debt."

"Rise, priest. You serve Logos, not me, but I will ask that you restore Marissa's honor and marry her to me. I cannot vow forever, but for what time I have remaining on the mortal ground, I would be her husband."

"And what if I forbid her to marry a shapeshifter?" Rafael demanded, glaring at Navarre. "You just did something strange to Father Dom's mind. How do I know you haven't done the same to Marissa's?"

Marissa felt the world whirl crazily and she reached out for Navarre. What did Navarre mean, *what time he had left*?

Chapter Twenty

AFTER A night of gnawing frustration, everything went to hell in a handbasket in less than three minutes. Nick had been prepared for action and sitting on go, too, and it still went down that way.

Menendez's helo left El Diablo Sinclair's compound, and Sinclair gathered his army of men and left in a hurry. So Jared put tracers on two of Sinclair's Hummers. Then Sam called. The sheriff of Twilight, Tennessee, was not happy.

Nick hadn't called Sam about finding Reed alive last night, nor had he returned Sam's numerous calls. Nick just couldn't bring himself to do it. After Bond had dropped her bomb about contacting the military regarding Reed Sinclair's activities, Nick had left her and walked for hours before diving into his bed in a stupor. The more he thought about it all, the more screwed up he became. He pressed the phone harder to his ear in order to hear Sam over the engine noises around the heliport. He paced alongside the metal building that housed supplies, a small store, and a restroom. Aragon and Annette were already on board the helo with the tracking equipment. He was just waiting for Jaymes and Stefanie to come out.

"Three hours tops," Sam said. "I'll be there. Once I murder you for *not* calling me, we'll figure out what in the hell is going on with your father."

"What's to figure out? He's a drug lord living in hog heaven, even has Menendez as a houseguest, so you might want to call that anonymous CIA contact and ask them what they know about Sinclair."

"I've already put in several calls," Sam said. "But I'm not buying this deal. I *know* Reed Sinclair. There's a reason. There's a damn good reason for what he's done."

"Not for me," Nick said. "There's no reason good enough and you know it."

Sam cursed. "I'll call when I hit Belize. Grayson is coming, too."

"What about Emerald and Megan? You can't leave them there. Twilight is too high-profile on the damned's radar screen."

"They're coming, too."

"Now that's real smart. You're going to put them in danger to go find out why a drug lord abandoned his kid and played dead for eight years?"

"Em and Meggie are going to stay hidden in Belize City while we see Reed. That's even safer than being here, where the damned last saw them both. I know there's no way that any of the undead who survived the fire and the tornado are going to forget there are two angels on the team, but sneering sarcasm isn't like you. What's going on?"

"I don't know," Nick said, and it was the truth. His head was spinning from the shit bouncing around in his brain. "Listen, you can see Reed, but I'm out of it and out of here. Just as soon as we have Marissa, I'm gone. You, Bond, and Grayson can string my father's ass up and shoot him but I don't want to see it happen."

"Who said anything about stringing his ass up?"

"Come on," Nick said. "What other option is there? He has to be taken out now that everyone knows he's alive, here, and running drugs. That's part of why I was just going to walk away without saying anything. I've got to go now. Menendez is already in the air and we still have to pick up Jared."

"Okay. But I'm telling you, there's a good damn reason for what Reed has done."

"Bye," Nick said, and hung up the phone. He turned to find Jaymes glaring at him.

"Nailing your father isn't why I called Grayson to check things out," she said. "And if you had listened to me last night instead of running off you would know that. I want to know what corruption there is at the top. What Commander Kingston did to Sam and his men years ago and what he tried to get me and Grayson to do to Sam now is wrong. Somebody besides Kingston is pulling those strings and I bet that person knows why your father is alive and well in Belize, too."

"Taking my father out may not have been your goal when you called, but there's no way to avoid it, and if you're honest with yourself, you'll admit it. Listen, I'm not blaming you. It is the right thing to do. It has to be done. I just can't handle watching it happen. As far as I'm concerned, Reed Sinclair died when Sam saw Vasquez mow him down with a machine gun."

"With so much underhanded manipulation going on in all of this, hasn't it occurred to you that your father is being forced into doing what he's doing?"

"Yeah, and all the Colombians are so desperate to channel drugs through Belize that they've tied my dear old dad hand and foot to his compound. Let's get real here. If my dad was a prisoner like Sam, I'd buy it, but the man I saw yesterday was free, armed, and in charge."

Jaymes shook her head. "Not the Colombians, Nick. The U.S. military could have their screws in your father and be pulling the strings. And you might want to keep in mind that there is more than just one kind of prison in this world. I think your problem is the little boy inside you doesn't want to hurt anymore, so he wants to run away. Take it from someone who knows. It doesn't work."

She walked off and left him there. Nick raked his hand through his hair, pressing his fingers hard against his scalp, sure the top of his head was about to explode. Why had he ever thought Staff Sergeant Jaymes Bond was even remotely interesting? Sure she was a looker, but damn, Christmas presents wrapped in barbed wire weren't worth opening.

What was with this "hurt little boy" crap?

"It's not easy, is it?" Stefanie said, exiting the metal building. "Having to take some of your own medicine. You wouldn't let me bury everything that happened to me at Corazón and run away, but somehow that's exactly what you want everyone to let you do."

"What is this? An Olympic eavesdropping competition?"

Pain crossed her features. "Word of advice. If you don't want to be heard then don't be yelling, on the phone or at Jaymes."

She turned away from him and Nick felt like a total son of a bitch.

"Wait, Stef." He ran up and caught her arm. When he swung her toward him, he saw the sheen of tears in her eyes, and it cut him to the quick. He set his hands on her shoulders and looked into her haunted blue eyes. "Damn, I'm sorry. I'm sorry for what I said last night and I'm sorry for just now. I'm screwing up all over and can't seem to stop it from happening."

"It's all right," she said, looking down.

"No, it's not all right. Stef, look at me." She brought her gaze back to his. "You're right about this shit. Maybe Jaymes is, too, okay. But more importantly, I can't believe that I'm the one hurting you." He leaned down and kissed her forehead. "I'm really, really sorry."

She brought her hand to his cheek and touched her fingers to his lips. "It's okay, really. You showed me something important about myself." She then stepped away and headed toward the helo.

He breathed a sigh of relief and jogged to catch up with her. "What?"

"That I can still care. I thought that part of me was dead."

"Good," he told her, part of him touched beyond words.

But there was another part of him that sank as if he were anchored to the *Titanic*. Was she hinting that she cared for him? If so, then he was in the worst situation imaginable. Except for this morning, his attraction for Jaymes had been helping him put his emotions for Stefanie into perspective. More and more he realized his feelings for Stef were deep, but closer to the friend end of the spectrum.

They were now too close to the helo to talk. She climbed on and he, having already completed his flight checklist, gave everything a second look and took the controls, more than ready to fly. Sometimes being in the air felt as if it were the only thing that kept him sane.

Within twenty minutes they had collected Jared and followed Menendez's tracer into Guatemala, which was where they all thought Herrera had Marissa. From the general direction of Sinclair's Hummer, he was heading the same way.

Nick had the feeling something really important was going to happen—and that something wasn't necessarily good. He might be meeting his dear old dad after all.

The world may have been spinning wildly, with everything spiraling out of control, but Marissa refused to give in to the vortex. She refused to faint. Stiffening her knees, she set her mind to putting the world back to rights. First with Navarre, then her brother, and then Father Dom.

"*Dios!*" She turned to Navarre. "You sit here. What do you mean about 'your time on earth'?"

He frowned, but then sat. "I don't expect the Guardian Council will allow a spirit warrior to remain upon the mortal ground forever."

Relief flooded her. "So you don't know for sure that you can't remain here like Jared and Aragon, *sí*?"

Navarre lifted a brow in surprise. "Aragon is here permanently? I know Jared is because only love saved him after he was bitten by a Tsara. I will have to find out about Aragon. Just before I was injured, the Guardian Council called for his execution because he left his duty and came to the mortal ground."

"This man isn't just a shapeshifter," Rafael cried. "He is mad! I forbid you to marry him."

Marissa swung around and planted her finger in Rafael's chest, pushing him back until he sat in a chair. "There will be no forbidding. I am my own person and I will marry the one I love. And I love Navarre. He is *not* mad, and you do not know everything there is to know. Nor do you know what I know. So sometimes you must close your mouth, be quiet, and listen. Navarre is a spirit warrior from the heavens. There are also two other warriors here on earth helping to fight Herrera's evil. That is where his strength comes from. That is why he changes to a wolf. That is why he was able to heal your wounds. Not that you've ever shown him gratitude."

Rafael just gaped at her.

She then faced Father Dom and pulled his cell phone from her pocket. Turning it on, she saw the *no signal* message again and turned it off in frustration. "We have waited too long for you to answer our questions, Father. How does keeping the *teléfono* secret protect Guatemala? How are you fighting Herrera and Menendez? And exactly who were you speaking to last night?"

Father Dom shook his head. "You put me in a very difficult situation. The answers are not simple and not so easy to give. Many lives are at stake. Herrera has kept his location secret, appearing before large groups of people at political events then disappearing as if evaporating into thin air. We know what he and Menendez are plotting, but we have yet to get proof to bring to the people. Herrera's sudden plans to marry and invite people into his home presented an opportunity that a very influential country that wishes to see democracy flourish in Guatemala wanted to take advantage of. A close associate of Menendez's arranged for me to perform the ceremony. We were to befriend his new wife and use her to get to Herrera, even if kidnapping was necessary, but then everything went wrong. I found out it was you Herrera was to marry and that he was forcing you. I knew I had to get you out of there or your *abuela* would never forgive me. But I failed, because you disappeared and those guards captured me."

"Langston," Marissa said, remembering Menendez's woman who'd purposely spilled punch on Marissa's sleeve. "Chanel Langston is the person you speak of. That means the country involved would be the United States, *sí*?"

"Shh! Child. Do not speak names out loud. The walls may have ears."

"So who were you speaking to last night?"

"You've said her name. She is the only contact. She will arrange for a large group of men to come and help us. All I have to do is to call her and tell her where we are. The phone's reception in the jungle can be unpredictable and I did not get a signal until last night, so I couldn't call for help before then. Or they would have come to the waterfall. I also couldn't have contacted your friends in America."

"How do we know that we can trust this woman and her army?" Rafael asked. "Have you known her for many years?"

"No, only for this past year, *pero* I know she can be trusted."

"I say we trust no one and set a trap for Herrera. Once he is dead, Marissa will be safe."

Marissa shook her head and put the phone back into her pocket. "I am sorry, Father Dom. There is no signal here, either. Besides, we need time to think. One day here will not harm any of us." She decided that it might just be a very lucky thing that there was no phone at the mission. It gave her the freedom to remain hidden from the world.

Father Dom disagreed. "Until we have her help we will not

be safe. I should take the phone and find a signal to call. Or even go to the village down the mountain to use the phone."

"No. We both know Herrera will have spies waiting for one of us to appear." Marissa shook her head. "I can't help but think that the fewer people who know where I am the better I will be. If we tell Chanel Langston and she tells the men who are to come, that means a lot of people are going to know where I am and there are many who wish to get Tío Luis's money and control of SINCO. *Dios,* I don't think I will ever be safe. There is a powerful sheik claiming that Tío Louis promised me in marriage to him. Even two of Herrera's guards were going to kidnap me and force me to marry one of them so they could become rich."

Navarre grunted with disgust. "You will no longer need to worry," he said, setting a hand on her shoulder and sending a flood of warmth through her. "Father Dom will marry us now. Then you will be safe and you will control the money and whatever else they are after."

Marissa started to tell Navarre that it wasn't that simple, but blinked instead. Wasn't it? Why shouldn't she herself take the fortune her twisted uncle had dumped on her and make him squirm in his grave by using it for doing good. She could even use it to fight monsters like him and Herrera.

She slipped her hand over Navarre's. "I would be honored to be your bride."

Rafael stood and cursed. "But he is a werewolf! How can you even think it? Surely there will be many problems with this. You will be persecuted, attacked by those who might fear him."

"There will be problems, *pero* we will face them and solve them. I will also have the means to protect us all," Marissa said, standing as well, more sure of this than of anything she'd ever been in her life. "I would be honored to be the bride of the Wolf, for he has proven himself by putting his life in danger again and again to save me and mine, even those who remain ungrateful to him. Navarre is pure and honest and noble and I consider myself very blessed that he has chosen me."

"Father, you cannot let this happen," Rafael cried. "What of her soul?"

"I fear that I was wrong in my belief about the shapeshifter, for he truly has seen the face of God. He is more noble than any mortal can hope to be. Marissa could marry no better, especially given that she is your *tío's* heir. I still have the license that I've yet to fill in. They could marry legally today."

"I don't know," said Rafael. "How can this be right?"

"Because I love him," Marissa said softly. "I am free to love him and I am free to choose him. *Dios*, It is more right than anything that has been forced upon me all of my life. Can you not see that?"

Rafael sighed. "*Sí*, I understand that. I have never known nor will I ever know that freedom."

Marissa found herself suddenly scooped up into Navarre's strong arms before she could speak to Rafael. He needed to realize that his future was not over because of the past.

Navarre swung her around, making her heart race with the energy of his excitement. "We will marry then, but not here. I will marry you among the beauty of the flowers at the top of the world and *then* we will find a mirror."

"Why would a blind man need a mirror?" Rafael asked.

Marrissa cheeks burned. Before she could think of an answer, the church door opened, and Señor and Señora Castillo entered, one carrying an overstuffed platter of food, the other a picnic basket. The delicious aroma of freshly baked sweet cakes flooded the air.

"*Amigos*, I hope you are very, very hungry," Señor Castillo said and smiled. "She kept making more and more cakes, saying 'those poor *niños* did not get enough to eat.'"

Rafael immediately went to relieve Señora Castillo of the tray, forgetting his question, and Navarre set Marissa on her feet. "I am hungry," he said. "Very hungry." He didn't need any help making it to where Rafael put down the sweet cakes and started eating.

It seemed to Marissa that the wedding was going to be delayed a little. She saw for the first time that Señor Castillo had a new bandage on his arm. "What happened?"

He rolled his eyes. "I burned myself with the torch fixing the pipes this morning. Stupid to do, no? I was not paying attention."

"I hope it was not bad," Marissa said.

"No. And I did not get sympathy for too long. The señora is already complaining that I left a mess on the porch. I will have to remember to put the torch up later. *Pero,* why does he use the altar cloth over his eyes?" Señor Castillo pointed to Navarre.

"The brightness of the sun hurts his eyes." Marissa said. "I am sorry, I didn't mean to disrespect anything sacred and I will replace it. I didn't have anything else close at hand and he was in pain."

"What is here is God's and belongs to all who are in need. *Pero,* I thought he was blind and could not see."

"He was injured and he hasn't been able to see, but this morning the light hurt."

Señor Castillo gave a huge, excited smile and called out to his wife. "Your prayers this morning worked! The blind *niño* saw light!"

Señora Castillo placed her hand over her heart. "We will soon see them all healed and happy. Father Dom tells me there will be a wedding today."

Marissa nodded and smiled, but then she saw the pain on

Rafael's face. He turned and quickly left the church, abandoning the food he had been enjoying. He clearly thought there would never be any healing or happiness for him. She gathered a plateful of the cakes. "I will take these to Rafael and be back in a minute."

"Do you wish for me to come with you?" Navarre asked, setting his food aside.

"No. I think I need to speak to him alone."

Señora Castillo came over and brought a big bar of chocolate. It was a golden-wrapped Goss Chocolate Bar made in Belize—her brother's favorite treat as a little boy. "You give this to the *niño* and you tell him, God heals all in time. I know, for in my life, I have lost everything and yet I still live to see the blessings that come every day."

"*Gracias,*" Marissa said, squeezing the woman's hand. She took the chocolate and the cakes and went in search of Rafael. She found him across the field at the ruins. He was staring up at the tall, crumbling pyramid and she shuddered. A fall from the top would be certain death.

"You should not follow me," Rafael said. "For where I will go one day, you will not want to be. And what I will do, you will not want to see."

"Then it is your decision to let evil win, *mi hermano*? You will give yourself over to their ways and let them use you over and over again? For the one place I do not want to be is in their twisted hell and what I do not want to see is their wicked deeds being passed on to others."

Rafael turned to face her, his body vibrating with the force of his emotion. "I will never! Never! Never be used again!"

"*Dios,* I pray not. Every day I pray for you and for our *hermana, madre,* and *abuela* that are now lost to us. But until you forgive yourself for what happened and realize there is more within you yet to be loved, then you are letting Herrera steal more from you than what he took before. Only now you are willingly giving it to him. Señora Castillo said to tell you God heals all things in time. She lost everything and yet she looks for the blessings of every day with a giving heart."

"It is easy for you to say all of that. You do not know what it is like."

"No, I don't, but does a person have to experience everything in order to understand or care? My *amiga* Stefanie suffered greatly from Herrera and from Tío Luis and she wanted nothing more than to die. Then she became angry, and now she wants to kill. I pray for her every day, too, in hopes she will realize that until she chooses to love again, evil is winning.

"Do you not understand that it is harder to say things to you *because* I have only imagined such pain and not lived it? But isn't this injury to you almost like Navarre's blindness? Maybe it is keeping you from seeing a future? If I, too, were blind, how could I help Navarre? And what sense would it make if I said to myself, I can't help him because I can see? We have both lost everyone in our *familia*, must we also lose each other? Do we have to let the evil poison us, or can we choose to live a different life?"

"Not wanting this life once I destroy Herrera is not letting evil win, but refusing to live with what is damaged beyond repair. A horse breaks his leg and it is humane to put the animal out of its misery. Do not ask me for more."

Marissa swallowed the huge lump of pain in her throat, forcing herself to understand that Rafael needed time. She set the plate of sweet cakes on the ground. "I brought these for you. Hopefully you will eat them before the ants do." Then she held out the huge bar of chocolate. "Señora Castillo sent this to you. Do you want it?"

He started to shake his head without looking then at the last second glanced out of the corner of his eye and his gaze widened. "A Goss Chocolate Bar? *Dios*, it has been years . . ."

He didn't say more as emotion cut off his voice. He took the candy bar, though.

"I hope you will stand with me when I marry Navarre. I would be honored to have my *hermano* at my side," she said, then left him alone with the chocolate and his memories of a time that wasn't so painful.

As she returned to the church and Navarre, she was amazed at how suddenly her life seemed to be gaining direction and purpose. Forever she had sat listless within the power of others and now she had a choice. She could choose what to do with her heart, her love, and her life, and she chose Navarre.

Now she needed to know why he couldn't stay here as Aragon and Jared had done—and just how much time they did have.

Herrera finally located Ysalane in a closet of the resort by following the smell of her Magic smoke. Along with her incense, she had a candle lit in front of her on the floor. Her hands were wrapped around the crystal jaguar and she had tears streaming down her face. It only gave him a moment's pause before he jerked her up by her hair. "You did not answer when I called, *puta!* Why do you hide from Herrera? Did you not learn years ago that it is only more pain for you?" He backhanded her and cut her lip. At least she was naked per his standard orders. He liked seeing the numerous scars he'd marked upon her body.

She opened her eyes and stared blankly at him, clutching her crystal jaguar. She'd never reacted so apathetically before and it gave him an uneasy feeling in his gut. Even when she'd accepted and sometimes invited him to inflict pain, there had always been emotion in her eyes. Hate, desire, resentment, love, a satisfying twist of mixed passions had always filled her gaze.

"Show me where the wolfman and Marissa are now."

She shook her head. "Ysalane cannot do it now."

He went to backhand her again, but Samir grabbed his

wrist. There was murder in the Vladarian's gaze. "It is my money being spent for the army. She will be mine to question until Marissa is found. How could you have expected to run SINCO when you can't even handle one servant properly?"

Rage filled Herrera. How dare Samir look down on him? Ysalane was his to do with as he chose. He bared his fangs but then lowered his hand. He couldn't let anything jeopardize his new deal with Samir, which meant he had to eat all of the Vladarian's shit with a smile. Herrera needed Menendez's army to take over the country after his election. He was already taking a big chance in losing the anonymous supporter Menendez had lined up, but it had been worth the gamble to take Menendez out of the game now. It was Herrera's hope that this anonymous backer would come to him once Herrera was in control.

Digging his nails into his palms, Herrera backed away from Ysalane. She had her eyes open now and was looking at him in complete shock. *You will pay for this,* he silently mouthed to her. And she would. She would pay dearly.

Samir pulled a handkerchief from his pocket and gently dabbed Ysalane's lip. "I won't apologize for Herrera's cruelty, for there is no excuse for such barbaric measures. There are many other ways to get what is needed. I must locate Marissa and her lover. One more time—you must tell me where they are."

Ysalane took the handkerchief from Samir and pressed it to her lip, more as a kiss than as a touch to her wound. Herrera dug his fangs into his gums.

"The wolfman killed Ysalane's jaguar last night," she said. "I must search for another whose soul is open to the magic and I can only do this at night. The jaguar can only see the wolfman at night because the wolfman is gone during the day."

"Then it will have to wait until tonight," Samir said. "You may go to my quarters and make use of my servants to see to your comfort. Tell them to find you something beautiful to wear, something befitting a woman of your talents. Come to me as soon as you can show me where Marissa is. You will be well rewarded for this, I promise."

"Ysalane thanks you." She collected her candle and her incense. Then with her jaguar clutched to her breasts she went to leave the room. At the last minute, she glanced back at Herrera. It was the first time he'd ever seen satisfaction in her eyes, but the malice that accompanied it wrapped an icy hand around his frozen soul.

He turned to Samir. "She is my *puta*. You will not touch her."

"Why would I want a woman as damaged and mutilated as you have made her? Even her Elan blood cannot cover the ugliness. I am smart enough to know that if I kill the goose that lays the golden eggs, I will have no more gold."

"As soon as you have Marissa, I get Ysalane back," Herrera said.

"Of course. Once I have Marissa, I will have no need for your goose," Samir said, smiling. "I will have my own."

And I will have them both, Herrera silently vowed, returning Samir's smile.

"Until Ysalane can tell me something, I want all five hundred men out looking for Marissa. She has to be found before morning. I'll need to return to the palace for the SINCO gathering and I want Marissa with me. Once they see that I have legal control of Vasquez's shares, it will make all the decisions go much smoother."

"Don't you mean when *we* return? And I thought the gathering was to plan *our* takeover of the Vladarian Order from Cinatas."

"Of course," Samir said. "Of course. You will have to let me lead them, though. The SINCO leaders respect me and know that they can trust me. You, they don't."

Samir immediately pulled out his phone to give orders to Colonel Estrada. Herrera ground his fangs again. Commanding Estrada was something else that Herrera should be doing. After all, it was going to be his army when Samir had Marissa. That was the deal. So why did it seem as if everything had been taken out of his hands since Samir had arrived?

Maybe Herrera would do well to set his own plans in motion now. Plans that would take care of Samir and clean house at SINCO, since they all seemed to be in Samir's pocket anyway. The meeting Samir had set up would be the perfect time to take out the old and put in the new.

Chapter Twenty-one

"GOD HAS brought you and your *hermano* to us," said Señora Castillo. "You are so like our Camina, young and passionate. I did not see her married because Menendez took her from us before she found her one true *novio*. And now I have the blessing of seeing you marry and wearing the *huipil* and looking *muy bonita*." She reached up and adjusted the wreath of flowers adorning Marissa's head. "Very, very beautiful."

Barefoot, wearing a simple cotton skirt and the elaborately embroidered shirt colored as brightly and vibrantly as a garden of wildflowers, Marissa felt more beautiful than she had in the expensive silk and lace dress Herrera had provided. And though it seemed unbelievable that she was really getting married in the middle of this nightmare, her heart still sang with the wonder of the love she had found in the darkness. That legally binding herself to Navarre was also the smartest thing she could do at the moment was only an added blessing.

She clasped Señora Castillo's hand. "I promise, I will repay your kindness. You and Señor Castillo have made this very special for me and Navarre, and I thank you."

"It is I who must thank you. You have brought us unexpected joy today. *Pero*, if you want to make me happier, then someday you and your husband will come back and visit us, *sí?* And bring your little *niños* and *niñas*, too."

"I will come back. The Misión Salida de Sol is a wonderful place. I wish things were different for you, though. I wish your Camina could come back to you. Can I ask what happened?"

"I told you she was very passionate, *sí?* She and her *hermano*, my Diego, were very smart, too. They went to the San Carlos University in Guatemala City and during their studies they became involved in a group that spoke out about the human rights tragedies occurring under the political regime. Camina and Diego found out very bad things about General Menendez and then they disappeared. We had hoped they were still alive, but then that hope was lost, and we visit their grave often with lots of flowers from the garden. We also pray and do what we can to fight against Menendez. One day I believe justice will be done. Now, no more talk of this. Señor Castillo and I have a surprise for you. We fixed this room for you and Navarre to share tonight. It was Camina's room. Father Dom and Rafael can stay in the church again and the señor and I will be upstairs."

Staring into the big mirror over the dresser, all Marissa could think about at that moment was having Navarre see her as he wished. To see himself touching her and for her to see him doing so, too. Her desire flared so strongly that she was sure Señora Castillo could read her mind. Her cheeks heated with embarrassment.

Was it wrong of her to be constantly thinking about Navarre that way? *Dios,* they were in danger. She knew Herrera searched for her. Her brother was hurting. Shouldn't all of those things be consuming her thoughts?

"You haven't had much time to think about where you two would sleep tonight," Señora Castillo said. "That is why you have me, no?" She smiled. "I know these things. It will be a long day and you and your *novio* will want to be alone, too. So I have a picnic packed for you two. There is a trail to a beautiful waterfall you must go to see after the ceremony."

The knock on the door was the signal that Father Dom had finished talking to Navarre. The time had come.

"Is the bride ready?" asked Señor Castillo.

"*Sí,* she is," Señora Castillo touched Marissa's cheek and then went and opened the door.

Marissa drew a deep breath and followed. Reaching the couple, she gave them both a kiss upon their wizened cheeks. "*Gracias,* from the bottom of my heart, I thank you."

They left the house together and went to the garden beside the church. The simple splendor of the lush flowers and bright butterflies beneath a blue, blue sky and golden sun was breathtaking. She knew it was the perfect place for her to marry Navarre. No walls hemmed her in. No locks kept her prisoner. No monsters lurked in the corners, at least for now. She'd heard the distant sound of a helicopter twice earlier, but then nothing came closer and all had been quiet for a long while.

For the moment, she could run and sing and dance in any direction she wanted and her heart reached out to embrace the freedom and beauty ringing in the air. Navarre stood quiet, strong, and noble at the end of the path. Father Dom was with him. She didn't see Rafael, but she wouldn't let his absence cast a shadow over this moment.

Navarre felt her presence, because he turned her way and held out his hand. She went to him, slipping her hand in his, and he leaned in to brush his lips against hers. "Father Dom has explained the depth and purpose of marriage to me and I am honored that you have given your heart to me. Though I may not see the beauty of your face as we pledge ourselves to one another, I can see your heart."

"And you have shown me yours. It's the heart that matters most."

Father Dom cleared his throat. "I almost feel unnecessary, except to make your pledge legal. Shall we begin?"

"Wait!" called Rafael from behind them.

Startled, Marissa turned to see her brother running toward them. He had something behind his back, and for a heart-stopping moment, fear that he might try to harm Navarre shot through her. Then when she looked into his eyes, she saw a glimmer of the brother who once made her smile no matter how badly she hurt and she relaxed.

Reaching her, he handed her a bouquet of bright flowers and gave her arm an encouraging squeeze. Then he turned to

Navarre. "You are a shapeshifter and I am the man of the family. I see problems, but I also see that she loves you. All I ask is that you guard her heart as well as you have protected her from Herrera's evil."

"I will not fail to do so," Navarre said.

Rafael nodded then stepped back, joining Señor and Señora Castillo.

Father Dom spoke of the sanctity of marriage and said a prayer.

Then, rather than stating vows for Navarre to repeat, Father Dom said, "Navarre, you may begin."

Navarre placed her hand over his heart. "I, Navarre, a Shadowman of the Blood Hunters, willfully take you, Marissa Isabella Tajeda Vasquez, in marriage. I vow to unite myself with you in body, in mind, and spirit. To hold and guard the gift of your love and your heart as my most sacred treasure. I will honor you from this day forth and I pledge my love to you for eternity."

His words, his voice, his heart wrapped around the very center of her soul and showed her she was only beginning to know her love for this man. She touched his golden amulet, then set her hand over his heart. Her tears fell.

"I, Marissa Isabella Tajeda Vasquez, willfully take you Navarre, Shadowman, Blood Hunter, wolf, to be my lawful husband in marriage. I pledge myself to you. My heart, which you have filled with the gentleness and protection of your love, will be one with your heart. My body, which you have inflamed with passion, will be one with your body. My spirit, which you have made soar with freedom, will be one with your spirit. I will treasure and honor you from this day forth and vow my soul to be united to yours forever."

"Navarre and Marissa, I ask that you join your right hands." When they did, Father Dom wrapped a silver rope loosely around their wrists. "May the Lord in his goodness strengthen you in your love for each other and fill you both with His blessings. What God has joined together here this day, let no man put asunder. I now pronounce you man and wife. You may kiss the bride."

Marissa expected Navarre to lightly kiss her. Instead, he wrapped his arms around her bottom and lifted her full against him as he brought her up to his height and kissed her soundly. She had no choice but to put her arms around his neck and to give herself over to his passion and commitment.

It wasn't until Señor Castillo began playing the marimba and Señora Castillo sang about love as she shook *chinchines* that Navarre ended the kiss. When Marissa looked up she found everyone had been watching, except Rafael. He'd left.

Father Dom shook his head and said dryly, "I have a feeling that if I had not married you two now, we would be doing this in the middle of the night."

Señor Castillo teased them as well about the passion of youth and Marissa thought she'd drown in embarrassment. That everyone now knew for certain she and Navarre would be intimate with each other made her tense inside. She knew it didn't make sense to feel that way because now that they were married, she could be with him without any hint of shame. Still, her stomach was knotted in a mixture of anticipation and discomfort.

Señora Castillo jabbed her husband in the side. "Tell them what you did at our wedding!"

"Will you never forgive me?" he said, smiling. "I was young, you were and still are irresistible, and I had waited years to be your husband."

"Bah. You know I forgave you long ago. And you know I only speak of it now because I will never forget, *sí*?" Señora Castillo sighed with satisfaction. "As soon as the priest said he could kiss the bride"—she gave her husband a sultry look—"he picked me up and carried me off. Left our families to celebrate our marriage without us, so he could begin loving me."

"And I haven't stopped yet," said Señor Castillo. "Besides, I already knew all of your family and all about you. It was time to love you as a man loves a woman."

She knew that if Navarre had any idea there was a mirror in the room they would share tonight, history would quickly repeat itself and she'd find herself carted off immediately. Her pulse raced and her body tingled and burned for him to do just that even though it would be mortifying. Was it wrong of her to want him so much?

More fire flamed Marissa's cheeks. She hadn't known Navarre years, only days. While she knew his heart and his courage and his noble spirit, she didn't know anything about his life in the spirit world. Shouldn't she want to know all of those things as much as she wanted his kiss and his touch? She did, but somehow whenever they were alone or had a stolen moment, they hadn't spoken of their lives. They'd thought only of pleasure and it was her fault. He was new to this world and she should be making sure everything was perfect for them. *Dios,* she loved him and vowed in her heart to make things right during their picnic today.

"Amazing!" Navarre said as he licked his lips and then his fingers. Nothing could compare to the pleasures he shared with Marissa, but the taste and satisfaction of food did come close. More than anything else, marrying Marissa had given him a great joy inside his heart and spirit. Pledging himself to her was the ultimate submission of his warrior's spirit, for his body, mind, and spirit became hers forever within the space of a heartbeat. Only he feared Marissa felt differently. He'd sensed her tension when he'd kissed her after their marriage and he wanted to ask her if she no longer felt pleasure with him, but wasn't sure how. So he spoke of the food instead. "What do you call this?"

"*Tamales dulces,* fruit with sweet cream."

Her answer reminded him of how he'd felt touching and

tasting her at the Green Water Jungle Resort. He started to tell her that, but then felt for another treat on his plate. "And this one?" he asked, biting into the mouthwatering treat. *Coward.* He could steal into her mind, but would she want him to do that? Somehow, unless he was giving her pleasure or protecting her from harm, it didn't seem right.

"*Pache,* it is a potato tamale with chicken and cheese. *Dios,* I do not know how you can eat so much. First the sweet cakes this morning and now this. I don't think I'll have room for the special dinner she is cooking for us tonight or even be able to walk back to the mission. Never have I had so much food in one day."

Navarre finished the *pache* then lay back upon the blanket to feel the warmth of the sun and frowned. He knew she had found the food as delicious as he had, but now it sounded as if she hadn't. Or that she could only enjoy it for a short time. Was that the reason mortals did not constantly indulge themselves? Was it the same for her in pleasures of the flesh?

Ask her now.

"Mortals have many great pleasures," Navarre said, then sighed. "It is now hard for me to imagine not enjoying them all of the time. Is this not the same for you?"

"*Sí,* but then if one constantly did nothing but feed one's pleasure, wouldn't that pleasure soon become not as pleasurable?"

"Has that happened with us?" His heart skipped a beat as it sometimes did when he feared what would follow. "I sensed your upset after I kissed you. Do you regret pledging yourself to me?"

"No! Never!" Marissa cried out, and he sat up quickly at the pain in her voice only to crash into her as she had apparently thrown herself his way. Her head hit his nose and he ended up on his back with her on top.

He wrapped his arms around her, his nose stinging. "By

Logos, I wish I could see. Maybe then I would know what was wrong. I am sorry to hurt you." He'd removed the cloth he'd worn over his eyes before the ceremony and had been very encouraged by the result. The sensation of seeing light did not cause him as much pain as before and the world now seemed to be gray rather than black.

"No. It is I who am sorry. *Dios mio,* nothing is wrong, Navarre. I just wanted everything to be perfect for you." As she scooted up his chest, she kissed his chin, his cheek, and then his lips. "I will always, always want you. In fact, I thought I was wanting you too much. It seems to be all I think about. When I saw the big mirror in the room Señora Castillo has ready for us to share tonight, I didn't think about how gracious and giving it was for her to do, even though I am very grateful. All I could think about was having you see yourself touch me in the mirror and me watching you do so." She drew a deep breath. "Then after the ceremony, when Señor Castillo said how he knew his wife years before he married her, I realized that I didn't know anything about your life before coming here and you only know a little about me, because my desire for you always gets in the way, and I think to myself I shouldn't let that happen. And—"

Filled with relief, he rolled her beneath him, cutting off her words. "The only thing you are thinking too much about is thinking that you think too much about pleasure. Do not all men and women enjoy pleasure and think about it?"

"*Sí.*"

"What if you don't think about it enough?"

"It's not possible," she said.

"Yes, it is possible, for I think about it more than you."

"You do?"

"Absolutely. There doesn't seem to be a moment that I am not aware of you or desiring you. But since you are worried"— he leaned down and brushed his lips over hers then moved to her neck—"go ahead and ask me anything and I will answer." He found the rise of her breasts and kissed his way across as he slid his hand under her shirt to caress the warmth of her stomach.

"Uh, where were you born?"

He pulled her shirt up and found her hardened pleasure points. "Eden where Adam loved Eve. If I only knew then what miracle Logos had wrought in creating woman." He suckled one breast with satisfaction then he filled his palm with the other and asked, "Where were you born?"

She gasped. "Be . . . lize . . . in . . . village."

"What else do we need to know?" He slid his hand down her stomach as he tongued her breast.

"Um . . . um . . . what are . . . the heavens like?"

He pulled the string keeping her skirt snug to her waist.

"Warm. Very warm, like you. Filled with beauty. Like you. But for Shadowmen who serve Logos's Guardian Forces it is a life of duty and purpose. We fight against Heldon's darkness, against the cold evil he perpetrates, against the chaotic hate with which he wants to rule the universe." He tugged her skirt down until he could feel the silken cloth covering her woman's flesh.

She gasped.

"Is there more?" he asked.

"More?" she whispered.

"Yes," he said then briefly kissed her thighs and stomach, scenting the sweetness of her desire. "Is there?"

"Wha . . . t?"

"More questions?" He pulled her panties off and spread her knees, wishing he could see the beauty of her. This time he kissed and lapped at her until her legs quivered at every lash of his tongue and she cried out his name, pulling at him to stop. He rose up, expecting to slide down his pants and join his throbbing flesh to hers. Instead she scooted to the side and sat up.

"*Sí*, there is more." She planted her hand in the center of his chest and pushed him onto his back. He then felt her looming over him. "I want to know what it is like to touch you everywhere that you touch me! I want to know what it is like to kiss you everywhere that you kiss me! And you are not to stop me until I know what you know, agreed?"

Her demand was so passionate that his pulse strangely raced with anticipation, somewhat akin to his eagerness in facing a worthy opponent, but far greater and more intimate than that. "Agreed," he said softly.

She then did to him what he had done to her. She brushed her lips over his, kissed him deeply then began kissing and licking her way down his throat to his chest. She ran her fingers beneath his shirt, lifting it up, and then urged him to take it off.

The feel of her lips and tongue on his chest and the brush of her silken hair over his skin made him crazy. Having her soft hands caressing and exploring his every muscle made him ache until the urge to push her onto her back and thrust himself into her overwhelmed him.

He reached for her.

"You promised," she said, pushing his hands back down. He bit his lip in consternation as the warrior in him wanted to rebel and take charge of bringing this torturous pleasure to fulfillment.

He lay back and groaned.

She moved lower, loosening his pants and pushing them down until he felt his swollen, throbbing flesh spring free. He already ached for her, but when she wrapped her velvet hands around him, stroking him, she ignited a fire of desire that had him shaking with the longing to assuage his need. Then she pressed her wet mouth to his hardened shaft, following with a sweep of her tongue, and his body arched like a bow, strung so tight that the least vibration would split it apart. Split him apart.

Never had he experienced such a rush of fierce pleasure or such an overwhelming vulnerability. He had to have her or he would surely perish.

"Now?" he cried out, trying to rise. "Have you satisfied your quest?"

"No." She pressed him back. "You promised."

She kissed his swollen hardness again, this time sucking on him. Sweat poured from his brow, his mind spun crazily, and his heart thundered. She did the same thing again, only this time it took much longer. His control snapped, his honed discipline faltered, and all of his strength melted into wild desperation. He was a warrior undone.

"Later," he said roughly, pulling her up to kiss her. Her hands braced against his shoulders and the soft swell of her breasts bounced against his chest. The brush and pressure of her body against his groin had him arching upward, crying out in need.

The more Marissa explored the nuances of Navarre's body, the more awed she became not only of his male beauty but also of the power and submission of intimacy. With her touch, her kiss, he became as defenseless and as needy as she became beneath his caresses. His passion and gentleness made her want things she didn't think she ever would. She'd seen pictures of things in the awful book Ysalane had forced upon her, and Marissa never would have imagined doing any of them. The thought of having a man's arousal in her mouth had made her shudder in revulsion. But with Navarre it was different. As she began her discovery of him, what it felt like to touch him everywhere, what it felt like to kiss him and see his passion become as needy and vulnerable as hers, the more she wanted to pleasure him with her mouth as he had pleasured her. Every part of the seductive dance of becoming one together was beautiful, and when he'd broken beneath her touch and cried for her, his body shaking with his need for her, all she could do was open herself to him.

She braced her hands on his shoulders and spread her knees over his hips. When he arched up, shouting from his hunger, she positioned herself and pressed downward. His arousal slid inside her, making her gasp from the heat and the thickness of his sex filling her. He groaned deeply and thrust them into a storm of passion. His mind penetrated hers in the midst of the fury and together their bodies spiraled into a frenzied cataclysm of fulfillment that left them both shaking, wrapped in each others' arms, hearts and spirits entwined in ecstasy.

They were one.

Chapter Twenty-two

"THAT'S IT? What about Reed Sinclair, a.k.a. El Diablo Sinclair?" Sam demanded, his cell phone plastered to his ear.

Nick tried to suck in a deep breath, but his muscles were too tied up in knots to do anything but clench tight from knees to hands to teeth. He could tell himself over and over again that he didn't give a shit why Reed had played dead for eight years, but something deep in his gut wasn't buying into what his mind wanted—a feeling that had worsened since Sam's and Grayson's arrival ten minutes ago via helo.

The team had settled on a remote helipad, a holding spot where they could keep a low profile and figure out what in hell was going on. Everything seemed to be happening, but not fast enough, and Sam may have just found out the reason why.

After leaving Sinclair's compound, Menendez had flown to a high-class resort not far from his estate, something that made little sense until Nick flew over Menendez's compound. The place was up in arms with snipers on the roof, heavy guards at the gates. He'd come to the conclusion that something bad was going on and Menendez wanted to be close to monitor it, but not in the middle of it. Nick had flown over both areas twice and didn't dare chance a third pass without raising suspicions.

Same with Sinclair's group. He and ten Hummerloads of men had crossed over the Belizean border into Guatemala and were now parked at a village on the fringes of a remote mountainous jungle area.

Sam hung up the phone, his expression one of angry determination, but then he'd arrived with a chip on his shoulder. Tension brewed in the air between them and Nick knew the only thing that would cut it would be a knock-down-drag-out over Reed. They'd talked about Emerald, Erin, and Megan and how they were probably the only three females on earth who would be upset at having to spend a day or two at an exclusive spa on the beach. Nick had explained the current situation with Menendez and Sinclair. Then Sam had received the CIA call.

"Well?" Nick demanded when Sam didn't immediately say anything.

"We've got a honeypot, a Joe the Sleeper, and if we blow them we're screwed."

"Run that by me again." Nick blinked, wondering which one of them had fallen off the deep end.

Jaymes laughed.

"Shit," said Grayson, speaking up for the first time. It was clear the sergeant first class wasn't quite comfortable operating on the edge of what his superiors might consider acceptable activity while on special leave. Both he and Staff Sergeant Bond had gotten time off with the particular intent to help with the tornado cleanup in Twilight. That didn't necessarily include a short junket to Belize.

"The translation is simple, but if you repeat it someone may have to kill you. We are in the middle of a CIA operation to take Menendez and Herrera out of the Guatemalan political arena. Two deep-cover operatives, one posing as an arms dealer and the other posing as Menendez's lover, have Menendez buying guns, enough to supply an army to 'assure' the safety of his political party after they 'win' the election. They've been waiting to tie Herrera to the deal before springing the trap."

"You're saying my father is this undercover arms dealer and not a drug lord?" Nick slammed his fist into his hand, wanting and needing the pain. None of this seemed real.

"Looks like."

Nick cursed. "Fine, but you know what? I don't care if he's wearing a white hat. It doesn't excuse being dead for eight years, does it?"

"No, but it's a start," Sam said.

"If an arms deal is what's on the table," Jaymes said, "then what in the hell is going on today? Is Sinclair camping out with the weapons waiting for Menendez and Herrera to show up?"

"Well," said Sam. "This is where it gets really interesting and why we're going to have to sit here and twiddle our thumbs for a while. Menendez got a call this morning from what may be the one loyal man left in his little army of rebels. It seems Herrera has commandeered Menendez's army and put Menendez on their hit list for a cool hundred million. The only apparent reason at this point is so the army can help capture a woman and a 'wolfman' who escaped from Herrera's compound two days ago. Tonight they are somehow supposed to be able to find the runaways and Menendez plans to take back his army."

"Marissa!" Annette said.

"She and Navarre have been safe from Herrera since then?" Stefanie cried with relief. "It is a real miracle. I have been so worried and . . . and . . . I . . . prayed. I prayed." There were tears in her eyes.

Nick knew that Stefanie never expected her prayers to be answered. He was glad they had been, for both Stefanie's and Marissa's sake.

"I knew that we could count on Navarre, even blind and delirious," Aragon said, slapping Jared on the back.

Jared grunted and shook his head. "That is why every night you have been on your knees, blaming yourself for Navarre's blindness and yelling at our brethren in the heavens for leaving Navarre defenseless upon the mortal ground."

"Can you blame me? Were he to be poisoned by a Tsara, you would be no more eager than I to execute him," Aragon replied.

"You would do that?" Annette asked, looking with horrified surprise at Aragon. "Kill your own friend?"

Aragon moved to her, cupped her cheek in his hand, and

said softly, "Yes. If every effort to save a damned brother fails, I would kill him. Do you know why?"

She shook her head.

"Pathos was once a Blood Hunter, my mentor. He became poisoned and turned into the greatest force for evil upon the mortal ground. We are embroiled in this battle with Cinatas and the Vladarians because of his master plan. I would never allow that to happen again."

Annette set her hand on Aragon's chest. "I can understand, but—"

"There aren't any buts," Stefanie said, a bitter edge to her voice. Aragon had apparently struck a raw nerve. "When wickedness takes root then there is no other choice but to kill the host."

Nick saw Stefanie look at her hands when she spoke. He knew better than the others how much she'd suffered and why she wanted revenge. Hell, he was the one who started her on this path and he would help her see it done, which meant getting to Herrera as soon as they had a handle on where he was, CIA operation or no. He hoped when the time came the others would be on board with that plan, because he wasn't going to let anyone or anything stop them from nailing the bastard.

"I might have agreed with you a week ago," Sam said. "But I'm living proof that isn't always true."

"As am I," said Jared.

"Yes," Stefanie said, "but then when you consider monsters like Cinatas and Herrera, there is no hope. And didn't they have to start out just like us?"

"There is no way for us to truly know the answer to that question," Jared said. "Only Logos's omniscience can discern the heart."

Sam scoffed. "Some folks you just know about. You don't have to ask. I wish your Logos's omniscience could tell us whether Cinatas survived Hades Mountain or not. I keep looking over my shoulder expecting him to make an appearance at any minute."

"I'm with you on that one," said Nick. "Did your contact know they are dealing with a vampire in Herrera?"

"The subject didn't come up," Sam replied. "And unless I'm face-to-face with someone and can feel them out beforehand, I won't be the one bringing it up."

"So what do they expect us to do?" Nick asked, going to the heart of the matter.

"Go back home," Sam said, "but I told them no can do. Not with Marissa and Navarre being hunted down. I did say we'd stay out of their hair if they'd notify us as soon as they located Marissa and Navarre."

"We'll see," said Nick. "I'm keeping Menendez and Sinclair in my sights. They move, I'm moving."

"I'm completely on board with that. If you want to win the game, you can't take your eye off the ball. Speaking of which, why don't you show me where these jokers are on the map."

"Over here." Nick directed Sam to the laptop screen he had set up in the helo. "This is a satellite blow-up of the area." He pointed out Menendez's location, where his estates were, and where Sinclair was currently cooling his heels.

"What do you want to bet Marrissa and Navarre are in the center of that mess?" Sam pointed to a remote jungle area that lay between Menendez's location and Sinclair's.

"I'd say you're right. I wish we could do an air search for them, but they'd probably duck out of sight at the first sound of the helo."

Sam laid a heavy hand on Nick's shoulder and Nick braced himself. He knew what was coming.

"If you alone had discovered your father alive, would you have told me?" Sam asked.

"I don't know," Nick said truthfully. "Maybe eventually, but not right away. Not until I worked through it myself."

"That pisses me off."

"Sorry, but finding out my father's living and breathing hasn't been a piece of cake."

"Where did I fail you?" Sam asked softly.

Nick jerked his head up to meet Sam's gaze. "Why in the hell would you ask that?"

Sam shrugged. "You obviously didn't feel that I was the person to come to when the world rocked."

"This has nothing to do with that, okay? Shit, you've been to hell and back recently. The past two days with Emerald have likely been the only real happiness you've had in over eight years. I wasn't about to dump on you right now because I find out some asshole mercenary has been playing dead. It's been going on for eight years, telling you could wait."

"Thanks for the thought, but when it comes to the fact that mercenary is Reed, then you thought wrong," Sam said.

"Gee, thanks."

"You're welcome. You'll also be thanking me when we find out why your father has done what he has, too."

"There isn't a single reason that would hold any water in my book."

"No? Have you forgotten what I said about Commander Kingston? What if the bastard was playing both your father and me? I couldn't come back here without causing a whole lot of people a lot of pain and trouble. Not to mention spending the rest of my days enjoying Leavenworth's hospitality. What if Reed had to play dead to keep me alive?"

Nick stared at Sam for a long moment, feeling bits and pieces inside of him crumble. He cursed long and hard. "Okay, you've proved me wrong. There is at least one reason I'd buy. If it's true, then Kingston is one son of a bitch I'm going to get my hands on." Nick made a mental note to pump Jaymes and Grayson for every drop of info he could get on their boss.

"The only thing that doesn't make sense in all of this is I

know Reed was dead. If I had had any doubt of that I would have been searching every inch of Central America, Kingston or no Kingston, consequences or not."

"I know you would. But you need to cut yourself some slack. You had a concussion, and were in bad shape after almost two years at the end of Vasquez's whip."

Sam shook his head. "We'll just have to see."

Nick was afraid they would. Now that Sam was here, though, Nick realized he was right. Walking away without finding out exactly why his father had played dead would have been the wrong thing to do.

"I know what you're thinking."

Stefanie looked up to see Jaymes had joined her on the edge of the heliport in the shade of some trees that she was doing her best to hide in. She didn't welcome the intrusion. Her mind was heavily weighing what Annette would think if she knew how close Stefanie had come to killing a man—for no other reason than he was like the men who'd stood by and watched her degradation at Herrera's and Vasquez's hands. "And what would that be?"

Jaymes sighed. "I know you want to be alone, but I can't let you think that you're all alone. I know a little about how you're feeling. You're thinking that you're evil because you pulled the trigger yesterday."

Stefanie clasped her hands tight. The woman was dead-on. "I suppose you're going to tell me I'm not because I subconsciously knew the safety was on. What if I had truly forgotten that fact and fully intended to kill the man?"

"No. I'm here to tell you that it doesn't matter either way. Fighting evil is a war and people die all the time in war, just for choosing the wrong side."

"So you're saying I wouldn't be a murderer if I had shot that guy yesterday? I'm not buying it."

"Then you're wearing the same rose-colored glasses as your sister. She needs them because every man that comes across her operating table, she has to fight equally hard to save. It's part of who she is and her oath as a doctor. She can't be a judge. But people like us have a different purpose. It's okay for us to wake up and smell the garbage. If that man had had half a chance to abuse or kill you yesterday, he would have done it in a heartbeat."

"You don't know that."

"Don't I? He's the one running around taking people by force at gunpoint. He made his choice in this battle. And there's no way in hell you can convince me that he would have intervened on your behalf if any one of his *amigos* had wanted to have a little fun with you even if he wasn't wicked enough to do it himself."

Stefanie shook her head. "I don't know. Maybe he would have."

"I *do* know. He was the man with the gun and he was the aggressor in the situation. He wasn't defending anything or anyone. He was up to no good. I can judge all of those things without a jury. If he hadn't gone down like a ton of bricks when I nailed him in the groin, but had tried to kill me, then I would have killed him without regret. I've killed before."

"That's different. You're a soldier."

"And you're not? But just so you clearly understand where I am coming from, I didn't kill in the line of duty. They claimed it was self-defense and I let the story ride because the truth would have done my mother in at the time. She'd already been through more than a mother should have to bear."

Stefanie studied Jayme's stark expression. There was a mixture of raw emotions—pain, anger, bitterness—on her face, but the one that stood out the most was hatred. "What do you mean?"

"Sometimes people really *are* guilty and justice isn't served. When that happens, and it is an absolute fact, then if you don't act you're almost just as guilty—especially if the crime happens again.

"When I was growing up, two seven-year-old girls disappeared four years apart. People thought they were runaways. Then my seven-year-old sister disappeared. We knew she hadn't run away. This time the killer didn't do as good a job of hiding the body, but he got off scot-free for killing my sister on a legal technicality. Then nothing could be found to tie him to the other missing girls. He walked around our small town with his head high, grinning from ear to ear because nobody could touch him. He was supposedly a war hero and there were a number of people who believed he wasn't guilty. They, like he, claimed that the DNA evidence was planted and that the eye-witnesses who'd seen him with my sister last were framing him. So I framed him. I was seventeen by the time the trial ended. Made up stories of him harassing me. Made it look as if he were stalking me. Got the police involved and set him up. Then when he came after me, I put a knife right through his heart and smiled when he died. I killed the man who molested and murdered my sister, and believe me, if anyone had stood by and watched what he did to my sister and didn't stop it, they would have died, too. So, does that make me evil?"

Stefanie set her hand on Jaymes's arm, realizing that she really wasn't alone. Not alone in her hatred, her anger, or her pain. "No. No, it doesn't."

"Some people might say so. Because he supposedly 'came' after me, everyone started looking harder into his life. Turned out his mother had inherited a piece of forested property in the next state years ago. They investigated and found the killer had built a cabin on the land. The other missing girls were buried there, along with all the evidence proving him guilty. If I hadn't acted they may or may not have discovered the truth. I don't ask myself that. I ask myself how many other little girls would have died before the police caught him."

Stefanie stood silent a moment as she considered what Jaymes was saying. The total control, or lack of visible emotion, from Jaymes resonated with Stefanie. There were some griefs so deep that if one were to let oneself fall into them, one would never recover. She was overwhelmed by the trust Jaymes put in her. If she had found the means to kill Herrera, then the vampire would never have been able to take Marissa. But where did a person draw the line? By not killing the man yesterday, had she opened up the window for harm to befall someone else in the future? It was something she needed to come to terms with, and fast. She glanced at Jaymes. The woman seemed lost in thought.

Stefanie touched her hand, understanding what Jaymes was saying. She also wanted to comfort the woman. "You did the right thing," Stefanie said. "But why did you become military? Since the killer was military it would seem you'd have gone for law enforcement or something."

Jaymes shook her head. "I decided to go for the heart of the issue. Internal affairs is my goal. I want to make sure guys who are twisted up don't make it back into civilian life."

"That's why you and Grayson were sent after Sam then. Internal Affairs is after Sam?"

"Yes. Only from what we've found out, it looks like Commander Kingston is the one who's corrupt."

"What are you going to do about it?"

"Not sure yet." Jaymes sighed and Stefanie could almost feel the heavy weight on the staff sergeant's shoulders. "That's part of why I requested emergency leave to help with the tornado cleanup. I won't be able to go back and let things ride, pretend I don't know who and what he is now. And I won't be able to just ask for a transfer, either. That would be like watching someone commit a crime and not try and stop it. Kingston is too entrenched in the upper echelon of the military chain for any solution to be simple and the only evidence is hearsay. All I do know is that I am going to do something. It may take time, but I *will* do something about it."

"We'd be with you," Stefanie said. "Me, Sam, Nick, everyone."

Jaymes met her gaze with a pointed one of her own. "We'll see. Sam isn't in a good position to get involved. All of you are already in over your heads with this demon and vampire battle. And Nick, I'm not really sure he's up for anything but burying his head in the sand since his father has surfaced."

"We'd be there," Stefanie insisted. "And you have to give Nick a chance. I'm learning he's the kind of guy to come through in the end."

"Maybe when it comes to flying. Anything on the ground, he's more like a blind bee in a flower garden." Jaymes nodded and left. She looked back over her shoulder. "That includes women—never mind. I'll just tell him what I think. Just remember to not judge yourself too harshly, okay?"

Stefanie felt an odd smile tug at the corners of her mouth. Jaymes's traumatic experience had given Stefanie a perspective she really needed. Also, she didn't think Nick would appreciate Jaymes's assessment of him, but the blind bee in a garden kind of fit him—especially when it came to women.

The moon cast faint shadows in the twilight and gave Herrera a sliver of hope that he'd survive the longest, most torturous day of his life. The most torturous *night* of his life could never be bested. It was the night of his eighteenth birthday. He'd been standing on the street, waiting for an easy mark to walk by so he could steal enough money to party that night. He'd had a special girl then. She wasn't like him. She lived in a house rather than a cardboard box. He wondered why she'd taken up with him, but when he found out she liked his dangerous edge and dark handsomeness, he didn't question it again. They were both facts.

That night, Vasquez's limo stopped on the corner and the next thing Herrera knew, he was snatched off the street by thugs. Bound, gagged, and blindfolded, he'd been taken to a room. His clothes had been cut from his body and Vasquez had used him over and over like a whore. Then Vasquez drank nearly every drop of blood from his body. Herrera thought he was in hell. He thought he would die. But he didn't die. His hell had only begun.

He spent the next ten years as Vasquez's blood slave and errand boy until he figured out he wasn't powerless—he could undermine Vasquez even as he ingratiated himself. He stole money and resources and framed others for the deeds. He secretly used the women Vasquez used and they never told. They knew they'd die a more horrible death than they could imagine if they did. And one by one he eliminated Vasquez's heirs, plotting for the day that he'd inherit it all through Marissa.

Everything that Samir had come in and taken over was Herrera's. He'd paid the price to have it year after year, and he couldn't wait to off the bastard. And it was a good thing Herrera had already put his plans in motion.

Ever since Herrera had hired the army and arranged for Menendez to die, Samir had surrounded himself with bodyguards as if Herrera couldn't be trusted. It was insulting. Herrera wouldn't kill Samir here. Well, he would have, but not once he realized anything he planned to do would be better served at the SINCO meeting tomorrow. Of course, it was against laws of the Vladarian Order for vampires to use fire bombs against one another, but these were extenuating circumstances.

Very extenuating.

Currently, Samir was on his cell phone commanding Colonel Estrada to bring most of his men in from the search so that they could be ready to act when Ysalane—

Speak of the *bruja*. Ysalane walked through the doors without even knocking, head held high as she pranced like a queen. She wore a gold dress and a ton of jewels, culminating in a small crown on her head, and she carried that crystal jaguar as if it were a god.

How dare she?

How dare she elevate herself as if she were better than him? The *puta* would pay. Before Samir could enter the room, Herrera crossed to Ysalane. Grabbed her breast and twisted. "You're a stupid, lazy *puta*. You deserve nothing. And very soon you and your precious jaguar are going to be in pieces all over the floor."

"Do you have news for me, Ysalane?" Samir said, entering the room from the balcony.

"Yes," Ysalane said then spat on Herrera.

Herrera's entire body went numb with shock. He couldn't believe it.

"Ysalane will only tell you if you promise me that pig will never come near me again and I will be rich enough to have my own compound and my own guards."

Samir laughed. "I see you've become a great deal wiser. The dress does make the woman after all. You have my promise."

"She is mine." Rage sent Herrera over the edge of reason. He drew his hidden dagger and went right for Ysalane's heart, but before he could take half a step or even raise the knife, a bodyguard had him on the floor, foot smashing his knife hand to the ground. "I am Hernan Cortes Herrera and I will kill you!"

"He will let you up," Samir said. "But only if you give me your word you'll not touch Ysalane. She is too important."

"Fine," Herrera sneered. "You have it." The words were forced from the guts of his humiliation.

"Let him up," Samir said.

Herrera rose up and slashed the guard's throat. "I did not say I wouldn't touch him." Herrera spat on the man.

"You're such a predictable, stupid creature, Herrera. Sometimes it is hard to despise you rather than pity you. For now we have more important things to attend. Ysalane, do you have news for me? I give you my word Herrera will not come near you and you shall have all the things you wish."

"Then Ysalane will tell you where the wolfman is."

Herrera clenched his knife and dug his fangs deep into his lip. Just a little longer. Just a little bit longer and everything would be his, including Ysalane. Death would be too good a punishment for her. He would see that she suffered the worst degradation possible in the farthest reaches of the damned.

"Excellent," said Samir. "Why don't you just whisper it to me? No need to shout it out to the world, now is there?"

Ysalane went to Samir and spoke so softly that not even Herrera's acute hearing could pick up the location.

Pain shot through Herrera's jaw, and he heard several teeth crack from the clenching of his jaw. He had to hold on. Just a little bit longer. Tomorrow would be his day to conquer and rule.

Chapter Twenty-three

WHEN SEÑOR Castillo played the marimba and Señora Castillo sang, it was very hard for Marissa to remember that they were barely holding a monster at bay. She would have to confront everything in the morning and make a decision about what to do. They had to find a way to stop Herrera and Menendez, and she still wasn't sure if going with Father Dom and Chanel Langston would be the right thing to do. She did know that no matter what, she had to find a way to contact Stefanie and Sam and the others. A flash of guilt streaked across her heart.

Though she knew Stefanie would be glad for the love Marissa had found, the fact that Stefanie and everyone could be harmed or still prisoners put a vise upon Marissa's happiness. But when she considered how fiercely Navarre had fought and protected her from Herrera, and recalled that Jared and Aragon would fight just as effectively for her friends, that vise eased a little. They had to be all right. They just had to be.

Marissa leaned into Navarre's embrace as Señora Castillo finished her song. A cool breeze caressed the twilight and from their "top of the world" location, she could see almost all of the stars across the horizon as they twinkled at the glowing ball of the moon bouncing just high enough to peek over the treetops.

Suddenly, she felt Navarre tense as if bracing for pain. His hand in hers shook and she felt hair pop from his skin. She glanced up at his face, thankful to see the change had not reached that far yet. Although the Castillos were very kind, everyone had thought it wise not to tell them of Navarre's wolf state.

Marissa leaned over and whispered, "You can't change now. It would frighten the Castillos."

"I know. I can't seem to stop it." His arm bulged and Marissa quickly jerked his arm off the table, setting it in her lap.

She smiled up at Señora Castillo. "I must talk to Navarre right now," she said, pulling Navarre up and away from the group. As she glanced at the others—they were all sitting outside in chairs on the Castillos' porch—she saw that Father Dom was no longer with them and Rafael had fallen asleep in the corner he'd practically hid in. Since participating in the ceremony her brother had completely withdrawn from everyone.

How long ago had Father Dom left?

"Do you want more sweet cakes before you sneak away?" Señor Castillo said, jumping up to serve them more.

"*Gracias,* no," Marissa said, pulling Navarre deeper into the shadows. She nearly tripped over the torch that was still sitting on the edge of the porch, but caught her balance and smiled. "I am still full from the wonderful dinner. We will have some when we get back."

Navarre's back arched and he groaned as he shifted into his full werewolf form.

"Is Navarre all right?" Señor Castillo asked, squinting into the darkness and moving their way.

Marissa shoved Navarre behind the house. "He's *muy bueno.* We'll be back soon."

"Leave them and come help me ready their room," said Señora Castillo. "The *novios* want to kiss beneath the stars like we used to do."

"Used to do?" Señor Castillo said. "We will fix that tonight, señora."

Marissa led Navarre away from the house, over to the Mayan ruins where their silhouettes wouldn't be discernible in the moonlight.

"I'm sorry," Navarre said, breathing heavily. "I thought I had all of this under control last night. I don't know why I can't stop it from happening now."

Marissa reached out to him, moving close and laying her head against his chest. "It's all right. We'll figure these things out, but it may take some time. We'll just stay here until you are better."

A noise from above them had Marissa pulling Navarre away from the wall. A rain of small rocks fell, accompanied by a cry of pain that sounded like Father Dom.

"What is it?" Navarre demanded, his wolf spirit suddenly appearing so he could see.

"I think that Father Dom must be up—"

"Help!" Another, larger shower of rocks brought Father Dom's pale face into view as he slid over the side of the crumbling pyramid.

Navarre pushed Marissa out of the way. She fell back from danger, watching as Navarre caught Father Dom, then absorbed the impact by rolling across the ground with the priest until they both came to a safe stop.

Marissa ran over to them. "*Dios!* I thought you would die."

"So did I, child. So did I."

"What were you doing up there? Señor Castillo told us it was not safe. And you go up there at night? Are you *loco*?"

"*Por favor,* I had to. I could not wait any longer. I climbed the steps until I received a phone signal. Only I could not get through to anyone. I left a message, but the *teléfono's* battery died and now I do not know if help will come or not."

Marissa grabbed the priest's shoulder and shook him before releasing her hold to pace in anger. "How could you do that? We were going to wait until *mañana* to call! Now we must leave here tonight."

"No, we must wait for their help. They are the only ones strong enough to fight Herrera and Menendez. You must believe me, I have lived here many years and I know how powerful and cruel the general and his men are. To do anything else would be *suicidio*. I know you heard the helicopters today. They are looking for us."

"I heard them, but they did not come close. We had time."

"How much time? Until morning? It is better to call for help before the trouble comes."

Marissa tried to think of what she, Navarre, and Rafael needed to do now. Father Dom could stay here, but she wasn't—

Loud, roaring screams reverberated through the night air. Several of them in a row. It was a jaguar. One that sounded as crazed as the animal last night had. It couldn't be. And just like last night, she felt a sudden sense of malevolence about her.

"There is danger," Navarre said, urging everyone in the direction of the Castillos' house. "I did not say anything last night but the creature that attacked you was possessed by an evil spirit. I believe the jaguar was sent to kill us."

"*Dios.*" Marissa's pulse pounded in her ears as she hurried at Navarre's side. "I thought I had imagined it last night. Who else but Herrera could be behind this?"

"A demonic shapeshifter?" asked Father Dom, his voice shaking with fear. He changed direction. "We must go to the church for protection."

"We need to get the others." Marissa slowed her step. The church was to the right. The house to the left.

Navarre urged her toward the church. "I will," he said. "You go and we'll be right there. I'll get Rafael first from the porch and have him bring the others. Then I will follow once I can change form again."

"But you'll be in danger—"

"Trust me. I fought the beast before, I can do so again. Now go with the priest."

Marissa still hesitated. The awful feeling suddenly filling her demanded that she hold on to Navarre and never let him go. It was silly. He'd only be a short distance away. She could stand on the steps of the church and watch him. It was only going to be a few minutes before he joined them.

"Be careful," she said, and hugged him. The jaguar screamed again, much closer this time. She and Father Dom broke into a run. As they reached the door, Father Dom went inside and headed directly to the altar where the large crucifix sat.

Marissa saw Navarre cross the field to the house. Then a sound more ominous than an animal roar chopped through the night. Helicopters. Several of them. But what could they expect to see at night?

Holding the crucifix, Father Dom joined her at the door.

Less than a minute later helicopters appeared against the twilit sky, their searchlights shining directly on the Misión Salida de Sol. Marissa kept the door slightly cracked to see what was happening, noticing that all lights at the Castillos' house had been extinguished. By all appearances the mountaintop looked deserted, but they didn't leave, and dread filled Marissa's heart.

Two figures suddenly materialized on the ground not more than fifteen feet from the church steps. Herrera and Samir!

Madre de Dios!

"They're here!" she whispered to Father Dom. "Herrera and his men are here."

She eased the door shut and locked it. Her pulse thundered as her mind raced for a solution. What could she do? Where could she hide? Urging Father Dom in front of her, she ran down the aisle, praying that Navarre and Rafael would stay hidden.

"There has to be a back way out. If we can get to the cover of the trees it will be harder for them to find us."

"No. That won't work, child. If they can't find you they will torture the Castillos until they get what they want. I brought this danger to them. I cannot allow them to be hurt. You have to give yourself up to Herrera. Señora Langston and her men will find and rescue you again. There is no other way to save the Castillos."

Marissa shook her head, unable to breathe. "I don't want anyone hurt. But I can't give myself to Herrera. There has to be another way. Navarre will die trying to save me. If we escape to the woods, Navarre and Rafael will likely try and do the same with the Castillos."

From outside they heard Señor Castillo yell, "What do you men want here? This is a church mission! Sacred ground!"

Marissa half turned and pain exploded in her head.

"Forgive me, child," Father Dom said, just as the world faded to black.

"They're both on the move," Nick shouted. Everyone came running from whatever corner of the heliport they had drifted to.

"Damn," said Sam. "I really wanted to hear back from the contact before this happened." The atmosphere was tense. They had to decide right now whether to follow a CIA directive to sit tight or to chance a mission they might never survive.

The blips on the computer screen appeared to be converging on the same point.

Nick cursed. "CIA operation or not, I'm taking the bird up and going for it. We're the only ones in this jig that really care what happens to Marissa and Navarre, and I think we need to be on scene for this showdown."

"We don't even know for sure that we're going to find Marissa and Navarre in the middle of that hornet's nest," Sam pointed out.

"Given the facts, what are the odds that they are?" Nick shot back.

"Fifty-fifty," Sam said.

"Exactly. I say those are good enough odds to save our friends."

"More than enough. Okay, since this is an operation, we have to pare it down and keep it simple so nobody gets shot in the confusion. Nick, you and I will move in. We leave the women here with Jared, Aragon, and Grayson——"

"Aragon and I go," Jared said. "Navarre is our brother. We go."

"We all go," said Annette. "My medical skill might be needed."

"I'm not staying behind, either," said Jaymes.

"I'm already in up to my neck," said Grayson. "No choice but to see this mission through." He grinned at Sam. "Besides, somebody has to keep you from getting into any more trouble."

Sam glared at everyone. "What part of simple didn't you all understand?"

Nobody answered Sam's question, they just piled into the helo.

Sam was still cursing. "This is about the stupidest thing I've ever let happen. When did this outfit lose a leader and become a democracy?"

Smiling, Nick powered up the bird and took it skyward.

Navarre reached the porch, his wolf spirit leading the way, and Rafael came running out of the house, gun in hand.

"I hear the jaguar. Where is everyone?" Rafael moved to the edge of the porch.

"Marissa and the priest are in the church," Navarre said. "You need to get the Castillos and take them there. I think this jaguar, like the one last night, is possessed with an evil spirit and Father Dom believes everyone will be safer at the church."

"Where are the señor and señora? I didn't see them— *Mierda*, I hear helicopters."

"We must hurry!" Navarre ran to the door, realizing they no longer had time for him to remain hidden. The older couple would just have to understand who and what he was. "The Castillos were here just a short time ago. They must be inside." Navarre called them as he stepped into the house.

No answer. He bounded up the stairs and called again. No answer. The sound of the helicopters grew louder. He grabbed a coat hanging on the door, planning to use it to pick up the Castillos' scent, and ran back outside. He felt Herrera's presence then, a pervading sense of darkness that seemed to drain the goodness from the air.

"Herrera is coming," he told Rafael.

Marissa's brother paled and grabbed at the porch railing. "We're not ready to fight yet."

"We will escape through the forest as we did before. You go to the church and I will find the Castillos."

Suddenly, lights flooded the area and Rafael ducked back into the shadows of the porch. "It's too late!" he cried, looking panicked. "We're too late."

"It is never too late," Navarre insisted. "Come with me. Keep to the shadows until we reach the woods. Then we'll go through the forest to the area in back of the church and get to Marissa and Father Dom that way."

"*Dios*, he's going to capture us again." Rafael didn't move, frozen in fear.

Navarre placed his hand on the young man's shoulder. "Look at me," he demanded. "I have been fighting for millennia. We can win, but you have to believe."

Rafael blinked. "We will win or die. I'll not be taken prisoner again. I will follow you."

They made it to the woods and were moving toward the church when they heard a crash through the brush up ahead and saw Señor Castillo run into the lit field. "What do you men want here? This is a church mission! Sacred ground!"

Two figures were standing in the field, too close to the church for Navarre's comfort. Herrera and another vampire. One of the hovering helicopters landed at the far end of the field. Armed men poured out.

"We're dead now," Rafael whispered.

"Glad to know we are in the right place, *amigo!*" Herrera said. "Now where are Marissa and the wolfman?"

"*Yo no sé,* I don't know who you are talking about," Señor Castillo said.

Herrera laughed. "Very amusing, *pero* I am not in the mood."

Suddenly Herrera appeared behind Señor Castillo with a knife raised and stabbed the old man in the shoulder.

Señor Castillo screamed and fell to his knees.

"Go to the back of the church, and escape with Marissa," Navarre told Rafael. "I will see this ended."

"Where are Marissa and the wolfman?" Herrera demanded.

"I am here, Herrera," Navarre shouted, stepping from the woods. "Marissa is not."

"Glad you are here for the party, wolfman, but I do not believe you'd leave Marissa," Herrera said. He sliced into Señor Castillo's other shoulder.

Navarre and his wolf spirit rushed forward, but before they could reach Herrera the church door opened.

"She is here," the priest shouted as he exited with Marissa in his arms. She didn't move or fight, but lay lifeless.

"No!" Navarre shouted, running harder and changing his direction toward Marissa. His mind reached out to hers, and thankfully sensed pain. She was dazed and confused. What had the priest done to her? *Marissa! Wake up! Fight! Run, love!*

Marissa felt Navarre's spirit and struggled to rise. Her head pounded with pain.

Why was Father Dom carrying her?

Suddenly, memory flooded back. Struggling to rise, she saw Navarre coming her way. Her worst nightmare was coming true. "Navarre!" she cried. "Run!"

Herrera and Samir appeared on the church steps in an instant.

Marissa fought to escape from Father Dom's hold, but Samir jerked her into his arms.

"She's mine," Samir yelled, baring his fangs.

Undaunted, Marissa balled her fists and pummeled the vampire in the face.

Herrera laughed. "All yours," he said.

Father Dom screamed and Marissa saw Herrera pull his knife out of Father Dom's back. The priest rolled down the church steps.

"I belong to Navarre," Marissa cried, fighting Samir's hold. "We are legally married."

"Free her!" Navarre shouted. Marissa glanced up to see him and his wolf spirit reach the steps, coming for her. Armed guards with their guns raised were right behind Navarre. He twisted and kicked, sending four of them flying backward, but more were on the way. In the distance, another helicopter arrived. Armed men were everywhere. He couldn't fight them all.

"No, Navarre. Run!"

Samir caught her wrist and wrenched it behind her. "You were legally mine six months ago, whore," he said. "I bought you and fixed a palace for you and now you have defiled it all." Samir pointed at Navarre. "Kill him, now."

"No!" Marissa yelled. "No!"

The advancing guards pointed their guns and fired. Navarre dove to the side and rolled, but bullets plowed into him. He stood, then jerked backward several times as his body changed from werewolf to mortal form before he fell to the ground, blood gushing from his wounds. His wolf spirit disappeared.

Marissa screamed in horror. She heard Herrera's laughter just before her heart squeezed so tight that she felt as if it had stopped beating. She wanted nothing more than to die, to join her spirit with Navarre's, and she gave herself over to the numbness stealing through her.

Chapter Twenty-four

HERRERA LAUGHED at Marissa's tortured scream. It was beautiful, perfectly pitched, a soul's final cry of ultimate pain and delivered so effectively that he wondered if she had actually died. From the look on Samir's face, he wondered, too. Surely, the whole world had heard her. So where was her handsome brother hiding? "Maybe you shouldn't have executed her lover in front of her, Samir. According to Vasquez's will, she has to be alive, well, and undamned in order for you to control SINCO and the money. Have you already killed her?"

As Marissa lay limp in his arms, Samir pressed his lips to her neck, where Herrera knew a vampire could detect the slightest sign of life.

"She has a faint pulse," Samir said. "I will see that she lives, for now. Once my attorneys break Vasquez's will, she'll be executed for her impurity, of course. My honor and the law demand it." He moved down the steps as Colonel Estrada and more guards arrived. "Impeccable timing, Estrada," Samir told the colonel.

"I serve to please, *comandante*," said the colonel, saluting Samir. "What do you want done next?"

"Whatever Herrera would like for you to do with the mess. You and your men may take orders from him tonight only. Tomorrow evening, I will inform you of where I want you and the men to establish a base." Samir turned and smiled at Herrera. "Come early tomorrow for the SINCO meeting and we'll discuss your payments for use of my new army. As useful as Colonel Estrada is, I may look into overtaking Venezuela's oil. Their recent meetings with the Russian infidels are too troubling to permit."

Disbelief froze Herrera on the church steps as Samir turned

and dashed across the field to a waiting helicopter. It lifted up, barely two feet off the ground, and wobbled wildly for a moment, giving Herrera hope it would crash and burn. Men who were on higher ground and hadn't had time to clear the rotors lost their heads before the helicopter evened out and took off.

Pay Samir! Pay that bastard for use of the army that was supposed to be Herrera's after getting Marissa? If it wasn't for Herrera, Samir wouldn't have had an army to use!

"What would you like for the men to do here, Herrera?" Colonel Estrada asked, as if he were speaking to a peon. No *jefe*, no *comandante*, not even a *señor!*

Herrera looked at the betrayer, wondering how he could eliminate them all in one strike. "Any word of Menendez?"

"No, *pero* I expect he has heard of our defection, so he will not return until he has enough men to assure his safety."

"You still have control of his estates?"

"*Sí.*"

"Then you and your men can return there for the moment and relax, perhaps even finish the celebration I interrupted last night, no?"

Colonel Estrada's his eyes narrowed with either confusion or suspicion. "*Muy bien.*"

Herrera smiled. "You will hear from me soon." And they would, just as long as it took him to arrange for their demise. A new day was about to dawn in the house of Hernan Cortes Herrera. He'd been too patient and played by the rules far too long.

Glancing over the reigning chaos as more men poured out of another helicopter, Herrera pulled out his cell phone and entered the church. Time to set his plans for SINCO's midnight meeting in motion. He'd try and get Marissa out before Samir's world came to an end. Having her would make things much easier for Herrera to gain control of it all, but if he didn't, it wouldn't matter.

From now on, he'd take everything by force. SINCO, Guatemala, Honduras, Nicaragua . . . the possibilities were limitless.

The continued fire of machine guns grabbed his attention, but before he could reach the doors, they burst open and General Menendez stood there, gun aimed, his face twisted with rage. "You die, *bastardo* traitor! You die!"

Herrera laughed and bared his fangs for the first time at the general. "I'm already dead, or undead. You can't kill a vampire, *pero* you dug your own grave, Otto. I cannot trust a man who keeps secret partners. I know once your army had enough power then you planned to assassinate me and rule yourself. I saw the evidence on your desk. The letter said, 'When you become *presidente* . . .' "

Menendez's eyes widened in surprise then he shook his head sadly as he stepped into the church. "That was an old letter, *amigo*, from when I campaigned in the last election. You should have asked me. This all could have been avoided. *Pero* now it is too late."

Herrera saw a dark figure fill the doorway. It was the old man whom he'd stabbed in the shoulder. The man lifted a machine gun and pointed it at Menendez's head. "You killed my Camina and Diego, Menendez. I now avenge my children's murders."

"Too late for you, *amigo*. But not for me," Herrera said, as Menendez turned and the old man pulled the trigger, ripping Menendez to shreds.

Herrera disappeared from the church and materialized outside. Colonel Estrada lay dead, his blood dripping down the church steps. That was one down and maybe not that many more to go. Soldiers Menendez had brought with him were chasing after the men who'd come with Samir. And yet another helicopter was landing at the far end of the field. Herrera assumed it was more of Menendez's forces. It appeared to be a night for retribution. All except for Samir. . . .

The scream of a jaguar very close by cut through the noise and sent a shiver down Herrera's spine. Before he could turn and look, a muzzle jabbed him in the back.

"Put your hands up and slowly turn around. I want you to see my face when I kill you, Herrera."

Did the idiot think he could gun down a vampire? Herrera spun about with an amused smile to face Marissa's brother. The man had a blanket wrapped around him and the gun he had pointed Herrera's way shook. That he was up and standing considering the torture he'd suffered was remarkable. "I wondered where you were hiding, *puto*."

"Preparing for your extinction. *Pero* I want it to happen slowly and painfully. You see, I listened very carefully to everything said about Tío Luis and I know a vampire's secrets."

"You must not have listened well, if you think a gun will harm me. Do you not know a *vampire* is invincible?"

"Except for silver and fire, no?" Rafael said.

The jaguar roared again, even closer, and they both jumped. But nothing appeared from the woods behind them.

Herrera shrugged. "True, *pero* you would have to catch me first." Herrera disappeared and materialized behind Rafael, thinking he would teach the man another lesson. Samir wouldn't be the only one enjoying raping a Vasquez tonight. The incomparable elixir of power that came with the act was just what Herrera needed. He roared with laughter, his mind already bubbling with excitement. Maybe he'd carry the *puto* into the church and take him there first.

Rafael turned around. The blanket fell from his shoulders just as he ignited a high-powered torch.

Herrera screamed in agony. Flames engulfed him as the fire burned across his neck and up to his face, setting his hair and shirt ablaze. Slapping at the fire, Herrera stumbled back but Rafael kept coming at him.

"*Por favor*, I forgot to tell you what else I know," Rafael said.

"When in pain a *vampire* cannot disappear, can he? And the greater the pain the more his strength disappears."

Herrera blindly turned to run, but Rafael kicked at his feet and sent him sprawling to the ground and pinned him in place with his foot. The torch cut into his back. Herrera screamed, crying for mercy.

"Where did he take my sister?" Rafael demanded.

"To his palace!"

The torch burned down his spine. His body convulsed.

"Where? What palace?"

"Sheik Rashad bin Samir Al Sabah in Kassim! You must rescue her at midnight! Not before then. Samir has a meeting. Mercy, *por favor*. End this torture."

"Turn over," Rafael demanded.

Herrera could barely move. His body shuddered with pain. His muscles refused to function. Rafael shoved him over with his foot.

"Mercy? You dare to beg for mercy, *bastardo*? I will give you the same mercy you gave me." Rafael put the full force of the torch to Herrera's groin.

More than when she returned to Corazón, a surreal, almost dizzying feeling gripped Stefanie. Tonight she wasn't facing ruins, but she might come face-to-face with a nightmare. Herrera might be here. The knife clipped to her bulletproof vest was close at hand and silver-plated. One thrust into Herrera's heart and he'd be dead. It almost seemed too humane.

She braced herself as Nick landed the helicopter at the far end of a field. She hoped and prayed they'd find Marissa and Navarre safe in the mess below. After seeing the bodies on the ground, Sam had tried to talk everyone into letting just the men out and for Jaymes to take the helicopter back up and wait until they'd assessed the danger of the situation before going in. Annette nixed that. There were men down, possibly dying, and if she could do something to save them, she had to. What if Marissa or Navarre were hurt?

Sam didn't argue more. Armed and geared, the men poured out of the helicopter. "Wait here until I signal it's okay," Sam shouted before taking off.

"Wait here, my ass," Annette said. She shoved a trauma pack into Stefanie's arms and grabbed another pack for herself. "Jamyes, you lead and we'll be your shadow. Get me to the closest body and we'll take it from there. Sam can kill us later."

Jaymes grinned. "I didn't know you had it in you, Doc." She grabbed up two machine guns, strapped one over her shoulder and anchored the other one in her hands, ready for action.

Stefanie noticed Sam had left his big silver-plated knife, the one he'd killed Vasquez with. She picked it up and put it in the med pack, planning to give it to him as soon as she saw him.

Keeping low, they ran from body to body with Annette cursing a blue streak at finding each one dead. Amid shouts and occasional gunfire, Stefanie heard the roar of a jaguar. So seemingly close that every time it screamed, she'd look around expectantly. They drew closer to the buildings and suddenly, from across the field, Stefanie heard Herrera laugh.

She knew it was him, recognized the malicious cruelty of it. He was here. A chill of fear rammed into the hard edge of her resolve for revenge and died. It was now or never. Dropping the trauma pack, she drew out Sam's huge knife and walked toward the sound of laughter.

"Where are you going?" hissed Annette.

Stefanie didn't look back. She didn't answer. To do anything but go after Herrera would crumble her strength. That laughter became a scream and Stefanie started to run. What in the hell was going on?

An abrupt tackle from behind brought her to the ground. It was Jaymes.

"What in the hell are you doing? Trying to get us both killed?"

Tears filled Stefanie's eyes and she shoved against Jaymes's hold. "Let me go," she cried. "I have to kill him. I must, or I will die. He's here. Herrera is here. Let me go."

"Easy," Jaymes said. "Where?"

"That screaming. That's him."

"We'll go together. Keep your head down."

"No. You go back and protect my sister."

"Aragon and Grayson showed up with Navarre. She's trying to save him. It's bad."

"Marissa?"

"Nothing yet. The men are searching. Let's go."

Jaymes led the way. They passed steps were bodies lay and Jaymes shoved her down as a man rounded the corner of the building and tried to fire on them. But Jaymes kicked the muzzle to the side and slammed the butt of her machine gun into his temple. He crumpled to the ground.

The screaming became a wild and mindless howl. Stefanie got to her feet and saw a man burning another man alive with a torch.

"Dear God!" Jaymes said, lifting her gun.

"No." Stefanie pushed her aside, then ran to the macabre tableau.

The man was so absorbed in his torture of Herrera that he didn't even notice her approach. She looked down at the tortured animal Herrera had become. She expected a flood of satisfaction to fill her, a moment of triumph to grip her. Instead, she felt nothing but a weary sickness inside. Her soul was in the same shape as Herrera's, screaming from the evil he'd burned her with, and killing him or anyone else wasn't going to help.

She knew the man with the torch had to be after revenge. There'd be no other reason to fry the vampire's dick. Was killing Herrera helping the man or damaging him more? Gripping her knife with both hands, she moved in, approaching Herrera's head. Herrera's gaze met hers a brief moment, in recognition and a plea for mercy. She fell to her knees and plunged the silver blade into his heart.

Herrera's screaming stopped. The man turned off the torch. The crying of her soul grew louder.

"*Gracias,*" said the torch man as he looked up at her. "I couldn't stop. I couldn't stop." Tears fell from his dark eyes, eyes that were familiar to her. Not only because of the desolation in them, but also because they were so like Marissa's. He threw the torch down and stumbled back from Herrera's body.

"I understand." She winced as she pulled her knife out.

"Didn't you just kill the wrong man?" Jaymes asked, eyes wide with horrified shock. She had her gun pointed at the torch man.

"No," said Stefanie, standing. "Not at all." She narrowed her gaze at Herrera's torturer. "Who are you?"

"Rafael Vasquez."

Stefanie's heart sank. A relation of Marissa's? But Marissa's family was dead. Still, if a man named Vasquez was torturing Herrera then . . . "Marissa," she gasped in pain. "Where is Marissa? What did Herrera do to her?" Regret that she hadn't picked up the torch and done more to Herrera flooded her.

"Who are you?" Rafael demanded.

"Stefanie Batista. Risa's friend. Where is she? What did Herrera do to her that made you torture him?"

"Stefanie! You came for Marissa!" the man cried. "*Gracias a Dios,* Herrera didn't have the chance to physically hurt Marissa, *pero* a vampire named Sheik Rashad bin Samir Al Sabah took her minutes ago. Herrera said to the sheik's palace in Kassim."

"Look out!" Jaymes yelled, and pulled Stefanie with her.

Stefanie swung her head around to see the danger. A jaguar was coming right at them, its eyes glowing red.

Rafael stumbled back. "*Mierda!* Herrera has returned as a beast! Kill it!"

"That's ridiculous," Jaymes said.

Still, Stefanie saw that Jaymes had the jaguar in her gun sights.

"It's an endangered species," Jaymes added. "I don't want to kill it unless it attacks. Everyone stand very still. Maybe it will go away."

"I tell you, it is possessed with *ojos rojos*," Rafael said, slowly moving backward.

With a loud snarl the jaguar leaped onto Herrera's body and sank its fangs into Herrera's neck. It tore out a chunk of flesh and began to feast.

"Shit," said Jaymes. "What do we do now? Go! Scat!" she yelled, shooing the cat.

The jaguar ignored her and continued to eat.

"We can't just sit here and let it eat him," Jaymes said.

"Then I suggest we go check on Navarre and tell everyone where Marissa is," Stefanie said.

Jaymes looked at her, horrified. "You can't be serious?"

Stefanie nodded her head. "Yes, I am. Not only does the bastard deserve it, but the body has to be destroyed to ensure the vampire's extinction. We were going to have to finish burning him anyway. Let the jaguar eat. Herrera fed off others his whole life in more gruesome ways than this."

They feared the war... state of being was too weakened from

Chapter Twenty-five

E VER SINCE their arrival at the mission, it had been foremost in Nick's mind that Sinclair could show up at any minute. The last he'd seen on the tracker monitor, Sinclair had been headed this way. But now that they'd found Navarre, thoughts of his father had taken a back burner.

Currently, he ran ahead of the group, gun ready, looking for danger. Grayson and Marissa's brother carried all of the medical supplies from the helo. Annette was behind them, keeping Navarre's and a priest's IV lines straight as Jared carried the priest and Aragon with Sam carried Navarre to the house at the mission where she'd set up a hospital. Jaymes, armed and alert, guarded the rear.

Sam had already called Emerald and Erin to search out all the info on the sheik they could find, and sent a message to his CIA contact that both Menendez and Herrera were dead.

Annette's skill as a doctor left Nick in awe. She knew just what to do and did it with precision and confidence. Navarre had six bullet wounds to his body, plus a graze on his right temple. The Blood Hunter's life hung precariously in the balance. She already had hyperviscous fluids pumping and hemostatic pressure bandages stemming some of his blood loss, but there were two major arteries that needed immediate intervention. She had decided his chances for survival were better if she repaired the arterial damage now rather than transporting him to the nearest hospital.

Jared and Aragon were extremely worried. They explained that as a Blood Hunter, Navarre's self-healing powers should have already stopped his blood loss and begun healing his tissue. That his hadn't meant something was seriously wrong. They feared the warrior's state of being was too weakened from his previous injury for him to survive the number of wounds he'd sustained. The moment they hit the house, Annette took charge.

Father Dom was stabilized, so he was placed on a couch she had dragged into the dining area. All the chairs were taken out and the table was positioned for surgery.

"There're sterile gloves and blankets in your pack, Nick," Annette said. "Put on the gloves and, keeping the top surface from touching anything else, spread a blanket on the dining table there and then on the countertop. Sam, get me four coat hangers, squeeze them flat and place them on the arms of the chandelier so that their hook is down to hold the IV bags. Stefanie, as soon as Nick has the counter ready, I want you to glove up and start putting out supplies, just like you did pretending to be my nurse to help me with my med exams, remember?"

"I'll never forget," Stefanie said.

"I've had training in battlefield trauma," Grayson said. "I can help."

"You're on," said Annette, giving him the task of setting up the surgical instruments. From that point on, she had everyone busy, until she declared she was ready. Then she kicked everyone out of the house except for Stefanie and Grayson.

"I am very worried about Señor and Señora Castillo," said Rafael. "They are the elderly couple who run the mission. I haven't seen the señora since before the attack, *pero* I saw Herrera stab Señor Castillo in the shoulder twice as he demanded to know where my sister was hiding."

"The priest is the only elderly man we've found," Sam said. "All the dead have been young, armed men."

Nick grunted. "We can hope they've hidden in the woods and have escaped harm. I suggest we spread out and search the area."

"Somebody should stay on guard here as well," added Jaymes.

"Would you mind that task, then?" asked Nick. Since

Jaymes and Stefanie had rejoined the group and declared Herrera dead, Nick had noticed a change in both women. Neither of them had given much detail regarding Herrera's demise, other than they had found him injured, Stefanie had put the silver blade through the vampire's heart, and a jaguar had attacked the body.

"I'll stay," Jaymes said without hesitation.

Superwoman was voluntarily taking a backseat? Nick lifted a curious brow and moved over to her. "You okay?"

She just glared at him and he held his hands up, backing off. "Don't say I didn't ask." If she didn't want to tell him why there were haunted shadows in her drop-dead purple eyes, he wasn't going to push the issue. He motioned to the men. They split into two groups and began searching the woods. It didn't take them long to hear the quiet weeping of a woman.

They found her in a cave turned into an emergency shelter not far from the mission. She was holding her husband in her arms, weeping and praying. Her husband was moaning deliriously. Blood covered them both. Nick could see that she'd bandaged her husband's shoulders, but blood had soaked through them. She screamed and tensed when they entered the cave, until she saw Rafael. Then she began speaking in rapid Spanish. General Menendez's name was mentioned several times. Her eyes were wild with fear.

"Tell her we just want to help and to take her husband to a doctor at her house," Sam said.

Rafael told her, but she shook her head no.

Nick frowned. "Why doesn't she want her husband to get help?"

"Fear of retribution. She says that her husband just killed Menendez and his men will now come back and kill him. She wants to stay hidden."

Sam smiled. "Her husband sounds like a hero to you doesn't he, Nick? And heroes really should have a nice place to retire."

"Yep," Nick said. "I vote we get them to that resort in Belize with Emerald for a while. Then if they want, later they can come back here or they can go to a new home where no one will know they had any connection to General Menendez."

"I vote for the rest of the team," said Sam. "Tell her that we'll take them out of here tonight, but she must let the doctor treat her husband."

"Dios," the woman said, answering Sam before Rafael could interpret. "Please do not lie to me. You will keep him safe?"

"They will," said Rafael as he set a hand on her shaking shoulder. "I stake my honor and my life on it."

Sighing in relief, she released her hold on her husband. Nick noted that the old man was pale, his pulse thready, but his breathing was even. They quickly brought the Castillos back to the house, but froze in the yard at the sight of Jaymes being held at gunpoint by . . . Reed Sinclair.

Nick was speechless, his body numb from shock.

"Son of a bitch," Sam muttered.

"Fuck," Reed said, lowering the gun. "Looks like I owe you an apology, Jaymes Bond. I assume you weren't lying about your name, either?"

"No," said Jaymes.

"You'll have to forgive my cynicism. But your name in combination with the story was frankly too hard to believe."

"I want my gun back," Jaymes said. She had yet to look Nick's way.

Reed rubbed his jaw. "Damn near took my head off without it. That's one hell of a kick you've got."

With every second that passed, a burning anger bubbled stronger and stronger inside of Nick. He hadn't seen his father in eight years and the bastard had yet to say a single word to him.

"Fuck this," Nick said, and swung around. His ass was out of here until Reed's ass left the premises.

"No, you don't," Sam said, clamping a hand down on Nick's

shoulder. "Why don't all of you go inside the Castillos' home through the back door and help Mr. and Mrs. Castillo until Nick and I settle a few things with El Diablo Sinclair?"

"You are sure you do not need us to stay?" Jared asked, glaring at Reed as he sniffed the air. "This man is not as you think he is."

"No," said Sam. "We'll handle this right now."

The others left and still Reed didn't say a word. Just stood there staring at them.

Since Sam hadn't let Nick leave, Nick's anger exploded. He went at Reed swinging like a gangster on steroids. "You cowardly son of a bitch!" Nick planted his fist in Reed's face and sent another uppercut to the stomach.

Reed didn't fight back, but just stood there.

"Damn you!" Nick yelled, clenching his fists in frustration. "Damn you!" Tears filled his eyes and his gut wrenched in pain. Everything he was shattered and fell at his feet. He couldn't even breathe.

"Aren't you going to say a damn word?" Sam demanded, coming forward and setting a hand on Nick's shoulder.

"What can I possibly say that is going to make any difference to either of you? I betrayed you both. I'm alive. I do what I do here. End of story. Go back home, live your lives, and forget you ever saw me."

"Fine," Nick said. "That's exactly what I wanted to do in the first place."

"Forget it," Sam said, grabbing Reed by his shirt and shoving him backward. "You two assholes can pretend you don't give a shit, but I can't. You were dead! I know it! I've lived every day for eight years churning my guts up over the sacrifice you made to rescue me. And you owe me! You owe me an explanation! I'm going to be your worst nightmare every minute of every damn day until I get it, because I don't believe a word of that shit you just spat out."

"Believe it," Reed said, but Nick could tell his father's cool, calm exterior was shaken. Sam released Reed, but stood staring at him. "Believe it," he said again, only this time he whispered, as if he could barely speak.

Could there possibly be a good enough reason to justify what his father had done? Had Nick's own resentment over his mother's death made it impossible for his father to come home?

"There're flowers on her grave," Nick said. "I planted them there. Daisies and forget-me-nots in the summer and roses in the winter. I found Mom's diary a couple of years ago. She loved you. She just didn't know how to show you. It wasn't your fault she died. I just felt that way for a while. I buried Grandma last year next to Grandpa. She died quietly in her sleep. Aneurysm. The dogwood tree at the cemetery shades them now. It blooms pink every spring."

Only Nick's ragged breaths could be heard in the following pause.

"I know," Reed whispered.

"What?" Nick said.

"I know," Reed said, louder. "I've . . . I've been to see."

Nick's heart skipped a beat. "When? When were you there?"

"Often. In the shadows at night. I saw you the night of your graduation. I saw you the night you first flew with your pilot's license. I've seen it all. I could go there right this minute and be back the next. You see, I was dead. Only my spirit still hovered above my body. I saw you check me for signs of life, Sam. I saw your anguish as you left. Before my spirit could be drawn away from this world, I was bitten by a vampire and came back to life. So maybe, though my heart had stopped beating, I wasn't exactly dead yet."

"Shit," said Sam. "Who bit you?"

"A woman. A villager."

Nick shook his head. "No," he whispered. Of all the reasons he could have possibly imagined, this he had never considered.

He took several steps back. "You're like them? You're like Vasquez and Herrera?"

"You know about them? About their vampirism?" Reed was clearly shocked.

"We not only know," Sam said, "but we're in the middle of a war with them. So it would be a good thing to start talking more about what you are. Are you another Vasquez? Did you know he was a vampire when you got me out of there?"

"No," said Reed. "No. I knew nothing about this shit until it happened to me. Would have sworn on my own soul that it was nothing more than ghost stories. But I'm not like them."

"How?" demanded Nick. "How can you avoid it?"

"It's complicated," Reed said. "Vampirism is kind of like a virus that changes a mortal's body into immortal, but there are several different strains of the virus. Often the Vladarian strain produces the serial killers of the vampire world. It took me quite a while to adjust to what I had been turned into, and by then I decided that Reed Sinclair of Twilight, Tennessee, was better off dead—because I wanted you, Nick, to have as normal a life as possible after your mother and I screwed things up so royally. Now, what do you all mean that you're in a battle with the Vladarians?"

Sam drew a deep breath. "About a month—"

"No," Nick said, interrupting Sam. "Don't tell him anything until he can explain why the vampire world lets monsters like Vasquez and Herrera live."

" 'Serial killer' is my terminology. In actuality, the vampire world is still mired in a medieval feudalistic society that is based on animalistic power. The Vladarians are the lords, or rock stars, if you will. The rest of us are the peasants. I can't take them out without bringing the wrath of the entire vampire world down upon my woman and her clan. But I can set them up to be dealt with by the mortal world. I'd been working for years with the CIA to trap Vasquez and Herrera by using Menendez."

The implications of what his father had revealed floored Nick, and at last he put himself in Reed's shoes. What would it have been like to wake up one day and be a peasant in a supernatural world?

Nick looked at his dad. He still had a lot of shit he had to work through, but Reed had hit upon the one reason Nick could swallow, hook, line, and sinker. "Thanks," he said. "Thanks for coming to my grad night and my first flight."

"I'd have come more often, but you started having a rather marked interest in women and I never knew what I'd pop in on."

Nick's jaw dropped and there was a suspicious noise from the side of the building, like a stifled laugh of the Jaymes Bond variety.

Sam shook his head. "Seems as if we don't know shit about what we're doing."

"Yeah, and ignorance will always bite your ass," Nick added. "Since I missed out on the sex ed, you think you could fill us in on the vamps?"

"I might be interested in some consulting work. Why don't you tell me how you've been dealing with the Vladarians? There have been a number of rumors among the peasants that a battle is brewing between the lords."

Nick shuddered at the thought his father would be considered a peasant, while bastards like Vasquez and Herrera were lords. "Have the vampires ever heard of the French Revolution?" Nick asked.

Reed grinned, showing fangs. "I tell anyone who will listen about it every chance I get."

"Shit," said Sam. "Do you have any idea how this complicates things? I think I was much better off with the idea that all vamps and demons were the bad guys."

Navarre's spirit hovered in what he thought was the twilit edges between the mortal and the spirit worlds. He couldn't see, but the darkness trying to steal over him was more than an absence of light. It was an absence of life. He clung to the pain knifing through his heart and body, knowing it was the only thing tethering him to the mortal world.

Marissa! Every fiber of his being cried out for her, but he couldn't reach her spirit, and feared it was because his existence in the mortal realm was fading.

It couldn't end this way. He couldn't bear it. He'd failed her. The moment she'd parted from him in the field, he'd felt her fear. He should have swept her into his arms and kept her with him, just as his instinct had been from the moment she'd heard the cry of his wolf spirit in Twilight.

Marissa! By Logos! How could he have failed her so?

He loved her beyond life, beyond all, and his spirit fell in abject grief to the very depths of his soul.

Marissa!

"I feel your pain, brother, and fear I am the cause."

"Sirius?" Navarre searched through the darkness until he sensed the warmth of the Pyrathian's leader. He hadn't had contact with his brethren in the spirit world since Draysius's firestrike. That he did now told him more than anything else that he'd lost Marissa. He'd failed to protect her from the vile Vladarians and she would now suffer the depths of hell.

Navarre's heart split in two.

There were no words for the agony consuming him.

Chapter Twenty-six

THE PAIN gripping Marissa's heart, body, and soul wouldn't let up. She felt she would die from it. She prayed she would die from it, but with every aching heartbeat death escaped her. All she could see as the helicopter whirled her away into the night was Navarre reaching for her, bullets ripping through him everywhere, and the blood.

Madre de Dios!

His wolf spirit had disappeared, instantly snuffed out, just as his life had been, for how could he have survived?

Healing is possible when death is not immediate or the injury grave.

Machine guns tearing his body apart could have only brought grave injury or death.

Everything inside her wrenched in agony and she curled into a ball on the floor of the helicopter as she cried, uncaring of the hard metal beneath her or the grit digging into her cheek. Navarre had told her Father Dom was not to be trusted, but she hadn't listened and Navarre had paid the price.

He had paid for her folly, for Father Dom's fear, for her tío's evil, and for the Vladarians' greed. Samir had ordered Navarre's cold-blooded murder.

Dios, she couldn't survive this. She didn't want to survive this. She opened her eyes.

Samir sat in the seat above where she lay, his black heart a mockery to the flowing white robes he wore. He was smiling and talking, communicating through the headpiece. She couldn't hear what he was saying over the throbbing drone of the helicopter's engine and blades, but it didn't matter. All that mattered was the realization that she hadn't truly understood her brother when all he wanted was to exact revenge and die.

Now she did. All she wanted was to kill Samir and then herself.

And she would. She would wait for the right moment and it would be over for Samir—and for her.

Marissa! Navarre's heart cried as he fought to return to his mortal form, but he knew now that his life, his existence was fading. His spirit writhed in pain, twisted in anguish, and he silently screamed. He didn't want to talk to Sirius. He didn't want to make any connection to the spirit world. He had to return to her. He had to. How could he have ever thought that to be with her for only a time was acceptable? He should have moved the heavens with his love for her and demanded the impossible rather than think he'd have to return to the spirit world one day. He hadn't.

He didn't deserve to love her. He could do nothing else but love her. Protecting her was more important than anything, even breaking his oath to the Guardian Forces.

"I am sorry for your blindness, brother. Yes, it is Sirius. I heard your pain and have come to you. It is all my fault," Sirius said. "I brought you to the mortal realm and left you, hoping to save you, and only caused you more pain. I did not realize you would be blind. Any warrior would be in pain and wish for death when faced with such weakness."

"No," Navarre whispered. "It is not the blindness. I failed. I failed to save the one I love from harm. There will never be anything for me but agony."

"What?" asked Sirius. "A loved one?"

"A mortal to whom I have pledged my heart. I failed her. My shame is nothing compared to the horror she will now suffer."

"I do not understand," said Sirius. "You must explain more. Did she die?"

"No. I have died. I have parted from the mortal realm," Navarre cried.

"You are mistaken, my brother. We are in the mortal realm," said Sirius. "I was searching the mortal world for York. He is lost. The depth of your pain thundered through the atmosphere at me. I had to come to help."

Navarre paused. "If I am still in the mortal realm, then why do I feel separated from my body?"

Navarre felt Sirius place both hands upon his spirit and delve inside him. "You've been gravely injured in the mortal realm and your warrior's strength is too weak from Draysius's firestrike to heal so great a harm," Sirius said.

Suddenly an infusion of hot strength seared through Navarre's spirit and he felt Sirius shudder in weakness. The Pyrathian had breathed Logos's gift of life into Navarre, a feat that severely drained a warrior's power.

Bright light surrounded Navarre and suddenly all of the brilliant colors of the world flooded into his mind. He could see. He could see Sirius's golden-winged image wavering in the blue atmosphere. They were in the mortal realm with the white clouds and mortal ground below. With the surge of strength, Navarre felt his spirit being drawn downward. Sirius stayed with him.

"I can see!" Sirius had healed and saved him. "You . . . you saved me at great cost to yourself," Navarre said, awed by the Pyrathian's sacrifice.

"No, Blood Hunter. I owed you. Now we are even."

"We will never be even," Navarre said. "I am eternally in your debt. I must find a way to stay in the mortal realm."

"When the Guardian Council learned of your blindness, and of the loss of your warrior's strength from the firestrike, they relieved you of your duty. They are not happy you are too weak to leave the mortal realm, but they have accepted this."

Navarre's flooding joy was cut short. "I am no longer blind, though. And what if my warrior's strength has also returned?"

"I doubt that is the case, for I didn't have that much

strength to give," Sirius said. "But I would not look to cross that bridge. Warriors are needed in the mortal realm and you can help us find York."

"York is lost?"

"Flynn said he was scratched by a Tsara and the wound would not heal. York couldn't cross through the spirit barrier, so Flynn came back for help from the brethren. When the Blood Hunters returned to the Solent, York was gone, and we have been unable to locate him. A very powerful and sinister mortal magic is involved."

"As soon as I save Marissa, I will find him. Sven must be beside himself."

"Sven doesn't know yet. He has gone into meditative seclusion. The Guardian Council has relieved him of his duties until they can review his decisions. Though I fully understand how the battle with the Vladarians has led to the loss of you, and your fellow Blood Hunters, the Council doesn't. Finding York will help, I hope."

"I'll find him," Navarre promised.

"Also, could you give a mortal woman a message for me?"

"Anything," said Navarre, though surprised not only by the request, but by the strange emotion in Sirius's voice. "Tell Stefanie Bastista, a mortal you fight with, that . . . tell her she is a worthy warrior."

Before Navarre could say anything else, Sirius disappeared, and Navarre was plunged into a world of physical pain beyond belief. He cried out from the shock.

Stefanie watched Annette battle to save Navarre, realizing for the first time the true depth of her sister's passion to fight for every life—and how much pain it must have caused Annette when Stefanie had wanted to give up on living. She also realized the lecture she'd given Annette about physically being willing to pick up a gun and fight was way off base. If Annette never touched a weapon in the war against evil, she would still be as valiant and courageous as any warrior who ever lived.

With steady hands she repaired Navarre's femoral artery, extracted a bullet from his chest close to his right lung, and now worked on a wound to his left shoulder, about a hand's width from his heart. His right leg was anchored to a board, keeping it straight. A tube drained excess fluid from Navarre's chest to keep pressure off his lungs, and Grayson monitored Navarre's vital signs. He'd made a top surgical nurse. Stefanie had done whatever they needed her to do, mainly finding supplies and getting drugs.

Though Stefanie knew Herrera had had to die, and that she'd had no choice but to plunge the knife into his heart, the very act of helping to save someone else eased the queasy feeling inside her a little. She thought of the golden-winged spirit warrior she'd seen, one who wore the Shadowman amulet. What would he think about what she'd done? When he told her to fight, was this what he meant?

"Marissa!" Navarre suddenly yelled, shocking everyone. His body began shaking.

"Vitals, Grayson!" Annette demanded.

"BP 85/50, pulse 130, respirations 22," Grayson called out.

"The sedative is wearing off. Stef, give him five milligrams of morphine IV stat! Increase the drip on the left arm's IV. Aragon! I need you and Jared!" She yelled the last.

Stefanie administered the drug as the warriors ran into the room. Marissa's brother and Jaymes were with them.

"Aragon, hold Navarre's left arm and shoulder. Jared, his legs. You two on the other side, be careful of the tubing. Keep him still. I'm almost finished suturing. This is going to hurt him, but I don't want to knock him out again. Not with his blood pressure that low."

The warriors latched on and Jaymes with Rafael carefully held down Navarre's right shoulder and arm. Stefanie noticed Marissa's brother was praying hard for Navarre.

Annette moved with precision, though it seemed to Stefanie that every stitch her sister made hurt her more than it did Navarre. He groaned some, and called for Marissa, but he wasn't fighting the treatment. He did continue to shiver badly and Stefanie found the thermometer.

"His temperature is ninety-seven."

"That's hypothermic for a Blood Hunter," Annette said. "Perfect slow metabolic state to give me time to patch him up, but now we need to warm him up before we lose him. Put the heat packs at his feet, head, and underarms."

Within moments of putting the packs in place, Navarre's shivering stopped and Annette finished the last stitch. "I've done all I can do. Now we pray for a miracle."

"I think I just missed witnessing a miracle." At the unfamiliar voice, everyone turned to see a woman who was a dead ringer for Nicole Kidman, but in camo and combat boots, standing just inside the doorway with Sam, Nick, and a man who was an older version of Nick. It would seem there was another miracle afoot.

"My father, Reed Sinclair," said Nick. "And his associate, Chanel Langston. They were working on Menendez and Herrera."

"Working on how?" asked Annette.

"He's Joe the sleeper and she was the honeypot," said Sam.

Chanel frowned. "Hopefully I'm more than that. Then again, somebody has to do the dirty work. It would seem I have you all to thank for tying up this operation neatly."

Stefanie considered Herrera and the jaguar. Not to mention the bodies littering the ground outside. "I'm not sure we had anything to do with it. It was pretty much over when we got here, each side doing the other in and then escaping."

"Señor Castillo, the owner of the mission here, took care of Menendez," Sam said. "He could use some sewing up if you're okay with leaving Navarre for a few minutes."

"I'll get my stuff," said Annette, crossing over to the medical supply packs.

"I see you found Father Dom," Chanel said. "I am glad to see him alive." She nodded to the priest, who quietly snored where he slept on the couch against the wall. "He will be all right, won't he?"

"Yes," said Stefani. "He's still knocked out from the pain medicine I gave him thirty minutes ago." It was hard to believe only that short amount of time had passed.

"Good," Chanel said. "I have too many deaths on my conscience already. There's one question left that I'm afraid to ask. Where is Marissa?"

"Taken," Rafael said. "Sheik Rashad bin Samir Al Sabah has taken her to Kassim."

Chanel stared at Rafael a moment. "You're not kidding, are you? Who are you?"

"I'm Marissa's *hermano*."

"From Herrera's dungeon? Glad you got out before Herrera could do his worst. We've heard things that—"

"*Mierda!* Enough talk. When can we go for Marissa?" Rafael demanded, looking at Nick. Stefanie examined Rafael more closely. Herrera had done something awful to him. A glance Chanel's way showed the woman studying Rafael with interest, as if she recognized some primal pain in him, too.

"We have to plan first," replied Nick. "That takes time."

"I have a trusted contact in neighboring Dubai so that would be a good base to operate from," said Reed.

"Marissa!" Navarre shouted as he abruptly sat up, sending everyone rushing to him.

Annette cursed, then laughed. "Here's the real miracle! His body is healing itself."

Everyone moved closer. Grayson's and Jaymes's mouths hung open.

Stefanie blinked in surprise and stared at Navarre in shock. His wounds appeared days old, not fresh from surgery. He was looking around at everyone, studying them carefully as if he could now see.

"Vampires can do that, too," said Reed Sinclair. His tone of voice and the look Nick leveled on him filled Stefanie with questions.

"Sirius healed me." Navarre focused on Aragon and Jared. "I am ready to go for Marissa now!"

Jared caught one of Navarre's arms, Aragon the other, and they gently pushed him back down on the table.

"*We* will go for Marissa now," Jared said.

"*You* will go when Annette allows you to," added Aragon.

Sam laughed. "When did you two buy into 'the doctor's never wrong'?"

Annette looked up from where she was examining Navarre. "Since Erin and I confiscated the online truffle order."

"Wimps," said Sam, glaring at the warriors.

"Meggie did say that the girls would rule and the men would drool," Nick added.

"Sounds like a story that I haven't heard yet," said Jaymes.

"Now *that* is a miracle, considering your eavesdropping habits," Nick said.

Grayson laughed while Jaymes glared at Nick.

The sparks flying confirmed to Stef that Nick and Jaymes were more than just new acquaintances battling vampires. It unsettled her somehow. Not that she could consider having a relationship with a man again after what happened to her. And she wasn't involved with Nick romantically—he was important to her, but not her lover. So why did she feel so confused? Blinking moisture from her eyes, she focused on helping her sister.

Annette removed Navarre's IV and untied his leg from the straight board. "Let me ease that chest tube out before you get up. At the rate you are healing, you'll likely be good as new by the time we reach Kassim tomorrow evening."

"Tomorrow evening!" Navarre said, incredulous. "It will take that long just to get to the Persian Gulf?" He frowned at Aragon. "We do it in a blink in the spirit realm."

"Welcome to the mortal world," Aragon told him.

"I can get you there faster than commercial or private," said Chanel.

"We need every edge we can get," said Nick.

"*Bien,*" said Rafael. "Herrera said we had to do it at midnight and not before. There is a SINCO meeting at that time and Samir will be distracted."

Stefanie swore she could have heard a pin drop in the sudden silence.

A meeting of the Vladarians seemed too good to be true. The team could eliminate a number of the Vladarian Order in one strike. But why had Herrera specified midnight?

Chapter Twenty-seven

THE SHARP poke in Marissa's side forced her to surface from her stupor. Her head throbbed from where Father Dom had hit her. Her body ached from the long journey to Kassim, and the strangling vise of pain gripping her heart only increased with every passing moment of awareness. If her desire to make Samir pay for killing Navarre wasn't so great, she would never move again.

"Wake up, *puta*."

Dios. Marissa shook her head, her heart suddenly thundering with surreal hope at the sound of Ysalane's voice. Could her entire escape have been a drug-induced dream or a nightmare and she would wake to find herself about to marry Herrera? She slitted her eyes open and saw the scarred Mayan woman, dressed in shimmering gold cloth and wearing more jewels than a queen. Her dark eyes were narrowed in hate and she clutched a sharp dagger in her hand.

Ysalane lowered the dagger to Marissa's throat. Marissa's heart didn't even skip a beat. She didn't care if she lived or died at the moment.

"Be warned. Ysalane will not let you kill el Sheik. My magic sees you will try. El Sheik is kind to Ysalane and she will keep him safe. I would kill you now, *pero* el Sheik says he must show you to others at a meeting later tonight."

Later tonight? "What time is it?

"Eight. The meeting is in four hours. Then"—Ysalane took the dagger and mimed cutting her own throat—"there will be nothing stopping Ysalane from protecting el Sheik. You remember that." She backed away toward the door. "I will tell the maids you are ready to be prepared. You stink."

"Prepared for what?" Marissa sat up abruptly. Dizziness and

nausea slammed into her. In her wavering vision, Ysalane just smiled and left.

Marissa vaguely remembered coming to the room located in Samir's harem earlier today. The dark-tinted windows dulled the bright sun and turquoise sea of the Persian Gulf to shades of light gray. Now it was dark outside and she castigated herself for not doing more to further her plans to kill Samir. She could have acted tonight.

The "harem" wasn't the decadent place she expected, but a separate part of the palace set aside for the women and young children to reside in. At least that was what she'd been told, and from what little she'd seen so far, it was true.

But just because Samir didn't appear to be the sexually depraved monster Herrera had been, didn't diminish his wickedness. He'd still executed Navarre—and if she could find a silver blade or a means to douse him in flames, she would eliminate Samir.

The bedroom held nothing useful for murder. She had checked that out before throbbing pain and exhaustion had made her lie down for a moment. She hadn't meant to fall asleep.

A loud knock at the door forced Marissa up. She crossed the room on unsteady feet and opened the door. Two women stood before her all dressed in loose jewel-encrusted loose clothing that consisted of a tunic over silk pants in dark, rich shades of blue and burgundy. They were about her age and both beautiful—dark hair, creamy skin, rich coffee-colored eyes.

They stared at her for a few moments, particularly at her low-cut shirt. Their eyes were wide with shock before they lowered their gazes in embarrassment.

"What do you want?" Marissa asked.

"We have come to welcome you to our home and help you to prepare for your important meeting with Rashid tonight," said one woman.

The other woman nodded in agreement. "In anticipation of

your arrival, appropriate clothes and jewels have been purchased for you to choose from. We will help you find something that suitably expresses Rashid's wealth and honor."

"Who are you?"

They blinked at her in surprise. "We are two of his wives," they said almost together.

This time it was Marissa who stared. She considered her marriage to Navarre, his passion, the intimacy between them, his promises to her. She couldn't imagine him sharing all of those things with someone else, too.

"Do not worry about this now," said one of the wives. "You will learn to accept life, but you must always carefully watch Fatima. You won't see her today. She's prostrate in her room after hearing you arrived."

"Fatima?"

"Rashid's third wife. She cannot be trusted, for she wishes her son to rule Kassim and he is the youngest of Rashid's male children. I am Ayisha and my Aman is firstborn."

"And I am Zaina. My sons Imaad and Omar are second and third in line to rule. May we call you Marissa?"

Marissa nodded and what followed was an odyssey of activity and cultural lessons that left Marissa filled with mixed emotions. Everywhere she looked she saw nothing but opulent luxury. Silks and gold, beautiful sculptures. It was unbelievable. They led her to the baths, gave her privacy when she asked, but as Marissa, wrapped tightly in her robe, passed another door there were women naked, bathing each other. Marissa hurried away, feeling something was as wrong here as it had been at Corazón de Rojo. Yet, at every turn she heard how kind Samir was, a fact that went against what she knew about Vladarian Vampires. Was Samir an oddity, or had her uncle and Herrera been the abnormal ones? These women idolized Samir, claimed to love him, and looked forward to the many more children he would give them.

Once she was "properly dressed" they instructed her on what she was allowed and not allowed to do under Kassim law while they ate a meal of perfectly prepared delicacies. Only silver forks and spoons accompanied the meal. No knives. Arming herself might take more ingenuity than she anticipated.

In the end, Marissa concluded that the palace was nothing more than a richly appointed prison, different from Corazón in some ways, but alike at its core.

They had yet to finish the meal when she received a summons from Samir. The women hurriedly thrust robes over her shoulders and wrapped a veil over her head, telling her she must not look other men in the eye at the meeting. It would be disrespectful. Then, wishing her well, they giggled as they escorted her to the harem's guarded entrance. It was eleven-fifteen.

As she walked, she had the eerie sense of being watched and thought once that she detected the sweet scent of Ysalane's Magic smoke. But she was past the point of fear or feeling. All she wanted was to see Samir dead and let her spirit find Navarre's in the afterlife. A servant led her all the way to the opposite end of the palace. He didn't speak and he didn't look at anything but her feet as he urged her along, until he directed her into a book-lined room. Samir sat at an elaborately expensive desk. Beside him stood two—she blinked twice to be sure—blue-tinged, grotesque-looking men with silver hair.

"I see you are now dressed more appropriately," said Samir. "You are a beautiful woman and I was quite enamored with the videos Vasquez showed of how devoutly you prayed for his soul. I would have enjoyed such services, but not from a whore." He motioned to a chair in front of his desk. "Please sit down. We have much business to attend before the SINCO meeting tonight, beginning with our marriage contract. My lawyers are currently working out the details of how to legally transfer your SINCO shares into my name. Once that is done then you will be beheaded for adultery."

Marissa didn't sit, but gripped the back of the chair, enraged. How did those women ever see any kindness in this cold, condescending . . . *bastardo*? "*Por favor,* I have consented to and married only *one* man. I have known *only* my husband. *I* am not guilty of adultery."

Samir stood and grabbed a paper and stabbed his finger on it. "According to Kassim and Vladarian law you became my wife when I purchased you from Vasquez six months ago."

"I am not a vampire and I am not a citizen of Kassim. I am Belizean. Your rules and your paper have nothing to do with me. I have learned that in the eyes of my God, my church, and my country, I cannot be married without my voluntary consent. According to my uncle's will, his SINCO shares belong to me now. Your paper is worthless and my lawyers are going to destroy SINCO." Marissa didn't have lawyers yet but she would.

Samir turned purple in the face. "Your lawyers? You obtained lawyers in the jungle?"

"No. When I was in America. My friends helped me. Did not Herrera tell you?" Marissa didn't know where her bald-faced lies were coming from, but she wasn't about to let herself be pushed around, especially by the man who had had Navarre killed.

"That is why Herrera gave you up to me so easily!" Samir cursed and turned to the blue man on his right. "Find out what she has done and stop it immediately!" He turned to the blue man on his right. "Herrera should be here any minute. Bring him to me."

Both blue men evaporated and Marissa tightened her grip on the back of the chair as her knees wobbled. Blue man number one would be a while searching because she hadn't done anything yet. Blue man number two and Herrera would be a problem. She had minutes to kill Samir.

"We are going to fix half of the legal problem immediately," Samir said, coming around his desk at her and baring his fangs. "Once you're infected, you'll be subject to Vladarian Law."

Marissa backed up, her heart slamming in fear. *NO! NO! NO!* her soul cried. She'd be separated from God and Navarre forever.

Cinatas found that the color black was growing on him, especially black velvet draped on the mischievous Sabrina. Unfortunately, he hadn't seen her since dinner. Valois was likely keeping the other Vladarians from seeing her. Cinatas had extended his visit with Valois just to spend some time with the woman. Why pop off when he would have had to pop back so soon?

Valois had done his best to limit Cinatas's access to his castle and Sabrina by filling just about every minute of every hour with some "royal" treat for his "honored" guest. They'd hunted twice, visited an exclusive brothel, gone to a gentleman's club and gamed much as the lords and ladies of the ton had done in their prime. They'd dined in exclusive restaurants and had practically polished off the imperial of Château Petrus. Cinatas had loved every minute of it, because he could tell Valois had hated every second. It was a wonder the Royal Vladarian hadn't ground his fangs to dust by now.

The showdown with the Vladarian oil cartel was about to commence. Currently, all those whom Valois had selected to participate in the coup were gathering at his castle. Then they would materialize en masse at Samir's palace.

Cinatas joined Valois where he spoke quietly in the corner with a group of Royals. They always kept themselves separated from the "great unwashed." The other Vladarians from different factions mingled about the room. Cinatas clapped Valois jovially on the back. "Boy, have we had a time," he said. "Hunting, gambling, whoring. I haven't had a minute to check with you on the Vasquez woman."

The Royals obviously didn't like to have their pastimes labeled so crudely. They looked at him as if he were shit on their shoes. Priceless, Cinatas thought.

"She's there," Valois said tightly, trying to slip away from the main group of the Royals and get Cinatas out of their lofty midst.

"She's where? Why haven't you told me?"

"She's at Samir's palace and I haven't told you because I just received the information myself. Samir keeps my informant chained to his side and he just now slipped free. The SINCO meeting is as scheduled."

"Excellent," Cinatas said. "Then I'll let you get back to your cronies." He looked down at his watch. "We leave in thirty minutes? Twelve sharp?"

"That is the plan," Valois said.

"In that case I'll go pour myself another glass of wine."

"Be my guest," Valois replied. "The Petrus is in the study. I will have a servant—"

"No need this time. I can get it." Before Valois could argue, Cinatas walked away smiling. He slipped into Valois's study, filled his glass to the brim, drinking the entire thing down. He had a feeling that he'd often avail himself of Valois's hospitality.

Focusing his mind on Samir's palace, Cinatas dematerialized. It wouldn't hurt to be a little early just to assure his interests were best served in the attack.

Navarre gripped Jared's shoulder. "Marissa is in trouble. I must go now."

After gaining access to the palace by sea, they'd split into two groups and hidden in the shadows, watching and waiting. Aragon, having seen a moving shadow on the other side of the gardens, had gone with Rafael to check it out. The others were on the far end of the palace.

"Go," Jared whispered. "I will be right behind you."

Navarre heard Jared whispering to the others as he ran toward the palace, shifting into his were form. Since Sirius's healing touch, he had complete control over changing forms at any time, as if his full Blood Hunter abilities had been restored.

He hadn't tried to cross the spirit barrier, and couldn't conceive of ever jeopardizing a future with Marissa just to find out if he'd regained his warrior's strength completely.

NO! NO! NO! The full force of Marissa's cry hit him.

I am coming! Navarre's mind shouted. *I am coming!*

Reaching a locked door, Navarre tore the handle off and wrenched the door open in seconds. The surprised guard inside didn't have to time to react before Navarre slammed him up against the wall and he slumped to the floor. Navarre ran hard in Marissa's direction.

Cinatas dropped himself into the middle of Samir's library and planted his fist into the sniveling Vladarian's face. He glanced at the Vasquez woman who was still backing up in horror. "Samir, what do we have here? It is a shame you left my coronation early." Cinatas snapped the vampire's head back with an uppercut to the jaw.

"Guards! Guards!" Samir yelled. "Who are you?"

"Don't you recognize me?" Cinatas smiled and let electricity crackle over his body before he launched a bolt and burned Samir's ear off. Samir screamed. "You really should have listened to me. I told you Marissa was mine to dispose of."

Samir gasped for air. "Cinatas? But . . . how? Your face . . ."

"Amazing, isn't it?" Cinatas sent another bolt. Samir's cheek sizzled.

"Stop!" Samir held his hand up to protect his face and Cinatas burned that, too.

Two guards ran into the room and Cinatas dropped them dead with an electric shock.

"I had to stop Herrera!" Samir cried. "Herrera took what

was mine. By Vladarian Law it was my right to get her back."

Cinatas smiled. "No it wasn't. I am Vladarian Law now. What you had to do was pay homage to me and you didn't."

Samir fell to his knees. "Forgive me. Hail, Cinatas. Hail, Cinatas."

"Too late," Cinatas said. Taking both hands, he aimed the full force of his power at Samir and began burning the vampire alive. Wonderful screams echoed off the walls until Samir erupted completely in flames and disappeared into extinction.

"*Beautiful,*" he said, then turned to the Vasquez woman and held out his hand. "Time to go."

"No! Never!"

Cinatas shook his head. "Samir disobeyed me. Do you really want a taste of what that was like?"

He heard a noise behind him and swung around, fingers aimed.

"We've got company," Nick whispered, catching Sam's and Jaymes's attention. He motioned to the shadows of three men crawling around the perimeter of the palace. They didn't spend a lot of time at any one place, but methodically bent down as if to check on something and moved on. They didn't look particularly concerned about watching their backs, either. And Nick thought for the second time that security surrounding the sheik's palace seemed much too lax.

At first he wondered if his father's contact in Dubai had that much power. But then Shareef had warned them repeatedly that the palace was heavily guarded.

So where were the guards?

"Marissa's in trouble, Navarre and I are going in." Jared's voice via the headset was low and clear. "Aragon and Grayson are checking shadows across the garden."

"Roger," Nick said, knowing Sam and Jaymes heard the report over their headsets. Shit. Why didn't anything ever go down easy and as planned? "Eighteen minutes to midnight. I'm going to move in and see what's up," Nick said.

"Take Jaymes and I'll watch your backs," Sam said.

Nick and Jaymes headed out. As they crouched by a bush, Nick muttered sarcastically under his breath, "Keep your ears open. Maybe you can hear what they're saying." He rolled and dashed to the perimeter before Jaymes could respond.

He had no sooner settled into a corner than Jaymes was right there behind him. His own damn shadow couldn't do better. He had to hand it to her, she was good at this shit.

"Can't hear words, but I damn well hear something ticking," Jaymes said.

"Ticking? His watch?" Nick shook off his thoughts and focused on the sounds. Before he could hear any ticking, ungodly screaming rent the air and kept going. Jaymes moved past him, closer to the wall then she grabbed his arm and jerked him forward. He nearly face-planted flashing red digits and an array of wires. A bomb. What if those shadows had been dropping a bomb every time they stopped?

"Fuck." He calculated the time. "They're set to go off at midnight."

"Sam," Nick said. "Jaymes has just discovered this place is wired and loaded. D-day. Midnight. We have exactly fifteen minutes to get our asses out of here."

Marissa saw Navarre's sleek, black were form fill the doorway and she gaped in disbelief. He was alive! The fire man who'd killed Samir turned.

"Watch out! He shoots fire!" she yelled. But she spoke too late. A bolt of fire headed right for Navarre's face.

Lightning quick, Navarre twisted to the side. The fire hit the silk walls, smoke and flames appeared. Navarre then dove. As he rolled, he grabbed a side table and used it as a shield against the subsequent streaks of fire. When the table erupted in flames from the force of the burning beams, Navarre threw the table at the man's face.

Navarre could see! His wolf spirit wasn't guiding him. He was alone and he could see!

"My face! My face! My face!" the man yelled wildly, backing away from the flames and continuing to scream even though he'd deflected the table and the fire hadn't touched him.

Navarre picked up another table and went after the fire man.

"Leave him! Get Marissa out! Bomb!" Jared yelled from the doorway.

The fire man disappeared, laughing.

Navarre turned her way.

"*Madre de Dios!* A bomb!" Marissa cried, running toward Navarre. "There're women and children in the harem! We can't leave them."

"Go that way," Jared yelled, pointing at the black windows then lifting one end of Samir's heavy desk. "Get the other end, Navarre."

They picked the desk up and threw it through the plate-glass window.

Navarre scooped her up and, with a running start, leaped out into the night, Jared right beside them.

As soon as they landed, far from the broken glass littering the ground, Jared yelled for Aragon. Sam showed up.

"Take everyone and go," Jared said. "I will clear the women and children from the building."

"Already in motion," said Sam. "Aragon is collecting any bombs around that part of the palace and throwing them in the sea. Everyone else is clearing the people out of the harem. We've eight minutes to D-day. Everyone clears out in four."

They all ran for the harem end of the palace. Jared and Navarre went after more bombs, and Marissa wanted to scream at fate. To bring him back to her, then put him in danger again was almost more than she could handle.

Women and children could be heard yelling and crying, trying to run back into the building. Marissa quickly realized they thought they were being kidnapped.

She ran forward, calling for Samir's wives. "Ayisha! Zaina! Get your children and run! These people are here to save you from a horrible danger! There is a bomb."

"Marissa?" called a woman from the darkness. "Is this the will of Rashid? He will come?"

Marissa swallowed the lump in her throat. Whatever Samir was to her and others, these women loved him and knew a different side of the Vladarian. "Yes!" she lied. "Now go! Hurry."

Order appeared in the chaos, and the women ran with their children, hurrying in the direction Nick and Jaymes sent them. They were exiting the side entrance to the palace, and once they passed to the other side of the surrounding concrete wall they would be somewhat protected from the blast.

She looked for Navarre, but didn't see him. Then she saw Rafael across the way, helping a little boy run toward safety and her heart swelled with hope for her brother . . . and for herself.

"Clear out in one minute!" Sam yelled.

Suddenly, someone grabbed her from behind and jerked her into the shadows, and she felt the blade of a knife against her throat.

"Ysalane will kill you now. You and your wolfman killed Samir."

Chapter Twenty-eight

"DIOS, WE did not do it," Marissa cried, remaining as still as possible so Ysalane's blade wouldn't slice her throat. "A vampire came, very handsome, very strong. He could shoot fire from his fingers and he burned Samir. Samir begged him to stop and this awful man would not. Samir called him 'Cinatas.' *Por favor*, you must believe me."

"Cinatas," Ysalane said. "Ysalane has heard of Cinatas. Herrera cursed him often. Cinatas killed Samir?"

"*Sí*, he burned him to death without mercy."

The knife eased from her throat.

"*Gracias*," Ysalane said. "I will kill Cinatas then. Herrera is dead, too. Ysalane's jaguar ate his carcass."

Marissa drew a tentative breath, and stepped away from Ysalane, then took another step. When she turned to face the woman, she was gone.

"Marissa!" Navarre yelled.

"*Aquí!* I am here!" she called, running toward him. He swept her up in his arms and ran. They cleared the gate. Somebody slammed and locked the steel doors.

Marissa couldn't even wait for the explosion. She wrapped her arms around Navarre's neck. "I love you, my husband."

He shifted to his mortal form. "And I love you, my wife."

The far end of the palace exploded just about the same time as a host of bombs went off in the sea. Marissa gave all of the fireworks a glance and decided she had something much more exciting to do. She kissed Navarre with all her heart, body, and soul, thankful to be the bride of the wolf.

The Palm, Jumeirah, Dubai, UAE

"This is a much different place than the jungle," Rafael said as Marissa joined him on the deck of the villa.

The luxury island they were on was manmade and shaped like a palm tree, a fact that Marissa's mind could barely comprehend. How could men build their own island in the ocean? The turquoise waters of the Persian Gulf glittered as far as she could see and the sun was so warm and beautiful that Marissa felt as if God were shining his love down on her. She wondered if Rafael could feel it, too.

"*Sí*, different and beautiful. There are so many places like that in the world that I would like to see. Wouldn't you?"

Rafael shrugged. "Perhaps."

Marissa drew a deep breath. "Perhaps" was a start, and much, much better than "I want to die." Ever since Ysalane told her that Herrera was dead, she worried about what Rafael would do next. She hoped he would find purpose in the fight against the Vladarians, and healing among the wonderful friends she'd made, but she was through giving lectures about what he should do. Not after she'd taken the dark road of wishing for death when she thought Samir had killed Navarre. She shivered every time she thought about it. If she hadn't wanted revenge, would she have taken her own life?

She prayed not, but she now understood the total despair that made one feel that way. She had to remember that feeling wasn't forever and that miracles did happen.

"Herrera is dead," Marissa said, "but there are others out there just as bad as he was."

"*Mierda*, I know." Rafael looked at his hands. "I may be one of them."

She grabbed his arm. "No. Never. You would never do what Herrera did."

"No?" he said harshly. "You did not see what I did to Herrera."

Marissa shook her head. "It doesn't matter. I do not have to know. Whatever you did wasn't bad enough for what he did to so many others. And do not ever think you are what he was. Would you do to the innocent what he did? Would you do to another what he did to you?"

"*Dios!* Never!"

"Then you are not like him. Not like any of them, but maybe you have the guts and the strength to see justice done, *sí?*"

Rafael stared hard at her for a long moment. Rage and anger and hate stormed in his dark eyes. "Do you question my honor, *hermana?*"

"No." She set her palm to his rough cheek. "I only ask that you not waste your resolve to exact justice from vampires like Herrera . . . and Samir. Join this fight against the evil and help save the innocent from suffering as you did."

He didn't answer, but she could see he was considering her challenge. It was enough for now. "I hear the others gathering. Let's go inside so we don't miss out on any of the news about last night. I am curious if any from SINCO survived. And just so you know, this burdensome inheritance is both of ours. I will need a lot of help in using it right."

"No," Rafael said. "I will help, *pero* I think you could take care of the world all by yourself."

Marissa grinned. "Maybe I could, but I wouldn't want to. I like having my brother, my friends, and my husband with me."

She went inside and sat next to Navarre, once again thanking God. She was surrounded by miracles and truly blessed. Rafael came inside, too, and leaned against the wall, not far from where Chanel Langston spoke on her cell phone. It had been a huge surprise to find Chanel waiting at the villa when they'd all arrived in the middle of the night. The moment the woman learned of the bombs, she got on the phone and Marissa didn't think she had been off since. It was unfortu-

nate that American voices had been heard among those helping the women and children escape, because now Kassim was
attempting to create an international incident out of Samir's
assassination.

Marissa had yet to meet their mysterious host, called Shareef.
He'd been absent when they had arrived back last night and was
still gone when they woke this morning. Most everyone had
slept for a couple of hours after the ordeal at the palace, and now
they had gathered, anxious to hear what the news would report
about the bombing of Samir's palace. The Vladarian Vampires
were to have met at midnight. The bombs went off at midnight.
Had any of the SINCO leaders been killed?

The TV screen practically covered an entire wall and the circle of couches facing it could seat many, which was a very good
thing because there were a lot of people. She watched the
newsperson's mouth move and saw the English words scroll
across the bottom of the screen, but they moved too fast for her
to read many of them.

Suddenly a face appeared on the screen and Marissa gripped
Navarre's hand. "It's him! It's the vampire who killed Samir."

Everyone focused on the television. "What are they saying?"
she asked after a moment of complete silence.

"It is confirmed the headless corpse that washed ashore on
Jumeirah Beach yesterday morning is that of Conrad Pitt, the
twenty-six-year old American cover model who has been
missing. Experts believe he was the victim of a brutal shark attack."

"*Dios,* I swear to you it is the vampire I saw last night. Samir
did not recognize him at first, then called him 'Cinatas' after
they started talking."

"Damn, what the hell do you think is going on?" Sam said.

"Oh my God," said Annette. "Is it possible he had a face
transplant?" She shook her head. "They haven't perfected the
surgery yet and he couldn't have healed that fast."

"Yes he could," said Reed Sinclair. "Vampires heal at a remarkable rate once free of incapacitating pain."

Marissa scooted closer to Navarre. The man might be Nick's father, but anyone who'd known her uncle was on her enemy list until proven otherwise.

"Bloody hell, you're serious, Nette," Emerald exclaimed.

"He stole a man's face?" asked Megan, who sat between Emerald and Sam.

"That's what we think, Meggie," said Stefanie.

"Gives me the creeps that I could pass Cinatas on the street and not even recognize him," Erin said from the couch she and Jared lounged on.

"Who is this Cinatas?" Rafael asked. He kept himself apart from the group, but still hovered on the fringes, giving Marissa hope that he would one day be sucked into the circle. "Should I know of him?"

"I don't know, either," Chanel said, touching Rafael's arm. She'd ended her call, but instead of joining the group she had leaned against the wall next to her brother, a fact that Marissa found very interesting.

"He is the wicked *jefe* of Tío Luis and Herrera and many more Vladarian Vampires," Marissa said.

Erin and Stefanie explained how the investigation of Cinatas and the Sno-Med Corporation had led to the discovery of the Vladarain Vampires and their high positions around the world.

"Are you saying they're trying to take over the . . . what? The whole world?" asked Jaymes, frowning.

"Go to the head of the class," said Nick.

"Knowing the history of the Vladarians," said Reed, "I would bet on it. Though it's only in this century they've made a coordinated effort to do it together. Before, it was always a one-man show."

"That would be because of Pathos," said Aragon. "The former Blood Hunter organized them into the force they are now."

Navarre abruptly tensed at Marissa's side. "York!" he said. "How could I have forgotten York?"

"What about York?" asked Jared and Aragon almost simultaneously.

"He is missing in the mortal realm," said Navarre. "Sirius said that York had been scratched by a Tsara. He wants us to find him."

"We will have to do so," said Aragon.

"Who is York? What is a Tsara?" asked Grayson. "My head is swimming from it all."

"A Tsara," said Sam, "is a spiritual assassin from hell."

"A Tsara tried to attack Erin," said Jared.

"Which you thankfully stopped," Erin said, leaning closer to Jared and setting her hand over her stomach. "Have I told you lately that I love you?"

Jared set his hand over Erin's. "The little one in here says you don't say it or show it enough. He says you need to give me the truffles to prove your love."

Most everyone laughed.

"That is just plain low, Jared," Nick said. "Using your unborn kid to extort chocolate from your wife."

Jared shrugged. "She stole it. She should be prepared for battle."

"He's right," said Aragon. "If she loved him she would—argh!"

Annette had elbowed Aragon in the stomach. "You do not want to go there, at all, period!"

"I don't?" Aragon frowned.

"No."

Aragon shrugged then smiled and leaned down to plant a heavy kiss on Annette's firm lips. "I just have to find somewhere else to go then."

Megan laughed. "Girls rule, men drool."

"Watch it, squirt," Nick said. "Or no more piggyback rides."

"Somebody want to explain truffles to the rest of us?" Jaymes asked.

"No!" everyone said in unison.

Meggie leaned forward, looking at Jaymes. "I'll tell you later," she whispered. "If you show me how to do karate kicks like you do."

"Deal," said Jaymes.

"Hey, look at the television," Annette said. "An explosion has demolished . . . what? A medical facility on a private island in the Persian Gulf? I thought they'd report about the palace."

The door opened and Marissa assumed the man who entered the room was their host, Shareef. Tall, dressed in white robes and wearing a white headdress with a black band, he was a commanding figure and mysteriously dark and alluring, almost scary.

He nodded toward the television. "You will not hear reports about Sheik Rashad bin Samir Al Sabah's death, or the attack on the palace. Not until they have sworn in his heir and are assured their rule is stabilized. I have, however, learned there were many men killed whose identities will not be known for quite a while. I have been to the island where the doctor and his staff were killed. He was a very good friend of mine and a brilliant plastic surgeon. They do not tell the whole story on the news. An explosion completely destroyed the facility, but the doctor, his family, and staff who lived on the island were all burned alive— in their beds as if their bodies had spontaneously combusted."

"Cinatas," almost everyone said together.

Shareef's grief and anger upon learning of Cinatas's powers were a palpable force. "This Cinatas must die! Forgive my inhospitality, but I must be alone in my grief. I have made arrangements for all of you to be guests for the next two days at Burj Al Arab with carte blanche at the Assawan Spa and Health

Club. I will then speak of this Cinatas—and where I can find him."

Reed Sinclair crossed the room and placed his hand on Shareef's shoulder. "I am sorry, my friend."

"Thank you. We will talk later about the Vladarians and this murderous leader of theirs. Change is coming to our world."

"Yes, it is. Change should have come long ago."

Marrissa saw that everyone, but mostly Sam and Nick, were studying Reed and Shareef with pointed interest. She hadn't understood the implications of the men's exchange, but it appeared to be significant. She would ask about it later. For now she wanted to respect their host's grief and go to Burj Al Arab. Perhaps she and Navarre would find a few moments alone together.

Marissa was sure she'd indulged in every bit of luxury there was in the world. The Burj Al Arab had to be heaven on earth. She and Navarre—as well as the others—had spent the day being pampered and beautified in the spa and being fed what could only be called ambrosia.

Over dinner they had discussed her plans for her inheritance, which included first assembling a team of lawyers to insure no one could come in and seize her shares. Now everyone had retired to their own rooms and she was finally alone with Navarre.

Dressed in a bathrobe, she drew a soft brush through her long hair, watching how the strands curled as they sprang free of the bristles. She stood in front of the dresser, looking into the mirror, wondering when Navarre was going to stop marveling over the remote control to the television and notice her waiting for him. Even though he could see now, she still had this wild idea of watching his hands caress her, in the mirror, to see him touching her and know that he saw, too.

"This is amazing. There is so much to see," Navarre said

from across the room. She heard the channels change several times.

She set down the brush, her heart beating wildly as she untied her sash. Then she shrugged and let the robe fall from her shoulders so that she stood naked in front of the mirror. Raising her arms up, she flung her long hair behind her so that her breasts could be fully seen. She wet her lips and then said loudly enough for Navarre to hear her over the television, "There are a lot of amazing things to discover," she said.

"Yes," he said. Suddenly the television went silent. She cut her glance to the side and saw a naked warrior, fully aroused, walking her way fast.

Dios, she knew what she was asking for, and it felt wonderful! He came up behind her and cupped her breasts, molding them with his hands as he worked his fingers over her nipples and gently plucked at her aching crests. She moaned softly. Raising her arms, she reached back and slid her fingers through his silky hair. He pressed his arousal against her and she wiggled her bottom back, asking for more, needing more.

"Watch me touch you," he said, easing one of his hands down to her sex and sliding his fingers against her sensitive flesh. Her body arched and shuddered from the burning pleasure melting her into a puddle of need.

It was incredible, feeling him and seeing him arouse her. She was so excited that she felt she could soar at any moment. Lowering her arms, she twisted away from him.

"My turn now," she said, urging him in front of her. "Put your hands behind your head." When he did, she peeked around from the side and watched herself caress his chest, touching the warm amulet that hung from his neck, loving every sculpted curve and bulge of his supple muscles. She worked her way down the trail of silky hair bisecting his stomach until she filled both of her hands with his hard, heated sex. She stroked him, watching his face, his fierce golden eyes.

Watching his hips undulate and thrust his erection harder into her hands. He was beautiful and—

He twisted in a flash, and before she could blink, he had her on the bed. Spreading her legs, he leaned down and tasted her sex, swirling his tongue quickly over her most sensitive spot before he thrust himself deep inside her. She expected a wild frenzy that would rocket them to heaven. Instead, he just held himself deep inside of her and eased up, looking down at her, his warm amulet between her breasts. She tingled everywhere in expectation.

"You are a miracle. I will never be able to see enough, touch enough, or love enough," he said. Then he kissed her thoroughly, his tongue thrusting deep and tangling with hers. He made love to her so slowly, so exquisitely that she experienced every nuance of his touch, every last vibration of pleasure. They drank, fully, every drop of pleasure that could be caressed from each other as their souls wrapped around each other and shuddered together in ecstasy. In his arms, her spirit soaring with his, Marissa found freedom, life, and love forever.